ROLF IN
THE WOODS

Skookum and the porcupine

ROLF IN THE WOODS

The Adventures of a Boy Scout with
Indian Quonab and Little Dog Skookum

WRITTEN AND ILLUSTRATED

BY

ERNEST THOMPSON SETON

SKYHORSE PUBLISHING

Skyhorse Publishing books may be purchased in bulk at special discounts for sales promotion, corporate gifts, fund-raising, or educational purposes. Special editions can also be created to specifications. For details, contact the Special Sales Department, Skyhorse Publishing, 307 West 36th Street, 11th Floor, New York, NY 10018 or info@skyhorsepublishing.com.

Skyhorse® and Skyhorse Publishing® are registered trademarks of Skyhorse Publishing, Inc.®, a Delaware corporation.

www.skyhorsepublishing.com

10 9 8 7 6 5 4 3 2 1

Library of Congress Cataloging-in-Publication Data is available on file.

ISBN: 978-1-62087-386-1

Printed in the United States of America

TO THE
BOY SCOUTS OF AMERICA

CONTENTS

Contents

Contents

ILLUSTRATIONS

Preface

IN THIS story I have endeavoured to realize some of the influences that surrounded the youth of America a hundred years ago, and made of them, first, good citizens, and, later, in the day of peril, heroes that won the battles of Lake Erie, Plattsburg, and New Orleans, and the great sea fights of Porter, Bainbridge, Decatur, Lawrence, Perry, and MacDonough.

I have especially dwelt in detail on the woodland and peace scouting in the hope that I may thus help other boys to follow the hard-climbing trail that leads to the higher uplands.

For the historical events of 1812–14, I have consulted among books chiefly, Theodore Roosevelt's *Naval War of 1812*, Peter S. Palmer's *History of Lake Champlain*, and Walter Hill Crockett's *A History of Lake Champlain*, 1909. But I found another and more personal mine of information. Through the kindness of my friend, Edmund Seymour, a native of the Champlain region, now a resident of New York, I went over all the historical ground with several unpublished manuscripts for guides, and heard from the children of the sturdy frontiersmen new tales of the war; and in getting more light and vivid personal memories, I was glad, indeed, to realize that not only were there valour and heroism on both sides, but also gentleness and courtesy. Histories written by either party at the time should be laid aside. They breathe the rancourous hate of the writers of the age — the fighters felt not so — and the many incidents given here of chivalry and consideration were actual happenings, related to me by the descendants of those who experienced them; and all assure me that these were a true reflex of the feelings of the day.

I am much indebted to Miss Katherine Palmer, of Plattsburg, for kindly allowing me to see the unpublished manuscript memoir of her grandfather, Peter Sailly, who was Collector of the Port of Plattsburg at the time of the war.

Preface

Another purpose in this story was to picture the real Indian with his message for good or for evil.

Those who know nothing of the race will scoff and say they never heard of such a thing as a singing and religious red man. Those who know him well, will say, "Yes, but you have given to your eastern Indian songs and ceremonies which belong to the western tribes, and which are of different epochs." To the latter I reply:

"You know that the western Indians sang and prayed in this way. How do you know that the eastern ones did not? We have no records, except those by critics, savagely hostile, and contemptuous of all religious observances but their own. The Ghost Dance Song belonged to a much more recent time, no doubt, but it was purely Indian, and it is generally admitted that the races of continental North America were of one stock, and had no fundamentally different customs or modes of thought."

The Sunrise Song was given to me by Frederick R. Burton, author of *American Primitive Music.* It is still in use among the Ojibwa.

The songs of the Wabanaki may be read in C. G. Leland's *Kuloskap the Master.*

The Ghost Dance Song was furnished by Alice C. Fletcher, whose *Indian Song and Story* will prove a revelation to those who wish to follow further.

ERNEST THOMPSON SETON.

ROLF IN THE WOODS

I

The Wigwam Under the Rock

T HE early springtime sunrise was near at hand as Quonab, the last of the Myanos Sinawa, stepped from his sheltered wigwam under the cliff that borders the Asamuk easterly, and, mounting to the lofty brow of the great rock that is its highest pinnacle, he stood in silence, awaiting the first ray of the sun over the sea water that stretches between Connecticut and Seawanaky.

His silent prayer to the Great Spirit was ended as a golden beam shot from a long, low cloud-bank over the sea, and Quonab sang a weird Indian song for the rising sun, an invocation to the Day God:

> *"O thou that risest from the low cloud
> To burn in the all above;
> I greet thee! I adore thee!"

Again and again he sang to the tumming of a small tom-tom, till the great refulgent one had cleared the cloud, and the red miracle of the sunrise was complete.

Back to his wigwam went the red man, down to his home tucked closed under the sheltering rock, and, after washing his hands in a basswood bowl, began to prepare his simple meal.

A tin-lined copper pot hanging over the fire was partly filled with water; then, when it was boiling, some samp or powdered corn and some clams were stirred in. While these were cooking, he took his smoothbore flint-lock, crawled gently over the ridge that screened his wigwam from the northwest wind, and peered with hawk-like eyes across the

---

* Original

Saga-je way-o-say jemo-say gezhik-om en-a-bid sh-keja e-na-bid sh-kora

3

broad sheet of water that, held by a high beaver-dam, filled the little valley of Asamuk Brook.

The winter ice was still on the pond, but in all the warming shallows there was open water, on which were likely to be ducks. None were to be seen, but by the edge of the ice was a round object which, although so far away, he knew at a glance for a muskrat.

By crawling around the pond, the Indian could easily have come within shot, but he returned at once to his wigwam, where he exchanged his gun for the weapons of his fathers, a bow and arrows, and a long fish-line. A short, quick stalk, and the muskrat, still eating a flagroot, was within thirty feet. The fish-line was coiled on the ground and then attached to an arrow, the bow bent — zip — the arrow picked up the line, coil after coil, and transfixed the muskrat. Splash! and the animal was gone under the ice.

But the cord was in the hands of the hunter; a little gentle pulling and the rat came to view, to be despatched with a stick and secured. Had he shot it with a gun, it had surely been lost.

He returned to his camp, ate his frugal breakfast, and fed a small, wolfish-looking yellow dog that was tied in the lodge. He skinned the muskrat carefully, first cutting a slit across the rear and then turning the skin back like a glove, till it was off to the snout; a bent stick thrust into this held it stretched, till in a day, it was dry and ready for market. The body, carefully cleaned, he hung in the shade to furnish another meal.

As he worked, there were sounds of trampling in the woods, and presently a tall, rough-looking man, with a red nose and a curling white moustache, came striding through brush and leaves. He stopped when he saw the Indian, stared contemptuously at the quarry of the morning chase, made a scornful remark about "rat-eater," and went on toward the wigwam, probably to peer in, but the Indian's slow, clear, "keep away!" changed his plan. He grumbled something about "copper-coloured tramp," and started away in the direction of the nearest farmhouse.

Securing the muskrat

II
Rolf Kittering and the Soldier Uncle

"A feller that chatters all the time is bound to talk a certain amount of drivel."
— *The Sayings of Si Sylvanne*

THIS was the Crow Moon, the white man's March. The Grass Moon was at hand, and already the arrow bands of black-necked honkers were passing northward from the coast, sending down as they flew the glad tidings that the Hunger Moon was gone, that spring was come, yea, even now was in the land. And the flicker clucked from a high, dry bough, the spotted wood-wale drummed on his chosen branch, the partridge drummed in the pine woods, and in the sky the wild ducks, winging, drummed their way. What wonder that the soul of the Indian should seek expression in the drum and the drum song of his race?

Presently, as though remembering something, he went quietly to the southward under the ridge, just where it breaks to let the brook go by, along the edge of Strickland's Plain, and on that hill of sliding stone he found, as he always had, the blue-eyed liver-leaf smiling, the first sweet flower of spring! He did not gather it, he only sat down and looked at it. He did not smile, or sing, or utter words, or give it a name, but he sat beside it and looked hard at it, and, in the first place, he went there knowingly to find it. Who shall say that its beauty did not reach his soul?

He took out his pipe and tobacco bag, but was reminded of something lacking — the bag was empty. He returned to his wigwam, and from their safe hanger or swinging shelf overhead, he took the row of stretched skins, ten muskrats and one mink, and set out along a path which led southward through the woods to the broad, open place called Strickland's Plain, across that, and over the next rock ridge to the little town and port of Myanos.

SILAS PECK
TRADING STORE

was the sign over the door he entered. Men and women were buying and selling, but the Indian stood aside shyly until all were served, and Master Peck cried out:

"Ho, Quonab! what have ye got for trade to-day?"

Quonab produced his furs. The dealer looked at them narrowly and said:

"They are too late in the season for primes; I cannot allow you more than seven cents each for the rats and seventy-five cents for the mink, all trade."

The Indian gathered up the bundle with an air of "that settles it," when Silas called out:

"Come now, I'll make it ten cents for the rats."

"Ten cents for rats, one dollar for mink, all cash, then I buy what I like," was the reply.

It was very necessary to Silas's peace that no customer of his should cross the street to the sign,

SILAS MEAD
TRADING STORE

So the bargain, a fair one now, was made, and the Indian went off with a stock of tobacco, tea, and sugar.

His way lay up the Myanos River, as he had one or two traps set along the banks for muskrats, although in constant danger of having them robbed or stolen by boys, who considered this an encroachment on their trapping grounds.

After an hour he came to Dumpling Pond, then set out for his home, straight through the woods, till he reached the Catrock line, and following that came to the farm and ramshackle house of Micky Kittering. He had been told that the man at this farm had a fresh deer hide for sale, and hoping to secure it, Quonab walked up toward the house. Micky was coming from the barn when he saw the Indian. They recognized each other at a glance. That was enough for Quonab; he turned away. The farmer remembered that he had been "insulted." He vomited a few oaths, and strode after the Indian, "To take it out of his hide"; his purpose was very clear. The Indian turned quickly, stood, and looked calmly at Michael.

Some men do not know the difference between shyness and cowardice, but they are apt to find it out unexpectedly. Something told the white man, "Beware! this red man is dangerous." He muttered something about, "Get out of that or I'll send for a constable." The Indian stood gazing coldly, till the farmer backed off out of sight, then he himself turned away to the woods.

Kittering was not a lovely character. He claimed to have been a soldier. He certainly looked the part, for his fierce white moustache was curled up like horns on his purple face, at each side of his red nose, in a most military style. His shoulders were square and his gait was swaggering, beside which, he had an array of swear words that was new and tremendously impressive in Connecticut. He had married late in life a woman who would have made him a good wife, had he allowed her. But, a drunkard himself, he set deliberately about bringing his wife to his own ways, and with most lamentable success. They had had no children, but some months before a brother's child, a fifteen-year-old lad, had become a charge on their hands, and, with any measure of good management, would have been a blessing to all. But Micky had gone too far. His original weak good-nature was foundered in rum. Always blustery and frothy, he divided the world in two — superior officers, before whom he grovelled, and inferiors, to whom he was a mouthy, foul-tongued, contemptible bully, in spite of a certain lingering kindness of heart that showed itself at such rare times when he was neither roaring drunk nor crucified by black reaction. His brother's child, fortunately, had inherited little of the paternal family traits, but in both body and brain favoured his mother, the daughter of a learned divine who had spent unusual pains on her book education, but had left her penniless and incapable of changing that condition.

Her purely mental powers and peculiarities were such that, a hundred years before, she might have been burned for a witch, and fifty years later might have been honoured as a prophetess. But she missed the crest of the wave both ways and fell in the trough; her views on religious matters procured neither a witch's grave nor a prophet's crown, but a sort of village contempt.

Rolf in the Woods

The Bible was her standard — so far so good — but she emphasized the wrong parts of it. Instead of magnifying the damnation of those who follow not the truth (as the village understood it), she was content to semi-quote:

"Those that are not against me are with me" and "A kind heart is the mark of His chosen." And then she made a final utterance, an echo really of her father: "If any man do anything sincerely, believing that thereby he is worshipping God, he *is* worshipping God."

Then her fate was sealed, and all who marked the blazing eyes, the hollow cheeks, the yet more hollow chest and cough, saw in it all the hand of an offended God destroying a blasphemer, and shook their heads knowingly when the end came.

So Rolf was left alone in life, with a common school education, a thorough knowledge of the Bible and of *Robinson Crusoe*, a vague tradition of God everywhere, and a deep distrust of those who should have been his own people.

The day of the little funeral he left the village of Redding to tramp over the unknown road to the unknown south where his almost unknown Uncle Michael had a farm and, possibly, a home for him.

Fifteen miles that day, a night's rest in a barn, twenty-five miles the next day, and Rolf had found his future home.

"Come in, lad," was the not unfriendly reception, for his arrival was happily fallen on a brief spell of good humour, and a strong, fifteen-year-old boy is a distinct asset on a farm.

III

Rolf Catches a Coon and Finds a Friend

AUNT PRUE, sharp-eyed and red-nosed, was actually shy at first, but all formality vanished as Rolf was taught the mysteries of pig-feeding, hen-feeding, calf-feeding, cow-milking, and launched by list only in a vast number of duties familiar to him from his babyhood. What a list there was! An outsider might have wondered if Aunt Prue was saving anything for herself, but Rolf was used to toil. He worked without ceasing and did his best, only to learn in time that the best could win no praise, only avert punishment. The spells of goodnature arrived more seldom in his uncle's heart. His aunt was a drunken shrew, and soon Rolf looked on the days of starving and physical misery with his mother as the days of his happy youth gone by.

He was usually too tired at night and too sleepy in the morning to say his prayers, and gradually he gave it up as a daily habit. The more he saw of his kinsfolk, the more wickedness came to view; and yet it was with a shock that he one day realized that some fowls his uncle brought home by night were there without the owner's knowledge or consent. Micky made a jest of it, and intimated that Rolf would have to "learn to do night work very soon." This was only one of the many things that showed how evil a place was now the orphan's home.

At first it was not clear to the valiant uncle whether the silent boy was a superior to be feared, or an inferior to be held in fear, but Mick's courage grew with non-resistance, and blows became frequent; although not harder to bear than the perpetual fault-finding and scolding of his aunt, and all the good his mother had implanted was being shrivelled by the fires of his daily life.

Rolf had no chance to seek for companions at the village store, but an accident brought one to him.

Rolf in the Woods

Before sunrise one spring morning he went, as usual, to the wood lot pasture for the cow, and was surprised to find a stranger, who beckoned him to come. On going near he saw a tall man with dark skin and straight black hair that was streaked with gray — undoubtedly an Indian. He held up a bag and said, "I got coon in that hole. You hold bag there, I poke him in." Rolf took the sack readily and held it over the hole, while the Indian climbed the tree to a higher opening, then poked in this with a long pole, till all at once there was a scrambling noise and the bag bulged full and heavy. Rolf closed its mouth triumphantly. The Indian laughed lightly, then swung to the ground.

"Now, what will you do with him?" asked Rolf.

"Train coon dog," was the answer.

"Where?"

The Indian pointed toward the Asamuk Pond.

"Are you the singing Indian that lives under Ab's Rock?"

"Ugh!* Some call me that. My name is Quonab."

"Wait for an hour and then I will come and help," volunteered Rolf impulsively, for the hunting instinct was strong in him.

The Indian nodded. "Give three yelps if you no find me." Then he shouldered a short stick, from one end of which, at a safe distance from his back, hung the bag with the coon. And Rolf went home with the cow.

He had acted on hasty impulse in offering to come, but now, in the normal storm state of the household, the difficulties of the course appeared. He cudgelled his brain for some plan to account for his absence, and finally took refuge unwittingly in ancient wisdom: "When you don't know a thing to do, don't do a thing." Also, "If you can't find the delicate way, go the blunt way."

So having fed the horses, cleaned the stable, and milked the cow, fed the pigs, the hens, the calf, harnessed the horses, cut and brought in wood for the woodshed, turned out the sheep, hitched the horses to the wagon, set the milk out in the creaming pans, put more corn to soak for the swill barrel, ground the house knife, helped to clear the breakfast things, replaced the fallen rails of a fence, brought up potatoes from the root cellar, all to the maddening music of a scolding tongue, he set out to take the cow back to the wood lot, sullenly resolved to return when ready.

---

*Ugh (yes) and wah (no) are Indianisms that continue no matter how well the English has been acquired.

IV

The Coon Hunt Makes Trouble for Rolf

NOT one hour, but nearly three, had passed before Rolf sighted the Pipestave Pond, as it was called. He had never been there before, but three short whoops, as arranged, brought answer and guidance. Quonab was standing on the high rock. When Rolf came he led down to the wigwam on its south side. It was like stepping into a new life. Several of the old neighbours at Redding were hunters who knew the wild Indians and had told him tales that glorified at least the wonderful woodcraft of the red man. Once or twice Rolf had seen Indians travelling through, and he had been repelled by their sordid squalour. But here was something of a different kind; not the Champlain ideal, indeed, for the Indian wore clothes like any poor farmer, except on his head and his feet; his head was bare, and his feet were covered with moccasins that sparkled with beads on the arch. The wigwam was of canvas, but it had one or two of the sacred symbols painted on it. The pot hung over the fire was tin-lined copper, of the kind long made in England for Indian trade, but the smaller dishes were of birch bark and basswood. The gun and the hunting knife were of white man's make, but the bow, arrows, snowshoes, tom-tom, and a quill-covered gun case were of Indian art, fashioned of the things that grow in the woods about.

The Indian led into the wigwam. The dog, although not fully grown, growled savagely as it smelled the hated white man odour. Quonab gave the puppy a slap on the head, which is Indian for, "Be quiet; he's all right," loosed the rope, and led the dog out. "Bring that," and the Indian pointed to the bag which hung from a stick between two trees. The dog sniffed suspiciously in the direction of the bag and growled, but he was not allowed to come near it. Rolf tried to make friends with the dog, but without success, and Quonab said, "Better let Skookum* alone. He make friends when he ready — maybe never."

"'Skookum" or "Skookum Chuck," in Chinook means "Troubled waters."

The two hunters now set out for the open plain, two or three hundred yards to the southward. Here the raccoon was dumped out of the sack, and the dog held at a little distance, until the coon had pulled itself together and began to run. Now the dog was released and chivvied on. With a tremendous barking he rushed at the coon, only to get a nip that made him recoil, yelping. The coon ran as hard as it could, the dog and hunters came after it; again it was overtaken, and, turning with a fierce snarl, it taught the dog a second lesson. Thus, running, dodging, and turning to fight, the coon got back to the woods, and there made a final stand under a small, thick tree; and, when the dog was again repulsed, climbed quickly up into the branches.

The hunters did all they could to excite the dog, until he was jumping about, trying to climb the tree, and barking uproariously. This was exactly what they wanted. Skookum's first lesson was learned — the duty of chasing the big animal of that particular smell, then barking up the tree it had climbed.

Quonab, armed with a forked stick and a cord noose, now went up the tree. After much trouble he got the noose around the coon's neck, then, with some rather rough handling, the animal was dragged down, manoeuvred into the sack, and carried back to camp, where it was chained up to serve in future lessons; the next two or three being to tree the coon, as before; in the next, the coon was to be freed and allowed to get out of sight, so that the dog might find it by trailing, and the last, in which the coon was to be trailed, treed, and shot out of the tree, so that the dog should have the final joy of killing a crippled coon, and the reward of a coon-meat feast. But the last was not to be, for the night before it should have taken place the coon managed to slip its bonds, and nothing but the empty collar and idle chain were found in the captive's place next morning.

These things were in the future however. Rolf was intensely excited over all he had seen that day. His hunting instincts were aroused. There had been no very obvious or repellant cruelty; the dog alone had suffered, but he seemed happy. The whole affair was so exactly in the line of his tastes that the boy was in a sort of ecstatic uplift, and already anticipating a real coon hunt, when the dog should be properly trained.

The Coon Hunt Makes Trouble for Rolf

The episode so contrasted with the sordid life he had left an hour before that he was spellbound. The very animal smell of the coon seemed to make his fibre tingle. His eyes were glowing with a wild light. He was so absorbed that he did not notice a third party attracted by the unusual noise of the chase, but the dog did. A sudden, loud challenge called all attention to a stranger on the ridge behind the camp. There was no mistaking the bloated face and white moustache of Rolf's uncle.

"So, you young scut! That is how you waste your time. I'll larn ye a lesson."

The dog was tied, the Indian looked harmless, and the boy was cowed, so the uncle's courage mounted high. He had been teaming in the nearby woods, and the black-snake whip was in his hands. In a minute its thong was lapped, like a tongue of flame, around Rolf's legs. The boy gave a shriek and ran, but the man followed and furiously plied the whip. The Indian, supposing it was Rolf's father, marvelled at his method of showing affection, but said nothing, for the Fifth Commandment is a large one in the wigwam. Rolf dodged some of the cruel blows, but was driven into a corner of the rock. One end of the lash crossed his face like a red-hot wire.

"Now I've got you!" growled the bully.

Rolf was desperate. He seized two heavy stones and hurled the first with deadly intent at his uncle's head. Mick dodged in time, but the second, thrown lower, hit him on the thigh. Mick gave a roar of pain. Rolf hastily seized more stones and shrieked out, "You come on one step and I'll kill you!"

Then that purple visage turned a sort of ashen hue. Its owner mouthed in speechless rage. He "knew it was the Indian who had put Rolf up to it. He'd see to it later," and muttering, blasting, frothing, the hoary-headed sinner went limping off to his loaded wagon.

V

Good-bye to Uncle Mike

"For counsel comes with the night, and action comes with the day;
But the gray half light, neither dark nor bright, is a time to hide away."

ROLF had learned one thing at least — his uncle was a coward. But he also knew that he himself was in the wrong, for he was neglecting his work, and he decided to go back at once and face the worst. He made little reply to the storm of scolding that met him. He would have been disappointed if it had not come. He was used to it; it made him feel at home once more. He worked hard and silently.

Mick did not return till late. He had been drawing wood for Horton that day, which was the reason he happened in Quonab's neighbourhood; but his road lay by the tavern, and when he arrived home he was too helpless to do more than mutter.

The next day there was an air of suspended thunder. Rolf overheard his uncle cursing "that ungrateful young scut — not worth his salt." But nothing further was said or done. His aunt did not strike at him once for two days. The third night Micky disappeared. On the next he returned with another man; they had a crate of fowls, and Rolf was told to keep away from "that there little barn."

So he did all morning, but he peeped in from the hayloft when a chance came, and saw a beautiful horse. Next day the "little barn" was open and empty as before.

That night this worthy couple had a jollification with some callers, who were strangers to Rolf. As he lay awake, listening to the carouse, he overheard many disjointed allusions that he did not understand, and some that he could guess at: "Night work pays better than day work any time," etc. Then he heard his own name and a voice, "Let's go up and settle it with him now." Whatever their plan, it was clear that the drunken crowd, inspired by the old ruffian, were intent on doing him bodily harm. He heard them stumbling and reeling up the steep stairs.

He heard, "Here, gimme that whip," and knew he was in peril, maybe of his life, for they were whiskey-mad. He rose quickly, locked the door, rolled up an old rag carpet, and put it in his bed. Then he gathered his clothes on his arm, opened the window, and lowered himself till his head only was above the sill, and his foot found a resting place. Thus he waited. The raucous breathing of the revellers was loud on the stairs; then the door was tried; there was some muttering; then the door was burst open and in rushed two, or perhaps three, figures. Rolf could  barely see in the gloom, but he knew that his uncle was one of them. The attack they made with whip and stick on that roll of rags in the bed would have broken his bones and left him shapeless, had he been in its place. The men were laughing and took it all as a joke, but Rolf had seen enough; he slipped to the ground and hurried away, realizing perfectly well now that this was "good-bye."

Which way? How naturally his steps turned northward toward Redding, the only other place he knew. But he had not gone a mile before he stopped. The yapping of a coon dog came to him from the near woods that lay to the westward along Asamuk. He tramped toward it. To find the dog is one thing, to find the owner another; but they drew near at last. Rolf gave the three yelps and Quonab responded.

"I am done with that crowd," said the boy. "They tried to kill me to-night. Have you got room for me in your wigwam for a couple of days?"

"Ugh, come," said the Indian.

That night, for the first time, Rolf slept in the outdoor air of a wigwam. He slept late, and knew nothing of the world about him till Quonab called him to breakfast.

VI

Skookum Accepts Rolf at Last

ROLF expected that Micky would soon hear of his hiding place and come within a few days, backed by a constable, to claim his runaway ward. But a week went by and Quonab, passing through Myanos, learned, first, that Rolf had been seen tramping northward on the road to Dumpling Pond, and was now supposed to be back in Redding; second, that Micky Kittering was lodged in jail under charge of horse-stealing and would certainly get a long sentence; third, that his wife had gone back to her own folks at Norwalk, and the house was held by strangers.

All other doors were closed now, and each day that drifted by made it the more clear that Rolf and Quonab were to continue together. What boy would not exult at the thought of it? Here was freedom from a brutal tyranny that was crushing out his young life; here was a dream of the wild world coming true, with gratification of all the hunter instincts that he had held in his heart for years, and nurtured in that single, ragged volume of *Robinson Crusoe*. The plunge was not a plunge, except it be one when an eagle, pinion-bound, is freed and springs from a cliff of the mountain to ride the mountain wind.

The memory of that fateful cooning day was deep and lasting. Never afterward did smell of coon fail to bring it back; in spite of the many evil incidents it was a smell of joy.

"Where are you going, Quonab?" he asked one morning, as he saw the Indian rise at dawn and go forth with his song drum, after warming it at the fire. He pointed up to the rock, and for the first time Rolf heard the chant for the sunrise. Later he heard the Indian's song for "Good Hunting," and another for "When His Heart Was Bad." They were prayers or praise, all addressed to the Great Spirit, or the Great Father, and it gave Rolf an entirely new idea of the red man, and a startling light on himself. Here was the Indian, whom no one considered anything but a hopeless pagan, praying to God for guidance at each step in life, while he himself, supposed to be a Christian, had not prayed regularly for months — was in danger of forgetting how.

Yet there was one religious observance that Rolf never forgot — that was to keep the Sabbath, and on that day each week he did occasionally say a little prayer his mother had taught him. He avoided being seen at such times and did not speak of kindred doings. Whereas Quonab neither hid nor advertised his religious practices, and it was only after many Sundays had gone that Quonab remarked:

"Does your God come only one day of the week? Does He sneak in after dark? Why is He ashamed that you only whisper to Him? Mine is here all the time. I can always reach Him with my song; all days are my Sunday."

The evil memories of his late life were dimming quickly, and the joys of the new one growing. Rolf learned early that, although one may talk of the hardy savage, no Indian seeks for hardship. Everything is done that he knows to make life pleasant, and of nothing is he more careful than the comfort of his couch. On the second day, under guidance of his host, Rolf set about making his own bed. Two logs, each four inches thick and three feet long, were cut. Then two strong poles, each six feet long, were laid into notches at the ends of the short logs. About seventy-five straight sticks of willow were cut and woven with willow bark into a lattice, three feet wide and six feet long. This, laid on the

poles, furnished a spring mattress, on which a couple of blankets made a most comfortable couch, dry, warm, and off the ground. In addition to the lodge cover, each bed had a dew cloth which gave perfect protection, no matter how the storm might rage outdoors. There was no hardship in it, only a new-found pleasure, to sleep and breathe the pure night air of the woods.

The Grass Moon — April — had passed, and the Song Moon was waxing, with its hosts of small birds, and one of Rolf's early discoveries was that many of these love to sing by night. Again and again the familiar voice of the song sparrow came from the dark shore of Asamuk, or the field sparrow trilled from the top of some cedar,

The Sunrise Song

occasionally the painted one, Aunakeu, the partridge, drummed in the upper woods, and nightly there was the persistent chant of Muckawis, the whip-poor-will, the myriad voices of the little frogs called spring-peepers, and the peculiar "*peent, peent*" from the sky, followed by a twittering, that Quonab told him was the love song of the swamp bird — the big snipe, with the fantail and long, soft bill, and eyes like a deer.

"Do you mean the woodcock?"

"Ugh, that's the name; Pah-dash-ka-anja we call it."

The waning of the moon brought new songsters, with many a nightingale among them. A low bush near the plain was vocal during the full moon with the sweet but disconnected music of the yellow-breasted chat. The forest rang again and again with a wild, torrential strain of music that seemed to come from the stars. It sent a peculiar thrill into Rolf's heart, and gave him a lump in his throat as he listened.

"What is that, Quonab?"

The Indian shook his head. Then, later, when it ended, he said: "That is the mystery song of someone. I never saw him."

There was a long silence, then the lad began, "There's no good hunting here now, Quonab. Why don't you go to the north woods, where deer are plentiful?"

The Indian gave a short shake of his head, and then, to prevent further talk, "Put up your dew cloth; the sea wind blows to-night."

He finished; both stood for a moment gazing into the fire. Then Rolf felt something wet and cold thrust into his hand. It was Skookum's nose. At last the little dog had made up his mind to accept the white boy as a friend.

VII

Memory's Harp and the Indian Drum

IN EARLY morning, or in dew time, before using his tom-tom, Quonab would tune it by warming it over the fire. On wet days it was so relaxed that he would tighten the back thongs. One day, after a thong tightening and warming, it sang so shrilly that Rolf turned to inquire, when crack! and the skin split open.

"It was old; I make a new one," was all its owner said.

That morning Rolf saw how it was made. A six-foot length of a four-inch hickory sapling was split and trimmed down to a long strip three inches wide and an inch thick in the middle, thin at the edges, rounded on one side, flat on the other. Then, flat side in, it was bent into a large hoop, and after treatment with hot water and steam to keep it from breaking, the hoop was reduced to fifteen inches across, and the ends, when thinned down, were lashed in place with some thongs cut from a rawhide and soaked in water till soft.

Raw buckskin is best for a tom-tom head, but having none, Quonab took an old calfskin from his storehouse under the rock. After this was softened by soaking over night in the pond, he covered the hairy side with a cream of quicklime and water. Next morning the hair was easily scraped off; then, after all fat and loose ends were removed from the hide, the hoop was set on it, and a circle cut out about five inches larger on all sides; a strong thong of rawhide was laced through the edge of this, and used as a puckering string when the loose flap was brought together on the upper side of the hoop. Now thongs were passed tightly across the back in four different places, so that they crossed in the centre, making eight rows of spokes. A final thong passed over and under these, in the centre, round and round, stretched the skin as much as desired. As soon as it dried out, the tension became very marked, and the sound of the ever-hardening rawhide took on almost a metallic character.

Rolf in the Woods

As the Indian tummed it Rolf felt strangely influenced. What was it in his nature that responded? He did not know, any more than the soldier knows, or the Salvationist knows, what power to sway the soul there is in the rhythmic, vibrant "tum-ta-tum-ta" of the big drum. But the power is there, and the wise halt not to seek the reason, but accept its help to make good their sway — the king who rules the army, the preacher who leads the Salvationists, and the medicine-man who would shape the red man's life.

Quonab sang at length his song of the long ago when his people, the Wabanaki, the Men of the Day-dawn, came westward, fighting their way, till they possessed all the country to the great Shatemuk, which white men call the Hudson. And, singing, he stirred his memory, till it opened up his heart. The silent Indian, like King William the Silent, got his reputation because of his behaviour at certain times. To strangers Indians are silent, reserved, and shy. Among themselves they are very human, some of them very talkative; and Rolf found that silent Quonab could, in the intimacy of camp life, become very outspoken when the right cord was touched in the very right way.

The song of the Wabanaki led Rolf to ask, "Did your people always live right here?" And then, in fragments, he got a history.

Long before the white man came, the Sinawa won and held this land from Quinnuhtekut to Shatemuk; then came the white men, Dutchmen from Manhattan and Englishmen from Massachusetts. First they made treaties; then, in time of peace, they gathered an army, and taking advantage of the truce and of the mid-winter festival that gathered all the tribe in the walled town of Petuquapen, the soldiers surrounded the place, and when the flames of their burning homes drove out the folk, they were slaughtered like deer in the snow-drifts.

"There stood the great village of my fathers," and the Indian pointed a quarter mile away to the level place next, the rock ridge that lies along the west of Strickland's Plain. "There stood the house of the mighty Amogerone, who was so honest that he thought all men were to be trusted, so trusted even the whites. That road away from the north was the moccasin trail, and where it forks to go to Cos Cob and Mya-nos, it ran ankle deep in blood that night; from that low mount to this the snow was black with bodies.

"How many perished? A thousand, mostly women and children. How many of the attack were killed? None, not one. Why should they? It was a time of peace. Our people were unprepared — were without guns. The enemy was in ambush.

"Only the brave Mayn Mayano escaped; he who bitterly opposed the Chief when the treaty was made — the 'Fighting Sagamore,' the English called him. Now all was open war for him. Many and many a scalp he took. He never feared to face double odds, and won and won, till he grew reckless. 'One Indian Sagamore is better than three white men,' he boldly proclaimed, and proved it again and again. But on an evil day, when armed only with a tomahawk, he attacked three soldiers wearing armour and bearing guns and pistols. The first he killed, the second disabled, but the third, a captain in a steel helmet that turned the tomahawk, had little ado to stand ten feet aside and shoot the brave Mayn Mayano through the heart. Yonder by that hill, on the highway to Stamford where he fell, his widow buried him. On the river that bears his name the remnant of his people lived, till all were gone but my father's lodge.

"Here Cos Cob, my father, brought me when a child, even as his grandfather once brought him, and showed me the place of our Royal Petuquapen. There along the plain it stretched, and there is the trail that ran so deep in blood. Here in the little swampy woods, where the ground was soft, the butchers piled our dead; close under that rocky hill beside the Asamuk, lie the murdered tribe. Our children used to come in the Wild Goose Moon to the top of that hill, because there, first of all, the little blue-eyes of spring used to show. I often come to find them, and as I sit I seem to hear the cry that rang in the night from the burning town, of mothers, of babies, killed like rabbits.

"But I remember, too, the brave Mayn Mayano. His spirit comes to help me as I sit and sing the songs of my people — not the war songs, but the songs of another land. I alone am left. A little while, and I shall be with them. Here have I dwelt, and here I would die." The Indian ceased and again became the silent one.

Rolf in the Woods

Late that day he took his new song-drum from its peg, went quietly to the top of the great rock, where he prayed, and the words of the song that he sang were:

"Father, we walk in darkness;
Father we do not understand;
Walking darkly, we bow the head."

VIII

The Law of Property Among Our Four-Footed Kin

NIGHT came down on the Asamuk woods, and the two in the wigwam were eating their supper of pork, beans, and tea, for the Indian did not, by any means object to the white man's luxuries, when a strange "yap-yurr" was heard out toward the plain. The dog was up at once with a growl. Rolf looked inquiringly, and Quonab said, "Fox," then bade the dog be still.

"Yap-yurr, yap-yurr," and then, "yurr, yeow," it came again and again. "Can we get him?" said the eager young hunter. The Indian shook his head.

"Fur no good now. An' that's a she-one, with young ones on the hillside."

"How do you know?" was the amazed inquiry.

"I know it's a she-one, 'cause she says:

yap yurr

If it was a he-one he'd say:

yap yurr

"And she has cubs, 'cause all have at this season. And they are on that hillside, because that's the nearest place where any fox den is, and they keep pretty much to their own hunting grounds. If another fox should come hunting on the beat of this pair, he'd have to fight for it. That is the way of the wild animals; each has his own run, and for that he will fight an outsider that he would be afraid of at any other place. One knows he is right — that braces him up; the other knows he is wrong — and that weakens him." Those were the Indian's views, expressed much less connectedly than here given, and they led Rolf on to a train of thought. He remembered a case that was much to the point.

Their little dog Skookum several times had been worsted by the dog on the Horton farm, when, following his master, he had come into the house yard. There was no question that the Horton dog was stronger. But Skookum had buried a bone under some bushes by the plain and next day the hated Horton dog appeared. Skookum watched him with suspicion and fear, until it was no longer doubtful that the enemy had smelled the hidden food and was going for it. Then Skookum, braced up by some instinctive feeling, rushed forward with bristling mane and gleaming teeth, stood over his *cache*, and said in plainest dog, "You can't touch that while I live!"

And the Horton dog — accustomed to domineer over the small yellow cur — growled contemptuously, scratched with his hind feet, smelled around an adjoining bush, and pretending not to see or notice, went off in another direction.

What was it that robbed him of his courage, but the knowledge that he was in the wrong?

Continuing with his host Rolf said, "Do you think they have any idea that it is wrong to steal?"

"Yes, so long as it is one of their own tribe. A fox will take all he can get from a bird or a rabbit or a woodchuck, but he won't go far on the hunting grounds of another fox. He won't go into another fox's den or touch one of its young ones, and if he finds a *cache* of food with another fox's mark on it, he won't touch it unless he is near dead of hunger."

"How do you mean they *cache* food and how do they mark it?"

"Generally they bury it under the leaves and soft earth, and the only mark is to leave their body scent. But that is strong enough, and every fox knows it."

"Do wolves make food *caches*?"

"Yes, wolves, cougars, weasels, squirrels, bluejays, crows, owls, mice, all do, and all have their own way of marking a place."

"Suppose a fox finds a wolf *cache*, will he steal from it?"

"Yes, always. There is no law between fox and wolf. They are always at war with each other. There is law only between fox and fox, or wolf and wolf."

"That is like ourselves, ain't it? We say, 'Thou shalt not steal,' and then when we steal the Indian's land or the Frenchman's ships, we say, 'Oh, that don't mean not steal from our enemies; they are fair game.'"

Quonab rose to throw some sticks on the fire, then went out to turn the smoke flap of the wigwam, for the wind was changed and another set was needed to draw the smoke. They heard several times again the high-pitched "yap-yurr," and once the deeper notes, which told that the dog fox, too, was near the camp, and was doubtless seeking food to carry home.

IX

Where the Bow Is Better Than the Gun

OF ALL popular errors about the Indians, the hardest to down is the idea that their women do all the work. They do the housework, it is true, but all the heavy labour beyond their strength is done by the men. Examples of this are seen in the frightful toil of hunting, canoeing, and portaging, besides a multitude of kindred small tasks, such as making snowshoes, bows, arrows, and canoes.

Each warrior usually makes his own bow and arrows, and if, as often happens, one of them proves more skilful and turns out better weapons, it is a common thing for others to offer their own specialty in exchange.

The advantages of the bow over the gun are chiefly its noiselessness, its cheapness, and the fact that one can make its ammunition anywhere. As the gun chiefly used in Quonab's time was the old-fashioned, smooth-bore flint-lock, there was not much difference in the accuracy of the two weapons. Quonab had always made a high-class bow, as well as high-class arrows, and was a high-class shot. He could set up ten clam shells at ten paces and break all in ten shots. For at least half of his hunting he preferred the bow; the gun was useful to him chiefly when flocks of wild pigeons or ducks were about, and a single charge of scattering shot might bring down a dozen birds.

But there is a law in all shooting — to be an expert, you must practise continually — and when Rolf saw his host shoot nearly every day at some mark, he tried to join in the sport.

It took not many trys to show that the bow was far too strong for him to use, and Quonab was persuaded at length to make an outfit for his visitor.

From the dry store hole under the rock, he produced a piece of common red cedar. Some use hickory; it is less liable to break and will stand more abuse, but it has not the sharp, clean action of cedar. The latter will send the arrow much farther, and so swiftly does it leave the string that it baffles the eye. But the cedar bow must be cared for like a delicate machine, overstring it, and it breaks; twang it without an arrow, and it sunders the cords; scratch it, and it may splinter; wet it, and it is dead; let it lie on the ground, even, and it is weakened. But guard it and it will serve you as a matchless servant, and as can no other timber in these woods.

Just where the red heart and the white sap woods join is the bowman's choice. A piece that reached from Rolf's chin to the ground was shaved down till it was flat on the white side and round on the red side, tapering from the middle, where it was one inch wide and one inch thick to the ends, where it was three fourths of an inch wide and five eighths of an inch thick, the red and white wood equal in all parts.

The string was made of sinew from the back of a cow, split from the long, broad sheath that lies on each side of the spine, and the bow strung for trial. Now, on drawing it (flat or white side in front), it was found that one arm bent more than the other, so a little more scraping was done on the strong side, till both bent alike.

Quonab's arrows would answer, but Rolf needed a supply of his own. Again there was great choice of material. The long, straight shoots of the arrowwood (*Viburnum dentatum*) supplied the ancient Indians, but Quonab had adopted a better way, since the possession of an axe made it possible. A 25-inch block of straight-grained ash was split and split until it yielded enough pieces. These were shaved down to one fourth of an inch thick, round, smooth, and perfectly straight. Each was notched deeply at one end; three pieces of split goose feather were lashed on the notched end, and three different kinds of arrows were made. All were alike in shaft and in feathering, but differed in the head. First, the target arrows: these were merely sharpened, and the points hardened by roasting to a brown colour. They would have been better with conical points of steel, but none of these were to be had. Second, the ordinary hunting arrows with barbed steel heads, usually bought ready-made, or filed out of a hoop: these were for use in securing such creatures as muskrats, ducks close at hand, or deer. Third, the bird bolts: these were left with a large, round, wooden head. They were intended for quail, partridges, rabbits, and squirrels, but also served very often, and most admirably, in punishing dogs, either the Indian's own when he was not living up to the rules and was too far off for a cuff or kick, or a farmer's dog that was threatening an attack.

Now the outfit was complete, Rolf thought, but one other touch was necessary. Quonab painted the feather part of the shaft bright red, and Rolf learned why. Not for ornament, not as an owner's mark, but as a *finding* mark. Many a time that brilliant red, with the white feather next to it, was the means of saving the arrow from loss. An uncoloured arrow among the sticks and leaves of the woods was usually hidden, but the bright-coloured shaft could catch the eye 100 yards away.

It was very necessary to keep the bow and arrows from the wet. For this, every hunter provides a case, usually of buckskin, but failing that they made a good quiver of birch bark laced with spruce roots for the arrows, and for the bow itself a long cover of tarpaulin.

Now came the slow drilling in archery; the arrow held and the bow drawn with three fingers on the cord — the thumb and little finger doing nothing. The target was a bag of hay set at twenty feet, until the beginner could hit it every time: then by degrees it was moved away until at the standard distance of forty yards he could do fair shooting, although of course he never shot as well as the Indian, who had practised since he was a baby.

There are three different kinds of archery tests: the first for aim: Can you shoot so truly as to hit a three-inch mark, ten times in succession, at ten paces?

Next for speed: Can you shoot so quickly and so far up, as to have five arrows in the air at once? If so, you are good: Can you keep up six? Then you are very good. Seven is wonderful. The record is said to be eight. Last for power: Can you pull so strong a bow and let the arrow go so clean that it will fly for 250 yards or will pass through a deer at ten paces? There is a record of a Sioux who sent an arrow through three antelopes at one shot, and it was not unusual to pierce the huge buffalo through and through; on one occasion a warrior with one shot pierced the buffalo and killed her calf running at the other side.

If you excel in these three things, you can down your partridge and squirrel every time; you can get five or six out of each flock of birds; you can kill your deer at twenty-five yards, and so need never starve in the woods where there is game.

Of course, Rolf was keen to go forth and try in the real chase, but it was many a shot he missed and many an arrow lost or broken, before he brought in even a red squirrel, and he got, at least, a higher appreciation of the skill of those who could count on the bow for their food.

For those, then, who think themselves hunters and woodmen, let this be a test and standard: Can you go forth alone into the wilderness where there is game, take only a bow and arrows for weapons, and travel afoot 250 miles, living on the country as you go?

X

Rolf Works Out with Many Results

"He is the dumbest kind of a dumb fool that ain't king in some little corner."

—Sayings of Si Syloanne

THE man who has wronged you will never forgive you, and he who has helped you will be forever grateful. Yes, there is nothing that draws you to a man so much as the knowledge that you have helped him.

Quonab helped Rolf, and so was more drawn to him than to many of the neighbours that he had known for years; he was ready to like him. Their coming together was accidental, but it was soon very clear that a friendship was springing up between them. Rolf was too much of a child to think about the remote future; and so was Quonab. Most Indians are merely tall children.

But there was one thing that Rolf did think of — he had no right to live in Quonab's lodge without contributing a fair share of the things needful. Quonab got his living partly by hunting, partly by fishing, partly by selling baskets, and partly by doing odd jobs for the neighbours. Rolf's training as a loafer had been wholly neglected, and when he realized that he might be all summer with Quonab he said bluntly:

"You let me stay here a couple of months. I'll work out odd days, and buy enough stuff to keep myself any way." Quonab said nothing, but their eyes met, and the boy knew it was agreed to.

Rolf went that very day to the farm of Obadiah Timpany, and offered to work by the day, hoeing corn and root crops. What farmer is not glad of help in planting time or in harvest? It was only a question of what did he know and how much did he want? The first was soon made clear; two dollars a week was the usual thing for boys in those times, and when he offered to take it half in trade, he was really getting three dollars a week and his board. Food was as low as wages, and at the end of a week, Rolf brought back to camp a sack of oatmeal, a sack of corn-meal, a bushel of potatoes, a lot of apples, and one dollar cash. The dollar went for tea and sugar, and the total product was enough to last them both a month; so Rolf could share the wigwam with a good conscience.

Of course, it was impossible to keep the gossipy little town of Myanos from knowing, first, that the Indian had a white boy for partner; and, later, that that boy was Rolf. This gave rise to great diversity of opinion in the neighbourhood. Some thought it should not be allowed, but Horton, who owned the land on which Quonab was camped, could not see any reason for interfering.

Ketchura Peck, spinster, however, did see many most excellent reasons. She was a maid with a mission, and maintained it to be an outrage that a Christian boy should be brought up by a godless pagan. She worried over it almost as much as she did over the heathen in Central Africa, where there are no Sunday schools, and clothes are as scarce as churches. Failing to move Parson Peck and Elder Knapp in the matter, and despairing of an early answer to her personal prayers, she resolved on a bold move, "An' it was only after many a sleepless, prayerful night," namely, to carry the Bible into the heathen's stronghold.

Thus it was that one bright morning in June she might have been seen, prim and proper — almost glorified, she felt, as she set her lips just right in the mirror — making for the Pipestave Pond, Bible in hand and spectacles clean wiped, ready to read appropriate selections to the unregenerate.

She was full of the missionary spirit when she left Myanos, and partly full when she reached the Orchard Street Trail; but the spirit was leaking badly, and the woods did appear so wild and lonely that she wondered if women had any right to be missionaries. When she came in sight of the pond, the place seemed unpleasantly different from Myanos and where was the Indian camp? She did not dare to shout; indeed, she began to wish she were home again, but the sense of duty carried her fully fifty yards along the pond, and then she came to an impassable rock, a sheer bank that plainly said, "Stop!" Now she must go back or up the bank. Her Yankee pertinacity said, "Try first up the bank," and she began a long, toilsome ascent, that did not end until she came out on a high, open rock which, on its farther side, had a sheer drop and gave a view of the village and of the sea.

Whatever joy she had on again seeing her home was speedily quelled in the fearsome discovery that she was night over the Indian camp, and the two inmates looked so utterly, dreadfully savage that she was thankful they had not seen her. At once she shrank back; but on recovering sufficiently to again peer down, she saw something roasting before the fire — "a tiny arm with a hand that bore five fingers," as she afterward said, and "a sickening horror came over her." Yes, she had heard of such things. If she could only get home in safety! Why had she tempted Providence thus? She backed softly and prayed only to escape. What, and never even deliver the Bible? "It would be wicked to return with it!" In a cleft of the rock she placed it, and then, to prevent the wind blowing off loose leaves, she placed a stone on top, and fled from the dreadful place.

That night, when Quonab and Rolf had finished their meal of corn and roasted coon, the old man climbed the rock to look at the sky. The book caught his eye at once, evidently hidden there carefully, and therefore in *cache*. A *cache* is a sacred thing to an Indian. He disturbed it not, but later asked Rolf, "That yours?"

"No."

It was doubtless the property of some one who meant to return for it, so they left it untouched. It rested there for many months, till the winter storms came down, dismantling the covers, dissolving the pages, but leaving such traces as, in the long afterward, served to identify the book and give the rock the other name, the one it bears to-day — "Bible Rock, where Quonab, the son of Cos Cob, used to live."

XI

The Thunder-storm and the Fire Sticks

WHEN first Rolf noticed the wigwam's place, he wondered that Quonab had not set it somewhere facing the lake, but he soon learned that it is best to have the morning sun, the afternoon shade, and shelter from the north and west winds.

The first two points were illustrated nearly every day; but it was two weeks before the last was made clear.

That day the sun came up in a red sky, but soon was lost to view in a heavy cloud-bank. There was no wind, and, as the morning passed, the day grew hotter and closer. Quonab prepared for a storm; but it came with unexpected force, and a gale of wind from the northwest that would indeed have wrecked the lodge, but for the great sheltering rock. Under its lea there was hardy a breeze; but not fifty yards away were two trees that rubbed together, and in the storm they rasped so violently that fine shreds of smoking wood were dropped and, but for the rain, would surely have made a blaze. The thunder was loud and lasted long, and the water poured down in torrents. They were ready for rain, but not for the flood that rushed over the face of the cliff, soaking everything in the lodge except the beds, which, being four inches off the ground, were safe; and lying on them the two campers waited patiently, or impatiently, while the weather raged for two drenching hours. And then the pouring became a pattering; the roaring, a swishing; the storm, a shower which died away, leaving changing patches of blue in the lumpy sky, and all nature calm and pleased, but oh, so wet! Of course the fire was out in the lodge and nearly all the wood was wet. Now Quonab drew from a small cave some dry cedar and got down his tinder-box with flint and steel to light up; but a serious difficulty appeared at once — the tinder was wet and useless.

Rolf in the Woods

These were the days before matches were invented. Every one counted on flint and steel for their fire, but the tinder was an essential, and now a fire seemed hopeless; at least Rolf thought so.

"Nana Bojou was dancing that time," said the Indian. "Did you see him make fire with those two rubbing trees? So he taught our fathers, and so make we fire when the tricks of the white man fail us."

Quonab now cut two pieces of dry cedar, one three fourths of an inch thick and eighteen inches long, round, and pointed at both ends; the other five eighths of an inch thick and flat. In the flat one he cut a notch and at the end of the notch a little pit. Next he made a bow of a stiff, curved stick, and a buckskin thong: a small pine knot was selected and a little pit made in it with the point of a knife. These were the fire-making sticks, but it was necessary to prepare the firewood, lay the fire, and make some fibre for tinder. A lot of fine cedar shavings, pounded up with cedar bark and rolled into a two-inch ball, made good tinder, and all was ready. Quonab put the bow thong once around the long stick, then held its point in the pit of the flat stick, and the pine knot on the top to steady it. Now he drew the bow back and forth, slowly, steadily, till the long stick or drill revolving ground smoking black dust out of the notch. Then faster, until the smoke was very strong and the powder filled the notch. Then he lifted the flat stick, fanning the powder with his hands till a glowing coal appeared. Over this he put the cedar tinder and blew gently, till it flamed, and soon the wigwam was aglow.

The whole time taken, from lifting the sticks to the blazing fire, was less than one minute.

This is the ancient way of the Indian; Rolf had often heard of it as a sort of semi-myth; never before had he seen it, and so far as he could learn from the books, it took an hour or two of hard work, not a few deft touches and a few seconds of time.

He soon learned to do it himself, and in the years which followed, he had the curious experience of showing it to many Indians who had forgotten how, thanks to the greater portability of the white man's flint and steel.

As they walked in the woods that day, they saw three trees that had been struck by lightning during the recent storm; all three were oaks.

The Thunder-storm and the Fire Sticks

Then it occurred to Rolf that he had never seen any but an oak struck by lightning. "Is it so, Quonab?"

"No, there are many others; the lightning strikes the oaks most of all, but it will strike the pine, the ash, the hemlock, the basswood, and many more. Only two trees have I never seen struck, the balsam and the birch."

"Why do they escape?"

"My father told me when I was a little boy it was because they sheltered and warmed the Star-girl, who was the sister of the Thunder-bird."

"I never heard that; tell me about it."

"Sometime maybe, not now."

XII

Hunting the Woodchucks

CORNMEAL and potatoes, with tea and apples, three times a day, are apt to lose their charm. Even fish did not entirely satisfy the craving for flesh meat. So Quonab and Rolf set out one morning on a regular hunt for food. The days of big game were over on the Asamuk, but there were still many small kinds and none more abundant than the woodchuck, hated of farmers. Not without reason. Each woodchuck hole in the field was a menace to the horses' legs. Tradition, at least, said that horses' legs and riders' necks had been broken by the steed setting foot in one of these dangerous pitfalls: besides which, each chuck den was the hub centre of an area of desolation whenever located, as mostly it was, in the cultivated fields. Undoubtedly the damage was greatly exaggerated, but the farmers generally agreed that the woodchuck was a pest.

Whatever resentment the tiller of the soil might feel against the Indian's hunting quail on his land, he always welcomed him as a killer of woodchucks.

And the Indian looked on this animal as fair game and most excellent eating.

Rolf watched eagerly when Quonab, taking his bow and arrows, said they were going out for a meat hunt. Although there were several fields with woodchucks resident, they passed cautiously from one to another, scanning the green expanse for the dark-brown spots that meant woodchucks out foraging. At length they found one, with a large and two small moving brown things among the clover. The large one stood up on its hind legs from time to time, ever alert for danger. It was a broad, open field, without cover; but close to the cleared place in which, doubtless, was the den, there was a ridge that Quonab judged would help him to approach.

Rolf in the Woods

Rolf was instructed to stay in hiding and make some Indian signs that the hunter could follow when he should lose sight of the prey. First, "Come on" (beckoning); and, second, "Stop" (hand raised, palm forward); "All right" (hand drawn across level and waist high); forefinger moved forward, level, then curved straight down, meant "gone in hole." But Rolf was not to sign anything or move, unless Quonab asked him by making the question sign (that is waving his hand with palm forward and spread fingers).

Quonab went back into the woods, then behind the stone walls to get around to the side next the ridge, and crawling so flat on his breast in the clover that, although it was but a foot high, he was quite invisible to any one not placed much above him.

In this way he came to the little ridge back of the woodchuck den, quite unknown to its occupants. But now he was in a difficulty. He could not see any of them. They were certainly beyond range of his bow, and it was difficult to make them seek the den without their rushing into it. But he was equal to the occasion. He raised one hand and made the query sign, and watching Rolf he got answer, "All well; they are there." (A level sweep of the flat hand and a finger pointing steadily.) Then he waited a few seconds and made exactly the same sign, getting the same answer.

He knew that the movement of the distant man would catch the eye of the old woodchuck; she would sit up high to see what it was, and when it came a second time she would, without being exactly alarmed, move toward the den and call the young ones to follow.

The hunter had not long to wait. He heard her shrill, warning whistle, then the big chuck trotted and waddled into sight, stopping occasionally to nibble or look around. Close behind her were the two fat cubs. Arrived near the den their confidence was restored, and again they began to feed, the young ones close to the den. Then Quonab put a blunt bird dart in his bow and laid two others ready. Rising as little as possible, he drew the bow. *'Tsip!* the blunt arrow hit the young chuck on the nose and turned him over. The other jumped in surprise and stood up. So did the mother. *'Tsip!* another bolt and the second chuck was kicking. But the old one dashed like a flash into the underground safety of her den. Quonab knew that she had seen nothing of him and would likely come forth very soon. He waited for some time; then the gray-brown muzzle of the fat old clover-stealer came partly to view; but it was not enough for a shot, and she seemed to have no idea of coming farther. The Indian waited what seemed like a long time, then played an ancient trick. He began to whistle a soft, low air. Whether the chuck thinks it is another woodchuck calling, or merely a pleasant sound, is not known, but she soon did as her kind always does, came out of the hole slowly and ever higher, till she was half out and sitting up, peering about.

This was Quonab's chance. He now drew a barbed hunting arrow to the head and aimed it behind her shoulders. *'Tsip!* and the chuck was transfixed by a shaft that ended her life a minute later, and immediately prevented that instinctive scramble into the hole, by which so many chucks elude the hunter, even when mortally wounded.

Now Quonab stood up without further concealment, and beckoned to Rolf, who came running. Three fat woodchucks meant abundance of the finest fresh meat for a week; and those who have not tried it have no idea what a delicacy is a young, fat, clover-fed woodchuck, pan-roasted, with potatoes, and served at a blazing camp-fire to a hunter who is young, strong, and exceedingly hungry.

XIII

The Fight with the Demon of the Deep

ONE morning, as they passed the trail that skirts the pond, Quonab pointed to the near water. There was something afloat like a small, round leaf, with two beads well apart, on it. Then Rolf noticed, two feet away, a larger floating leaf, and now he knew that the first was the head and eyes, the last the back, of a huge snapping turtle. A moment more and it quickly sank from view. Turtles of three different kinds were common, and snappers were well known to Rolf; but never before had he seen such a huge and sinister-looking monster of the deep.

"That is Bosikado. I know him; he knows me," said the red man. "There has long been war between us; some day we will settle it. I saw him here first three years ago. I had shot a duck; it floated on the water. Before I could get to it something pulled it under, and that was the last of it. Then a summer duck came with young ones. One by one he took them, and at last got her. He drives all ducks away, so I set many night lines for him. I got some little snappers, eight and ten pounds each. They were good to eat, and three times already I took Bosikado on the hooks, but each time when I pulled him up to the canoe, he broke my biggest line and went down. He was as broad as the canoe; his claws broke through the canoe skin; he made it bulge and tremble. He looked like the devil of the lake. *I was afraid!*

"But my father taught me there is only one thing that can shame a man — that is to be afraid, and I said I will never let fear be my guide. I will seek a fair fight with Bosikado. He is my enemy. He made me afraid once; I will make him much afraid. For three years we have been watching each other. For three years he has kept all summer ducks away, and robbed my fish-lines, my nets, and my muskrat traps. Not often do I see him — mostly like to-day.

"Before Skookum I had a little dog, Nindai. He was a good little dog. He could tree a coon, catch a rabbit, or bring out a duck, although he was very small. We were very good friends. One time I shot a duck; it fell into the lake; I called Nindai. He jumped into the water and swam to the duck. Then that duck that I thought dead got up and flew away, so I called Nindai. He came across the water to me. By and by, over that deep place, he howled and splashed. Then he yelled, like he wanted me. I ran for the canoe and paddled quick; I saw my little dog Nindai go down. Then I knew it was that Bosikado again. I worked a long time with a pole, but found nothing; only five days later one of Nindai's paws floated down the stream. Some day I will tear open that Bosikado!

"Once I saw him on the bank. He rolled down like a big stone to the water. He looked at me before he dived, and as we looked in each other's eyes I knew he was a Manito; but he is evil, and my father said, 'When an evil Manito comes to trouble you, you must kill him.'

"One day, when I swam after a dead duck, he took me by the toe, but I reached shallow water and escaped him; and once I drove my fish-spear in his back, but it was not strong enough to hold him. Once he caught Skookum's tail, but the hair came out; the dog has not since swum across the pond.

"Twice I have seen him like to-day and might have killed him with the gun, but I want to meet him fighting. Many a time I have sat on the bank and sung to him the 'Coward's Song,' and dared him to come and fight in the shallow water where we are equals. He hears me. He does not come.

"I know he made me sick last winter; even now he is making trouble with his evil magic. But my magic must prevail, and some day we shall meet. He made me afraid once. *I will make him much afraid, and will meet him in the water.*"

Not many days were to pass before the meeting. Rolf had gone for water at the well, which was a hole dug ten feet from the shore of the lake. He had learned the hunter's cautious trick of going silently

and peering about, before he left cover. On a mud bank in a shallow bay, some fifty yards off, he described a peculiar gray and greenish form that he slowly made out to be a huge turtle, sunning itself. The more he looked and gauged it with things about, the bigger it seemed. So he slunk back quickly and silently to Quonab. "He is out sunning himself — Bosikado — on the bank!"

The Indian rose quickly, took his tomahawk and a strong line. Rolf reached for the gun, but Quonab shook his head. They went to the lake. Yes! There was the great, goggle-eyed monster, like a mud-coloured log. The bank behind him was without cover. It would be impossible to approach the watchful creature within striking distance before he could dive. Quonab would not use the gun; in this case he felt he must atone by making an equal fight. He quickly formed a plan; he fastened the tomahawk and the coiled rope to his belt, then boldly and silently slipped into the lake, to approach the snapper from the water side — quite the easiest in this case, not only because the snapper would naturally watch on the land side, but because there was a thick clump of rushes behind which the swimmer could approach.

Then, as instructed, Rolf went back into the woods, and came silently to a place whence he could watch the snapper from a distance of twenty yards.

The boy's heart beat fast as he watched the bold swimmer and the savage reptile. There could be little doubt that the creature weighed a hundred pounds. It is the strongest for its size and the fiercest of all reptiles. Its jaws, though toothless, have cutting edges, a sharp beak, and power to the crushing of bones. Its armour makes it invulnerable to birds and beasts of prey. like a log it lay on the beach, with its long alligator tail stretched up the bank and its serpentine head and tiny wicked eves vigilantly watching the shore. Its shell, broad and ancient, was fringed with green moss, and its scaly armpits exposed, were decked with leeches, at which a couple of peelweets pecked with eager interest, apparently to the monster's satisfaction. Its huge limbs and claws were

in marked contrast to the small, red eyes. But the latter it was that gave the thrill of unnervement.

Sunk down nearly out of sight, the Indian slowly reached the reeds. Here he found bottom, and pausing, he took the rope in one hand, the tomahawk in the other, and dived, and when he reappeared he was within ten yards of the enemy, and in water but four feet deep.

With a sudden rush the reptile splashed into the pond and out of sight, avoiding the rope noose. But Quonab clutched deep in the water as it passed, and seized the monster's rugged tail. Then it showed its strength. In a twinkling that mighty tail was swung sidewise, crushing the hand with terrible force against the sharp-edged points of the back armour. It took all the Indian's grit to hold on to that knife-edged war club. He dropped his tomahawk, then with his other hand swung the rope to catch the turtle's head, but it lurched so quickly that the rope missed again, slipped over the shell, and, as they struggled, encircled one huge paw. The Indian jerked it tight, and they were bound together. But now his only weapon was down at the bottom and the water all muddied. He could not see, but plunged to grope for the tomahawk. The snapper gave a great lurch to escape, releasing the injured hand, but jerking the man off his legs. Then, finding itself held by a forepaw, it turned with gaping, hissing jaws, and sprang on the foe that struggled in the bottom of the water.

The snapper has the bulldog habit to seize and hold till the piece tears out. In the muddy water it had to seize in the dark, and finding first the left arm of its foe, fastened on with fierce beak and desperate strength. At this moment Quonab recovered his tomahawk; rising into the air he dragged up the hanging snapper, and swung the weapon with all the force of his free arm. The blow sank through the monster's shell, deep into its back, without any visible effect, except to rob the Indian of his weapon, as he could not draw it out.

Then Rolf rushed into the water to help. But Quonab gasped, "No, no, go back — I'm alone."

The creature's jaws were locked on his arm, but its front claws, tearing downward and outward, were demolishing the coat that had protected it, and long lines of mingled blood were floating on the waves.

After a desperate plunge toward shallow water, Quonab gave another wrench to the tomahawk — it moved, loosed; another, and it was free. Then "chop, chop, chop," and that long, serpentine neck was severed; the body, waving its great scaly legs and lashing its alligator tail, went swimming downward, but the huge head, blinking its bleary, red eyes and streaming with blood, was clinched on his arm. The Indian made for the bank, hauling the rope that held the living body, and fastened it to a tree, then drew his knife to cut the jaw muscles of the head that ground its beak into his flesh. But the muscles were protected by armour plates and bone; he could not deal a stab to end their power. In vain he fumbled and slashed, until in a spasmodic quiver the jaws gaped wide and the bloody head fell to the ground. Again it snapped, but a tree branch bore the brunt; on this the strong jaws clinched, and so remained.

For over an hour the headless body crawled, or tried to crawl, always toward the lake. And now they could look at the enemy. Not his size so much as his weight surprised them. Although barely four feet long, he was so heavy that Rolf could not lift him. Quonab's scratches were many but slight; only the deep bill wound made on his arm and the bruises of the jaws were at all serious, and of these he made light. Headed by Skookum in full 'yap,' they carried the victim's body to camp; the grim head, still clutching the stick, was decorated with three feathers, then set on a pole near the wigwam. And the burden of the red man's song when next he sang was:

> "Bosikado, mine enemy was mighty,
> But I went into his country
> And made him afraid!"

XIV

Selectman Horton Appears at the Rock

SUMMER was at its height on the Asamuk. The wood thrush was nearing the end of its song; a vast concourse of young robins in their speckled plumage joined chattering every night in the thickest cedars; and one or two broods of young ducks were seen on the Pipestave Pond.

Rolf had grown wonderfully well into his wigwam life. He knew now exactly how to set the flap so as to draw out all the smoke, no matter which way the wind blew; he had learned the sunset signs, which tell what change of wind the night might bring. He knew without going to the shore whether the tide was a little ebb, with poor chances, or a mighty outflow that would expose the fattest oyster beds. His practiced fingers told at a touch whether it was a turtle or a big fish on his night line; and by the tone of the tom-tom he knew when a rainstorm was at hand.

Being trained in industry, he had made many improvements in their camp, not the least of which was to clean up and bum all the rubbish and garbage that attracted hordes of flies. He had fitted into the camp partly by changing it to fit himself, and he no longer felt that his stay there was a temporary shift. When it was to end, he neither knew nor cared. He realized only that he was enjoying life as he never had done before. His canoe had passed a lot of rapids and was now in a steady, unbroken stream — but it was the swift shoot before the fall. A lull in the clamour does not mean the end of war, but a new onset preparing; and, of course, it came in the way least looked for.

Selectman Horton stood well with the community; he was a man of good judgment, good position, and kind heart. He was owner of all the woods along the Asamuk, and thus the Indian's landlord on the Indian's ancestral land. Both Rolf and Quonab had worked for Horton, and so they knew him well, and liked him for his goodness.

Rolf in the Woods

It was Wednesday morning, late in July, when Selectman Horton, clean-shaven and large, appeared at the wigwam under the rock.

"Good morrow to ye both!" Then without wasting time he plunged in. "There's been some controversy and much criticism of the selectmen for allowing a white lad, the child of Christian parents, the grandson of a clergyman, to leave all Christian folk and folds, and herd with a pagan, to become, as it were, a mere barbarian. I hold not, indeed, with those that out of hand would condemn as godless a good fellow like Quonab, who, in my certain knowledge and according to his poor light, doth indeed maintain in some kind a daily worship of a sort. Nevertheless, the selectmen, the magistrates, the clergy, the people generally, and above all the Missionary Society, are deeply moved in the matter. It hath even been made a personal charge against myself, and with much bitterness I am held up as unzealous for allowing such a nefarious stronghold of Satan to continue on mine own demesne, and harbour one, escaped, as it were, from grace. Acting, therefore, not according to my heart,

but as spokesman of the Town Council, the Synod of Elders, and the Society for the Promulgation of Godliness among the Heathen, I am to state that you, Rolf Kittering, being without kinsfolk and under age, are in verity a ward of the parish, and as such, it hath been arranged that you become a member of the household of the most worthy Elder Ezekiel Peck, a household filled with the spirit of estimable piety and true doctrine; a man, indeed, who, notwithstanding his exterior coldness and severity, is very sound in all matters regarding the Communion of Saints, and, I may even say in a measure a man of fame for some most excellent remarks he hath passed on the shorter catechism, beside which he hath gained much approval for having pointed out two hidden meanings in the 27th verse of the 12th chapter of Hebrews; one whose very presence, therefore, is a guarantee against levity, laxity, and false preachment.

"There, now, my good lad, look not so like a colt that feels the whip for the first time. You will have a good home, imbued with the spirit of a most excellent piety that will be ever about you."

"Like a colt feeling the whip," indeed! Rolf reeled like a stricken deer. To go back as a chore-boy drudge was possible, but not alluring; to leave Quonab, just as the wood world was opening to him, was devastating; but to exchange it all for bondage in the pious household of

Selectman Horton Appears at the Rock

Old Peck, whose cold cruelty had driven off all his own children, was an accumulation of disasters that aroused him.

"I won't go!" he blurted out, and gazed defiantly at the broad and benevolent selectman.

"Come now, Rolf, such language is unbecoming. Let not a hasty tongue betray you into sin. This is what your mother would have wished. Be sensible; you will soon find it was all for the best. I have ever liked you, and will ever be a friend you can count on.

"Acting, not according to my instructions, but according to my heart, I will say further that you need not come *now*, you need not even give answer now, but think it over. Nevertheless, remember that on or before Monday morning next, you will be expected to appear at Elder Peck's, and I fear that, in case you fail, the messenger next arriving will be one much less friendly than myself. Come now, Rolf, be a good lad, and remember that in your new home you will at least be living for the glory of God."

Then, with a friendly nod, but an expression of sorrow, the large, black messenger turned and tramped away.

Rolf slowly, limply, sank down on a rock and stared at the fire. After awhile Quonab got up and began to prepare the mid-day meal. Usually Rolf helped him. Now he did nothing but sullenly glare at the glowing coals. In half an hour the food was ready. He ate little; then went away in the woods by himself. Quonab saw him lying, on a flat rock, looking at the pond, and throwing pebbles into it. Later Quonab went to Myanos. On his return he found that Rolf had cut up a great pile of wood, but not a word passed between them. The look of sullen anger and rebellion on Rolf's face was changing to one of stony despair. What was passing in each mind the other could not divine.

The evening meal was eaten in silence; then Quonab smoked for an hour, both staring into the fire. A barred owl hooted and laughed over their heads, causing the dog to jump up and bark at the sound that ordinarily he would have heeded not at all. Then silence was restored, and the red man's hidden train of thought was in a flash revealed.

"Rolf, let's go to the North Woods!"

It was another astounding idea. Rolf had realized more and more how much this valley meant to Quonab, who worshipped the memory of his people.

Rolf in the Woods

"And leave all this?" he replied, making a sweep with his hand toward the rock, the Indian trail, the site of bygone Petuquapen, and the graves of the tribe.

For reply their eyes met, and from the Indian's deep chest came the single word, "Ugh." One syllable, deep and descending, but what a tale it told of the slowly engendered and strong-grown partiality, of a struggle that had continued since the morning when the selectman came with words of doom, and of friendship's victory won.

Rolf realized this, and it gave him a momentary choking in his throat, and, "I'm ready if you really mean it."

"Ugh! I go, but some day come back."

There was a long silence, then Rolf, "When shall we start?" and the answer, "To-morrow night."

XV

Bound for the North Woods

WHEN Quonab left camp in the morning he went heavy laden, and the trail he took led to Myanos. There was nothing surprising in it when he appeared at Silas Peck's counter and offered for sale a pair of snowshoes, a bundle of traps, some dishes of birch bark and basswood, and a tom-tom, receiving in exchange some tea, tobacco, gunpowder, and two dollars in cash. He turned without comment, and soon was back in camp. He now took the kettle into the woods and brought it back filled with bark, fresh chipped from a butternut tree. Water was added, and the whole boiled till it made a deep brown liquid. When this was cooled he poured it into a flat dish, then said to Rolf: "Come now, I make you a Sinawa."

With a soft rag the colour was laid on. Face, head, neck, and hands were all at first intended, but Rolf said, "May as well do the whole thing." So he stripped off; the yellow brown juice on his white skin turned it a rich copper colour, and he was changed into an Indian lad that none would have taken for Rolf Kittering. The stains soon dried, and Rolf, re-clothed, felt that already he had burned a bridge.

Two portions of the wigwam cover were taken off; and two packs were made of the bedding. The tomahawk, bows, arrows, and gun, with the few precious food pounds in the copper pot, were divided between them and arranged into packs with shoulder straps; then all was ready. But there was one thing more for Quonab; he went up alone to the rock. Rolf knew what he went for, and judged it best not to follow.

The Indian lighted his pipe, blew the four smokes to the four winds, beginning with the west, then he sat in silence for a time. Presently the prayer for good hunting came from the rock:

> "Father lead us!
> Father, help us!
> Father, guide us to the good hunting."

Rolf in the Woods

And when that ceased a barred owl hooted in the woods, away to the north.

"Ugh! good," was all he said as he rejoined Rolf; and they set out, as the sun went down, on their long journey due northward, Quonab, Rolf, and Skookum. They had not gone a hundred yards before the dog turned back, raced to a place where he had a bone in *cache* and rejoining them trotted along with his bone.

The high road would have been the easier travelling, but it was very necessary to be unobserved, so they took the trail up the brook Asamuk, and after an hour's tramp came out by the Cat-Rock road that runs westerly. Again they were tempted by the easy path, but again Quonab decided on keeping to the woods. Half an hour later they were halted by Skookum treeing a coon. After they had secured the dog, they tramped on through the woods for two hours more, and then, some eight miles from the Pipestave, they halted, Rolf, at least, tired out. It was now midnight. They made a hasty double bed of the canvas cover over a pole above them, and slept till morning, cheered, as they closed their drowsy eyes, by the "Hoo, Hoo, Hoo, Hoo, yah, hoo," of their friend, the barred owl, still to the northward.

The sun was high, and Quonab had breakfast ready before Rolf awoke. He was so stiff with the tramp and the heavy pack that it was with secret joy he learned that they were to rest, concealed in the woods, that day, and travel only by night, until in a different region, where none knew or were likely to stop them. They were now in York State, but that did not by any means imply that they were beyond pursuit.

As the sun rose high, Rolf went forth with his bow and blunt arrows, and then, thanks largely to Skookum, he succeeded in knocking over a couple of squirrels, which, skinned and roasted, made their dinner that day. At night they set out as before, making about ten miles. The third night they did better, and the next day being Sunday, they kept out of sight. But Monday morning, bright and clear, although it was the first morning when they were sure of being missed, they started to tramp openly along the highway, with a sense of elation that they had not hitherto known on the journey. Two things impressed Rolf by their novelty: the curious stare of the country folk whose houses and teams they passed, and the violent antagonism of the dogs. Usually the latter could be quelled by shaking a stick at them, or by pretending to pick up a stone, but one huge and savage brindled mastiff kept following and barking just out of stick range, and managed to give Skookum a mauling, until Quonab drew his bow and let fly a blunt arrow that took the brute on the end of the nose, and sent him howling homeward, while Skookum got a few highly satisfactory nips at the enemy's rear. Twenty miles they made that day and twenty-five the next, for now they were on good roads, and their packs were lighter. More than once they found kind farmer folk who gave them a meal. But many times Skookum made trouble for them. The farmers did not like the way he behaved among their hens. Skookum never could be made to grasp the fine zoological distinction between partridges which are large birds and fair game, and hens which are large birds, but not fair game. Such hair splitting was obviously unworthy of study, much less of acceptance.

Soon it was clearly better for Rolf, approaching a house, to go alone, while Quonab held Skookum. The dogs seemed less excited by Rolf's smell, and remembering his own attitude when tramps came to one or another of his ancient homes, he always asked if they would let him work for a meal, and soon remarked that his success was better when he sought first the women of the house, and then, smiling to show his very white teeth, spoke in clear and un-Indian English, which had the more effect coming from an evident Indian.

"Since I am to be an Indian, Quonab, you must give me an Indian name," he said after one of these episodes.

"Ugh! Good! That's easy! You are 'Nibowaka,' the wise one." For the Indian had not missed any of the points, and so he was named.

Twenty or thirty miles a day they went now, avoiding the settlements along the river. Thus they saw nothing of Albany, but on the tenth day they reached Fort Edward, and for the first time viewed the great Hudson. Here they stayed as short a time as might be, pushed on by Glen's Falls, and on the eleventh night of the journey they passed the old, abandoned fort, and sighted the long stretch of Lake George, with its wooded shore, and glimpses of the mountains farther north.

The farmers did not like the way Skookum behaved among their hens

Bound for the North Woods

Now a new thought possessed them — "If only they had the canoe that they had abandoned on the Pipe-stave." It came to them both at the sight of the limitless water, and especially when Rolf remembered that Lake George joined with Champlain, which again was the highway to all the wilderness.

They camped now as they had fifty times before, and made their meal. The bright blue water dancing near was alluring, inspiring; as they sought the shore Quonab pointed to a track and said, "Deer." He did not show much excitement, but Rolf did, and they returned to the camp fire with a new feeling of elation — they had reached the Promised Land. Now they must prepare for the serious work of finding a hunting ground that was not already claimed.

Quonab, remembering the ancient law of the woods, that parcels off the valleys, each to the hunter first arriving, or succeeding the one who had, was following his own line of thought. Rolf was puzzling over means to get an outfit, canoe, traps, axes, and provisions. The boy broke silence.

"Quonab, we must have money to get an outfit; this is the beginning of harvest; we can easily get work for a month. That will feed us and give us money enough to live on, and a chance to learn something about the country."

The reply was simple, "You are Nibowaka."

The farms were few and scattered here, but there were one or two along the lake. To the nearest one with standing grain Rolf led the way. But their reception, from the first brush with the dog to the final tilt with the farmer, was unpleasant — "He didn't want any darn red-skins around there. He had had two St. Regis Indians last year, and they were a couple of drunken good-for-nothings."

The next was the house of a fat Dutchman, who was just wondering how he should meet the compounded accumulated emergencies of late hay, early oats, weedy potatoes, lost cattle, and a prospective increase of his family, when two angels of relief appeared at his door in copper-coloured skins.

"Cahn yo work putty goood?"

"Yes, I have always lived on a farm," and Rolf showed his hands, broad and heavy for his years.

"Cahn yo mebby find my lost cows, which I haf not find, already yet?"

Rolf in the Woods

Could they! It would be fun to try.

"I giff yo two dollars you pring dem putty kvick."

So Quonab took the trail to the woods, and Rolf started into the potatoes with a hoe, but he was stopped by a sudden outcry of poultry. Alas! It was Skookum on an ill-judged partridge hunt. A minute later he was ignominiously chained to a penitential post, nor left it during the travellers' sojourn.

In the afternoon Quonab returned with the cattle, and as he told Rolf he saw *five deer*, there was an unmistakable hunter gleam in his eye.

Three cows in milk, and which had not been milked for two days, was a serious matter, needing immediate attention. Rolf had milked five cows twice a day for five years, and a glance showed old Van Trumper that the boy was an expert.

"Good, good! I go now make feed swine."

He went into the outhouse, but a tow-topped, red-cheeked girl ran after him. "Father, father, mother says — " and the rest was lost.

"Myn Hemel! Myn Hemel! I thought it not so soon," and the fat Dutchman followed the child. A moment later he reappeared, his jolly face clouded with a look of grave concern. "Hi yo big Injun, yo cahn paddle canoe?" Quonab nodded. "Den coom. Annette, pring Tomas und Hendrik." So the father carried two-year-old Hendrik, while the Indian carried six-year-old Tomas, and twelve-year-old Annette followed in vague, uncomprehended alarm. Arrived at the shore the children were placed in the canoe, and then the difficulties came fully to the father's mind — he could not leave his wife. He must send the

children with the messenger — In a sort of desperation, "Cahn you dem childen take to de house across de lake, and pring back Mrs. Callan? Tell her Marta Van Trumper need her right now mooch very kvick." The Indian nodded. Then the father hesitated, but a glance at the Indian was enough. Something said, "He is safe," and in spite of sundry wails from the little ones left with a dark stranger, he pushed off the canoe: "Yo take care for my babies," and turned his brimming eyes away.

The farmhouse was only two miles off, and the evening calm; no time was lost: what woman will not instantly drop all work and all interests, to come to the help of another in the trial time of motherhood?

Within an hour the neighbour's wife was holding hands with the mother of the banished tow-heads. He who tempers the wind and appoints the season of the wild deer hinds had not forgotten the womanhood beyond the reach of skilful human help, and with the hard and lonesome life had conjoined a sweet and blessed compensation. What would not her sister of the city give for such immunity; and long before that dark, dread hour of night that brings the ebbing life force low, the wonderful miracle was complete; there was another tow-top in the settler's home, and all was well.

XVI

Life with the Dutch Settler

THE Indians slept in the luxuriant barn of logs, with blankets, plenty of hay, and a roof. They were more than content, for now, on the edge of the wilderness, they were very close to wild life. Not a day or a night passed without bringing proof of that.

One end of the barn was portioned off for poultry. In this the working staff of a dozen hens were doing their duty, which, on that first night of the "brown angels' visit," consisted of silent slumber, when all at once the hens and the new hands were aroused by a clamorous cackling, which speedily stopped. It sounded like a hen falling in a bad dream, then regaining her perch to go to sleep again. But next morning the body of one of these highly esteemed branches of the egg-plant was found in the corner, partly devoured. Quonab examined the headless hen, the dust around, and uttered the word, "Mink."

Rolf said, "Why not skunk?"

"Skunk could not climb to the perch."

"Weasel then."

"Weasel would only suck the blood, and would kill three or four."

"Well, coon."

"Coon would carry him away, so would fox or wildcat, and a marten would not come into the building by night."

There was no question, first, that it was a mink, and, second, that he was hiding about the barn until the hunger pang should send him again to the hen house. Quonab covered the hen's body with two or

65

three large stones so that there was only one approach. In the way of this approach he buried a "number one" trap.

That night they were aroused again; this time by a frightful screeching, and a sympathetic, inquiring cackle from the fowls.

Arising, quickly they entered with a lantern. Rolf then saw a sight that gave him a prickling in his hair. The mink, a large male, was caught by one front paw. He was writhing and foaming, tearing, sometimes at the trap, sometimes at the dead hen, and sometimes at his own imprisoned foot, pausing now and then to utter the most ear-piercing shrieks, then falling again in crazy animal fury on the trap, splintering his sharp white teeth, grinding the cruel metal with bruised and bloody jaws, frothing, snarling, raving mad. As his foemen entered he turned on them a hideous visage of inexpressible fear and hate, rage and horror. His eyes glanced back green fire in the lantern light; he strained in renewed efforts to escape; the air was rank with his musky smell. The impotent fury of his struggle made a picture that continued in Rolf's mind. Quonab took a stick and with a single blow put an end to the scene, but never did Rolf forget it, and never afterward was he a willing partner when the trapping was done with those relentless jaws of steel.

A week later another hen was missing, and the door of the hen house left open. After a careful examination of the dust, inside and out of the building, Quonab said, "Coon." It is very unusual for coons to raid a hen house. Usually it is some individual with abnormal tastes, and once he begins, he is sure to come back. The Indian judged that he might be back the next night, so prepared a trap. A rope was passed from the door latch to a tree; on this rope a weight was hung, so that the door was self-shutting, and to make it self-locking he leaned a long pole against it inside. Now he propped it open with a shingle platform, so set that the coon must walk on it once he was inside, and so release the door. The trappers thought they would hear in the night when the door closed, but they were sleepy; they knew nothing until next morning. Then they found that the self-shutter had shut, and inside, crouched in one of the nesting boxes, was a tough, old fighting coon. Strange to tell, he had not touched a second hen. As soon as he found himself a prisoner he had experienced a change of heart, and presently his skin was nailed on the end of the barn and his meat was hanging in the larder.

Life with the Dutch Settler

"Is this a marten," asked little Annette. And when told not, her disappointment elicited the information that old Warren, the storekeeper, had promised her a blue cotton dress for a marten skin.

"You shall have the first one I catch," said Rolf.

Life in Van Trumper's was not unpleasant. The mother was going about again in a week. Annette took charge of the baby, as well as of the previous arrivals. Hendrik senior was gradually overcoming his difficulties, thanks to the unexpected help, and a kindly spirit made the hard work not so very hard. The shyness that was at first felt toward the Indians wore off, especially in the case of Rolf, he was found so companionable; and the Dutchman, after puzzling over the combination of brown skin and blue eyes, decided that Rolf was a half-breed.

August wore on not unpleasantly for the boy, but Quonab was getting decidedly restless. He could work for a week as hard as any white man, but his race had not risen to the dignity of patient, unremitting, life-long toil.

"How much money have we now, Nibowaka?" was one of the mid-August indications of restlessness. Rolf reckoned up; half a month for Quonab, $15.00; for himself, $10.00; for finding the cows $2.00 — $27.00 in all. Not enough.

Three days later Quonab reckoned up again. Next day he said: "We need two months' open water to find a good country and build a shanty." Then did Rolf do the wise thing; he went to fat Hendrik and told him all about it. They wanted to get a canoe and an outfit, and seek for a trapping or hunting ground that would not encroach on those already possessed, for the trapping law is rigid; even the death penalty is not considered too high in certain cases of trespass, provided the injured party is ready to be judge, jury, and executioner. Van Trumper was able to help them not a little in the matter of location — there was no use trying on the Vermont side, nor anywhere near Lake Champlain, nor near Lake George; neither was it worth while going to the far North, as the Frenchmen came in there, and they were keen hunters, so that Hamilton County was more promising than any other, but it was almost inaccessible, remote from all the great waterways, and of course without roads; its inaccessibility was the reason why it was little known.

So far so good; but happy Hendrik was unpleasantly surprised to learn that the new help were for leaving at once. Finally he made this offer: If they would stay till September 1st, and so leave all in "good shape fer der vinter," he would, besides the wages agreed, give them the canoe, one axe, six mink traps, and a fox trap now hanging in the barn, and carry them in his wagon as far as the five-mile portage from Lake George to Schroon River, down which they could go to its junction with the upper Hudson, which, followed up through forty miles of rapids and hard portages, would bring them to a swampy river that enters from the southwest, and ten miles up this would bring them to Jesup's Lake, which is two miles wide and twelve miles long. This country abounded with game, but was so hard to enter that after Jesup's death it was deserted.

There was only one possible answer to such an offer — they stayed.

In spare moments Quonab brought the canoe up to the barn, stripped off some weighty patches of bark and canvas and some massive timber thwarts, repaired the ribs, and when dry and gummed, its weight was below one hundred pounds; a saving of at least forty pounds on the soggy thing he crossed the lake in that first day on the farm.

September came. Early in the morning Quonab went alone to the lakeside; there on a hill top he sat, looking toward the sunrise, and sang a song of the new dawn, beating, not with a tom-tom — he had none — but with one stick on another. And when the sunrise possessed the earth he sang again the hunter's song:

> "Father, guide our feet,
> Lead us to the good hunting."

Then he danced to the sound, his face skyward, his eyes closed, his feet barely raised, but rythmically moved. So went he three times round to the chant in three sun circles, dancing a sacred measure, as royal David might have done that day when he danced around the Ark of the Covenant on its homeward journey. His face was illumined, and no man could have seen him then without knowing that this was a true heart's worship of a true God, who is in all things He has made.

XVII

Canoeing on the Upper Hudson

"There is only one kind of a man I can't size up; that's the feller that shets up and says nothing."

—*The Sayings of Sylvanne*

A SETTLER, named Hulett had a scow that was borrowed by the neighbours whenever needed to take a team across the lake. On the morning of their journey, the Dutchman's team and wagon, the canoe and the men, were aboard the scow, Skookum took his proper place at the prow, and all was ready for "good-bye." Rolf found it a hard word to say. The good old Dutch mother had won his heart, and the children were like his brothers and sisters.

"Coom again, lad; coom and see us kvick." She kissed him, he kissed Annette and the three later issues. They boarded the scow to ply the poles till the deep water was reached, then the oars. An east wind springing up gave them a chance to profit by a wagon-cover rigged as a sail, and two hours later the scow was safely landed at West Side, where was a country store, and the head of the wagon road to the Schroon River.

As they approached the door, they saw a rough-looking man slouching against the building, his hands in his pockets, his blear eyes taking in the new-comers with a look of contemptuous hostility. As they passed, he spat tobacco juice on the dog and across the feet of the men.

Old Warren who kept the store was not partial to Indians, but he was a good friend of Hendrik and very keen to trade for fur, so the new trappers were well received; and now came the settling of accounts. Flour, oatmeal, pork, potatoes, tea, tobacco, sugar, salt, powder, ball, shot, clothes, lines, an inch-auger, nails, knives, awls, needles, files, another axe, some tin plates, and a frying-pan were selected and added to Hendrik's account.

"If I was you, I'd take a windy-sash; you'll find it mighty convenient in cold weather." The store keeper led them into an outhouse where there was a pile of six-lighted window-frames all complete. So the awkward thing was added to their load.

"Can't I sell you a fine rifle?" and he took down a new, elegant small bore of the latest pattern. "Only twenty-five dollars." Rolf shook his head; "Part down, and I'll take the rest in fur next spring." Rolf was sorely tempted; however, he had an early instilled horror of debt. He steadfastly said: "No." But many times he regretted it afterward! The small balance remaining was settled in cash.

As they were arranging and selecting, they heard a most hideous yelping outdoors, and a minute later Skookum limped in, crying as if half-killed. Quonab was out in a moment.

"Did you kick my dog?"

The brutal loafer changed countenance as he caught the red man's eye. "Naw! Never touched him; hurted himself on that rake."

It was obviously a lie, but better to let it pass, and Quonab came in again.

Then the rough stranger appeared at the door and growled: "Say, Warren! Ain't you going to let me have that rifle? I guess my word's as good as the next man's."

"No," said Warren, "I told you, no!"

"Then you can go to blazes, and you'll never see a cent's worth of fur from the stuff I got last year."

"I don't expect to," was the reply; "I've learned what your word's worth." And the stranger slouched away.

"Who vas he?" asked Hendrik.

"I only know that his name is Jack Hoag; he's a little bit of a trapper and a big bit of a bum; stuck me last year. He doesn't come out this way; they say he goes out by the west side of the mountains."

New light on their course was secured from Warren, and above all, the important information that the mouth of Jesup's River was marked by an eagle's nest in a dead pine. "Up to that point keep the main stream, and don't forget next spring I'm buying fur."

The drive across Five-mile portage was slow. It took over two hours to cover it, but late that day they reached the Schroon.

Here the Dutchman said "Good-bye: Coom again some noder time." Skookum saluted the farmer with a final growl, then Rolf and Quonab were left alone in the wilderness.

Canoeing on the Upper Hudson

It was after sundown, so they set about camping for the night. A wise camper always prepares bed and shelter in daylight, if possible. While Rolf made a fire and hung the kettle, Quonab selected a level, dry place between two trees, and covered it with spruce boughs to make the beds, and last a low tent was made by putting the lodge cover over a pole between the trees. The ends of the covers were held down by loose green logs quickly cut for the purpose, and now they were safe against weather.

Tea, potatoes, and fried pork, with maple syrup and hard-tack, made their meal of the time, after which there was a long smoke. Quonab took a stick of red willow, picked up in the daytime, and began shaving it toward one end, leaving the curling shreds still on the stick. When these were bunched in a fuzzy mop, he held them over the fire until they were roasted brown; then, grinding all up in his palm with some tobacco, and filling his pipe he soon was enveloped in that odour of woodsy smoke called the "Indian smell," by many who do not know whence or how it comes. Rolf did not smoke. He had promised his mother that he would not until he was a man, and something brought her back home now

with overwhelming force; that was the beds they had made of fragrant balsam boughs. "Cho-ko-tung or blister tree" as Quonab called it. His mother had a little sofa pillow, brought from the North — a "northern pine" pillow they called it, for it was stuffed with pine needles of a kind not growing in Connecticut. Many a time had Rolf as a baby pushed his little round nose into that bag to inhale the delicious odour it gave forth, and so it became the hallowed smell of all that was dear in his babyhood, and it never lost its potency. Smell never does. Oh, mighty aura! that, in marching by the nostrils, can reach and move the soul; how wise the church that makes this power its handmaid, and through its incense overwhelms all alien thought when the worshipper, wandering, doubting, comes again to see if it be true, that here doubt dies. Oh, queen of memory that is master of the soul! How fearful should we be of letting evil thought associated grow with some recurrent odour that we love. Happy, indeed, are they that find some ten times pure and consecrated fragrance, like the pine, which entering in is master of their moods, and yet through linking thoughts has all its power, uplifting, full of sweetness and blessed peace. So came to Rolf his medicine tree.

Rolf in the Woods

The balsam fir was his tree of hallowed memory. Its odour never failed, and he slept that night with its influence all about him.

Starting in the morning was no easy matter. There was so much to be adjusted that first day. Packs divided in two, new combinations to trim the canoe, or to raise such and such a package above a possible leak. The heavy things, like axes and pans, had to be fastened to the canoe or to packages that would float in case of an upset. The canoe itself had to be gummed in one or two places; but they got away after three hours, and began the voyage down the Schroon.

This was Rolf's first water journey. He had indeed essayed the canoe on the Pipestave Pond, but that was a mere ferry. This was real travel. He marvelled at the sensitiveness of the frail craft; the delicacy of its balance; its quick response to the paddle; the way it seemed to shrink from the rocks; and the unpleasantly suggestive bend-up of the ribs when the bottom grounded upon a log. It was a new world for him. Quonab taught him never to enter the canoe except when she was afloat; never to rise in her or move along without hold of the gunwale; never to make a sudden move; and he also learned that it was easier to paddle when there were six feet of water underneath than when only six inches.

In an hour they had covered the five miles that brought them to the Hudson, and here the real labour began, paddling up stream. Before long they came to a shallow stretch with barely enough water to float the canoe. Here they jumped out and waded in the stream, occasionally lifting a stone to one side, till they reached the upper stretch of deep water and again went merrily paddling. Soon they came to an impassable rapid, and Rolf had his first taste of a real carry or portage. Quonab's eye was watching the bank as soon as the fierce waters appeared; for the first question was, where shall we land? and the next, how far do we carry? There are no rapids on important rivers in temperate America that have not been portaged more or less for ages. No canoe man portages without considering most carefully when, where, and how to land. His selection of the place, then, is the result of careful study. He cannot help leaving some mark at the place, slight though it be, and the next man looks for that mark to save himself time and trouble.

Canoeing on the Upper Hudson

"Ugh" was the only sound that Rolf heard from his companion, and the canoe headed for a flat rock in the pool below the rapids. After landing, they found traces of an old camp fire. It was near noon now, so Rolf prepared the meal while Quonab took a light pack and went on to learn the trail. It was not well marked; had not been used for a year or two, evidently, but there are certain rules that guide one. The trail keeps near the water, unless there is some great natural barrier, and it is usually the easiest way in sight. Quonab kept one eye on the river, for navigable water was the main thing, and in about one hundred yards he was again on the stream's edge, at a good landing above the rapid.

After the meal was finished and the Indian had smoked, they set to work. In a few loads each, the stuff was portaged across, and the canoe was carried over and moored to the bank.

The cargo replaced, they went on again, but in half an hour after passing more shoal water, saw another rapid, not steep, but too shallow to float the canoe, even with both men wading. Here Quonab made what the Frenchmen call a *demi-charge*. He carried half the stuff to the bank; then, wading, one at each end, they hauled the canoe up the portage and reloaded her above. Another strip of good going was succeeded by a long stretch of very swift water that was two or three feet deep and between shores that were densely grown with alders. The Indian landed, cut two light, strong poles, and now, one at the bow, the other at the stern, they worked their way foot by foot up the fierce current until safely on the upper level.

Yet one more style of canoe propulsion was forced on them. They came to a long stretch of smooth, deep, very swift water, almost a rapid — one of the kind that is a joy when you are coming down stream. It differed from the last in having shores that were not alder-hidden, but open gravel banks. Now did Quonab take a long, strong line from his war sack. One end he fastened, not to the bow, but to the forward part of the canoe, the other to a buckskin band which he put across his breast. Then, with Rolf in the stern to steer and the Indian hauling on the bank, the canoe was safely "tracked" up the "strong waters."

Thus they fought their way up the hard river, day after day, making sometimes only five miles after twelve hours' toilsome travel. Rapids, shoals, portages, strong waters, abounded, and before they had covered the fifty miles to the forks of Jesup's River, they knew right well why the region was so little entered.

It made a hardened canoe man of Rolf, and when, on the evening of the fifth day, they saw a huge eagle's nest in a dead pine tree that stood on the edge of a long swamp, both felt they had reached their own country, and were glad.

XVIII

Animal Life Along the River

IT MUST not be supposed that, because it has not been duly mentioned, they saw no wild life along the river. The silent canoe man has the best of opportunities. There were plenty of deer tracks about the first camp, and that morning, as they turned up the Hudson, Rolf saw his first deer. They had rounded a point in rather swift water when Quonab gave two taps on the gunwale, the usual sign, "Look out," and pointed to the shore. There, fifty yards away on the bank, gazing at them, was a deer. Stock still he stood, like a red statue, for he was yet in the red coat. With three or four strong strokes, Quonab gave a long and mighty forward spurt; then reached for his gun. But the deer's white flag went up. It turned and bounded away, the white flag the last thing to disappear. Rolf sat spellbound. It was so sudden; so easy; it soon melted into the woods again. He trembled after it was gone.

Many a time in the evening they saw muskrats in the eddies, and once they glimpsed a black, shiny something like a monstrous leech rolling up and down as it travelled in the stream. Quonab whispered, "Otter," and made ready his gun, but it dived and showed itself no more.

At one of the camps they were awakened by an extraordinary tattoo in the middle of the night — a harsh rattle close by their heads; and they got up to find that a porcupine was rattling his teeth on the frying-pan in an effort to increase the amount of salt that he could taste on it. Skookum, tied to a tree, was vainly protesting against the intrusion and volunteered to make a public example of the invader. The campers did not finally get rid of the spiny one till all their kitchen stuff was hung beyond his reach.

Once they heard the sharp, short bark of a fox, and twice or thrice the soft, sweet, moaning call of the gray wolf out to hunt. Wild fowl abounded, and their diet was varied by the ducks that one or other of the hunters secured at nearly every camp.

On the second day they saw three deer, and on the third morning Quonab loaded his gun with buckshot, to be ready, then sallied forth at dawn. Rolf was following, but the Indian shook his head, then said: "Don't make fire for half an hour."

In twenty minutes Rolf heard the gun, then later the Indian returned with a haunch of venison, and when they left that camp they stopped a mile up the river to add the rest of the venison to their cargo. Seven other deer were seen, but no more killed; yet Rolf was burning to try his hand as a hunter. Many other opportunities he had, and improved some of them. On one wood portage he, or rather Skookum, put up a number of ruffed grouse. These perched in the trees above their heads and the travellers stopped. While the dog held their attention Rolf with blunt arrows knocked over five that proved most acceptable as food. But his thoughts were now on deer, and his ambition was to go out alone and return with a load of venison.

Another and more thrilling experience followed quickly. Rounding a bend in the early dawn they sighted a black bear and two cubs rambling along the gravelly bank and stopping now and then to eat something that turned out to be crayfish.

Quonab had not seen a bear since childhood, when he and his father hunted along the hardwood ridges back of Myanos, and now he was excited. He stopped paddling, warned Rolf to do the same, and let the canoe drift backward until out of sight; then made for the land. Quickly tying up the canoe he took his gun and Rolf his hunting arrows, and, holding Skookum in a leash, they dashed into the woods. Then, keeping out of sight, they ran as fast and as silently as possible in the direction of the bears. Of course, the wind was toward the hunters, or they never could have got so near. Now they were opposite the family group and needed only a chance for a fair shot. Sneaking forward with the utmost caution, they were surely within twenty-five yards, but still the bushes screened the crab-eaters. As the hunters sneaked, the old bear stopped and sniffed suspiciously; the wind changed; she got an unmistakable whiff; then gave a loud warning "Koff! Koff! Koff! Koff!" and ran as fast as she could. The hunters knowing they were discovered rushed out, yelling as loudly as possible, in hopes of making the bears tree. The old bear ran like a horse with Skookum yapping bravely in her rear. The young ones, left behind, lost sight of her, and, utterly bewildered by the noise, made for a tree conveniently near and scrambled up into the branches. "Now," Rolf thought, judging by certain tales he had heard, "that old bear will come back and there will be a fight."

"Is she coming back?" he asked nervously.

The Indian laughed. "No, she is running yet. Black bear always a coward; they never fight when they can run away."

The little ones up the tree were, of course, at the mercy of the hunters, and in this case it was not a broken straw they depended on, but an ample salvation. "We don't need the meat and can't carry it with us; let's leave them," said Rolf, but added, "Will they find their mother?"

"Yes, bime-by; they come down and squall all over woods. She will hang round half a mile away and by night all will be together."

Their first bear hunt was over. Not a shot fired, not a bear wounded, not a mile travelled, and not an hour lost. And yet it seemed much more full of interesting thrills than did any one of the many stirring bear hunts that Rolf and Quonab shared together in the days that were to come.

XIX

The Footprint on the Shore

JESUP'S RIVER was a tranquil stream that came from a region of swamps, and would have been easy canoeing but for the fallen trees. Some of these had been cut years ago, showing that the old trapper had used this route. Once they were unpleasantly surprised by seeing a fresh chopping on the bank, but their mourning was changed into joy when they found it was beaver-work.

Ten miles they made that day. In the evening they camped on the shore of Jesup's Lake, proud and happy in the belief that they were the rightful owners of it all. That night they heard again and again the howling of wolves, but it seemed on the far side of the lake. In the morning they went out on foot to explore, and at once had the joy of seeing five deer, while tracks showed on every side. It was evidently a paradise for deer, and there were in less degree the tracks of other animals — mink in fair abundance, one or two otters, a mountain lion, and a cow moose with her calf. It was thrilling to see such a feast of possibilities. The hunters were led on and on, revelling in the prospect of many joys before them, when all at once they came on something that turned their joy to grief — *the track of a man*; the fresh imprint of a cowhide boot. It was maddening. At first blush, it meant some other trapper ahead of them with a prior claim to the valley; a claim that the unwritten law would allow. They followed it a mile. It went striding along the shore at a great pace, sometimes running, and keeping down the west shore. Then they found a place where he had sat down and broken a lot of

79

clam shells, and again had hastened on. But there was no mark of gun-stock or other weapon where he sat; and why was he wearing boots? The hunters rarely did.

For two miles the Indian followed with Rolf, and sometimes found that the hated stranger had been running hard. Then they turned back, terribly disappointed. At first it seemed a crushing blow. They had three courses open to them — to seek a location farther north, to assume that one side of the lake was theirs, or to find out exactly who and what the stranger was. They decided on the last. The canoe was launched and loaded, and they set out to look for what they hoped they would not find, a trapper's shanty on the lake.

After skirting the shore for four or five miles and disturbing one or two deer, as well as hosts of ducks, the voyagers landed and there still they found that fateful boot-mark steadily tramping southward. By noon they had reached the south end of the west inlet that leads to another lake, and again an examination of the shore showed the footmarks, here leaving the lake and going southerly. Now the travellers retired to the main lake and by noon had reached the south end. At no point had they seen any sign of a cabin, though both sides of the lake were in plain view all day. The travelling stranger was a mystery, but he did not live here and there was no good reason why they should not settle.

Where? The country seemed equally good at all points, but it is usually best to camp on an outlet. Then when a storm comes up, the big waves do not threaten your canoe, or compel you to stay on land. It is a favourite crossing for animals avoiding the lake, and other trappers coming in are sure to see your cabin before they enter.

Which side of the outlet? Quonab settled that — the west. He wanted to see the sun rise, and, not far back from the water, was a hill with a jutting, rocky pinnacle. He pointed to this and uttered the one word, "Idaho." Here, then, on the west side, where the lake enters the river, they began to clear the ground for their home.

XX

The Trapper's Cabin

"It's a smart fellow that knows what he can't do."

—The Sayings of Si Sylvanne

I SUPPOSE every trapper that ever lived, on first building a cabin, said, "Oh, any little thing will do, so long as it has a roof and is big enough to lie down in." And every trapper has realized before spring that he made a sad mistake in not having it big enough to live in and store goods in. Quonab and Rolf were new at the business, and made the usual mistake. They planned their cabin far too small; 10 × 12 ft., instead of 12 × 20 ft. they made it, and 6-ft. walls, instead of 8-ft. walls. Both were expert axemen. Spruce was plentiful and the cabin rose quickly. In one day the walls were up. An important thing was the roof. What should it be? Overlapping basswood troughs, split shingles, also called shakes, or clay? By far the easiest to make, the warmest in winter and coolest in summer, is the clay roof. It has three disadvantages: It leaks in long-continued wet weather; it drops down dust and dirt in dry weather; and is so heavy that it usually ends by crushing in the log rafters and beams, unless they are further supported on posts, which are much in the way. But its advantages were so obvious that the builders did not hesitate. A clay roof it was to be.

When the walls were five feet high, the doorway and window were cut through the logs, but leaving in each case one half of the log at the bottom of the needed opening. The top log was now placed, then rolled over bottom up, while half of its thickness was cut away to fit over the door: a similar cut out was made over the window. Two flat pieces of spruce were prepared for door jambs and two shorter ones for window jambs. Auger holes were put through, so as to allow an oak pin to be driven through the jamb into each log, and the doorway and window opening were done.

Rolf in the Woods

In one corner they planned a small fireplace, built of day and stone. Not stone from the lake, as Rolf would have had it, but from the hillside; and why? Quonab said that the lake stone was of the water spirits, and would not live near fire, but would burst open; while the hillside stone was of the sun and fire spirit, and in the fire would add its heat.

The facts are that lake stone explodes when greatly heated and hill stone does not; and since no one has been able to improve upon Quonab's explanation, it must stand for the present.

The plan of the fireplace was simple. Rolf had been present at the building of several, and the main point was to have the chimney large enough, and the narrowest point just above the fire.

The eaves logs, end logs, and ridge logs were soon in place; then came the cutting of small poles, spruce and tamarack, long enough to reach from ridge to eaves, and in sufficient number to completely cover the roof. A rank sedge meadow near by afforded plenty of coarse grass with which the poles were covered deeply; and lastly clay dug out with a couple of hand-made, axe-hewn wooden spades was thrown evenly on the grass to a depth of six inches; this, when trampled flat, made a roof that served them well.

The chinks of the logs when large were filled with split pieces of wood; when small they were plugged with moss. A door was made of hewn planks, and hinged very simply on two pins; one made by letting the plank project as a point, the other by nailing on a pin after the door was placed; both pins fitting, of course, into inch auger holes.

A floor was not needed, but bed bunks were, and in making these they began already to realize that the cabin was too small. But now after a week's work it was done. It had a sweet fragrance of wood and moss, and the pleasure it gave to Rolf at least was something he never again could expect to find in equal measure about any other dwelling he might make.

Quonab laid the fire carefully, then lighted his pipe, sang a little crooning song about the "home spirits," which we call "household gods," walked around the shanty, offering the pipestem to each of the four winds in turn, then entering lighted the fire from his pipe, threw some tobacco and deer hair on the blaze, and the house-warming was ended.

Nevertheless, they continued to sleep in the tent they had used all along, for Quonab loved not the indoors, and Rolf was growing daily more of his mind.

XXI

Rolf's First Deer

ANXIOUS to lose no fine day they had worked steadily on the shanty, not even going after the deer that were seen occasionally over the lake, so that now they were out of fresh meat, and Rolf saw a chance he long had looked for. "Quonab, I want to go out alone and get a deer, and I want your gun."

"Ugh! you shall go. To-night is good."

"To-night" meant evening, so Rolf set out alone as soon as the sun was low, for during the heat of the day the deer are commonly lying in some thicket. In general, he knew enough to travel up wind, and to go as silently as possible. The southwest wind was blowing softly, and so he quickened his steps southwesterly which meant along the lake. Tracks and signs abounded; it was impossible to follow any one trail. His plan was to keep on silently, trusting to luck, nor did he have long to wait. Across a little opening of the woods to the west he saw a movement in the bushes, but it ceased, and he was in doubt whether the creature, presumably a deer, was standing there or had gone on. "Never quit till you are sure," was one of Quonab's wise adages. Rolf was bound to know what it was that had moved. So he stood still and waited. A minute passed; another; many; a long time; and still he waited, but got no further sign of life from the bush. Then he began to think he was mistaken; yet it was good huntercraft to *find out what that was*. He tried the wind several times, first by wetting his finger, which test said "southwest"; second, by tossing up some handfuls of dried grass, which said "yes, southwest, but veering southerly in this glade." So he knew he might crawl silently to the north side of that bush. He looked to the priming of his gun and began a slow and stealthy stalk, selecting such openings as might be passed without effort or movement of bushes or likelihood of sound. He worked his way step by step; each time his foot was lifted he set it down again only after trying the footing. At each step he paused to look and listen. It was only one hundred yards to the interesting spot, but Rolf was fifteen minutes in covering the distance, and more than once, he got a great start as a chicadee flew out or a woodpecker tapped. His heart beat louder and louder, so it seemed everything near must hear; but he kept on his careful stalk, and at last had reached the thicket that had given him such thrills and hopes. Here he stood and watched for a full minute. Again he tried the wind, and proceeded to circle slowly to the west of the place.

After a long, tense crawl of twenty yards he came on the track and sign of a big buck, perfectly fresh, and again his heart worked harder; it seemed to be pumping his neck full of blood, so he was choking. He judged it best to follow this hot trail for a time, and holding his gun ready cocked he stepped softly onward. A bluejay cried out, "jay, jay!" with startling loudness, and seemingly enjoyed his pent-up excitement. A few steps forward at slow, careful stalk, and then behind him he heard a loud whistling hiss. Instantly turning he found himself face to face with a great, splendid buck in the short blue coat. There not thirty yards away he stood, the creature he had been stalking so long, in plain view now, broadside on. They gazed each at the other, perfectly still for a few seconds, then Rolf without undue movement brought the gun to bear, and still the buck stood gazing. The gun was up, but oh, how disgustingly it wabbled and shook! and the steadier Rolf tried to hold it, the more it trembled, until from that wretched gun the palsy spread all over his body; his breath came tremulously, his legs and arms were shaking, and at last, as the deer moved its head to get a better view and raised its tail, the lad, making an effort at self-control, pulled the trigger. *Bang!* and the buck went lightly bounding out of sight.

Poor Rolf; how disgusted he felt; positively sick with self-contempt. Thirty yards, standing, broadside on, full daylight, a big buck, a clean miss. Yes, there was the bullet hole in a tree, five feet above the deer's

head. "I'm no good; I'll never be a hunter," he groaned, then turned and slowly tramped back to camp. Quonab looked inquiringly, for, of course, he heard the shot. He saw a glum and sorry-looking youth, who in response to his inquiring look gave merely a head-shake, and hung up the gun with a vicious bang.

Quonab took down the gun, wiped it out, reloaded it, then turning to the boy said: "Nibowaka, you feel pretty sick. Ugh! You know why? You got a good chance, but you got buck fever. It is always so, every one the first time. You go again to-morrow and you get your deer."

Rolf made no reply. So Quonab ventured, "You want *me* to go?" That settled it for Rolf; his pride was touched.

"No; I'll go again in the morning."

In the dew time he was away once more on the hunting-trail. There was no wind, but the southwest was the likeliest to spring up. So he went nearly over his last night's track. He found it much easier to go silently now when all the world was dew wet, and travelled quickly. Past the fateful glade he went, noted again the tree torn several feet too high up, and on. Then the cry of a bluejay rang out; this is often a notification of deer at hand. It always is warning of something doing, and no wise hunter ignores it.

Rolf stood for a moment listening and peering. He thought he heard a scraping sound; then again the bluejay, but the former ceased and the jay-note died in the distance. He crept cautiously on again for a few minutes; another opening appeared. He studied this from a hiding place; then far across he saw a little flash near the ground. His heart gave a jump; he studied the place, saw again the flash and then made out the head of a deer, a doe that was lying in the long grass. The flash was made by its ear shaking off a fly. Rolf looked to his priming, braced himself, got fully ready, then gave a short, sharp whistle; instantly the doe rose to her feet; then another appeared, a small one; then a young buck, all stood gazing his way. Up went the gun, but again its muzzle began to wabble. Rolf lowered it, said grimly and savagely to himself, "*I will not shake this time.*" The deer stretched themselves and began slowly walking toward the lake. All had disappeared but the buck. Rolf gave another whistle that turned the antler-bearer to a statue. Controlling himself with a strong "*I will*" he raised the gun, held it steadily, and fired. The buck gave a gathering spasm, a bound, and disappeared. Rolf felt sick again with disgust, but he reloaded, then hastily went forward.

Rolf in the Woods

There was the deep imprint showing where the buck had bounded at the shot, but no blood. He followed, and a dozen feet away found the next hoof marks and on them a bright-red stain; on and another splash; and more and shortening bounds, till one hundred yards away — yes, there it lay; the round, gray form, quite dead, shot through the heart.

Rolf gave a long, rolling war cry and got an answer from a point that was startlingly near, and Quonab stepped from behind a tree.

"I got him," shouted Rolf.

The Indian smiled. "I knew you would, so I followed; last night I knew you must have your shakes, so let you go it alone."

Very carefully that deer was skinned, and Rolf learned the reason for many little modes of procedure.

After the hide was removed from the body (not the head or legs), Quonab carefully cut out the broad sheath of tendon that cover the muscles, beginning at the hip bones on the back and extending up to the shoulders; this is the *sewing sinew*. Then he cut out the two long fillets of meat that lie on each side of the spine outside (the loin) and the two smaller ones inside (the tenderloin). These, with the four quarters, the heart, and the kidneys, were put into the hide. The entrails, head, neck, legs, feet, he left for the foxes, but the hip bone or sacrum he hung in a tree with three little red yarns from them, so that the Great Spirit would be pleased and send good hunting. Then addressing the head he said: "Little brother, forgive us. We are sorry to kill you. Behold! We give you the honour of red streamers." Then bearing the rest they tramped back to camp.

The meat wrapped in sacks to keep off the flies was hung in the shade, but the hide he buried in the warm mud of a swamp hole, and three days later, when the hair began to slip, he scraped it clean. A broad ash wood hoop he had made ready and when the green rawhide was strained on it again the Indian had an Indian drum.

It was not truly dry for two or three days and as it tightened on its frame it gave forth little sounds of click and shrinkage that told of the strain the tensioned rawhide made. Quonab tried it that night as he sat by the fire softly singing:

"Ho da ho — he da he."

Rolf's First Deer

But the next day before sunrise he climbed the hill and sitting on the sun-up rock he hailed the Day God with the invocation, as he had not sung it since the day they left the great rock above the Asamuk, and followed with the song:

> "Father, we thank thee;
> We have found the good hunting.
> There is meat in the wigwam."

XXII

The Line of Traps

NOW that they had the cabin for winter, and food for the present, they must set about the serious business of trapping and lay a line of deadfalls for use in the coming cold weather. They were a little ahead of time, but it was very desirable to get their lines blazed through the woods in all proposed directions in case of any other trapper coming in. Most fur-bearing animals are to be found along the little valleys of the stream: beaver, otter, mink, muskrat, coon, are examples. Those that do not actually live by the water seek these places because of their sheltered character and because their prey lives there; of this class are the lynx, fox, fisher, and marten that feed on rabbits and mice. Therefore a line of traps is usually along some valley and over the divide and down some other valley back to the point of beginning.

So, late in September, Rolf and Quonab, with their bedding, a pot, food for four days, and two axes, alternately followed and led by Skookum, set out along a stream that entered the lake near their cabin. A quarter mile up they built their first deadfall for martens. It took them one hour and was left unset. The place was under a huge tree on a neck of land around which the stream made a loop. This tree they blazed on three sides. Two hundred yards up another good spot was found and a deadfall made. At one place across a neck of land was a narrow trail evidently worn by otters. "Good place for steel trap, bime-by," was Quonab's remark.

From time to time they disturbed deer, and in a muddy place where a deer path crossed the creek, they found, among the numerous small hoof prints, the track of wolves, bears, and a mountain lion, or panther. At these little Skookum sniffed fearsomely, and showed by his bristly mane that lie was at least much impressed.

After five hours' travel and work they came to another stream joining on, and near the angle of the two little valleys they found a small tree that was chewed and scratched in a remarkable manner for three to six feet up.

"Bear tree," said Quonab, and by degrees Rolf got the facts about it.

The bears, and indeed most animals, have a way of marking the range that they consider their own. Usually this is done by leaving their personal odour at various points, covering the country claimed, but in some cases visible marks are added. Thus the beaver leaves a little dab of mud, the wolf scratches with his hind feet, and the bear tears the signal tree with tooth and claw. Since this is done from time to time, when the bear happens to be near the tree, it is kept fresh as long as the region is claimed. But it is especially done in midsummer when the bears are pairing, and helps them to find suitable companions for all are then roaming the woods seeking mates; all call and leave their mark on the sign post, so the next bear, thanks to his exquisite nose, can tell at once the sex of the bear that called last and by its track tell which way it travelled afterward.

In this case it was a bear's register, but before long Quonab showed Rolf a place where two long logs joined at an angle by a tree that was rubbed and smelly, and showed a few marten hairs, indicating that this was the sign post of a marten and a good place to make a deadfall.

Yet a third was found in an open, grassy glade, a large, white stone on which were pellets left by foxes. The Indian explained:

"Every fox that travels near will come and smell the stone to see who of his kind is around, so this is a good place for a fox-trap; a steel trap, of course, for no fox will go into a deadfall."

And slowly Rolf learned that these habits are seen in some measure in all animals; yes, down to the mice and shrews. We see little of it because our senses are blunt and our attention untrained; but the naturalist and the hunter always know where to look for the four-footed inhabitants and by them can tell whether or not the land is possessed by such and such a furtive tribe.

XXIII

The Beaver Pond

AT THE noon halt they were about ten miles from home and had made fifteen deadfalls for marten, for practice was greatly reducing the time needed for each.

In the afternoon they went on, but the creek had become a mere rill and they were now high up in a more level stretch of country that was more or less swampy. As they followed the main course of the dwindling stream, looking ever for signs of fur-bearers, they crossed and recrossed the water. At length Quonab stopped, stared, and pointed at the rill, no longer clear but clouded with mud. His eyes shone as he jerked his head up stream and uttered the magic word, "Beaver."

They tramped westerly for a hundred yards through a dense swamp of alders, and came at last to an irregular pond that spread out among the willow bushes and was lost in the swampy thickets. Following the stream they soon came to a beaver dam, a long, curving bank of willow branches and mud, tumbling through the top of which were a dozen tiny streams that reunited their waters below to form the rivulet they had been following.

Red-winged blackbirds were sailing in flocks about the pond; a number of ducks were to be seen, and on a dead tree, killed by the backed up water, a great blue heron stood. Many smaller creatures moved or flitted in the lively scene, while far out near the middle rose a dome-like pile of sticks, a beaver lodge, and farther three more were discovered. No beaver were seen, but the fresh cut sticks, the floating branches peeled of all the bark, and the long, strong dam in good repair were enough to tell a practised eye that here was a large colony of beavers in undisturbed possession.

In those days beaver was one of the most valued furs. The creature is very easy to trap; so the discovery of the pond was like the finding of a bag of gold. They skirted its uncertain edges and

Rolf in the Woods

Quonab pointed out the many landing places of the beaver; little docks they seemed, built up with mud and stones with deep water plunge holes alongside. Here and there on the shore was a dome-shaped ant's nest with a pathway to it from the pond, showing, as the Indian said, that here the beaver came on sunny days to lie on the hill and let the swarming ants come forth and pick the vermin from their fur. At one high point projecting into the still water they found a little mud pie with a very strong smell; this, the Indian said, was a *castor cache,* the sign that, among beavers, answers the same purpose as the bear tree among bears.

Although the pond seemed small they had to tramp a quarter of a mile before reaching the upper end and here they found another dam, with its pond. This was at a slightly higher level and contained a single lodge; after this they found others, a dozen ponds in a dozen successive rises, the first or largest and the second only having lodges, but all were evidently part of the thriving colony, for fresh cut trees were seen on every side. "Ugh, good; we get maybe fifty beaver," said the Indian, and they knew they had reached the Promised Land.

Rolf would gladly have spent the rest of the day exploring the pond and trying for a beaver, when the eventide should call them to come forth, but Quonab said, "Only twenty deadfall; we should have one hundred and fifty." So making for a fine sugar bush on the dry ground west of the ponds they blazed a big tree, left a deadfall there, and sought the easiest way over the rough hills that lay to the east, in hopes of reaching the next stream leading down to their lake.

XXIV

The Porcupine

SKOOKUM was a partly trained little dog; he would stay in camp when told, if it suited him; and would not hesitate to follow or lead his master, when he felt that human wisdom was inferior to the ripe product of canine experience covering more than thirteen moons of recollection. But he was now living a life in which his previous experience must often fail him as a guide. A faint rustling on the leafy ground had sent him ahead at a run, and his sharp, angry bark showed that some hostile creature of the woods had been discovered. Again and again the angry yelping was changed into a sort of yowl, half anger, half distress. The hunters hurried forward to find the little fool charging again and again a huge porcupine that was crouched with its head under a log, its hindquarters exposed but bristling with spines; and its tail lashing about, left a new array of quills in the dog's mouth and face each time he charged. Skookum was a plucky fighter, but plainly he was nearly sick of it. The pain of the quills would, of course, increase every minute and with each movement. Quonab took a stout stick and threw the porcupine out of its retreat (Rolf supposed to kill it when the head was exposed) but the spiny one, finding a new and stronger enemy, wasted no time in galloping at its slow lumbering pace to the nearest small spruce tree and up that it scrambled to a safe place in the high branches.

Now the hunters called the dog. He was a sorry-looking object, pawing at his muzzle, first with one foot, then another, trying to unswallow the quills in his tongue, blinking hard, uttering little painful grunts and whines as he rubbed his head upon the ground or on his forelegs. Rolf held him while Quonab, with a sharp jerk, brought out quill after quill. Thirty or forty of the poisonous little daggers were plucked from his trembling legs, head, face, and nostrils, but the dreadful ones were those in his lips and tongue. Already they were deeply sunk in the soft,

quivering flesh. One by one those in the lips were withdrawn by the strong fingers of the red man, and Skookum whimpered a little, but he shrieked outright when those in the tongue were removed. Rolf had to work hard to hold him, and any one not knowing the case might have thought that the two men were deliberately holding the dog to administer the most cruel torture.

But none of the quills had sunk very deep. All were got out at last and the little dog set free.

Now Rolf thought of vengeance on the quill-pig snugly sitting in the tree near by.

Ammunition was too precious to waste, but Rolf was getting ready to climb when Quonab said: "No, no; you must not. Once I saw white man climb after the Kahk; it waited till he was near, then backed down, lashing its tail. He put up his arm to save his face. It speared his arm in fifty places and he could not save his face, so he tried to get down, but the Kahk came faster, lashing him; then he lost his hold and dropped. His leg was broken and his arm was swelled up for half a year. They are very poisonous. He nearly died."

"Well, I can at least chop him down," and Rolf took the axe.

"Wah!" Quonab said, "no; my father said you must not kill the Kahk, except you make sacrifice and use his quills for household work. It is bad medicine to kill the Kahk."

So the spiny one was left alone in the place he had so ably fought for. But Skookum, what of him? He was set free at last. To be wiser? Alas, no! Before one hour he met with another porcupine and remembering only his hate of the creature repeated the same sad mistake, and again had to have the painful help, without which he must certainly have died. Before night, however, he began to feel his real punishment and next morning no one would have known the pudding-headed thing that sadly followed the hunters, for the bright little dog that a day before had run so joyously through the woods. It was many a long day before he fully recovered and at one time his life was in the balance; and yet to the last of his days he never fully realized the folly of his insensate attacks on the creature that fights with its tail.

"It is ever so," said the Indian. "The lynx, the panther, the wolf, the fox, the eagle, all that attack the Kahk must die. Once my father saw a bear that was killed by the quills. He had tried to bite the Kahk; it filled his mouth with quills that he could not spit out. They sunk deeper and his jaws swelled so he could not open or shut his mouth to eat; then he starved. My people found him near a fish pond below a rapid. There were many fish. The bear could kill them with his paw but not eat, so with his mouth wide open and plenty about him, he died of starvation in that pool.

"There is but one creature that can kill the Kahk that is the Ojeeg, the big fisher weasel. He is a devil. He makes very strong medicine; the Kahk cannot harm him. He turns it on its back and tears open its smooth belly. It is ever so. We not know, but my father said, that it is because when in the flood Nana Bojou was floating on the log with Kahk and Ojeeg, Kahk was insolent and wanted the highest place, but Ojeeg was respectful to Nana Bojou, he bit the Kahk to teach him a lesson and got lashed with the tail of many stings. But the Manito drew out the quills and said: 'It shall be ever thus; the Ojeeg shall conquer the Kahk and the quills of Kahk shall never do Ojeeg any harm.'"

XXV

The Otter Slide

IT WAS late now and the hunters camped in the high, cool woods. Skookum whined in his sleep so loudly as to waken them once or twice. Near dawn they heard the howling of wolves and the curiously similar hooting of a horned owl. There is, indeed, almost no difference between the short opening howl of a she-wolf and the long hoot of the owl. As he listened, half awake, Rolf heard a whirr of wings which stopped overhead, then a familiar chuckle. He sat up and saw Skookum sadly lift his misshaped head to gaze at a row of black-breasted grouse or partridge on a branch above, but the poor doggie was feeling too sick to take any active interest. They were not the ruffed grouse, but a kindred kind, new to Rolf. As he gazed at the perchers, he saw Quonab rise gently, go to the nearest willow and cut a long slender rod at least twelve feet long; on the top of this he made a short noose of cord. Then he went cautiously under the watching grouse, the spruce partridges, and reaching up slipped the noose over the neck of the first one; a sharp jerk then tightened the noose and brought the grouse tumbling out of the tree, while its companions merely clucked their puzzlement, but made no effort to escape.

A short, sharp blow put the captive out of pain. The rod was reached again and a second, the lowest always, was jerked down, and the trick repeated till three grouse were secured. Then only did it dawn on the others that they were in a most perilous neighbourhood, so they took flight.

Rolf sat up in amazement. Quonab dropped the three birds by the fire and set about preparing breakfast.

"These are fool hens," he explained. "You can mostly get them this way; sure, if you have a dog to help, but the ruffed grouse is no such fool."

Rolf in the Woods

Rolf dressed the birds and as usual threw the entrails to Skookum. Poor little dog! He was, indeed, a sorry sight. He looked sadly out of his bulging eyes, feebly moved his swollen jaws, but did not touch the food he once would have pounced on. He did not eat because he could not open his mouth.

At camp the trappers made a log trap and continued the line with blazes and deadfalls, until, after a mile, they came to a broad tamarack swamp, and, skirting its edge, found a small, outflowing stream that brought them to an eastward-facing hollow. Everywhere there were signs of game, but they were not prepared for the scene that opened as they cautiously pushed through the thickets into a high, hardwood bush. A deer rose out of the grass and stared curiously at them; then another and another until nearly a dozen were in sight; still farther many others appeared; to the left were more, and movements told of yet others to the right. Then their white flags went up and all loped gently away on the slope that rose to the north. There may have been twenty or thirty deer in sight, but the general effect of all their white tails bobbing away, was that the woods were full of deer. They seemed to be there by the hundreds and the joy of seeing so many beautiful live things was helped in the hunters by the feeling that this was their own hunting-ground. They had, indeed, reached the land of plenty.

The stream increased as they marched; many springs and some important rivulets joined on. They found some old beaver signs but none new; and they left their deadfalls every quarter mile or less.

The stream began to descend more quickly until it was in a long, narrow valley with steep clay sides and many pools. Here they saw again and again the tracks and signs of otter and coming quietly round a turn that opened a new reach they heard a deep splash, then another and another.

The hunters' first thought was to tie up Skookum, but a glance showed that this was unnecessary. They softly dropped the packs and the

sick dog lay meekly down beside them. Then they crept forward with hunter caution, favoured by an easterly breeze. Their first thought was of beaver, but they had seen no recent sign, nor was there anything that looked like a beaver pond. The measured *splash, splash, splash* — was not so far ahead. It might be a bear snatching fish, or — no, that was too unpleasant — a man baling out a canoe. Still the slow *splash, splash,* went on at intervals, not quite regular.

Now it seemed but thirty yards ahead and in the creek.

With the utmost care they crawled to the edge of the clay bank, and opposite they saw a sight but rarely glimpsed by man. Here were six otters; two evidently full-grown, and four seeming young of the pair, engaged in a most hilarious and human game of tobogganing down a steep clay hill to plump into a deep part at its foot.

Plump went the largest, presumably the father; down he went, to reappear at the edge, scramble out and up an easy slope to the top of the twenty-foot bank. *Splash, splash, splash,* came three of the young ones; splash, splash, the mother and one of the cubs almost together.

"Scoot" went the big male again, and the wet fur slopping and rub-bing on the long clay chute made it greasier and slipperier every time.

Splash, plump, splash — splash, plump, splash, went the otter family gleefully, running up the bank again, eager each to be first, it seemed, and to do the chute the oftenest.

The gambolling grace, the obvious good humour, the animal hilar-ity of it all, was absorbingly amusing. The trappers gazed with pleasure that showed how near akin are naturalist and hunter. Of course, they had some covetous thought connected with those glossy hides, but this was September still, and even otter were not yet prime.

Shoot, plump, splash, went the happy crew with apparently unabated joy and hilarity. The slide improved with use and the otters seemed tireless; when all at once a loud but muffled yelp was heard and Skookum, forget-ting all caution, came leaping down the bank to take a hand.

With a succession of shrill, birdy chirps the old otters warned their young. *Plump, plump, plump,* all shot into the pool, but to reappear, swimming with heads out, for they were but slightly alarmed. This was too much for Quonab; he levelled his flintlock; *snap, bang,* it went, pointed at the old male, but he dived at the snap and escaped. Down the bank now rushed the hunters, joined by Skookum, to attack the otters in the pool, for it was small and shallow; unless a burrow led from it, they were trapped.

But the otters realized the peril. All six dashed out of the pool, down the open, gravelly stream the old ones uttering loud chirps that rang like screams. Under the fallen logs and brush they glided, dodging beneath roots and over banks, pursued by the hunters, each armed with a club and by Skookum not armed at all.

The otters seemed to know where they were going and distanced all but the dog. Forgetting his own condition Skookum had almost overtaken one of the otter cubs when the mother wheeled about and, hissing and snarling, charged. Skookum was lucky to get off with a slight nip, for the otter is a dangerous fighter. But the unlucky dog was sent howling back to the two packs that he never should have left.

The hunters now found an open stretch of woods through which Quonab could run ahead and intercept the otters as they bounded on down the stream bed, pursued by Rolf, who vainly tried to deal a blow with his club. In a few seconds the family party was up to Quonab, trapped it seemed, but there is no more desperate assailant than an otter fighting for its young. So far from being cowed the two old ones made a simultaneous, furious rush at the Indian. Wholly taken by surprise, he missed with his club, and sprang aside to escape their jaws. The family dashed around then past him, and, urged by the continuous chirps of the mother, they plunged under a succession of log jams and into a willow swamp that spread out into an ancient beaver lake and were swallowed up in the silent wilderness.

XXVI

Back to the Cabin

AT THE far end of the long swamp the stream emerged, now much larger, and the trappers kept on with their work. When night fell they had completed fifty traps, all told, and again they camped without shelter overhead.

Next day Skookum was so much worse that they began to fear for his life. He had eaten nothing since the sad encounter. He could drink a little, so Rolf made a pot of soup, and when it was cool the poor doggie managed to swallow some of the liquid after half an hour's patient endeavour.

They were now on the home line; from a hill top they got a distant view of their lake, though it was at least five miles away. Down the creek they went, still making their deadfalls at likely places and still seeing game tracks at the muddy spots. The creek came at length to an extensive, open, hardwood bush, and here it was joined by another stream that came from the south, the two making a small river. From then on they seemed in a land of game; trails of deer were seen on the ground everywhere, and every few minutes they started one or two deer. The shady oak wood itself was flanked and varied with dense cedar swamps such as the deer love to winter in, and after they had tramped through two miles of it, the Indian said, "Good! Now we know where to come in winter when we need meat."

Rolf in the Woods

At a broad, muddy ford they passed an amazing number of tracks, mostly deer, but a few of panther, lynx, fisher, wolf, otter, and mink.

In the afternoon they reached the lake. The stream, quite a broad one here, emptied in about four miles south of the camp. Leaving a deadfall near its mouth they followed the shore and made a log trap every quarter mile just above the high water mark.

When they reached the place of Rolf's first deer they turned aside to see it. The gray jays had picked a good deal of the loose meat. No large animal had troubled it, and yet in the neighbourhood they found the tracks of both wolves and foxes.

"Ugh," said Quonab, "they smell it and come near, but they know that a man has been here; they are not very hungry, so keep away. This is good for trap."

So they made two deadfalls with the carrion half way between them. Then one or two more traps and they reached home, arriving at the camp just as darkness and a heavy rainfall began.

"Good," said Quonab, "our deadfalls are ready; we have done all the work our fingers could not do when the weather is very cold, and the ground too hard for stakes to be driven. Now the traps can get weathered before we go round and set them. Yet we need some strong medicine, some trapper charm."

Next morning he went forth with fish-line and fish-spear; he soon returned with a pickerel. He filled a bottle with cut-up shreds of this, corked it up, and hung it on the warm, sunny side of the shanty. "That will make a charm that every bear will come to," he said, and left it to the action of the sun.

XXVII

Sick Dog Skookum

GETTING home is always a joy; but walking about the place in the morning they noticed several little things that were wrong. Quonab's lodge was down, the paddles that stood against the shanty were scattered on the ground, and a bag of venison hung high at the ridge was opened and empty.

Quonab studied the tracks and announced "a bad old black bear; he has rollicked round for mischief, upsetting things. But the venison he could not reach; that was a marten that ripped open the bag."

"Then that tells what we should do; build a storehouse at the end of the shanty," said Rolf, adding, "it must be tight and it must be cool."

"Maybe! Sometime before winter," said the Indian; "but now we should make another line of traps while the weather is fine."

"No," replied the lad, "Skookum is not fit to travel now. We can't leave him behind, and we can make a storehouse in three days."

The unhappy little dog was worse than ever. He could scarcely breathe, much less eat or drink, and the case was settled.

First they bathed the invalid's head in water as hot as he could stand it. This seemed to help him so much that he swallowed eagerly some soup that they poured into his mouth. A bed was made for him in a sunny place and the hunters set about the new building.

In three days the storehouse was done, excepting the chinking. It was October now, and a sharp night frost warned them of the hard white moons to come. Quonab, as he broke the ice in a tin cup and glanced at the low-hung sun, said: "The leaves are falling fast; snow comes soon; we need another line of traps."

He stopped suddenly; stared across the lake. Rolf looked, and here came three deer, two bucks and a doe, trotting, walking, or lightly clearing obstacles, the doe in advance; the others, rival followers. As they kept along the shore, they came nearer the cabin. Rolf glanced at

Rolf in the Woods

Quonab, who nodded, then slipped in, got down the gun, and quickly glided unseen to the river where the deer path landed. The bucks did not actually fight, for the season was not yet on, but their horns were clean, their necks were swelling, and they threatened each other as they trotted after the leader. They made for the ford as for some familiar path, and splashed through, almost without swimming. As they landed, Rolf waited a clear view, then gave a short sharp *Hist!* It was like a word of magic, for it turned the three moving deer to three stony-still statues. Rolf's sights were turned on the smaller buck, and when the great cloud following the bang had cleared away, the two were gone and the lesser buck was kicking on the ground some fifty yards away.

"We have found the good hunting; the deer walk into camp," said Quonab; and the product of the chase was quickly stored, the first of the supplies to be hung in the new storehouse.

The entrails were piled up and covered with brush and stones. "That will keep off ravens and jays; then in winter the foxes will come and we can take their coats."

Now they must decide for the morning. Skookum was somewhat better, but still very sick, and Rolf suggested: "Quonab, you take the gun and axe and lay a new line. I will stay behind and finish up the cabin for the winter and look after the dog." So it was agreed. The Indian left the camp alone this time and crossed to the east shore of the lake; there to follow up another stream as before and to return in three or four days to the cabin.

XXVIII

Alone in the Wilderness

ROLF began the day by giving Skookum a bath as hot as he could stand it, and later his soup. For the first he whined feebly and for the second faintly wagged his tail; but clearly he was on the mend.

Now the chinking and moss-plugging of the new cabin required all his attention. That took a day and looked like the biggest job on hand, but Rolf had been thinking hard about the winter. In Connecticut the wiser settlers used to bank their houses for the cold weather; in the Adiron-dacks he knew it was far, far colder, and he soon decided to bank the two shanties as deeply as possible with earth. A good spade made of white oak, with its edge hardened by roasting it brown, was his first necessity, and after two days of digging he had the cabin with its annex buried up to "the eyes" in fresh, clean earth.

A stock of new, dry wood for wet weather helped to show how much too small the cabin was; and now the heavier work was done, and Rolf had plenty of time to think.

Which of us that has been left alone in the wilderness does not remember the sensations of the first day! The feeling of self-dependency, not unmixed with unrestraint; the ending of civilized thought; the total reversion to the primitive; the nearness of the wood-folk; a sense of intimacy; a recurrent feeling of awe at the silent inexorability of all around; and a sweet pervading sense of mastery in the very freedom. These were among the feelings that swept in waves through Rolf, and when the first

night came, he found such comfort — yes, he had to confess it — in the company of the helpless little dog whose bed was by his own.

But these were sensations that come not often; in the four days and nights that he was alone they lost all force.

The hunter proverb about "strange beasts when you have no gun" was amply illustrated now that Quonab had gone with their only fire-arm. The second night before turning in (he slept in the shanty now), he was taking a last look at the stars, when a large, dark form glided among the tree trunks between him and the shimmering lake; stopped, gazed at him, then silently disappeared along the shore. No wonder that he kept the shanty door closed that night, and next morning when he studied the sandy ridges he read plainly that his night visitor had been not a lynx or a fox, but a prowling cougar or panther.

On the third morning as he went forth in the still early dawn he heard a snort, and looking toward the spruce woods, was amazed to see towering up, statuesque, almost grotesque, with its mulish ears and antediluvian horns, a large bull moose.

Rolf was no coward, but the sight of that monster so close to him set his scalp a-prickling. He felt so helpless without any firearms. He stepped into the cabin, took down his bow and arrows, then gave a contemptuous "Humph; all right for partridge and squirrels, but give me a rifle for the woods!" He went out again; there was the moose stand-ing as before. The lad rushed toward it a few steps, shouting; it stared unmoved. But Rolf was moved, and he retreated to the cabin. Then remembering the potency of fire he started a blaze on the hearth. The thick smoke curled up on the still air, hung low, made swishes through the grove, until a faint air current took a wreath of it to the moose. The great nostrils drank in a draught that conveyed terror to the creature's soul, and wheeling it started at its best pace to the distant swamp, to be seen no more.

Five times, during these four days, did deer come by and behave as though they knew perfectly well that this young human was harmless, entirely without the power of the far-killing mystery.

How intensely Rolf wished for a gun. How vividly came back the scene in the trader's store, when last month he had been offered a beau-tiful rifle for twenty-five dollars, to be paid for in fur next spring, and savagely he blamed himself for not realizing what a chance it was. Then and there he made resolve to be the owner of a gun as soon as another chance came, and to *make* that chance come right soon.

One little victory he had in that time. The creature that had torn open the venison bag was still around the camp; that was plain by the further damage on the bag hung in the storehouse, the walls of which were not chinked. Mindful of Quonab's remark, he set two marten traps, one on the roof, near the hole that had been used as entry; the other on a log along which the creature must climb to reach the meat. The method of setting is simple; a hollow is made, large enough to receive the trap as it lies open; on the pan of the trap some grass is laid smoothly; on each side of the trap a piece of prickly brush is placed, so that in leaping over these the creature will land on the lurking snare. The chain was made fast to a small log.

Although so seldom seen there is no doubt that the marten comes out chiefly by day. That night the trap remained unsprung; next morning as Rolf went at silent dawn to bring water from the lake, he noticed a long, dark line that proved to be ducks. As he sat gazing he heard a sound in the tree beyond the cabin. It was like the scratching of a squirrel climbing about. Then he saw the creature, a large, dark squirrel, it seemed. It darted up this tree and down that, over logs and under brush, with the lightning speed of a lightning squirrel, and from time to time it stopped still as a bump while it gazed at some far and suspicious object. Up one trunk it went like a brown flash, and a moment later, out, cackling from its top, flew two partridges. Down to the ground, sinuous, graceful, incessantly active flashed the marten. Along a log it raced in undulating leaps; in the middle it stopped as though frozen, to gaze intently into a bed of sedge; with three billowy bounds its sleek form reached the sedge, flashed in and out again with a mouse in its snarling jaws; a side leap now, and another squeaker was squeakless, and another. The three were slain, then thrown aside, as the brown terror scanned a flight of ducks passing over. Into a thicket of willow it

disappeared and out again like an eel going through the mud, then up a tall stub where woodpecker holes were to be seen. Into the largest it went so quickly Rolf could scarcely see how it entered, and out in a few seconds bearing a flying squirrel whose skull it had crushed. Dropping the squirrel it leaped after it, and pounced again on the quivering form with a fearsome growl; then shook it savagely, tore it apart, cast it aside. Over the ground it now undulated, its shining yellow breast like a target of gold. Again it stopped. Now in pose like a pointer, exquisitely graceful, but oh, so wicked! Then the snaky neck swung the cobra head in the breeze and the brown one sniffed and sniffed, advanced a few steps, tried the wind and the ground. Still farther and the concentrated interest showed in its outstretched neck and quivering tail. Bounding into a thicket it went, when out of the other side there leaped a snowshoe rabbit away and away for dear life. Jump, jump, jump; twelve feet at every stride, and faster than the eye could follow, with the marten close behind. What a race it was, and how they twinkled through the brush! The rabbit is, indeed, faster, but courage counts for much, and his was low; but luck and his good stars urged him round to the deer trail crossing of the stream; once there he could not turn. There was only one course. He sprang into the open river and swam for his life. And the marten — why should it go in? It hated the water; it was not hungry; it was out for sport, and water sport is not to its liking. It braced its sinewy legs and halted at the very brink, while bunny crossed to the safe woods.

Back now came Wahpestan, the brown death, over the logs like a winged snake, skimming the ground like a sinister shadow, and heading for the cabin as the cabin's owner watched. Passing the body of the squirrel it paused to rend it again, then diving into the brush came out so far away and so soon that the watcher supposed at first that this was another marten. Up the shanty corner it flashed, hardly appearing to

snowshoe

climb, swung that yellow throat and dark-brown muzzle for a second, then made toward the entry.

Rolf sat with staring eyes as the beautiful demon, elegantly spurning the roof sods, went at easy, measured bounds toward the open chink — toward its doom. One, two, three — clearing the prickly cedar bush, its forefeet fell on the hidden trap; clutch, a savage shriek, a flashing — a struggle baffling the eyes to follow, and the master of the squirrels was himself under mastery.

Rolf rushed forward now. The little demon in the trap was frothing with rage and hate; it ground the iron with its teeth; it shrieked at the human foeman coming.

The scene must end, the quicker the better, and even as the marten itself had served the flying squirrel and the mice, and as Quonab served the mink, so Rolf served the marten and the woods was still.

XXIX

Snowshoes

"THATS for Annette," said Rolf, remembering his promise as he hung the stretched marten skin to dry.

"Yi! Yi! Yi!" came three yelps, just as he had heard them the day he first met Quonab, and crossing the narrow lake he saw his partner's canoe.

"We have found the good hunting," he said, as Rolf steadied the canoe at the landing and Skookum, nearly well again, wagged his entire ulterior person to welcome the wanderer home. The first thing to catch the boy's eye was a great, splendid beaver skin stretched on a willow hoop. "Ho, ho!" he exclaimed.

"Ugh; found another pond."

"Good, good," said Rolf as he stroked the first beaver skin he had ever seen in the woods.

"This is better," said Quonab, and held up the two bark-stones, castors, or smell-glands that are found in every beaver and which for some hid reason have an irresistible attraction for all wild animals. To us the odour is slight, but they have the power of intensifying, perpetuating, and projecting such odorous substances as may be mixed with them. No trapper considers his bait to be perfect without a little of the mysterious castor. So that that most stenchable thing they had already concocted of fish-oil, putrescence, sewer-gas, and sunlight, when commingled and multiplied with the dried-up powder of a castor, was intensified into a rich, rancid, gas-exhaling hell-broth as rapturously bewitching to our furry brothers as it is poisonously nauseating to ourselves — seductive afar like the sweetest music, inexorable as fate, insidious as laughing-gas, soothing and numbing as absinthe — this, the lure and caution-luller, is the fellest trick in all the trappers'

Annette

code. As deadly as inexplicable, not a few of the states have classed it with black magic and declared its use a crime.

But no such sentiment prevailed in the high hills of Quonab's time, and their preparations for a successful trapping season were nearly perfect. Thirty deadfalls made by Quonab, with the sixty made on the first trip and a dozen steel traps, were surely promise of a good haul. It was nearly November now; the fur was prime; then why not begin? Because the weather was too fine. You must have frosty weather or the creatures taken in the deadfalls are spoiled before the trapper can get around.

Already a good, big pile of wood was cut; both shanty and storeroom were chinked, plugged, and banked for the winter. It was not safe yet to shoot and store a number of deer, but there was something they could do. Snowshoes would soon be a necessary of life; and the more of this finger work they did while the weather was warm, the better.

Birch and ash are used for frames; the former is less liable to split, but harder to work. White ash was plentiful on the near flat, and a small ten-foot log was soon cut and split into a lot of long laths. Quonab of course took charge; but Rolf followed in everything. Each took a lath and shaved it down evenly until an inch wide and three quarters of an inch thick. The exact middle was marked, and for ten inches at each side of that it was shaved down to half an inch in thickness. Two flat crossbars, ten and twelve inches long, were needed and holes to receive these made half through the frame. The pot was ready boiling and by using a cord from end to end of each lath they easily bent it in the middle and brought the wood into touch with the boiling water. Before an hour the steam had so softened the wood, and robbed it of spring, that it was easy to make it into any desired shape. Each lath was cautiously bent round; the crossbars slipped into their prepared sockets; a temporary lashing of cord kept all in place; then finally the frames were set on a level place with the fore end raised two inches and a heavy log put on the frame to give the upturn to the toe.

Here they were left to dry and the Indian set about preparing the necessary thongs. A buckskin rolled in wet, hardwood ashes had been left in the mud hole. Now after a week the hair was easily scraped off and the hide, cleaned and trimmed of all loose ends and tags, was spread out — soft, white, and supple. Beginning outside, and following round and round the edge, Quonab cut a thong of rawhide as nearly as possible a quarter inch wide. This he carried on till there were many yards of it, and the hide was all used up. The second deer skin was much smaller and thinner. He sharpened his knife and cut it much finer, at least half the width of the other. Now they were ready to lace the shoes, the finer for the fore and back parts, the heavy for the middle on which the wearer treads. An expert squaw would have laughed at the rude snowshoes that were finished that day, but they were strong and serviceable.

Naturally the snowshoes suggested a toboggan. That was easily made by splitting four thin boards of ash, each six inches wide and ten feet long. An up-curl was steamed on the prow of each, and rawhide lashings held all to the crossbars.

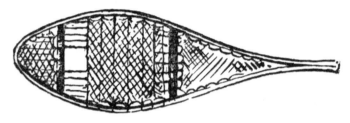

XXX

Catching a Fox

"As to wisdom, a man ain't a spring; he's a tank, an' gives out only what he gathers."

—The Sayings of Si Sylvanne

QUONAB would not quit his nightly couch in the canvas lodge so Rolf and Skookum stayed with him. The dog was himself again, and more than once in the hours of gloom dashed forth in noisy chase of something which morning study of the tracks showed to have been foxes. They were attracted partly by the carrion of the deer, partly by the general suitability of the sandy beach for a gambolling place, and partly by a foxy curiosity concerning the cabin, the hunters, and their dog.

One morning after several night arousings and many raids by Skookum, Rolf said: "Fox is good now; why shouldn't I add some fox pelts to that?" and he pointed with some pride to the marten skin.

"Ugh, good; go ahead; you will learn," was the reply.

So getting out the two fox traps Rolf set to work. Noting where chiefly the foxes ran or played he chose two beaten pathways and hid the traps carefully, exactly as he did for the marten; then selecting a couple of small cedar branches he cut these and laid them across the path, one on each side of the trap, assuming that the foxes following the usual route would leap over the boughs and land in disaster. To make doubly sure he put a piece of meat by each trap and half-way between them set a large piece on a stone.

Then he sprinkled fresh earth over the pathway and around each trap and bait so he should have a record of the tracks.

Foxes came that night, as he learned by the footprints along the beach, but never one went near his traps. He studied the marks; they slowly told him all the main facts. The foxes had come as usual, and frolicked about. They had discovered the bait and the traps at once — how could such sharp noses miss them — and as quickly noted that the traps were suspicious-smelling iron things, that man-scent, hand, foot, and body, were very evident all about; that the only inducement to go forward was some meat which was coarse and cold, not for a moment to be compared with the hot juicy mouse meat that abounded in every meadow. The foxes were well fed and unhungry. Why should they venture into such evident danger? In a word, walls of stone could not have more completely protected the ground and the meat from the foxes than did the obvious nature of the traps; not a track was near, and many afar showed how quickly they had veered off.

"Ugh, it is always so," said Quonab. "Will you try again?"

"Yes, I will," replied Rolf, remembering now that he had omitted to deodorize his traps and his boots.

He made a fire of cedar and smoked his traps, chains, and all. Then taking a piece of raw venison he rubbed it on his leather gloves and on the soles of his boots, wondering how he had expected to succeed the night before with all these man-scent killers left out. He put fine, soft moss under the pan of each trap, then removed the cedar brush, and gently sprinkled all with fine, dry earth. The set was perfect; no human eye could have told that there was any trap in the place. It seemed a foregone success.

"Fox don't go by eye," was all the Indian said, for he reckoned it best to let the learner work it out.

In the morning Rolf was up eager to see the results. There was nothing at all. A fox had indeed come within ten feet at one place, but behaved then as though positively amused at the childishness of the whole smelly affair. Had a man been there on guard with a club, he could not have kept the spot more wholly clear of foxes. Rolf turned

away baffled and utterly puzzled. He had not gone far before he heard a most terrific yelping from Skookum, and turned to see that trouble-seeking pup caught by the leg in the first trap. It was more the horrible surprise than the pain, but he did howl.

The hunters came quickly to the rescue and at once he was freed, none the worse, for the traps have no teeth; they merely hold. It is the long struggle and the starvation chiefly that are cruel, and these every trapper should cut short by going often around his line.

Now Quonab took part. "That is a good setting for some things. It would catch a coon, a mink, or a marten — or a dog — but not a fox or a wolf. They are very clever. You shall see."

The Indian got out a pair of thick leather gloves, smoked them in cedar, also the traps. Next he rubbed his moccasin soles with raw meat and selecting a little bay in the shore he threw a long pole on the sand, from the line of high, dry shingle across to the water's edge. In his hand he carried a rough stake. Walking carefully on the pole and standing on it, he drove the stake in at about four feet from the shore; then split it, and stuffed some soft moss into the split. On this he poured three or four drops of the "smell-charm." Now he put a lump of spruce gum on the pan of the trap, holding a torch under it till the gum was fused, and into this he pressed a small, flat stone.

The chain of the trap he fastened to a ten-pound stone of convenient shape, and sank the stone in the water half-way between the stake and the shore. Last he placed the trap on this stone, so that when open everything would be under water except the flat stone on the pan. Now he returned along the pole and dragged it away with him.

Thus there was now no track or scent of human near the place.

The setting was a perfect one, but even then the foxes did not go near it the following night; they must become used to it. In their code, "A strange thing is always dangerous." In the morning Rolf was inclined to scoff. But Quonab said: "Wah! No trap goes first night."

They did not need to wait for the second morning. In the middle of the night Skookum rushed forth barking, and they followed to see a wild struggle, the fox leaping to escape and fast to his foot was the trap with its anchor stone a-dragging.

Then was repeated the scene that ended the struggle of mink and marten. The creature's hind feet were tied together and his body hung from a peg in the shanty. In the morning they gloated over his splendid fur and added his coat to their store of trophies.

XXXI

Following the Trap Line

THAT night the moon changed. Next day came on with a strong north wind. By noon the wild ducks had left the lake. Many long strings of geese passed southeastward, honking as they flew. Colder and colder blew the strong wind, and soon the frost was showing on the smaller ponds. It snowed a little, but this ceased. With the clearing sky the wind fell and the frost grew keener.

At daybreak, when the hunters rose, it was very cold. Everything but the open lake was frozen over, and they knew that winter was come; the time of trapping was at hand. Quonab went at once to the pinnacle on the hill, made a little fire, then chanting the "Hunter's Prayer," he cast into the fire the whiskers of the fox and the marten, some of the beaver castor, and some tobacco. Then descended to prepare for the trail — blankets, beaver-traps, weapons, and food for two days, besides the smell-charm and some fish for bait.

Quickly the deadfalls were baited and set; last the Indian threw into the trap chamber a piece of moss on which was a drop of the "smell," and wiped another drop on each of his moccasins. "Phew," said Rolf.

"That make a trail the marten follow for a month," was the explanation. Skookum seemed to think so too, and if he did not say "phew," it was because he did not know how.

Very soon the little dog treed a flock of partridge and Rolf with blunt arrows secured three. The breasts were saved for the hunters' table, but the rest with the offal and feathers made the best of marten baits and served for all the traps, till at noon they reached the beaver pond. It was covered with ice too thin to bear, but the freshly used landing places were easily selected. At each they set a strong, steel beaver-trap, concealing it amid some dry grass, and placing in a split stick a foot away a piece of moss in which were a few drops of the magic lure. The ring on the trap chain was slipped over a long, thin, smooth pole which was driven deep in the mud, the top pointing away from the deep water. The plan was old and proven. The beaver, eager to investigate that semi-friendly smell, sets foot in the trap; instinctively when in danger he dives for the deep water; the ring slips along the pole till at the bottom and there it jams so that the beaver cannot rise again and is drowned.

In an hour the six traps were set for the beavers; presently the hunters, skirmishing for more partridges, had much trouble to save Skookum from another porcupine disaster.

They got some more grouse, baited the traps for a couple of miles, then camped for the night.

Before morning it came on to snow and it was three inches deep when they arose. There is no place on earth where the first snow is more beautiful than in the Adirondacks. In early autumn nature seems to prepare for it Green leaves are cleared away to expose the berry bunches in red; rushbeds mass their groups, turn golden brown and bow their heads to meet the silver load; the low hills and the lines of various Christmas trees are arrayed for the finest effect: the setting is perfect and the scene, but it lacks the limelight yet. It needs must have the lavish blaze of white. And when it comes like the veil on a bride, the silver mountings on a charger's trappings, or the golden fire in a sunset, the shining crystal robe is the finishing, the crowning glory, without which all the rest must fail, could have no bright completeness. Its beauty stirred the hunters though it found no better expression than Rolf's simple words, "Ain't it fine," while the Indian gazed in silence.

There is no other place in the eastern woods where the snow has such manifold tales to tell, and the hunters that day tramping found themselves dowered over night with the wonderful power of the hound to whom each trail is a plain record of every living creature that has passed within many hours. And though the first day after a storm has less to tell than the second, just as the second has less than the third, there was no lack of story in the snow. Here sped some antlered buck,

trotting along while yet the white was flying. There went a fox, sneaking across the line of march, and eying distrustfully that deadfall. This broad trail with many large tracks not far apart was made by one of Skookum's friends, a knight of many spears. That bounding along was a marten. See how he quartered that thicket like a hound, here he struck our odour trail. Mark, how he paused and whiffed it; now away he goes; yes, straight to our trap.

"It's down; hurrah!" Rolf shouted, for there, dead under the log, was an exquisite marten, dark, almost black, with a great, broad, shining breast of gold.

They were going back now toward the beaver lake. The next trap was sprung and empty; the next held the body of a red squirrel, a nuisance always and good only to rebait the trap he springs. But the next held a marten, and the next a white weasel. Others were unsprung, but they had two good pelts when they reached the beaver lake. They were in high spirits with their good luck, but not prepared for the marvellous haul that now was theirs. *Each of the six traps* held a big beaver, dead, drowned, and safe. Each skin was worth five dollars, and the hunters felt rich. The incident had, moreover, this pleasing significance: It showed that these beavers were unsophisticated, so had not been hunted. Fifty pelts might easily be taken from these ponds.

The trappers reset the traps; then dividing the load, sought a remote place to camp, for it does not do to light a fire near your beaver pond. One hundred and fifty pounds of beaver, in addition to their packs, was not a load to be taken miles away; within half a mile on a lower level they selected a warm place, made a fire, and skinned their catch. The bodies they opened and hung in a tree with a view to future use, but the pelts and tails they carried on.

They made a long, hard tramp that day, baiting all the traps and reached home late in the night.

XXXII

The Antler-bound Bucks

IN THE man-world, November is the month of gloom, despair, and many suicides.

In the wild world, November is the Mad Moon. Many and diverse the madnesses of the time, but none more insane than the rut of the white-tailed deer. Like some disease it appears, first in the swollen necks of the antler-bearers, and then in the feverish habits of all. Long and obstinate combats between the bucks now characterize the time; neglecting even to eat, they spend their days and nights in rushing about and seeking to kill.

Their horns, growing steadily since spring, are now of full size, sharp, heavy, and cleaned of the velvet; in perfection. For what? Has Nature made them to pierce, wound, and destroy? Strange as it may seem, these weapons of offence are used for little but defence; less as spears than as bucklers they serve the deer in battles with its kind. And the long, hard combats are little more than wrestling and pushing bouts; almost never do they end fatally. When a mortal thrust is given, it is rarely a gaping wound, but a sudden springing and locking of the ant-lers, whereby the two deer are bound together, inextricably, hopelessly, and so suffer death by starvation. The records of deer killed by their rivals and left on the duel-ground are few; very few and far between. The records of those killed by interlocking are numbered by the scores.

There were hundreds of deer in this country that Rolf and Quonab claimed. Half of them were bucks, and at least half of these engaged in combat some times or many times a day, all through November; that is to say, probably a thousand duels were fought that month within ten miles of the cabin. It was not surprising that Rolf should witness some of them, and hear many more in the distance.

They were living in the cabin now, and during the still, frosty nights, when he took a last look at the stars before turning in, Rolf formed the habit of listening intently for the voices of the gloom. Sometimes it was the "hoo-hoo" of the horned-owl; once or twice it was the long, smooth howl of the wolf; but many times it was the rattle of antlers that told of two bucks far up in the hardwoods, trying out the all-important question, "Which is the better buck?"

One morning he heard still an occasional rattle at the same place as the night before. He set out alone, after breakfast, and coming cautiously near, peered into a little, open space to see two bucks with heads joined, slowly, feebly pushing this way and that. Their tongues were out; they seemed almost exhausted, and the trampled snow for an acre about plainly showed that they had been fighting for hours; that indeed these were the ones he had heard in the night. Still they were evenly matched, and the green light in their eyes told of the ferocious spirit in each of these gentle-looking deer.

Rolf had no difficulty in walking quite near. If they saw him, they gave slight heed to the testimony of their eyes, for the unenergetic struggle went on until, again pausing for breath, they separated, raised their heads a little, sniffed, then trotted away from the dreaded enemy so near. Fifty yards off, they turned, shook their horns, seemed in doubt whether to run away, join battle again, or attack the man. Fortunately the first was their choice, and Rolf returned to the cabin.

Quonab listened to his account, then said: "You might have been killed. Every buck is crazy now. Often they attack man. My father's brother was killed by a Mad Moon buck. They found only his body, torn to rags. He had got a little way up a tree, but the buck had pinned him. There were the marks, and in the snow they could, see how he held on to the deer's horns and was dragged about till his strength gave out. He had no gun. The buck went off. That was all they knew. I would rather trust a bear than a deer."

The Indian's words were few, but they drew a picture all too realistic. The next time Rolf heard the far sound of a deer fight, it brought back the horror of that hopeless fight in the snow, and gave him a new and different feeling for the antler-bearer of the changing mood.

The Antler-bound Bucks

It was two weeks after this, when he was coming in from a trip alone on part of the line, when his ear caught some strange sounds in the woods ahead; deep, sonorous, semi-human they were. Strange and weird wood-notes in winter are nearly sure to be those of a raven or a jay; if deep, they are likely to come from a raven.

"Quok, quok, ha, ha, ha — hreww, hrrr, hooop, hooop," the diabolic noises came, and Rolf, coming gently forward, caught a glimpse of sable pinions swooping through the lower pines.

"Ho, ho, ho— yah — hew - w - w - w" came the demon laughter of the death birds, and Rolf soon glimpsed a dozen of them in the branches, hopping or sometimes flying to the ground. One alighted on a brown bump. Then the bump began to move a little. The raven was pecking away, but again the brown bump heaved and the raven leaped to a near perch. "Wah — wah — wah - wo - hoo —yow-wow— rrrrrr-rrrr-rrrr" — and the other ravens joined in.

Rolf had no weapons but his bow, his pocket knife, and a hatchet. He took the latter in his hand and walked gently forward; the hollow-voiced ravens "haw - hawed," then flew to safe perches where they chuckled like ghouls over some extra-ghoulish joke.

The lad, coming closer, witnessed a scene that stirred him with mingled horror and pity. A great, strong buck — once strong, at least — was standing, staggering, kneeling there; sometimes on his hind legs, spasmodically heaving and tugging at a long gray form on the ground, the body of another buck, his rival, dead now, with a broken neck, as it proved, but bearing big, strong antlers with which the antlers of the living buck were interlocked as though riveted with iron, bolted with clamps of steel. With all his strength, the living buck could barely move his head, dragging his adversary's body with him. The snow marks showed that at first he had been able to haul the carcass many yards; had nibbled a little at shoots and twigs; but that was when he was stronger, was long before. How long? For days, at least, perhaps a week, that wretched buck was dying hopelessly a death that would not come. His gaunt sides, his parched and lolling tongue, less than a foot from the snow and yet beyond reach, the filmy eye, whose opaque veil of death was illumined again with a faint fire of fighting green as the new foe came.

Rolf in the Woods

The ravens had picked the eyes out of the dead buck and eaten a hole in its back. They had even begun on the living buck, but he had been able to use one front foot to defend his eyes; still his plight could scarce have been more dreadful. It made the most pitiful spectacle Rolf had ever seen in wild life; yes, in all his life. He was full of compassion for the poor brute. He forgot it as a thing to be hunted for food; thought of it only as a harmless, beautiful creature in dire and horrible straits; a fellow-being in distress; and he at once set about being its helper. With hatchet in hand he came gently in front, and selecting an exposed part at the base of the dead buck's antler he gave a sharp blow with the hatchet. The effect on the living buck was surprising. He was roused to vigorous action that showed him far from death as yet. He plunged, then pulled backward, carrying with him the carcass and the would-be rescuer. Then Rolf remembered the Indian's words: "You can make strong medicine with your mouth." He spoke to the deer, gently, softly. Then came nearer, and tapped on the horn he wished to cut; softly speaking and tapping he increased his force, until at last he was permitted to chop seriously at that prison bar. It took many blows, for the antler stuff is very thick and strong at this time, but the horn was loose at last. Rolf gave it a twist and the strong buck was free. Free for what?

Oh, tell it not among the folk who have been the wild deer's friend! Hide it from all who blindly believe that gratitude must always follow good-will! With unexpected energy, with pent-up fury, with hellish purpose, the ingrate sprang on his deliverer, aiming a blow as deadly as was in his power.

Wholly taken by surprise, Rolf barely had time to seize the murderer's horns and ward them off his vitals. The buck made a furious lunge. Oh! what foul fiend was it gave him then such force? — and Rolf went down. Clinging for dear life to those wicked, shameful horns, he yelled as he never yelled before: "Quonab, Quonab! Help me, oh, help me!" But he was pinned at once, the fierce brute above him pressing on his chest, striving to bring its horns to bear; his only salvation had been that their wide spread gave his body room between. But the weight on his chest was crushing out his force, his life; he had no breath to call again. How the ravens chuckled, and "haw-hawed" in the tree!

The buck's eyes gleamed again with the emerald light of murderous hate, and he jerked his strong neck this way and that with the power of

"Quonab, Quonab! Help me!"

madness. It could not last for long. The boy's strength was going fast; the beast was crushing in his chest.

"Oh, God, help me!" he gasped, as the antlered fiend began again struggling for the freedom of those murderous horns. The brute was almost free, when the ravens rose with loud croaks, and out of the woods dashed another to join the fight A smaller deer? No; what? Rolf knew not, nor how, but in a moment there was a savage growl and Skookum had the murderer by the hind leg. Worrying and tearing he had not the strength to throw the deer, but his teeth were sharp, his heart was in his work, and when he transferred his fierce attack to parts more tender still, the buck, already spent, reared, wheeled, and fell. Before he could recover Skookum pounced upon him by the nose and hung on like a vice. The buck could swing his great neck a little, and drag the dog, but he could not shake him off. Rolf saw the chance, rose to his tottering legs, seized his hatchet, stunned the fierce brute with a blow. Then finding on the snow his missing knife he gave the hunter stroke that spilled the red life-blood and sank on the ground to know no more till Quonab stood beside him.

XXXIII

A Song of Praise

ROLF was lying by a fire when he came to, Quonab bending over him with a look of grave concern. When he opened his eyes, the Indian smiled; such a soft, sweet smile, with long, ivory rows in its background.

Then he brought hot tea, and Rolf revived so he could sit up and tell the story of the morning.

"He is an evil Manito," and he looked toward the dead buck. "We must not eat him. You surely made medicine to bring Skookum."

"Yes, I made medicine with my mouth," was the answer. "I called, I yelled, when *he* came at me."

"It is a long way from here to the cabin," was Quonab's reply. "I could not hear you; Skookum could not hear you; but Cos Cob, my father, told me that when you send out a cry for help, you send medicine, too, that goes farther than the cry. May be so; I do not know: my father was very wise."

"Did you see Skookum come, Quonab?"

"No; he was with me hours after you left, but he was restless and whimpered. Then he left me and it was a long time before I heard him bark. It was the 'something-wrong' bark. I went. He brought me here."

"He must have followed my track all 'round the line."

After an hour they set out for the cabin. The ravens "Ha-ha-ed" and "Ho-ho-ed" as they went. Quonab took the fateful horn that Rolf had chopped off, and hung it on a sapling with a piece of tobacco and a red yarn streamer, to appease the evil spirit that surely was near. There it hung for years after, until the sapling grew to a tree that swallowed the horn, all but the tip, which rotted away.

Skookum took a final sniff at his fallen enemy, gave the body the customary expression of a dog's contempt, then led the procession homeward.

Rolf in the Woods

Not that day, not the next, but on the first day of calm, red, sunset sky, went Quonab to his hill of worship; and when the little fire that he lit sent up its thread of smoke, like a plumb-line from the red cloud over him, he burnt a pinch of tobacco, and, with face and arms upraised in the red light, he sang a new song:

> "The evil one set a trap for my son,
> But the Manito saved him;
> In the form of a Skookum he saved him."

XXXIV

The Birch-bark Vessels

ROLF was sore and stiff for a week afterward; so was Skookum. There were times when Quonab was cold, moody, and silent for days. Then some milder wind would blow in the region of his heart and the bleak ice surface melted into running rills of memory or kindly emanation.

Just before the buck adventure, there had been an unpleasant time of chill and aloofness. It arose over little. Since the frost had come, sealing the waters outside, Quonab would wash his hands in the vessel that was also the bread pan. Rolf had New England ideas of propriety in cooking matters, and finally he forgot the respect due to age and experience. That was one reason why he went out alone that day. Now, with time to think things over, the obvious safeguard would be to have a wash bowl; but where to get it? In those days, tins were scarce and expensive. It was the custom to look in the woods for nearly all the necessaries of life; and, guided by ancient custom and experience, they seldom looked in vain. Rolf had seen, and indeed made, watering troughs, pig troughs, sap troughs, hen troughs, etc., all his life, and he now set to work with the axe and a block of basswood to hew out a trough for a wash bowl. With adequate tools he might have made a good one; but, working with an axe and a stiff arm, the result was a very heavy, crude affair. It would indeed hold water, but it was almost impossible to dip it into the water hole, so that a dipper was needed.

When Quonab saw the plan and the result, he said: "In my father's lodge we had only birch bark. See; I shall make a bowl." He took from

the storehouse a big roll of birch bark, gathered in warm weather (it can scarcely be done in cold), for use in repairing the canoe. Selecting a good part he cut out a square, two feet each way, and put it in the big pot which was full of boiling water. At the same time he soaked with it a bundle of wattap, or long fibrous roots of the white spruce, also gathered before the frost came, with a view to canoe repairs in the spring.

While these were softening in the hot water, he cut a couple of long splints of birch, as nearly as possible half an inch wide and an eighth of an inch thick, and put them to steep with the bark. Next he made two or three straddle pins or clamps, like clothes pegs, by splitting the ends of some sticks which had a knot at one end.

Now he took out the spruce roots, soft and pliant, and selecting a lot that were about an eighth of an inch in diameter, scraped off the bark and roughness, until he had a bundle of perhaps ten feet of soft, even, white cords.

The bark was laid flat and cut as below.

The rounding of (A) and (B) is necessary, for the holes of the sewing would tear the piece off if all were on the same line of grain. Each corner was now folded and doubled on itself (C), then held so with a straddle pin (D). The rim was trimmed so as to be flat where it crossed the fibre of the bark, and arched where it ran along. The pliant rods of birch were bent around this, and using the large awl to make holes, Quonab sewed the rim rods to the bark with an over-lapping stitch that made a smooth finish to the edge, and the birch-bark wash pan was complete. (E.) Much heavier bark can be used if the plan (F) (G) be followed, but it is hard to make it water-tight.

So now they had a wash pan and a cause of friction was removed. Rolf found it amusing as well as useful to make other bark vessels of varying sizes for dippers and dunnage. It was work that he could do now while he was resting and recovering and he became expert. After watching a fairly successful attempt at a box to hold fish-hooks and

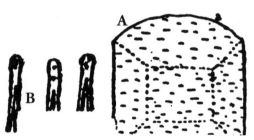

tackle, Quonab said: "In my father's lodge these would bear quill work in colours."

"That's so," said Rolf, remembering the birch-bark goods often sold by the Indians. "I wish we had a porcupine now."

"Maybe Skookum could find one," said the Indian, with a smile.

"Will you let me kill the next Kahk we find?"

"Yes, if you use the quills and burn its whiskers."

"Why burn its whiskers?"

"My father said it must be so. The smoke goes straight to the All-above; then the Manito knows we have killed, but we have remembered to kill only for use and to thank Him."

It was some days before they found a porcupine, and when they did, it was not necessary for them to kill it. But that belongs to another chapter.

They saved its skin with all its spears and hung it in the storehouse. The quills with the white bodies and ready-made needle at each end are admirable for embroidering, but they are white only.

"How can we dye them, Quonab?"

"In the summer are many dyes; in winter they are hard to get. We can get some."

So forth he went to a hemlock tree, and cut till he could gather the inner pink bark, which, boiled with the quills, turned them a dull pink; similarly, alder bark furnished rich orange, and butternut bark a brown. Oak chips, with a few bits of iron in the pot, dyed black.

"Must wait till summer for red and green," said the Indian. "Red comes only from berries; the best is the blitum. We call it squaw-berry and mis-caw-wá, yellow comes from the yellow root."*

---

* *Hydrostis.*

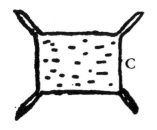 C
 D
 E

Rolf in the Woods

But black, white, orange, pink, brown, and a dull red made by a double dip of orange and pink, are a good range of colour. The method in using the quills is simple. An awl to make holes in the bark for each; the rough parts behind are concealed afterward with a lining of bark stitched over them; and before the winter was over, Rolf had made a birch-bark box, decorated lid and all, with porcupine quill work, in which he kept the sable skin that was meant to buy Annette's new dress, the costume she had dreamed of, the ideal and splendid, almost unbelievable vision of her young life, ninety-five cents' worth of cotton print.

There was one other point of dangerous friction. Whenever it fell to Quonab to wash the dishes, he simply set them on the ground and let Skookum lick them off. This economical arrangement was satisfactory to Quonab, delightful to Skookum, and apparently justified by the finished product, but Rolf objected. The Indian said: "Don't he eat the same food as we do? You cannot tell if you do not see."

Whenever he could do so, Rolf washed the doubtful dishes over again, yet there were many times when this was impossible, and the situation became very irritating. But he knew that the man who loses his temper has lost the first round of the fight, so, finding the general idea of uncleanness without avail, he sought for some purely Indian argument.

As they sat by the evening fire, one day, he led up to talk of his mother — of her power as a medicine woman, of the many evil medicines that harmed her. "It was evil medicine for her if a dog licked her hand or touched her food. A dog licked her hand and the dream dog came to her three days before she died." After a long pause, he added, "In some ways I am like my mother."

Two days later, Rolf chanced to see his friend behind the shanty give Skookum the pan to clean off after they had been frying deer fat. The Indian had no idea that Rolf was near, nor did he ever learn the truth of it.

F G

The Birch-bark Vessels

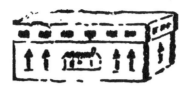

That night, after midnight, the lad rose quietly, lighted the pine splints that served them for a torch, rubbed some charcoal around each eye to make dark rings that should supply a horror-stricken look. Then he started in to pound on Quonab's tom-tom, singing:

"Evil spirit leave me;
Dog-face do not harm me."

Quonab sat up in amazement. Rolf paid no head, but went on, bawling and drumming and staring upward into vacant space. After a few minutes Skookum scratched and whined at the shanty door. Rolf rose, took his knife, cut a bunch of hair from Skookum's neck and burned it in the torch, then went on singing with horrid solemnity:

"Evil spirit leave me;
Dog-face do not harm me."

At last he turned, and seeming to discover that Quonab was looking on, said:

"The dream dog came to me. I thought I saw him lick deer grease from the frying pan behind the shanty. He laughed, for he knew that he made evil medicine for me. I am trying to drive him away, so he cannot harm me. I do not know. I am like my mother. She was very wise, but she died after it."

Now Quonab arose, cut some more hair from Skookum, added a pinch of tobacco, then, setting it ablaze, he sang in the rank odour of the burning weed and hair, his strongest song to kill ill magic; and Rolf, as he chuckled and sweetly sank to sleep, knew that the fight was won. His friend would never, never more install Skookum in the high and sacred post of pot-licker, dishwasher, or final polisher.

XXXV

Snaring Rabbits

THE deepening snow about the cabin was marked in all the thickets by the multitudinous tracks of the snowshoe rabbits or white hares. Occasionally the hunters saw them, but paid little heed. Why should they look at rabbits when deer were plentiful?

"You catch rabbit?" asked Quonab one day when Rolf was feeling fit again.

"I can shoot one with my bow," was the answer, "but why should I, when we have plenty of deer?"

"My people always hunted rabbits. Sometimes no deer were to be found; then the rabbits were food. Sometimes in the enemy's country it was not safe to hunt, except rabbits, with blunt arrows, and they were food. Sometimes only squaws and children in camp — nothing to eat; no guns; then the rabbits were food."

"Well, see me get one," and Rolf took his bow and arrow. He found many white bunnies, but always in the thickest woods. Again and again he tried, but the tantalizing twigs and branches muffled the bow and turned the arrow. It was hours before he returned with a fluffy snowshoe rabbit.

"That is not our way." Quonab led to the thicket and selecting a place of many tracks he cut a lot of brush and made a hedge across with half a dozen openings. At each of these openings he made a snare of strong cord tied to a long pole, hung on a crotch, and so arranged that a tug at the snare would free the pole which in turn would hoist the snare and the creature in it high in the air.

Next morning they went around and found that four of the snares had each a snow-white rabbit hanging by the neck. As he was handling these, Quonab felt a lump on the hind leg of one. He carefully cut it open and turned out a curious-looking object about the size of an acorn, flattened, made of flesh and covered with hair, and nearly the shape of a large bean. He gazed at it, and, turning to Rolf, said with intense meaning:

"Ugh! we have found the good hunting. This is the Peeto-wab-oos-once, the little medicine rabbit. Now we have strong medicine in the lodge. You shall see."

He went out to the two remaining snares and passed the medicine rabbit through each. An hour later, when they returned, they found a rabbit taken in the first snare.

"It is ever so," said the Indian. "We can always catch rabbits now. My father had the Peeto-wab-i-ush once, the little medicine deer, and so he never failed in hunting but twice. Then he found that his papoose, Quonab, had stolen his great medicine. He was a very wise papoose. He killed a chipmunk each of those days."

"Hark! what is that?" A faint sound of rustling branches, and some short animal noises in the woods had caught Rolf's ear, and Skookum's, too, for he was off like one whose life is bound up in a great purpose.

The Little Medicine Rabbit

"Yap, yap, yap," came the angry sound from Skookum. Who can say that animals have no language? His merry "Yip, yip, yip," for partridge up a tree, or his long, hilarious, "Yow, yow, yow," when despite all orders he chased some deer, were totally distinct from the angry "Yap, yap," he gave for the bear up the tree, or the "Grrryap-grryap," with which he voiced his hatred of the porcupine.

But now it was the "Yap, yap," as when he had treed the bears.

"Something up a tree," was the Indian's interpretation, as they followed the sound. Something up a tree! A whole menagerie it seemed to Rolf when they got there. Hanging by the neck in the remaining snare, and limp now, was a young lynx, a kit of the year. In the adjoining tree, with Skookum circling and yapping 'round the base, was a savage old lynx. In the crotch above her was another young one, and still higher was a third, all looking their unutterable disgust at the noisy dog below; the mother, indeed, expressing it in occasional hisses, but none of them daring to come down and face him. The lynx is very good fur and very easy prey. The Indian brought the old one down with a shot; then, as fast as he could reload, the others were added to the bag, and, with the one from the snare, they returned laden to the cabin.

Snaring Rabbits

The Indian's eyes shone with a peculiar light. "Ugh! Ugh! My father told me; it is great medicine. You see, now, it does not fail."

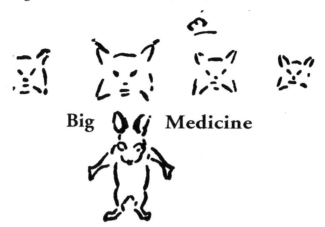

Big Medicine

XXXVI

Something Wrong at the Beaver Traps

ONCE a week they had run the trap lines, and their store of furs was increasing finely. They had taken twenty-five beavers and counted on getting two or three each time they went to the ponds. But they got an unpleasant surprise in December, on going to the beaver grounds, to find all the traps empty and unmistakable signs that some man had been there and had gone off with the catch. They followed the dim trail of his snowshoes, half hidden by a recent wind, but night came on with more snow, and all signs were lost.

The thief had not found the line yet, for the haul of marten and mink was good. But this was merely the beginning.

The trapper law of the wilderness is much like all primitive laws; first come has first right, provided he is able to hold it. If a strong rival comes in, the first must fight as best he can. The law justifies him in anything he may do, if he succeeds. The law justifies the second in anything he may do, except murder. That is, the defender may shoot to kill; the offender may not.

But the fact of Quonab's being an Indian and Rolf supposedly one would turn opinion against them in the Adirondacks, and it was quite likely that the rival considered them trespassers on his grounds, although the fact that he robbed their traps without removing them, and kept out of sight, rather showed the guilty conscience of a self-accused poacher.

He came in from the west, obviously; probably the Racquet River country; was a large man, judging by his foot and stride, and understood trapping; but lazy, for he set no traps. His principal object seemed to be to steal.

And it was not long before he found their line of marten traps, so his depredations increased. Primitive emotions are near the surface at all times, and under primitive conditions are very ready to appear. Rolf and Quonab felt that now it was war.

XXXVII

The Pekan or Fisher

THERE was one large track in the snow that they saw several times; it was like that of a marten, but much larger. "Pekan," said the Indian, "the big marten; the very strong one, that fights without fear.

"When my father was a papoose he shot an arrow at a pekan. He did not know what it was; it seemed only a big black marten. It was wounded, but sprang from the tree on my father's breast. It would have killed him, but for the dog; then it would have killed the dog, but my grandfather was near.

"He made my father eat the pekan's heart, so his heart might be like it. It sought no fight, but it turned, when struck, and fought without fear. That is the right way; seek peace, but fight without fear. That was my father's heart and mine." Then glancing toward the west he continued in a tone of menace: "That trap robber will find it so. We sought no fight, but some day I kill him."

The big track went in bounds, to be lost in a low, thick woods. But they met it again.

They were crossing a hemlock ridge a mile farther on, when they came to another track which was first a long, deep furrow, some fifteen inches wide, and in this were the wide-spread prints of feet as large as those of a fisher.

"Kahk," said Quonab, and Skookum said "Kahk," too, but he did it by growling and raising his back hair, and doubtless also by sadly remembering. His discretion seemed as yet embryonic, so Rolf slipped his sash through the dog's collar, and they followed the track, for the porcupine now stood in Rolf's mind as a sort of embroidery outfit.

They had not followed far before another track joined on — the track of the fisher-pekan; and soon after they heard in the woods ahead scratching sounds, as of something climbing, and once or twice a faint, far, fighting snarl.

Quickly tying the over-valiant Skookum to a tree, they crept forward, ready for anything, and arrived on the scene of a very peculiar action.

Action it was, though it was singularly devoid of action. First, there was a creature, like a huge black marten or a short-legged black fox, standing at a safe distance, while, partly hidden under a log, with hind quarters and tail only exposed, was a large porcupine. Both were very still, but soon the fisher snarled and made a forward lunge. The porcupine, hearing the sounds or feeling the snow dash up on that side, struck with its tail; but the fisher kept out of reach. Next a feint was made on the other side, with the same result; then many, as though the fisher were trying to tire out the tail or use up all its quills.

Sometimes the assailant leaped on the log and teased the quill-pig to strike upward, while many white daggers already sunk in the bark showed that these tactics had been going on for some time.

Now the two spectators saw by the trail that a similar battle had been fought at another log, and that the porcupine trail from that was spotted with blood. How the fisher had forced it out was not then clear, but soon became so.

After feinting till the Kahk would not strike, the pekan began a new manœuvre. Starting on the opposite side of the log that protected the spiny one's nose, he burrowed quickly through the snow and leaves. The log was about three inches from the ground, and before the porcupine could realize it, the fisher had a space cleared and seized the spiny one by its soft, unspiny nose. Grunting and squealing it pulled back and lashed its terrible tail. To what effect? Merely to fill the log around with quills. With all its strength the quill-pig pulled and writhed, but the fisher was stronger. His claws enlarged the hole and when the victim ceased from exhaustion, the fisher made a forward dash and changed his hold from the tender nose to the still more tender throat of the porcupine. His hold was not deep enough and square enough to seize the windpipe, but he held on. For a minute or two the struggles of Kahk were of desperate energy and its lashing tail began to be short of spines, but a red stream trickling from the wound was sapping its strength. Protected by the log, the fisher had but to hold on and play a waiting game.

The Pekan or Fisher

The heaving and backward pulling of Kahk were very feeble at length; the fisher had nearly finished the fight. But he was impatient of further delay and backing out of the hole he mounted the log, displaying a much scratched nose; then reaching down with deft paw, near the quill-pig's shoulder, he gave a sudden jerk that threw the former over on its back, and before it could recover, the fisher's jaws closed on its ribs, and crushed and tore. The nerveless, almost quilless tail could not harm him there. The red blood flowed and the porcupine lay still. Again and again as he uttered chesty growls the pekan ground his teeth into the warm flesh and shook and worried the unconquerable one he had conquered. He was licking his bloody chops for the twentieth time, gloating in gore, when *crack* went Quonab's gun, and the pekan had an opportunity of resuming the combat with Kahk far away in the Happy Hunting.

"Yap, yap, yap!" and in rushed Skookum, dragging the end of Rolf's sash which he had gnawed through in his determination to be in the fight, no matter what it cost; and it was entirely due to the fact that the porcupine was belly up, that Skookum did not have another hospital experience.

This was Rolf's first sight of a fisher, and he examined it as one does any animal — or man — that one has so long heard described in superlative terms that it has become idealized into a semi-myth. This was the desperado of the woods; the weird black cat that feared no living thing. This was the only one that could fight and win against Kahk.

They made a fire at once, and while Rolf got the mid-day meal of tea and venison, Quonab skinned the fisher. Then he cut out its heart and liver. When these were cooked he gave the first to Rolf and the second to Skookum, saying to the one, "I give you a pekan heart," and to the dog, "That will force all of the quills out of you if you play the fool again, as I think you will."

In the skin of the fisher's neck and tail they found several quills, some of them new, some of them dating evidently from another fight of the same kind, but none of them had done any damage. There was no inflammation or sign of poisoning. "It is ever so," said Quonab, "the quills cannot hurt him." Then, turning to the porcupine, he remarked, as he prepared to skin it:

"Ho, Kahk! You see now it was a big mistake you did not let Nana Bojou sit on the dry end of that log."

XXXVIII

The Silver Fox

THEY were returning to the cabin, one day, when Quonab stopped and pointed. Away off on the snow of the far shore was a moving shape to be seen.

"Fox, and I think silver fox; he so black. I think he lives there."

"Why?"

"I have seen many times a very big fox track, and they do not go where they do not live. Even in winter they keep their own range."

"He's worth ten martens, they say?" queried Rolf.

"Ugh! fifty."

"Can't we get him?"

"Can try. But the water set will not work in winter; we must try different."

This was the plan, the best that Quonab could devise for the snow: Saving the ashes from the fire (dry sand would have answered), he selected six open places in the woods on the south of the lake, and in each made an ash bed on which he scattered three or four drops of the smell-charm. Then, twenty-five yards from each, on the north or west side (the side of the prevailing wind) he hung from some sapling a few feathers, a partridge wing or tail with some red yarns to it. He left the places unvisited for two weeks, then returned to learn the progress of act one.

Judging from past experience of fox nature and from the few signs that were offered by the snow, this is what had happened: A fox came along soon after the trappers left, followed the track a little way, came to the first opening, smelled the seductive danger-lure, swung around it, saw the dangling feathers, took alarm, and went off. Another of the places had been visited by a marten. He had actually scratched in the ashes. A wolf had gone around another at a safe distance.

Another had been shunned several times by a fox or by foxes, but they had come again and again and at last yielded to the temptation to investigate the danger-smell; finally had rolled in it, evidently wallowing in an abandon of delight. So far, the plan was working there.

The next move was to set the six strong fox traps, each thoroughly smoked, and chained to a fifteen-pound block of wood.

Approaching the place carefully and using his blood-rubbed glove, Quonab set in each ash pile a trap. Under its face he put a wad of white rabbit fur. Next he buried all in the ashes, scattered a few bits of rabbit and a few drops of smell-charm, then dashed snow over the place, renewed the dangling feathers to lure the eye; and finally left the rest to the weather.

Rolf was keen to go the next day, but the old man said: "Wah! no good! No trap go first night; man smell too strong." The second day there was a snowfall, and the third morning Quonab said, "Now seem like good time."

The first trap was untouched, but there was clearly the track of a large fox within ten yards of it.

The second was gone. Quonab said, with surprise in his voice, "Deer!" Yes, truly, there was the record. A deer — a big one — had come wandering past; his keen nose soon apprised him of a strong, queer appeal near by. He had gone unsuspiciously toward it, sniffed and pawed the unaccountable and exciting nose medicine; then *snap!* and he had sprung a dozen feet, with that diabolic smell-thing hanging to his foot. Hop, hop, hop, the terrified deer had gone into a slashing windfall. Then the drag had caught on the logs, and, thanks to the hard and taper hoofs, the trap had slipped off and been left behind, while the deer had sought safer regions.

In the next trap they found a beautiful marten dead, killed at once by the clutch of steel. The last trap was gone, but the tracks and the marks told a tale that any one could read; a fox had been beguiled and had gone off, dragging the trap and log. Not far did they need to go; held in a thicket they found him, and Rolf prepared the mid-day meal while Quonab gathered the pelt. After removing the skin the Indian cut

deep and carefully into the body of the fox and removed the bladder. Its contents sprinkled near each of the traps was good medicine, he said; a view that was evidently shared by Skookum.

More than once they saw the track of the big fox of the region, but never very near the snare. He was too dever to be fooled by smell-spells or kidney products, no matter how temptingly arrayed. The trappers did, indeed, capture three red foxes; but it was at cost of great labour. It was a venture that did not pay. The silver fox was there, but he took too good care of his precious hide. The slightest hint of a man being near was enough to treble his already double wariness. They would never have seen him near at hand, but for a stirring episode that told a tale of winter hardship.

XXXIX

The Humiliation of Skookum

I F SKOOKUM could have been interviewed by a newspaper man, he would doubtless have said: "I am a very remarkable dog. I can tree partridges. I'm death on porcupines. I am pretty good in a dog fight; never was licked in fact: but my really marvellous gift is my speed; I'm a terror to run."

Yes, he was very proud of his legs, and the foxes that came about in the winter nights gave him many opportunities of showing what he could do. Many times over *he very nearly caught a fox*. Skookum did not know that these wily ones were playing with him; but they were, and enjoyed it immensely.

The self-sufficient cur never found this out, and never lost a chance of *nearly* catching a fox. The men did not see those autumn chases because they were by night; but foxes hunt much by day in winter, perforce, and are often seen; and more than once they witnessed one of these farcical races.

And now the shining white furnished background for a much more important affair.

It was near sundown one day when a faint fox bark was heard out on the snow-covered ice of the lake.

"That's for me," Skookum seemed to think, and jumping up, with a very fierce growl, he trotted forth; the men looked first from the window. Out on the snow, sitting on his haunches, was their friend, the big, black silver fox.

Quonab reached for his gun and Rolf tried to call Skookum, but it was too late. *He* was out to catch that fox; *their* business was to look on and applaud. The fox sat on his haunches, grinning apparently, until Skookum dashed through the snow within twenty yards. Then, that shining, black fox loped gently away, his huge tail level out behind him, and Skookum, sure of success, raced up, within six or seven yards. A few more leaps now, and the victory would be won. But somehow he could not close that six- or seven-yard gap. No matter how he strained and leaped, the great black brush was just so far ahead. At first they had headed for the shore, but the fox wheeled back to the ice and up and down. Skookum felt it was because escape was hopeless, and he redoubled his effort. But all in vain. He was only wearing himself out, panting noisily now. The snow was deep enough to be a great disadvantage, more to dog than to fox, since weight counted as such a handicap. Unconsciously Skookum slowed up. The fox increased his headway; then audaciously turned around and sat down in the snow.

This was too much for the dog. He wasted about a lungful of air in an angry bark, and again went after the enemy. Again the chase was round and round, but very soon the dog was so wearied that he sat down, and now the black fox actually came back and barked at him.

It was maddening. Skookum's pride was touched. He was in to win or break. His supreme effort brought him within five feet of that white-tipped brush. Then, strange to tell, the big black fox put forth his large reserve of speed, and making for the woods, left Skookum far behind. Why? The cause was clear. Quonab, after vainly watching for a chance to shoot, that would not endanger the dog, had, under cover, crept around the lake and now was awaiting in a thicket. But the fox's keen nose had warned him. He knew that the funny part was over, so ran for the woods and disappeared as a ball tossed up the snow behind him.

Poor Skookum's tongue was nearly a foot long as he walked meekly ashore. He looked depressed; his tail was depressed; so were his ears; but there was nothing to show whether he would have told that reporter that he "wasn't feeling up to his usual, to-day," or "Didn't you see me get the best of him?"

XL

The Rarest of Pelts

THEY saw that silver fox three or four times during the winter, and once found that he had had the audacity to jump from a high snowdrift onto the storehouse and thence to the cabin roof, where he had feasted on some white rabbits kept there for deadfall baits. But all attempts to trap or shoot him were vain, and their acquaintance might have ended as it began, but for an accident.

It proved a winter of much snow. Heavy snow is the worst misfortune that can befall the wood folk in fur. It hides their food beyond reach, and it checks their movements so they can neither travel far in search of provender nor run fast to escape their enemies. Deep snow then means fetters, starvation, and death. There are two ways of meeting the problem: stilts and snowshoes. The second is far the better. The caribou, and the moose have stilts; the rabbit, the panther, and the lynx wear snowshoes. When there are three or four feet of soft snow, the lynx is king of all small beasts, and little in fear of the large ones. Man on his snowshoes has most wild four-foots at his mercy.

Skookum, without either means of meeting the trouble was left much alone in the shanty. Apparently, it was on one of these occasions that the silver fox had driven him nearly frantic by eating rabbits on the roof above him.

The exasperating robbery of their trap line had gone on irregularly all winter, but the thief was clever enough or lucky enough to elude them.

They were returning to the cabin after a three days' round, when they saw, far out on the white expanse of the lake, two animals, alternately running and fighting. "Skookum and the fox," was the first thought that came, but on entering the cabin Skookum greeted them in person.

Rolf in the Woods

Quonab gazed intently at the two running specks and said: "One has no tail. I think it is a peeshoo (lynx) and a fox."

Rolf was making dinner. From time to time he glanced over the lake and saw the two specks, usually running. After dinner was over, he said, "Let's sneak 'round and see if we can get a shot."

So, putting on their snowshoes and keeping out of sight, they skimmed over the deer crossing and through the woods, till at a point near the fighters, and there they saw something that recalled at once the day of Skookum's humiliation.

A hundred yards away on the open snow was a huge lynx and their old friend, the black and shining silver fox, face to face; the fox desperate, showing his rows of beautiful teeth, but sinking belly deep in the snow as he strove to escape. Already he was badly wounded. In any case he was at the mercy of the lynx who, in spite of his greater weight, had such broad and perfect snowshoes that he skimmed on the surface, while the fox's small feet sank deep. The lynx was far from fresh, and still stood in some awe of those rows of teeth that snapped like traps when he came too near. He was minded, of course, to kill his black rival, but not to be hurt in doing so. Again and again there was in some sort a closing fight, the wearied fox plunging breathlessly through the treacherous, relent-less snow. If he could only get back to cover, he might find a corner to protect his rear and have some fighting chance for life. But wherever he turned that huge cat faced him, doubly armed, and equipped as a fox can never be for the snow.

No one could watch that plucky fight without feeling his sympathies go out to the beautiful silver fox. Rolf, at least, was for helping him to escape, when the final onset came. In another dash for the woods the fox plunged out of sight in a drift made soft by sedge sticking through, and before he could recover, the lynx's jaws closed on the back of his neck and the relentless claws had pierced his vitals.

The justification of killing is self-preservation, and in this case the proof would have been the lynx making a meal of the fox. Did he do so? Not at all. He shook his fur, licked his chest and paws in a self-congratulatory way, then giving a final tug at the body, walked calmly over the snow along the shore.

Quonab put the back of his hand to his mouth and made a loud squeaking, much like a rabbit caught in a snare. The lynx stopped,

The fox, sinking deep, was hopelessly overmatched

wheeled, and came trotting straight toward the promising music. Unsuspectingly he came within twenty yards of the trappers. The flintlock banged and the lynx was kicking in the snow.

The beautiful silver fox skin was very little injured and proved of value almost to double their catch so far; while the lynx skin was as good as another marten.

They now had opportunity of studying the tracks and learned that the fox had been hunting rabbits in a thicket when he was set on by the lynx. At first he had run around in the bushes and saved himself from serious injury, for the snow was partly packed by the rabbits. After perhaps an hour of this, he had wearied and sought to save himself by abandoning the lynx's territory, so had struck across the open lake. But here the snow was too soft to bear him at all, and the lynx could still skim over. So it proved a fatal error. He was strong and brave. He fought at least another hour here before the much stronger, heavier lynx had done him to death. There was no justification. It was a clear case of tyrannical murder, but in this case vengeance was swift and justice came sooner than its wont.

Moose
Maple

XLI

The Enemy's Fort

"It pays 'boat once in a hundred times to git mad, but there ain't any way of tellin' beforehand which is the time."

— *The Sayings of Si Sylvanne*

IT GENERALLY took two days to run the west line of traps. At a convenient point they had built a rough shack for a half-way house. On entering this one day, they learned that since their last visit it had been occupied by some one who chewed tobacco. Neither of them had this habit. Quonab's face grew darker each time fresh evidence of the enemy was discovered, and the final wrong was added soon.

Some trappers mark their traps; some do not bother. Rolf had marked all of theirs with a file, cutting notches on the iron. Two, one, three, was their mark, and it was a wise plan, as it turned out.

On going around the west beaver pond they found that all six traps had disappeared. In some, there was no evidence of the thief; in some, the tracks showed clearly that they were taken by the same interloper that had bothered them all along, and on a jagged branch was a short blue yarn.

"Now will I take up his trail and kill him," said the Indian.

Rolf had opposed extreme measures, and again he remonstrated. To his surprise, the Indian turned fiercely and said: "You know it is white man. If he was Indian would you be patient? No!"

"There is plenty of country south of the lake; maybe he *was* here first."

"*You know he was not.* You should eat many pekan hearts. I have sought peace, now I fight."

He shouldered his pack, grasped his gun, and his snow-shoes went *tssape, tssape, tssape,* over the snow.

Skookum was sitting by Rolf. He rose to resume the march, and trotted a few steps on Quonab's trail. Rolf did not move; he was dazed by the sudden and painful situation. Mutiny is always worse than war. Skookum looked back, trotted on, still Rolf sat staring. Quonab's figure was lost in the distance; the dog's was nearly so. Rolf moved not. All the events of the last year were rushing through his mind; the refuge he had found with the Indian; the incident of the buck fight and the tender nurse the red man proved. He wavered. Then he saw Skookum coming back on the trail. The dog trotted up to the boy and dropped a glove, one of Quonab's. Undoubtedly the Indian had lost it; Skookum had found it on the trail and mechanically brought it to the nearest of his masters. Without that glove Quonab's hand would freeze. Rolf rose and sped along the other's trail. Having taken the step, he found it easy to send a long halloo, then another and another, till an answer came. In a few minutes Rolf came up. The Indian was sitting on a log, waiting. The glove was handed over in silence, and received with a grunt.

After a minute or two, Rolf said, "Let's get on," and started on the dim trail of the robber.

For an hour or two they strode in silence. Then their course rose as they reached a rocky range. Among its bare, wind-swept ridges all sign was lost, but the Indian kept on till they were over and on the other side. A far cast in the thick, windless woods revealed the trail again, surely the same, for the snowshoe was two fingers wider on every side, and a hand-breadth longer than Quonab's; besides the right frame had been

broken and the binding of rawhide was faintly seen in the snow mark. It was a mark they had seen all winter, and now it was headed as before for the west.

When night came down, they camped in a hollow. They were used to snow camps. In the morning they went on, but wind and snow had hidden their tell-tale guide.

What was the next move? Rolf did not ask, but wondered.

Quonab evidently was puzzled.

At length Rolf ventured: "He surely lives by some river — that way — and within a day's journey. This track is gone, but we may strike a fresh one. We'll know it when we see it."

The friendly look came back to the Indian's face. "You are Nibowaka."

They had not gone half a mile before they found a fresh track — their old acquaintance. Even Skookum showed his hostile recognition. And in a few minutes it led them to a shanty. They slipped off their snowshoes, and hung them in a tree. Quonab opened the door without knocking. They entered, and in a moment were face to face with a lanky, ill-favoured white man that all three, including Skookum, recognized as Hoag, the man they had met at the trader's.

That worthy made a quick reach for his rifle, but Quonab covered him and said in tones that brooked no discussion, "Sit down!"

Hoag did so, sullenly, then growled: "All right; my partners will be here in ten minutes."

Rolf was startled. Quonab and Skookum were not.

"We settled your partners up in the hills," said the former, knowing that one bluff was as good as another. Skookum growled and sniffed at the enemy's legs. The prisoner made a quick move with his foot.

"You kick that dog *again* and it's your last kick," said the Indian.

"Who's kicked yer dog, and what do you mean coming here with yer cutthroat ways? You'll find there's law in this country before yer through," was the answer.

"That's what we're looking for, you trap robber, you thief. We're here first to find our traps; second to tell you this: the next time you come on our line there'll be meat for the ravens. Do you suppose I don't know them?" and the Indian pointed to a large pair of snowshoes with long heels and a repair lashing on the right frame. "See that blue yarn," and the Indian matched it with a blue sash hanging to a peg.

"Yes, them belongs to Bill Hawkins; he'll be 'round in five minutes now."

The Indian made a gesture of scorn; then taming to Rolf said: "Look 'round for our traps." Rolf made a thorough search in and about the shanty and the adjoining shed. He found some traps but none with his mark; none of a familiar make even.

"Better hunt for a squaw and papoose," sneered Hoag, who was utterly puzzled by the fact that now Rolf was obviously a white lad.

But all the search was vain. Either Hoag had not stolen the traps or had hidden them elsewhere. The only large traps they found were two of the largest size for taking bear.

Hoag's torrent of bad language had been quickly checked by the threat of turning Skookum loose on his legs, and he looked such a grovelling beast that presently the visitors decided to leave him with a warning.

The Indian took the trapper's gun, fired it off out of doors, not in the least perturbed by the possibility of its being heard by Hoag's partners. He knew they were imaginary. Then changing his plan, he said "Ugh! You find your gun in half a mile on our trail. But don't come farther and don't let me see the snowshoe trail on the divide again. Them ravens is awful hungry."

Skookum, to his disappointment, was called off and, taking the trapper's gun for a time, they left it in a bush and made for their own country.

XLII

Skookum's Panther

"WHY are there so few deer tracks now?"

"Deer yarded for winter," replied the Indian; "no travel in deep snow."

"We'll soon need another," said Rolf, which unfortunately was true. They could have killed many deer in early winter, when the venison was in fine condition, but they had no place to store it. Now they must get it as they could, and of course it was thinner and poorer every week.

They were on a high hill some days later. There was a clear view and they noticed several ravens circling and swooping.

"Maybe dead deer; maybe deer yard," said the Indian.

It was over a thick, sheltered, and extensive cedar swamp near the woods where last year they had seen so many deer, and they were not surprised to find deer tracks in numbers, as soon as they got into its dense thicket.

A deer yard is commonly supposed to be a place in which the deer have a daily "bee" at road work all winter long and deliberately keep the snow hammered down so they can run on a hard surface everywhere within its limits. The fact is, the deer gather in a place where there is plenty of food and good shelter. The snow does not drift here, so the deer, by continually moving about, soon make a network of tracks in all directions, extending them as they must to seek more food. They may, of course, leave the yard at any time, but at once they encounter the dreaded obstacle of deep, soft snow in which they are helpless.

Once they reached the well-worn trails, the hunters took off their snowshoes and went gently on these deer paths. They saw one or two disappearing forms, which taught them the thick cover was hiding many more. They made for the sound of the ravens, and found that the feast of the sable birds was not a deer but the bodies of three, quite recently killed.

Rolf in the Woods

Quonab made a hasty study of the signs and said, "Panther."

Yes, a panther, cougar, or mountain lion also had found the deer yard; and here he was living, like a rat in a grocer shop with nothing to do but help himself whenever he felt like feasting.

Pleasant for the panther, but hard on the deer; for the killer is wasteful and will often kill for the joy of murder.

Not a quarter of the carcasses lying here did he eat; he was feeding at least a score of ravens, and maybe foxes, martens, and lynxes as well.

Before killing a deer, Quonab thought it well to take a quiet prowl around in hopes of seeing the panther. Skookum was turned loose and encouraged to display his talents.

Proud as a general with an ample and obedient following, he dashed ahead, carrying fresh dismay among the deer, if one might judge from the noise. Then he found some new smell of excitement, and voiced the new thrill in a new sound, one not unmixed with fear. At length his barking was far away to the west in a rocky part of the woods. Whatever the prey, it was treed, for the voice kept one place.

The hunters followed quickly and found the dog yapping furiously under a thick cedar. The first thought was of porcupine; but a nearer view showed the game to be a huge panther on the ground, not greatly excited, disdaining to climb, and taking little notice of the dog, except to curl his nose and utter a hissing kind of snarl when the latter came too near.

But the arrival of the hunters gave a new colour to the picture. The panther raised his head, then sprang up a large tree and ensconced himself on a fork, while the valorous Skookum reared against the trunk, threatening loudly to come up and tear him to pieces.

This was a rare find and a noble chance to conserve their stock of deer, so the hunters went around the tree seeking for a fair shot. But every point of view had some serious obstacle. It seemed as though the

branches had been told off to guard the panther's vitals, for a big one always stood in the bullet's way.

After vainly going around, Quonab said to Rolf: "Hit him with something, so he'll move."

Rolf always was a good shot with stones, but he found none to throw. Near where they stood, however, was an unfreezing spring, and the soggy snow on it was easily packed into a hard, heavy snowball. Rolf threw it straight, swift, and by good luck it hit the panther square on the nose and startled him so that he sprang right out of the tree and flopped into the snow.

Skookum was on him at once, but got a slap on the ear that changed his music, and the panther bounded away out of sight with the valiant Skookum ten feet behind, whooping and yelling like mad.

It was annoyance rather than fear that made that panther take to a low tree while Skookum boxed the compass, and made a beaten dog path all around him. The hunters approached very carefully now, making little sound and keeping out of sight. The panther was wholly engrossed with observing the astonishing impudence of that dog, when Quonab came quietly up, leaned his rifle against a tree and fired. The smoke cleared to show the panther on his back, his legs convulsively waving in the air, and Skookum tugging valiantly at his tail.

"My panther," he seemed to say; "whatever would you do without me?"

A panther in a deer yard is much like a wolf shut up in a sheepfold. He would probably have killed all the deer that winter, though there were ten times as many as he needed for food; and getting rid of him was a piece of good luck for hunters and deer, while his superb hide made a noble trophy that in years to come had unexpected places of honour.

XLIII

Sunday in the Woods

ROLF still kept to the tradition of Sunday, and Quonab had in a manner accepted it. It was a curious fact that the red man had far more toleration for the white man's religious ideas than the white man had for the red's.

Quonab's songs to the sun and the spirit, or his burning of a tobacco pinch, or an animal's whiskers were to Rolf but harmless nonsense. Had he given them other names, calling them hymns and incense, he would have been much nearer respecting them. He had forgotten his mother's teaching: "If any man do anything sincerely, believing that thereby he is worshipping God, he is worshipping God." He disliked seeing Quonab use an axe or a gun on Sunday, and the Indian, realizing that such action made "evil medicine" for Rolf, practically abstained. But Rolf had not yet learned to respect the red yarns the Indian hung from a deer's skull, though he did come to understand that he must let them alone or produce bad feeling in camp.

Sunday had become a day of rest and Quonab made it also a day of song and remembrance.

They were sitting one Sunday night by the fire in the cabin, enjoying the blaze, while a storm rattled on the window and door. A white-footed mouse, one of a family that lived in the shanty, was trying how close he could come to Skookum's nose without being caught, while Rolf looked on. Quonab was lying back on a pile of deer skins, with his pipe in his mouth, his head on the bunk, and his hands clasped back of his neck.

There was an atmosphere of content and brotherly feeling; the evening was young, when Rolf broke silence:

"Were you ever married, Quonab?"

"Ugh," was the Indian's affirmative.

"Where?"

"Myanos."

Rolf in the Woods

Rolf did not venture more questions, but left the influence of the hour to work. It was a moment of delicate poise, and Rolf knew a touch would open the door or double bar it. He wondered how he might give that touch as he wished it. Skookum still slept. Both men watched the mouse, as, with quick movements it crept about. Presently it approached a long birch stick that stood up against the wall. High hanging was the song-drum. Rolf wished Quonab would take it and let it open his heart, but he dared not offer it; that might have the exact wrong effect. Now the mouse was behind the birch stick. Then Rolf noticed that the stick if it were to fall would strike a drying line, one end of which was on the song-drum peg. So he made a dash at the mouse and displaced the stick; the jerk it gave the line sent the song-drum with hollow bumping to the ground. The boy stooped to replace it; as he did, Quonab grunted and Rolf turned to see his hand stretched for the drum. Had Rolf officiously offered it, it would have been refused; now the Indian took it, tapped and warmed it at the fire, and sang a song of the Wabanaki. It was softly done, and very low, but Rolf was close, for almost the first time in any long rendition, and he got an entirely new notion of the red music. The singer's face brightened as he tummed and sang with peculiar grace notes and throat warbles of "Kaluscap's war with the magi," and the spirit of his people, rising to the sweet magic of melody, came shining in his eyes. He sang the lovers' song, "The Bark Canoe."*

> "While the stars shine and falls the dew,
> I seek my love in bark canoe."

And then the cradle song, "The Naked Bear Shall Never Catch Thee."

When he stopped, he stared at the fire; and after a long pause Rolf ventured, "My mother would have loved your songs."

Whether he heard or not, the warm emanation surely reached the Indian, and he began to answer the question of an hour before:

"Her name was Gamowini, for she sang like the sweet night bird at Asamuk. I brought her from her father's house at Saugatuck. We lived at Myanos. She made beautiful baskets and moccasins. I fished and trapped; we had enough. Then the baby came. He had big round eyes, so we called him Wee-wees, 'our little owl,' and we were very happy. When Gamowini sang to her baby, the world seemed full of sun. One

---

* See F. R. Burton's "American Primitive Music."

day when Wee-wees could walk she left him with me and she went to Stamford with some baskets to sell. A big ship was in the harbour. A man from the ship told her that his sailors would buy all her baskets. She had no fear. On the ship they seized her for a runaway slave, and hid her till they sailed away.

"When she did not come back I took Wee-wees on my shoulder and went quickly to Stamford. I soon found out a little, but the people did not know the ship, or whence she came, or where she went, they said. They did not seem to care. My heart grew hotter and wilder. I wanted to fight. I would have killed the men on the dock, but they were many. They bound me and put me in jail for three months. When I came out Wee-wees was dead. They did not care. I have heard nothing since. Then I went to live under the rock, so I should not see our first home. I do not know; she may be alive. But I think it killed her to lose her baby."

The Indian stopped; then rose quickly. His face was hard set. He stepped out into the snowstorm and the night. Rolf was left alone with Skookum.

Sad, sad, everything seemed sad in his friend's life, and Rolf, brooding over it with wisdom beyond his years, could not help asking: "Had Quonab and Gamowini been white folk, would it have happened so? Would his agony have been received with scornful indifference?" Alas! he knew it would not. He realized it would have been a very different tale, and the sequent questions that would not down, were, "Will this bread cast on the waters return after many days?" "Is there a God of justice and retribution?" "On whom will the flail of vengeance fall for all these abominations?"

Two hours later the Indian returned. No word was spoken as he entered. He was not cold. He must have walked far. Rolf prepared for bed. The Indian stooped, picked up a needle from the dusty ground, one that had been lost the day before, silently handed it to his companion, who gave only a recognizant "Hm," and dropped it into the birch-bark box.

XLIV

The Lost Bundle of Furs

THREE had been a significant cessation of robbery on their trap line after the inconclusive visit to the enemy's camp. But a new and extreme exasperation arose in the month of March, when the alternation of thaw and frost had covered the snow with a hard crust that rendered snowshoes unnecessary and made it easy to run anywhere and leave no track.

They had gathered up a fisher and some martens before they reached the beaver pond. They had no beaver traps now, but it was interesting to call and see how many of the beavers were left, and what they were doing.

Bubbling springs on the bank of the pond had made open water at several places, now that the winter frost was weakening. Out of these the beavers often came, as was plainly seen in the tracks, so the trappers approached them carefully.

They were scrutinizing one of them from behind a log, Quonab with ready gun, Rolf holding the unwilling Skookum, when the familiar broad, flat head appeared. A large beaver swam around the hole, sniffed and looked, then silently climbed the bank, evidently making for a certain aspen tree that he had already been cutting. He was in easy range, and the gunner was about to fire when Rolf pressed his arm and pointed. Here, wandering through the wood, came a large lynx. It had not seen or smelt any of the living creatures ahead, as yet, but speedily sighted the beaver now working away to cut down his tree.

As a pelt, the beaver was worth more than the lynx, but the naturalist is strong in most hunters, and they watched to see what would happen.

The lynx seemed to sink into the ground, and was lost to sight as soon as he knew of a possible prey ahead. And now he began his stalk. The hunters sighted him once as he crossed a level opening in the snow.

Rolf in the Woods

He seemed less than four inches high as he crawled. Logs, ridges, trees, or twigs, afforded ample concealment, till his whiskers appeared in a thicket within fifteen feet of the beaver.

All this was painfully exciting to Skookum, who, though he could not see, could get some thrilling whiffs, and he strained forward to improve his opportunities. The sound of this slight struggle caught the beaver's ear. It stopped work, wheeled, and made for the water hole. The lynx sprang from his ambush, seized the beaver by the back, and held on; but the beaver was double the lynx's weight, the bank was steep and slippery, the struggling animals kept rolling down hill, nearer and nearer the hole. Then, on the very edge, the beaver gave a great plunge, and splashed into the water with the lynx clinging to its back. At once they disappeared, and the hunters rushed to the place, expecting them to float up and be an easy prey; but they did not float. At length it was clear that the pair had gone under the ice, for in water the beaver was master.

After five minutes it was certain that the lynx must be dead. Quonab cut a sapling and made a grappler. He poked this way and that way under the ice, until at length he felt something soft. With the hatchet they cut a hole over the place and then dragged out the body of the lynx. The beaver, of course, escaped and was probably little the worse.

While Quonab skinned the catch, Rolf prowled around the pond and soon came running back to tell of a remarkable happening.

At another open hole a beaver had come out, wandered twenty yards to a mound which he had castorized, then passed several hard wood trees to find a large poplar or aspen, the favourite food tree. This he had begun to fell with considerable skill, but for some strange reason, perhaps because alone, he had made a miscalculation, and when the tree came crashing down, it had fallen across his back, killed him, and pinned him to the ground.

It was an easy matter for the hunters to remove the log and secure his pelt, so they left the beaver pond, richer than they had expected.

Next night, when they reached their half-way shanty, they had the best haul they had taken on this line since the memorable day when they got six beavers.

The morning dawned clear and bright. As they breakfasted, they noticed an extraordinary gathering of ravens far away to the north, beyond any country they had visited. At least twenty or thirty of the birds were sailing in great circles high above a certain place, uttering a deep, sonorous croak, from time to time. Occasionally one of the ravens would dive down out of sight.

"Why do they fly above that way?"

"That is to let other ravens know there is food here. Their eyes are very good. They can see the signal ten miles away, so all come to the place. My father told me that you can gather all the ravens for twenty miles by leaving a carcass so they can see it and signal each other."

"Seems as if we should look into that. Maybe another panther," was Rolf's remark.

The Indian nodded; so leaving the bundle of furs in a safe place with the snowshoes, that they carried on a chance, they set out over the hard crust. It was two or three miles to the ravens' gathering, and, as before, it proved to be over a cedar brake where was a deer yard.

Skookum knew all about it. He rushed into the woods, filled with the joy of martial glory. But speedily came running out again as hard as he could, yelling "yow, yow, yow!" for help, while swiftly following behind him were a couple of gray wolves. Quonab waited till they were within forty yards; then, seeing the men, the wolves slowed up and veered; Quonab fired; one of the wolves gave a little, dog-like yelp. Then they leaped into the bushes and were lost to view.

A careful study of the snow showed one or two trifling traces of blood. In the deer yard they found at least a dozen carcasses of deer killed by the wolves, but none very recent. They saw but few deer and nothing more of the wolves, for the crust had made all the country easy, and both kinds fled before the hunters.

Exploring a lower level of willow country in hopes of finding beaver delayed them, and it was afternoon when they returned to the half-way shanty, to find everything as they left it, *except that their pack of furs had totally disappeared.*

Of course, the hard crust gave no sign of track. Their first thought was of the old enemy, but, seeking far and near for evidence, they found pieces of an ermine skin, and a quarter mile farther, the rest of it, then, at another place, fragments of a muskrat's skin. Those made it look like

the work of the trapper's enemy, the wolverine, which, though rare, was surely found in these hills. Yes! There was a wolverine scratch mark, and here another piece of the rat skin. It was very clear who was the thief.

"He tore up the cheapest ones of the lot anyway," said Rolf.

Then the trappers stared at each other significantly — *only the cheap ones destroyed*; why should a wolverine show such discrimination? There was no positive sign of wolverine; in fact, the icy snow gave no sign of anything. There was little doubt that the torn furs and the scratch marks were there to mislead; that this was the work of a human robber, almost certainly Hoag.

He had doubtless seen them leave in the morning, and it was equally sure, since he had had hours of start, he would now be far away.

"Ugh! Give him few days to think he safe, then I follow and settle all," and this time the Indian clearly meant to end the matter.

XLV

The Subjugation of Hoag

"A feller as weeps for pity and never does a finger-tap to help it 'bout as much use as an overcoat on a drowning man."

— *The Sayings of Si Sylvann*e

SOME remarkable changes of weather made some remarkable changes in their plan and saved their enemy from immediate molestation. For two weeks it was a succession of thaws and there was much rain. The lake was covered with six inches of water; the river had a current above the ice, that was rapidly eating the latter away. Everywhere there were slush and wet snow that put an end to travel and brought on the spring with a rush.

Each night there was, indeed, a trifling frost, but each day's sun seemed stronger, and broad, bare patches of ground appeared on all sunny slopes.

On the first crisp day the trappers set out to go the rounds, knowing full well that this was the end of the season. Henceforth for six months deadfall and snare would lie idle and unset.

They went their accustomed line, carrying their snow-shoes, but rarely needing them. Then they crossed a large track to which Quonab pointed, and grunted affirmatively as Rolf said "Bear?" Yes! the bears were about once more; their winter sleep was over. Now they were fat and the fur was yet prime; in a month they would be thin and shedding. Now is the time for bear hunting with either trap or dog.

Doubtless Skookum thought the party most fortunately equipped in the latter respect, but no single dog is enough to bay a bear. There must be three or four to bother him behind, to make him face about and fight; one dog merely makes him run faster.

They had no traps, and knowing that a spring bear is a far traveller, they made no attempt to follow.

Rolf in the Woods

The deadfalls yielded two martens, but one of them was spoiled by the warm weather. They learned at last that the enemy had a trap-line, for part of which he used their deadfalls. He had been the rounds lately and had profited at least a little by their labours.

The track, though two days old, was not hard to follow, either on snow or ground. Quonab looked to the lock of his gun; his lower lip tightened and he strode along.

"What are you going to do, Quonab? Not shoot?"

"When I get near enough," and the dangerous look in the red man's eye told Rolf to be quiet and follow.

In three miles they passed but three of his marten traps — very lazy trapping — and then found a great triangle of logs by a tree with a bait and signs enough to tell the experienced eye that, in that corner, was hidden a huge steel trap for bear.

They were almost too late in restraining the knowledge-hunger of Skookum. They went on a mile or two and realized in so doing that, however poor a trapper the enemy might be, he was a good tramper and knew the country.

At sundown they came to their half-way shelter and put up there for the night. Once when Rolf went out to glimpse the skies before turning in, he heard a far tree creaking and wondered, for it was dead calm. Even Skookum noticed it. But it was not repeated. Next morning they went on.

There are many quaint sounds in the woods at all times, the rasping of trees, at least a dozen different calls by jays, twice as many by ravens, and occasional notes from chicadees, grouse, and owls. The quadrupeds in general are more silent, but the red squirrel is ever about and noisy, as well as busy.

Far-reaching sounds are these echoes of the woods — some of them very far. Probably there were not five minutes of the day or night when some weird, woodland chatter, scrape, crack, screech, or whistle did not reach the keen ears of that ever-alert dog. That is, three hundred times a day his outer ear submitted to his inner ear some report of things a-doing, which same report was as often for many days disregarded as of no interest or value. But this did not mean that he missed anything; the steady tramp, tramp of their feet, while it dulled all sounds for the hunter, seemed to have no effect on Skookum. Again the raspy squeal of some far tree reached his inmost brain, and his hair rose as he stopped and gave a low "woof."

The hunters held still; the wise ones always do, when a dog says "Stop!" They waited. After a few minutes it came again — merely the long-drawn creak of a tree bough, wind-rubbed on its neighbour.

And yet, "Woof, woof, woof," said Skookum, and ran ahead.

"Come back, you little fool!" cried Rolf.

But Skookum had a mind of his own. He trotted ahead, then stopped, paused, and sniffed at something in the snow. The Indian picked it up. It was the pocket jackscrew that every bear trapper carries to set the powerful trap, and without which, indeed, one man cannot manage the springs.

He held it up with "Ugh! Hoag in trouble now." Clearly the rival trapper had lost this necessary tool.

But the finding was an accident. Skookum pushed on. They came along a draw to a little hollow. The dog, far forward, began barking and angrily baying at something. The men hurried to the scene to find on the snow, fast held in one of those devilish engines called a bear trap — the body of their enemy — Hoag, the trapper, held by a leg, and a hand in the gin he himself had been setting.

A fierce light played on the Indian's face. Rolf was stricken with horror. But even while they contemplated the body, the faint cry was heard again coming from it.

"He's alive; hurry!" cried Rolf. The Indian did not hurry, but he came. He had vowed vengeance at sight; why should he haste to help?

The implacable iron jaws had clutched the trapper by one knee and the right hand. The first thing was to free him. How? No man has power enough to force that spring. But the jackscrew!

"Quonab, help him! For God's sake, come!" cried Rolf in agony, forgetting their feud and seeing only the tortured, dying man.

The Indian gazed a moment, then rose quickly, and put on the jackscrew. Under his deft fingers the first spring went down, but what about the other? They had no other screw. The long buckskin line they always carried was quickly lashed round and round the down spring to hold it. Then the screw was removed and put on the other spring; it bent, and the jaws hung loose. The Indian forced them wide open, drew out the mangled limbs, and the trapper was free, but so near death, it seemed they were too late.

Rolf spread his coat. The Indian made a fire. In fifteen minutes they were pouring hot tea between the victim's lips. Even as they did, his feeble throat gave out again the long, low moan.

The weather was mild now. The prisoner was not actually frozen, but numbed and racked. Heat, hot tea, kindly rubbing, and he revived a little.

At first they thought him dying, but in an hour he recovered enough to talk. In feeble accents and broken phrases they learned the tale:

"Yest — m-m-m. Yesterday — no; two or three days back — m-m-m-m-m — I dunno; I was a goin' — roun' me traps — me bear traps. Didn't have no hick; m-m-m (yes, I'd like another sip; ye ain't got no whiskey — no?) m-m-m. Nothing in any trap, and when I come to this un — oh-h — m-m; I seen — the bait was stole by birds, an' the pan — m-m-m; an' the pan, m-m-m — (yes, that's better) — an' the pan laid bare. So I starts in to cover it with — ce-ce-dar; the on'y thing I c'd get — m-m-m-m — wuz leanin' over — to fix tother side — when me foot slipped on — the — ice — ev'rything was icy — an' — m-m-m-m — I lost — me balance — me knee hit the pan — O Lord — how I suffer! — m-m-m — an' it grabbed me — knee an' — h-h-hand — " His voice died to a whisper and ceased; he seemed sinking.

Quonab got up to hold him. Then, looking at Rolf, the Indian shook his head as though to say all was over; but the poor wretch had a woodman's constitution, and in spite of a mangled, dying body, he revived again. They gave him more hot tea, and again he began in a whisper:

"I hed one arm free an' — an' — an' — I might — a — got out — m-m — but I hed no wrench — I lost it — some place — m-m-m-m.

"Then — I yelled — I dun — no — maybe some un might hear — it kin-kin-kinder eased me — to yell — m-m-m."

"Say — make that yer dog keep — away — will yer — I dunno — it seems like a week — must a fainted some — m-m-m — I yelled — when I could."

There was a long pause. Rolf said, "Seems to me I heard you last night, when we were up there. And the dog heard you, too. Do you want me to move that leg around?"

The Subjugation of Hoag

"M-m-m — yeh — that's better — say, you air — white — ain't ye? Ye won't leave me — coz — I done some mean things — m-m-m. Ye won't, will ye?"

"No, you needn't a worry — we'll stay by ye."

Then he muttered, they could not tell what. He closed his eyes. After long silence he looked around wildly and began again:

"Say — I done you dirt — but don't leave me — don't leave me." Tears ran down his face and he moaned piteously. "I'll — make it — right — you're white, ain't ye?"

Quonab rose and went for more firewood. The trapper whispered, "I'm scared o' him — now — he'll do me — say, I'm jest a poor ole man. If I do live — through — this — m-m-m-m — I'll never walk again. I'm crippled sure."

It was long before he resumed. Then he began: "Say, what day is it — Friday! — I must — been two days in there — m-m-m — I reckoned it was a week. When — the — dog came I thought it was wolves. Oh — ah, didn't care much — m-m-m. Say, ye won't leave me — coz — coz — I treated — ye mean. I — ain't had no I-I-luck." He went off into a stupor, but presently let out a long, startling cry, the same as that they had heard in the night. The dog growled; the men stared. The wretch's eyes were rolling again. He seemed delirious.

Quonab pointed to the east, made the sun-up sign, and shook his head at the victim. And Rolf understood it to mean that he would never see the sunrise. But they were wrong.

The long night passed in a struggle between death and the tough make-up of a mountaineer. The waxing light of dawn saw death defeated, retiring from the scene. As the sun rose high, the victim seemed to gain considerably in strength. There was no immediate danger of an end.

Rolf said to Quonab: "Where shall we take him? Guess you better go home for the toboggan, and we'll fetch him to the shanty."

But the invalid was able to take part in the conversation. "Say, don't take me there. Ah — want to go home. 'Pears like — I'd be better at home. My folks is out Moose River way. I'd never get out if I went in there," and by "there" he seemed to mean the Indian's lake, and glanced furtively at the unchanging countenance of the red man.

"Have you a toboggan at your shanty?" asked Rolf.

"Yes — good enough — it's on the roof — say," and he beckoned feebly to Rolf, "let him go after it — don't leave me — he'll kill me," and he wept feebly in his self pity.

So Quonab started down the mountain — a sinewy man — a striding form, a speck in the melting distance.

XLVI

Nursing Hoag

IN TWO hours the red man reached the trapper's shanty, and at once, without hesitation or delicacy, set about a thorough examination of its contents. Of course there was the toboggan on the roof, and in fairly good condition for such a shiftless owner.

There were bunches of furs hanging from the rafters, but not many, for fur-taking is hard work; and Quonab, looking suspiciously over them, was not surprised to see the lynx skin he had lost, easily known by the absence of wound and the fur still in points as it had dried from the wetting. In another bundle, he discovered the beaver that had killed itself, for there was the dark band across its back.

The martens he could not be sure of, but he had a strong suspicion that most of this fur came out of his own traps.

He tied Hoag's blankets on the toboggan, and hastened back to where he left the two on the mountain.

Skookum met him long before he was near. Skookum did not enjoy Hoag's company.

The cripple had been talking freely to Rolf, but the arrival of the Indian seemed to suppress him.

With the wounded man on the toboggan, they set out. The ground was bare in many places, so that the going was hard; but, fortunately, it was all; down hill, and four hours' toil brought them to the cabin.

They put the sick man in his bunk; then Rolf set about preparing a meal, while Quonab cut wood.

After the usual tea, bacon, and flour cakes, all were feeling refreshed. Hoag seemed much more like himself. He talked freely, almost cheerfully, while Quonab, with Skookum at his feet, sat silently smoking and staring into the fire.

After a long silence, the Indian turned, looked straight at the trap-per, and, pointing with his pipestem to the furs, said, "How many is ours?"

Hoag looked scared, then sulky, and said: "I dunno what ye mean. I'm a awful sick man. You get me out to Lyons Falls all right, and ye can have the hull lot," and he wept.

Rolf shook his head at Quonab, then turned to the sufferer and said: "Don't you worry; we'll get you out all right. Have you a good canoe?"

"Pretty fair; needs a little fixing."

The night passed with one or two breaks, when the invalid asked for a drink of water. In the morning he was evidently recovering, and they began to plan for the future.

He took the first chance of whispering to Rolf, "Can't you send him away? I'll be all right with you." Rolf said nothing.

"Say," he continued, "say, young feller, what's yer name?"

"Rolf Kittering."

"Say, Rolf, you wait a week or ten days, and the ice'll be out; then I'll be fit to travel. There ain't on'y a few carries between here an' Lyons Falls."

After a long pause, due to Quonab's entry, he continued again: "Moose River's good canoeing; ye can get me out in five days; me folks is at Lyons Falls." He did not say that his folks consisted of a wife and boy that he neglected, but whom he counted on to nurse him now.

Rolf was puzzled by the situation.

"Say! I'll give ye all them furs if ye git me out." Rolf gave him a curious look — as much as to say, "Ye mean *our* furs."

Again the conversation was ended by the entry of Quonab.

Rolf stepped out, taking the Indian with him. They had a long talk, then, as Rolf reentered, the sick man began:

Nursing Hoag

"You stay by me, and git me out. I'll give ye my rifle" — then, after a short silence — "an' I'll throw in all the traps an' the canoe."

"I'll stay by you," said Rolf, "and in about two weeks we'll take you down to Lyons Falls. I guess you can guide us."

"Ye can have all them pelts," and again the trapper presented the spoils he had stolen, "an' you bet it's your rifle when ye get me out."

So it was arranged. But it was necessary for Quonab to go back to their own cabin. Now what should he do? Carry the new lot of fur there, or bring the old lot here to dispose of all at Lyons Falls?

Rolf had been thinking hard. He had seen the evil side of many men, including Hoag. To go among Hoag's people with a lot of stuff that Hoag might claim was running risks, so he said:

"Quonab, you come back in not more than ten days. We'll take a few furs to Lyons Falls so we can get supplies. Leave the rest of them in good shape, so we can go out later to Warren's. We'll get a square deal there, and we don't know what at Lyon's."

So they picked out the lynx, the beaver, and a dozen martens to leave, and making the rest into a pack, Quonab shouldered them, and followed by Skookum, trudged up the mountain and was lost to view in the woods.

The ten days went by very slowly. Hoag was alternately querulous, weeping, complaining, unpleasantly fawning, or trying to insure good attention by presenting again and again the furs, the gun, and the canoe.

Rolf found it pleasant to get away from the cabin when the weather was fine. One day, taking Hoag's gun, he travelled up the nearest stream for a mile, and came on a big beaver pond. Round this he scouted and soon discovered a drowned beaver, held in a trap which he recognized at once, for it had the ("' ' '") mark on the frame. Then he found an empty trap with a beaver leg in it, and another, till six traps were found. Then he gathered up the six and the beaver, and returned to the cabin to be greeted with a string of complaints:

"Ye didn't ought to leave me like this. I'm paying ye well enough. I don't ax no favours," etc.

"See what I got," and Rolf showed the beaver. "An' see what I found;" then he showed the traps. "Queer, ain't it," he went on, "we had six traps just like them, and I marked the face just like these, and they all disappeared, and there was a snowshoe trail pointing this way. You haven't got any crooked neighbours about here, have you?"

The trapper looked sulky and puzzled, and grumbled, "I bet it was Bill Hawkins done it," then relapsed into silence.

XLVII

Hoag's Home-coming

"When it comes to personal feelin's better let yer friends do the talkin' and jedgin'. A man can't handle hit own case any more than a delirious doctor kin give hisself the right physic."

— *The Sayings of Si Sylvanne*

THE coming of springtime in the woods is one of the gentlest, sweetest advents in the world. Sometimes there are heavy rains which fill all the little rivers with an overflood that quickly eats away the ice and snow, but usually the woodland streams open slowly and gradually. Very rarely is there a spate, an upheaval, and a cataclysmal sweep that bursts the ice and ends its reign in an hour or two. That is the way of the large rivers, whose ice is free and floating. The snow in the forest melts slowly, and when the ice is attacked, it goes gradually, gently, without uproar. The spring comes in the woods with swelling of buds and a lengthening of drooping catkins, with honking of wild geese, and cawing of crows coming up from the lower countries to divide with their larger cousins, the ravens, the spoils of winter's killing.

The small birds from the South appear with a few short notes of spring, and the pert chicadees that have braved it all winter, now lead the singing with their cheery "I told you so" notes, till robins and black-birds join in, and with their mors ambitious singing make all the lesser roundelays forgot.

Once the winter had taken a backward step spring found it easy to turn retreat into panic and rout; and the ten days Quonab stayed away were days of revolutionary change. For in them semi-winter gave place to smiling spring, with all the snow-drifts gone, except perhaps in the shadiest hollows of the woods.

It was a bright morning, and a happy one for Rolf, when he heard the Indian's short "Ho," outside, and a minute later had Skookum dancing and leaping about him. On Hoag the effect was quite different.

Rolf in the Woods

He was well enough to be up, to hobble about painfully on a stick; to be exceedingly fault-finding, and to eat three hearty meals a day; but the moment the Indian appeared, he withdrew into himself, and became silent and uneasy. Before an hour passed, he again presented the furs, the gun, the canoe, and the traps to Rolf, on condition that he should get him out to his folks.

All three were glad to set out that very day on the outward trip to Lyons Falls.

Down Little Moose River to Little Moose Lake and on to South Branch of Moose, then by the Main Moose, was their way. The streams were flush; there was plenty of water, and this fortunately reduced the number of carries; for Hoag could not walk and would not hobble. They sweat and laboured to carry him over every portage; but they covered the fifty miles in three days, and on the evening of the third, arrived at the little backwoods village of Lyons Falls.

The change that took place in Hoag now was marked and unpleasant. He gave a number of orders, where, the day before, he would have made whining petitions. He told them to "land easy, and don't bump my canoe." He hailed the loungers about the mill with an effusiveness that they did not respond to. Their cool, "Hello, Jack, are you back?" was little but a passing recognition. One of them was persuaded to take Rolf's place in carrying Hoag to his cabin. Yes, his folks were there, but they did not seem overjoyed at

his arrival. He whispered to the boy, who sullenly went out to the river and returned with the rifle, Rolf's rifle now, the latter supposed, and would have taken the bundle of furs had not Skookum sprung on the robber and driven him away from the canoe.

And now Hoag showed his true character. "Them's my furs and my canoe," he said to one of the mill hands, and turning to the two who had saved him, he said: "An' you two dirty, cutthroat, redskin thieves, you can get out of town as fast as ye know how, or I'll have ye jugged," and all the pent-up hate of his hateful nature frothed out in words insulting and unprintable.

"Talks like a white man," said Quonab coldly. Rolf was speechless. To toil so devotedly, and to have such filthy, humiliating words for thanks! He wondered if even his Uncle Mike would have shown so vile a spirit.

Hoag gave free rein to his tongue, and found in his pal, Bill Hawkins, one with ready ears to hear his tale of woe. The wretch began to feel himself frightfully ill-used. So, fired at last by the evermore lurid story of his wrongs, the "partner" brought the magistrate, so they could swear out a warrant, arrest the two "outlaws," and especially secure the bundle of "Hoag's furs" in the canoe.

Old Silas Sylvanne, the mill-owner and pioneer of the place, was also its magistrate. He was tall, thin, black-looking, a sort of Abe Lincoln in type, physically, and in some sort, mentally. He heard the harrowing tale of terrible crime, robbery, and torture, inflicted on poor harmless Hoag by these two ghouls in human shape; he listened, at first shocked, but little by little amused.

"You don't get no warrant till I hear from the other side," he said. Rolf and Quonab came at call. The old pioneer sized up the two, as they stood, then, addressing Rolf, said:

"Air you an Injun?"

"No, sir."

"Air you half-breed?"

"No, sir."

"Well, let's hear about this business," and he turned his piercing eyes full on the lad's face.

Rolf told the simple, straight story of their acquaintance with Hoag, from the first day at Warren's to their arrival at the Falls. There is never any doubt about the truth of a true story, if it be long enough, and this true story, presented in its nakedness to the shrewd and kindly old hunter, trader, mill-owner and magistrate, could have only one effect.

"Sonny," he said, slowly and kindly, "I know that ye have told me the truth. I believe every word of it. We all know that Hoag is the meanest cuss and biggest liar on the river. He's a nuisance, and always was. He only *promised* to give ye the canoe and the rifle, and since he don't want to, we can't help it. About the trouble in the woods, you got two witnesses to his one, and ye got the furs and the traps; it's just as well ye left the other furs behind, or ye might have had to divide 'em; so keep them and call the hull thing square. We'll find ye a canoe to get out of this gay metropolis, and as to Hoag, ye needn't a-worry; his travelling days is done."

Rolf in the Woods

A man with a bundle of high-class furs is a man of means in any frontier town. The magistrate was trader, too, so they set about disposing of their furs and buying the supplies they needed.

The day was nearly done before their new canoe was gummed and ready with the new supplies. When dealing, old Sylvanne had a mild, quiet manner, and a peculiar way of making funny remarks that led some to imagine he was "easy" in business; but it was usual to find at the end that he had lost nothing by his manners, and rival traders shunned an encounter with Long Sylvanne of the unruffled brow.

When business was done — keen and complete — he said: "Now, I'm a goin' to give each of ye a present," and handed out two double-bladed jackknives, new things in those days, wonderful things, precious treasures in their eyes, sources of endless joy; and even had they known that one marten skin would buy a quart of them, their pleasant surprise and childish joy would not have been in any way tempered or alloyed.

"Ye better eat with me, boys, an' start in the morning." So they joined the miller's long, continuous family, and shared his evening meal. Afterward as they sat for three hours and smoked on the broad porch that looked out on the river, old Sylvanne, who had evidently taken a fancy to Rolf, regaled them with a long, rambling talk on "fellers and things," that was one of the most interesting Rolf had ever listened to. At the time it was simply amusing; it was not till years after that the lad realized by its effect on himself, its insight, and its hold on his memory, that Si Sylvanne's talk was real wisdom. Parts of it would not look well in print; but the rugged words, the uncouth Saxonism, the obscene phrase, were the mere oaken bucket in which the pure and precious waters were hauled to the surface.

"Looked like he had ye pinched when that shyster got ye in to Lyons Falls. Wall, there's two bad places for Jack Hoag; one is where they don't know him at all, an' take him on his looks; an't other is where they know him through and through for twenty years, like we hev. A smart rogue kin put up a false front fer a year or maybe two, but given twenty year to try him, for and bye, summer an' winter, an' I reckon a man's make is pretty well showed up, without no dark corners left unexplored.

"Not that I want to jedge him harsh, coz I don't know what kind o' maggots is eatin' his innards to make him so ornery. I'm bound to suppose he has 'em, or he wouldn't act so dum like it. So I says, go slow and gentle before puttin' a black brand on any feller; as my mother used to say, never say a bad thing till ye ask, 'Is it true, is it kind, is it necessary?' An' I tell you, the elder I git, the slower I jedge; when I wuz your age, I wuz a steel trap on a hair trigger, an' cocksure. I tell you, there ain't anythin' wiser nor a sixteen-year-old boy, 'cept maybe a fifteen-year-old girl.

"Ye'll genilly find, lad, jest when things looks about as black as they kin look, that's the sign of luck a-comin' your way, pervidin' ye hold steady, keep cool and kind; *something happens* every time to make it all easy. There's always a way, an' the stout heart will find it.

"Ye may be very sure o' this, boy, yer never licked till ye think ye air; an' if ye won't think it, ye can't be licked.

"It's just the same as being sick. I seen a lot o' doctorin' in my day, and I'm forced to believe there ain't any sick folks 'cept them that *thinks* they air sick.

"The older I git, the more I'm bound to consider that most things is inside, anyhow, and what's outside don't count for much.

"So it stands to reason when ye play the game for what's inside, ye win over all the outside players. When ye done kindness to Hoag, ye mightn't a meant it, but ye was bracin' up the goodness in yerself, or bankin' it up somewher' on the trail ahead, where it was needed. And he was simply chawin' his own leg off, when he done ye dirt. I ain't much o' a prattlin' Christian, but I reckon as a cold-blooded, business proposition it pays to lend the neighbour a hand; not that I go much on gratitude. It's scarcer'n snowballs in hell — which ain't the point; but I take notice there ain't any man'll hate ye more'n the feller that knows he's acted mean to ye. An' there ain't any feller more ready to fight yer battles than the chap that by some dum accident has hed the luck to help ye, even if he only done it to spite some one else —which 'minds me o' McCarthy's bull pup that saved the drowning kittens by mistake, and ever after was a fightin' cat protector, whereby he lost the chief joy o' his life, which had been cat-killin'. An' the way they cured the cat o' eatin' squirrels was givin' her a litter o' squirrels to raise.

"I tell ye there's a lot o' common-sense an' kindness in the country, only it's so dum slow to git around; while the cussedness and meanness always acts like they felt the hell fire sizzlin' their hind-end whiskers, an' knowed they had jest so many minutes to live an' make a record. There's where a man's smart that fixes things so he kin hold out a long time, fer the good stuff in men's minds is what lasts; and the feller what can stay with it hez proved hisself by stayin'. How'd ye happen to tie up with the Injun, Rolf?"

"Do ye want me to tell it long or short?" was the reply.

"Wall, short, fer a start," and Silas Sylvanne chuckled.

So Rolf gave a very brief account of his early life.

"Pretty good," said the miller; "now let's hear it long."

And when he had finished, the miller said: "I've seen yer tried fer most everything that goes to make a man, Rolf, an' I hev my own notion of the results. You ain't goin' to live ferever in them hills. When ye've hed yer fling an' want a change, let me know."

Early next day the two hunters paddled up the Moose River with a good canoe, an outfit of groceries, and a small supply of ready cash.

"Good-bye, lad, good-bye! Come back again and yell find we improve on acquaintance; an' don't forget I'm buying fur," was Si Sylvanne's last word. And as they rounded the point, on the way home, Rolf turned in the canoe, faced Quonab, and said: "Ye see there *are* some good white men left;" but the Indian neither blinked, nor moved, nor made a sound.

XLVIII

Rolf's Lesson in Trailing

THE return journey was hard paddling against strong waters, but otherwise uneventful. Once over any trail is enough to fix it in the memory of a woodman. They made no mistakes and their loads were light, so the portages were scarcely any loss of time, and in two days they were back at Hoag's cabin.

Of this they took possession. First, they gathered all things of value, and that was little since the furs and bedding were gone, but there were a few traps and some dishes. The stuff was made in two packs; now it was an overland journey, so the canoe was hidden in a cedar thicket, a quarter of a mile inland. The two were about to shoulder the packs, Quonab was lighting his pipe for a start, when Rolf said:

"Say, Quonab! That fellow we saw at the Falls claimed to be Hoag's partner. He may come on here and make trouble if we don't head him off. Let's burn her," and he nodded toward the shanty.

"Ugh!" was the reply.

They gathered some dry brush and a lot of birch bark, piled them up against the wall inside, and threw plenty of firewood on this. With flint and steel Quonab made the vital spark, the birch bark sputtered, the dry, resinous logs were easily set ablaze, and soon great volumes of smoke rolled from the door, the window, and the chimney; and Skookum, standing afar, barked pleasantly aloud.

The hunters shouldered their packs and began the long, upward slope. In an hour they had reached a high, rocky ridge. Here they stopped to rest, and, far below them, marked with grim joy a twisted, leaning column of thick black smoke.

That night they camped in the woods and next day rejoiced to be back again at their own cabin, their own lake, their home.

Several times during the march they had seen fresh deer tracks, and now that the need of meat was felt, Rolf proposed a deer hunt.

Rolf in the Woods

Many deer die every winter; some are winter-killed; many are devoured by beasts of prey, or killed by hunters; their numbers are at low ebb in April, so that now one could not count on finding a deer by roaming at random. It was a case for trailing.

Any one can track a deer in the snow. It is not very hard to follow a deer in soft ground, when there are no other deer about. But it is very hard to take one deer trail and follow it over rocky ground and dead leaves, never losing it or changing off, when there are hundreds of deer tracks running in all directions.

Rolf's eyes were better than Quonab's, but experience counts for as much as eyes, and Quonab was leading. They picked out a big buck track that was fresh — no good hunter kills a doe at this season. They Knew it for a buck, because of its size and the roundness of the toes.

Before long, Rolf said: "See, Quonab, I want to learn this business; let me do the trailing, and you set me right if I get off the line."

Within a hundred yards, Quonab gave a grunt and shook his head. Rolf looked surprised, for he was on a good, fresh track.

Quonab said but one word, "Doe."

Yes, a closer view showed the tracks to be a little narrower, a little closer together, and a little sharper than those he began with.

Back went Rolf to the last marks that he was sure of, and plainly read where the buck had turned aside.

For a time, things went along smoothly, Quonab and Skookum following Rolf. The last was getting very familiar with that stub hoof on the left foot. At length they came to the "fumet" or "sign;" it was all in one pile. That meant the deer had stood, so was unalarmed; and warm; that meant but a few minutes ahead. Now, they must use every precaution for this was the crux of the hunt.

Of this much only they were sure — the deer was within range now, and to get him they must see him before he saw them.

Skookum was leashed. Rolf was allowed to get well ahead, and crawling cautiously, a step at a time, he went, setting down his moccasined foot only after he had tried and selected a place. Once or twice he threw into the air a tuft of dry grass to make sure that the wind was right, and by slow degrees he reached the edge of a little opening. Across this he peered long, without entering it. Then he made a sweep with his hand and pointed, to let Quonab know the buck had gone

across and he himself must go around. But he lingered still and with his eyes swept the near woods. Then, dim gray among the gray twigs, he saw a slight movement, so slight it might have been made by the tail of a tomtit. But it fixed his attention, and out of this gray haze he slowly made out the outline of a deer's head, antlers, and neck. A hundred yards away, but "take a chance when it comes" is hunter wisdom. Rolf glanced at the sight, took steady aim, fired, and down went the buck behind a log. Skookum whined and leaped high in his eagerness to see. Rolf restrained his impatience to rush forward, at once reloaded, then all three went quickly to the place. Before they were within fifty yards, the deer leaped up and bounded off. At seventy-five yards, it stood for a moment to gaze. Rolf fired again; again the buck fell down, but jumped to its feet and bounded away.

They went to the two places, but found no blood. Utterly puzzled, they gave it up for the day, as already the shades of night were on the woods, and in spite of Skookum's voluble offer to solve and settle everything, they returned to the cabin.

"What do you make of it, Quonab?'

The Indian shook his head, then: "Maybe touched his head and stunned him, first shot; second, wah! I not know."

"I know this," said Rolf. "I touched him and I mean to get him in the morning." True to this resolve, he was there again at dawn, but examined the place in vain for a sign of blood. The red rarely shows up much on leaves, grass, or dust; but there are two kinds of places that the hunter can rely on as telltales— stones and logs. Rolf followed the deer track, now very dim, till at a bare place he found a speck of blood on a pebble. Here the trail joined onto a deer path, with so many tracks that it was hard to say which was the right one. But Rolf passed quickly along to a log that crossed the runway, and on that log he found a drop of dried-up blood that told him what he wished to know.

Now he had a straight run of a quarter of a mile, and from time to time he saw a peculiar scratching mark that puzzled him. Once he found a speck of blood at one of these scratches but no other evidence that the buck was touched.

A wounded deer is pretty sure to work down hill, and Quonab, leaving Skookum with Rolf, climbed a lookout that might show whither the deer was heading.

After another half mile, the deer path forked; there were buck trails on both, and Rolf could not pick out the one he wanted. He went a few yards along each, studying the many marks, but was unable to tell which was that of the wounded buck.

Now Skookum took a share in it. He had always been forbidden to run deer and knew it was a contraband amusement, but he put his nose to that branch of the trail that ran down hill, followed it for a few yards, then looked at Rolf, as much as to say: "You poor nose-blind creature; don't you know a fresh deer track when you smell it? Here it is; this is where he went."

Rolf stared, then said, "I believe he means it;" and followed the lower trail. Very soon he came to another scrape, and, just beyond it, found the new, velvet-covered antler of a buck, raw and bloody, and splintered at the base.

From this on, the task was easier, as there were no other tracks, and this was pointing steadily down hill.

Soon Quonab came striding along. He had not seen the buck, but a couple of jays and a raven were gathered in a thicket far down by the stream. The hunters quit the trail and made for that place. As they drew near, they found the track again, and again saw those curious scrapes.

Every hunter knows that the bluejay dashing about a thicket means that hidden there is game of some kind, probably deer. Very, very slowly and silently they entered that copse. But nothing appeared until there was a rush in the thickest part and up leaped the buck. This was too much for Skookum. He shot forward like a wolf, fastened on one hind leg, and the buck went crashing head over heels. Before it could rise, another shot ended its troubles. And now a careful study shed the light desired. Rolf's first shot had hit the antler near the base, breaking it, except for the skin on one side, and had stunned the buck. The second shot had broken a hind leg. The scratching places he had made were efforts to regain the use of this limb, and at one of them the deer had fallen and parted the sag of skin by which the antler hung.

It was Rolf's first important trailing on the ground; it showed how possible it was, and how quickly he was learning the hardest of all the feats of woodcraft.

XLIX

Rolf Gets Lost

EVERY ONE who lives in the big woods gets lost at some time. Yes, even Daniel Boone did sometimes go astray. And whether it is to end as a joke or a horrible tragedy depends entirely on the way in which the person takes it. This is, indeed, the grand test of a hunter and scout, the trial of his knowledge, his muscle, and, above everything, his courage; and, like all supreme trials, it comes without warning.

The wonderful flocks of wild pigeons had arrived. For a few days in May they were there in millions, swarming over the ground in long-reaching hordes, walking along, pecking and feeding, the rearmost flying on ahead, ever to the front. The food they sought so eagerly now was chiefly the seeds of the slippery elm, tiny nuts showered down on wings like broad-brimmed hats. And when the flock arose at some alarm, the sound was like that of the sea beach in a storm.

There seemed to be most pigeons in the low country southeast of the lake, of course, because, being low, it had most elms. So Rolf took his bow and arrows, crossed in the canoe, and confidently set about gathering in a dozen or two for broilers.

It is amazing how well the game seems to gauge the range of your weapon and keep the exact safe distance. It is marvellous how many times you may shoot an arrow into a flock of pigeons and never kill one. Rolf went on and on, always in sight of the long, straggling flocks on the ground or in the air, but rarely within range of them. Again and again he fired a random shot into the distant mass, without success for two hours. Finally a pigeon was touched and dropped, but it rose as he ran forward, and flew ten yards, to drop once more. Again he rushed at it, but it fluttered out of reach and so led him on and on for about half an hour's breathless race, until at last he stopped, took deliberate aim, and killed it with an arrow.

Rolf in the Woods

Now a peculiar wailing and squealing from the woods far ahead attracted him. He stalked and crawled for many minutes before he found out, as he should have known, that it was caused by a mischievous bluejay.

At length he came to a spring in a low hollow, and leaving his bow and arrows on a dry log, he went down to get a drink.

As he arose, he found himself face to face with a doe and a fat, little yearling buck, only twenty yards away. They stared at him, quite unalarmed, and, determining to add the yearling to his bag, Rolf went back quietly to his bow and arrows.

The deer were just out of range now, but inclined to take a curious interest in the hunter. Once when he stood still for a long time, they walked forward two or three steps; but whenever he advanced, they trotted farther away.

To kill a deer with an arrow is quite a feat of woodcraft, and Rolf was keen to show his prowess; so he kept on with varying devices, and was continually within sight of the success that did not actually arrive.

Then the deer grew wilder and loped away, as he entered another valley that was alive with pigeons.

He was feeling hungry now, so he plucked the pigeon he had secured, made a fire with the flint and steel he always carried, then roasted the bird carefully on a stick, and having eaten it, felt ready for more travel.

The day was cloudy, so he could not see the sun; but he knew it was late, and he made for camp.

The country he found himself in was entirely strange to him, and the sun's whereabouts doubtful; but he knew the general line of travel and strode along rapidly toward the place where he had left the canoe.

After two hours' tramping, he was surprised at not seeing the lake through the trees, and he added to his pace.

Three hours passed and still no sign of the water.

He began to think he had struck too far to the north; so corrected his course and strode along with occasional spells of trotting. But another hour wore away and no lake appeared.

Rolf Gets Lost

Then Rolf knew he was off his bearings. He climbed a tree and got a partial view of the country. To the right was a small hill. He made for that. The course led him through a hollow. In this he recognized two huge bass-wood trees, that gave him a reassuring sense. A little farther he came on a spring, strangely like the one he had left some hours ago. As he stooped to drink, he saw deer tracks, then a human track. He studied it. Assuredly: it was his own track, though now it seemed on the south side instead of the north. He stared at the dead gray sky, hoping for sign of sun, but it gave no hint. He tramped off hastily toward the hill that promised a lookout. He went faster and faster. In half an hour the woods opened a little, then dipped. He hastened down, and at the bottom found himself standing by the same old spring, though again it had changed its north bearing.

He was stunned by this succession of blows. He knew now he was *lost in the woods;* had been tramping in a circle.

The spring whirled around him; it seemed now north and now south. His first impulse was to rush madly north-westerly, as he understood it. He looked at all the trees for guidance. Most moss should be on the north side. It would be so, if all trees were perfectly straight and evenly exposed, but alas! none are so. All lean one way or another, and by the moss he could prove any given side to be north. He looked for the hemlock top twigs. Tradition says they *always point easterly*; but now they differed among themselves as to which was east.

Rolf got more and more worried. He was a brave boy, but grim fear came into his mind as he realized that he was too far from camp to be heard; the ground was too leafy for trailing him; without help he could not get away from that awful spring. His head began to swim, when all at once he remembered a bit of advice his guide had given him long ago: "Don't get scared when you're lost. Hunger don't kill the lost man, and it ain't cold that does it; it's *being afraid.* Don't be afraid, and everything will come out all right."

So, instead of running, Rolf sat down to think it over.

"Now," said he, "I went due southeast all day from the canoe." Then he stopped; like a shock it came to him that he had not seen the sun all day. *Had he really gone southeast?* It was a devastating thought, enough to unhinge some men; but again Rolf said to himself. "Never mind, now; don't get scared, and it'll be all right. In the morning the sky will be clear."

As he sat pondering, a red squirrel chippered and scolded from a near tree; closer and closer the impudent creature came to sputter at the intruder.

Rolf drew his bow, and when the blunt arrow dropped to the ground, there also dropped the red squirrel, turned into acceptable meat. Rolf put this small game into his pocket, realizing that this was his supper.

It would soon be dark now, so he prepared to spend the night.

While yet he could see, he gathered a pile of dry wood into a sheltered hollow. Then he made a wind-break and a bed of balsam boughs. Flint, steel, tinder, and birch bark soon created a cheerful fire, and there is no better comforter that the lone lost man can command.

The squirrel roasted in its hide proved a passable supper, and Rolf curled up to sleep. The night would have been pleasant and uneventful, but that it turned chilly, and when the fire burnt low, the cold awakened him, so he had a succession of naps and fire-buildings.

Soon after dawn, he heard a tremendous roaring, and in a few minutes the wood was filled again with pigeons.

Rolf was living on the country now, so he sallied forth with his bow. Luck was with him; at the first shot he downed a big, fat cock. At the second he winged another, and as it scrambled through the brush, he rushed headlong in pursuit. It fluttered away beyond reach, half-flying, half-running, and Rolf, in reckless pursuit, went sliding and tumbling down a bank to land at the bottom with a horrid jar. One leg was twisted under him; he thought it was broken, for there was a fearful pain in the lower part. But when he pulled himself together he found no

broken bones, indeed, but an ankle badly sprained. Now his situation was truly grave, for he was crippled and incapable of travelling.

He had secured the second bird, and crawling painfully and slowly back to the fire, he could not but feel more and more despondent and gloomy as the measure of his misfortune was realized.

"There is only one thing that can shame a man, that is to be afraid." And again, "There's always a way out." These were the sayings that came ringing through his head to his heart; one was from Quonab, the other from old Sylvanne. Yes, there's always a way, and the stout heart can always find it.

Rolf prepared and cooked the two birds, made a breakfast of one and put the other in his pocket for lunch, not realizing at the time that his lunch would be eaten on this same spot. More than once, as he sat, small flocks of ducks flew over the trees due northward. At length the sky, now clear, was ablaze with the rising sun, and when it came, it was *in Rolf's western sky.*

Now he comprehended the duck flight. They were really heading southeast for their feeding grounds on the Indian Lake, and Rolf, had he been able to tramp, could have followed, but his foot was growing worse. It was badly swollen, and not likely to be of service for many a day — perhaps weeks — and it took all of his fortitude not to lie down and weep over this last misfortune.

Again came the figure of that grim, kindly, strong old pioneer, with the gray-blue eyes and his voice was saying: "Jest when things looks about as black as they can look, if ye hold steady, keep cool and kind, something sure happens to make it all easy. There's always a way and the stout heart will find it."

What way was there for him? He would die of hunger and cold before Quonab could find him, and again came the spectre of fear. If only he could devise some way of letting his comrade know. He shouted once or twice, in the faint hope that the still air might carry the sound, but the silent wood was silent when he ceased.

Then one of his talks with Quonab came to mind. He remembered how the Indian, as a little papoose, had been lost for three days. Though, then but ten years old, he had built a smoke fire that brought him help. Yes, that was the Indian way; two smokes means "I am lost;" "double for trouble."

For a while Rolf was sunk in despair

Rolf Gets Lost

Fired by this new hope, Rolf crawled a little apart from his camp and built a bright fire, then smothered it with rotten wood and green leaves. The column of smoke it sent up was densely white and towered above the trees.

Then painfully he hobbled and crawled to a place one hundred yards away, and made another smoke. Now all he could do was wait.

A fat pigeon, strayed from its flock, sat on a bough above his camp, in a way to tempt Providence. Rolf drew a blunt arrow to the head and speedily had the pigeon in hand for some future meal.

As he prepared it, he noticed that its crop was crammed with the winged seed of the slippery elm, so he put them all back again into the body when it was cleaned, knowing well that they are a delicious food and in this case would furnish a welcome variant to the bird itself.

An hour crawled by. Rolf had to go out to the far fire, for it was nearly dead. Instinctively he sought a stout stick to help him; then remembered how Hoag had managed with one leg and two crutches. "Ho!" he exclaimed. "That is the answer — this is the 'way.'"

Now his attention was fixed on all the possible crutches. The trees seemed full of them, but all at impossible heights. It was long before he found one that he could cut with his knife. Certainly he was an hour working at it; then he heard a sound that made his blood jump.

From far away in the north it came, faint but reaching; "Ye-hoo-o."

Rolf dropped his knife and listened with the instinctively open mouth that takes all pressure from the eardrums and makes them keen. It came again: "Ye-hoo-o." No mistake now, and Rolf sent the ringing answer back:

"Ye-hoo-o, ye-hoo-o."

In ten minutes there was a sharp "yap, yap," and Skookum bounded out of the woods to leap and bark around Rolf, as though he knew all about it; while a few minutes later, came Quonab striding.

"Ho, boy," he said, with a quiet smile, and took Rolf's hand. "Ugh! That was good," and he nodded to the smoke fire. "I knew you were in trouble."

"Yes," and Rolf pointed to the swollen ankle.

Rolf in the Woods

The Indian picked up the lad in his arms and carried him back to the little camp. Then, from his light pack, he took bread and tea and made a meal for both. And, as they ate, each heard the other's tale.

"I was troubled when you did not come back last night, for you had no food or blanket. I did not sleep. At dawn I went to the hill, where I pray, and looked away southeast where you went in the canoe. I saw nothing. Then I went to a higher hill, where I could see the northeast, and even while I watched, I saw the two smokes, so I knew my son was alive."

"You mean to tell me I am northeast of camp?"

"About four miles. I did not come very quickly, because I had to go for the canoe and travel here.

"How do you mean by canoe?" said Rolf, in surprise.

"You are only half a mile from Jesup River," was the reply. "I soon bring you home."

It was incredible at first, but easy of proof. With the hatchet they made a couple of serviceable crutches and set out together.

In twenty minutes they were afloat in the canoe; in an hour they were safely home again.

And Rolf pondered it not a little. At the very moment of blackest despair, the way had opened, and it had been so simple, so natural, so effectual. Surely, as long as he lived, he would remember it — "There is always a way, and the stout heart will find it."

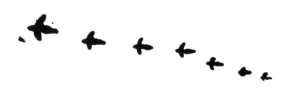

L

Marketing the Fur

IF ROLF had been at home with his mother, she would have rubbed his black and swollen ankle with goose grease. The medical man at Stamford would have rubbed it with a carefully prepared and secret ointment. His Indian friend sang a little crooning song and rubbed it with deer's fat. All different, and all good, because each did something to reassure the patient, to prove that big things were doing on his behalf, and each helped the process of nature by frequent massage.

Three times a day, Quonab rubbed that blackened ankle. The grease saved the skin from injury, and in a week Rolf had thrown his crutches away.

The month of May was nearly gone; June was at hand; that is, the spring was over.

In all ages, man has had the impulse, if not the habit, of spring migration. Yielding to it he either migrated or made some radical change in his life. Most of the Adirondack men who trapped in the winter sought work on the log drives in spring; some who had families and a permanent home set about planting potatoes and plying the fish nets. Rolf and Quonab having neither way open, yet feeling the impulse, decided to go out to Warren's with the fur.

Quonab wanted tobacco — and a change.

Rolf wanted a rifle, and to see the Van Trumpers — and a change.

So June 1st saw them all aboard, with Quonab steering at the stern, and Skookum bow-wowing at the bow, bound for the great centre of Warren's settlement — one store and three houses, very wide apart.

There was a noble flush of water in the streams, and, thanks to their axe work in September, they passed down Jesup's River without a pause, and camped on the Hudson that night, fully twenty-five miles from home.

Rolf in the Woods

Long, stringing flocks of pigeons going north were the most numerous forms of life. But a porcupine on the bank and a bear in the water aroused Skookum to a pitch of frightful enthusiasm and vaulting ambition that he was forced to restrain.

On the evening of the third day they landed at Warren's and found a hearty welcome from the trader, who left a group of loafers and came forward:

"Good day to ye, boy. My, how ye have growed."

So he had. Neither Rolf nor Quonab had remarked it, but now they were much of the same height. "Wall, an' how'd ye make out with yer hunt? —Ah, that's fine!" as each of them dropped a fur pack on the counter. "Wall, this is fine; we must have a drink on the head of it," and the trader was somewhat nonplused when both the trappers refused. He was disappointed, too, for that refusal meant that they would get much better prices for their fur. But he concealed his chagrin and rattled on: "I reckon I'll sell you the finest rifle in the country this time," and he knew by Rolf's face that there was business to do in that line.

Now came the listing of the fur, and naturally the bargaining was between the shrewd Yankee boy and the trader. The Indian stood shyly aside, but he did not fail to help with significant grunts and glances.

"There, now," said Warren, as the row of martens were laid out side by side, "thirty martens — a leetle pale — worth three dollars and fifty cents each, or, to be generous, we'll say four dollars." Rolf glanced at Quonab, who, unseen by the trader shook his head, held his right hand out, open hollow up, then raised it with a jerk for two inches.

Quickly Rolf caught the idea and said, "No, I don't reckon them pale. I call them prime dark, every one of them." Quonab spread his hand with all five fingers pointed up, and Rolf continued, "They are worth five dollars each, if they're worth a copper."

Marketing the Fur

"Phew!" said the trader, "you forget fur is an awful risky thing; what with mildew, moth, mice, and markets, we have a lot of risk. But I want to please you, so let her go; five each. There's a fine black fox; that's worth forty dollars."

"I should think it is," said Rolf, as Quonab, by throwing to his right an imaginary pinch of sand, made the sign "refuse."

They had talked over the value of that fox skin and Rolf said, "Why, I know of a black fox that sold for two hundred dollars."

"Where?"

"Oh, down at Stamford."

"Why, that's near New York."

"Of course; don't you send your fur to New York?"

"Yes, but it costs a lot to get it there."

"Now," said Warren, "if you'll take it in trade, I'll meet you half-way and call it one hundred dollars."

"Make it one hundred and twenty-five dollars and I'll take a rifle, anyway."

"Phew!" whistled the trader. "Where *do* ye get such notions?"

"Nothing wrong about the notion; old Si Sylvanne offered me pretty near that, if I'd come out his way with the stuff."

This had the desired effect of showing that there were other traders. At last the deal was closed. Besides the fox skin, they had three hundred dollars' worth of fur. The exchange for the fox skin was enough to buy all the groceries and dry goods they needed. But Rolf had something else in mind.

He had picked out some packages of candies, some calico prints and certain bright ribbons, when the trader grasped the idea. "I see; yer goin' visitin'. Who is it? Must be the Van Trumpers!"

Rolf nodded and now he got some very intelligent guidance. He did not buy Annette's dress, because part of her joy was to be the expedition

in person to pick it out; but he stocked up with some gorgeous pieces of jewellery that were ten cents each, and ribbons whose colours were as far beyond expression as were the joys they could create in the backwoods female heart.

Proudly clutching his new rifle, and carrying in his wallet a memorandum of three hundred dollars for their joint credit, Rolf felt himself a person of no little importance. As he was stepping out of the store, the trader said, "Ye didn't run across Jack Hoag agin, did ye?"

"Did we? Hmph!" and Rolf told briefly of their experience with that creature.

"Just like him, just like him; served him right; he was a dirty cuss. But, say; don't you be led into taking your fur out Lyons Falls way. They're a mean lot in there, and it stands to reason I can give you better prices, being a hundred miles nearer New York."

And that lesson was not forgotten. The nearer New York the better the price; seventy-five dollars at Lyons Falls; one hundred and twenty-five dollars at Warren's; two hundred dollars at New York. Rolf pondered long and the idea was one which grew and bore fruit.

LI

Back at Van Trumper's

"NIBOWAKA" — Quonab always said "Nibowaka" when he was impressed with Rolf's astuteness — "what about the canoe and stuff?"

"I think we better leave all here. Callan will lend us a canoe." So they shouldered the guns, Rolf clung to his, and tramped across the portage, reaching Callan's in less than two hours.

"Why, certainly you can have the canoe, but come in and eat first," was the kindly backwoods greeting. However, Rolf was keen to push on; they launched the canoe at once and speedily were flashing their paddles on the lake.

The place looked sweetly familiar as they drew near. The crops in the fields were fair; the crop of chickens at the barn was good; and the crop of children about the door was excellent.

"Mein Hemel! Mein Hemel!" shouted fat old Hendrik, as they walked up to the stable door. In a minute he was wringing their hands and smiling into great red, white, and blue smiles. "Coom in, coom in, lad. Hi, Marta, here be Rolf and Quonab. Mein Hemel! Mein Hemel! What am I now so happy."

"Where's Annette?" asked Rolf.

"Ach, poor Annette, she fever have a little; not mooch, some," and he led over to a corner where on a low cot lay Annette, thin, pale, and listless.

She smiled faintly, in response, when Rolf stooped and kissed her.

"Why, Annette, I came back to see you. I want to take you over to Warren's store, so you can pick out that dress. See, I brought you my first marten and I made this box for you; you must thank Skookum for the quills on it."

Rolf in the Woods

"Poor chile; she bin sick all spring," and Marta used a bunch of sedge to drive away the flies and mosquitoes that, bass and treble, hovered around the child.

"What ails her?" asked Rolf anxiously.

"Dot ve do not know," was the reply.

"Maybe there's some one here can tell," and Rolf glanced at the Indian.

"Ach, sure! Have I you that not always told *all-vays* — eet is so. All-vays, I want sumpin bad mooch. I prays de good Lord and all-vays, all-vays, two times now, He it send by next boat. Ach, how I am spoil," and the good Dutchman's eyes filled with tears of thankfulness.

Quonab knelt by the sufferer. He felt her hot, dry hand; he noticed her short, quick breathing, her bright eyes, and the untouched bowl of mush by her bed.

"Swamp fever," he said. "I bring good medicine." He passed quietly out into the woods. When he returned, he carried a bundle of snake-root which he made into tea.

Annette did not wish to touch it, but her mother persuaded her to take a few sips from a cup held by Rolf.

"Wah! this not good," and Quonab glanced about the close, fly-infested room. "I must make lodge." He turned up the cover of the bedding; three or four large, flat brown things moved slowly out of the light. "Yes, I make lodge."

It was night now, and all retired; the newcomers to the barn. They had scarcely entered, when a screaming of poultry gave a familiar turn to affairs. On running to the spot, it proved not a mink or coon, but Skookum, up to his old tricks. On the appearance of his masters, he fled with guilty haste, crouched beneath the post that he used to be, and soon again was, chained to.

In the morning Quonab set about his lodge, and Rolf said: "I've got to go to Warren's for sugar." The sugar was part truth and part blind. As soon as he heard the name swamp fever, Rolf remembered that, in Redding, Jesuit's bark (known later as quinine) was the sovereign remedy. He had seen his mother administer it many times, and, so far as he knew, with uniform success. Every frontier (or backwoods, it's the same) trader carries a stock of medicine, and in two hours Rolf left Warren's counter with twenty-five pounds of maple sugar and a bottle of quinine extract in his pack.

Back at Van Trumper's

"You say she's bothered with the flies; why don't you take some of this new stuff for a curtain?" and the trader held up a web of mosquito gauze, the first Rolf had seen. That surely was a good idea, and ten yards snipped off was a most interesting addition to his pack. The amount was charged against him, and in two hours more he was back at Van Trumper's.

On the cool side of the house, Quonab had built a little lodge, using a sheet for cover. On a low bed of pine boughs lay the child. Near the door was a smouldering fire of cedar, whose aromatic fumes on the lazy wind reached every cranny of the lodge.

Sitting by the bed head, with a chicken wing to keep off the few mosquitoes, was the Indian. The child's eyes were closed; she was sleeping peacefully. Rolf crept gently forward, laid his hand on hers, it was cool and moist. He went into the house with his purchases; the mother greeted him with a happy look: Yes, Annette was a little better; she had slept quietly ever since she was taken outdoors. The mother could not understand. Why should the Indian want to have her surrounded by pine boughs? why cedar-smoke? and why that queer song? Yes, there it was again. Rolf went out to see and hear. Softly tumming on a tin pan, with a muffled stick, the Indian sang a song. The words which Rolf learned in the after-time were:

> "Come, Kaluskap, drive the witches;
> Those who came to harm the dear one."

Annette moved not, but softly breathed, as she slept, a sweet, restful slumber, the first for many days.

"Vouldn't she be better in de house?" whispered the anxious mother.

"No, let Quonab do his own way," and Rolf wondered if any white man had sat by little Wee-wees to brush away the flies from his last bed.

LII

Annette's New Dress

"Deep feelin's ain't any count by themselves; work 'em off, an' ye're some-body; weep 'em off an' you'd be more use with a heart o' stone."
— *The Sayings of Si Sylvanne*

"QUONAB, I am going out to get her a partridge."

"Ugh, good."

So Rolf went off. For a moment he was inclined to grant Skookum's prayer for leave to follow, but another and better plan came in mind. Skookum would most likely find a mother partridge, which none should kill in June, and there was a simple way to find a cock; that was, listen. It was now the evening calm, and before Rolf had gone half a mile he heard the distant *Thump, thump, thump, thump — rrrrrr* of a partridge, drumming. He went quickly and cautiously toward the place, then waited for the next drumming. It was slow in coming, so he knelt down by a mossy, rotten log, and struck it with his hands to imitate the thump and roll of the partridge. At once this challenge procured response.

Thump — thump — thump, thump rrrrrrrrrr it came, with martial swing and fervour, and crawling nearer, Rolf spied the drummer, pompously strutting up and down a log some forty yards away. He took steady aim, not for the head — with a strange gun, at forty yards — but for the body. At the crack, the bird fell dead, and in Rolf's heart there swelled up a little gush of joy, which he believed was all for the sake of the invalid, but which a finer analysis might have proved to be due quite as much to pride in himself and his newly bought gun.

Night was coming on when he got back, and he found the Dutch parents in some excitement. "Dot Indian he say no bring Annette indoors for de night. How she sleep outdoors — like dog — like nigger — like

213

tramp? Yah, it is bad, ain't it?" and poor old Hendrik looked sadly upset and mystified.

"Hendrik, do you suppose God turns out worse air in the night than in the day?"

"Ach, dunno."

"Well, you see Quonab knows what he's doing."

"Yah."

"Well, let him do it. He or I'll sleep alongside the child; she'll be all right," and Rolf thought of those horrible brown crawlers under the bedding indoors.

Rolf had much confidence in the Indian as a doctor, but he had more in his own mother. He was determined to give Annette the quinine, yet he hesitated to interfere. At length, he said: "It is cool enough now; I will put these thin curtains round her bed."

"Ugh, good!" but the red man sat there while it was being done.

"You need not stay now; I'll watch her, Quonab."

"Soon, give more medicine," was the reply that Rolf did not want. So he changed his ruse. "I wish you'd take that partridge and make soup of it. I've had my hands in poison ivy, so I dare not touch it."

"Ach, dot shall *I* do. Dot kin myself do," and the fat mother, laying the recent baby in its cradle, made cumbrous haste to cook the bird.

"Foiled again," was Rolf's thought, but his Yankee wit was with him. He laid one hand on the bowl of snake-root tea. It was lukewarm. "Do you give it hot or cold, Quonab?"

"Hot."

"I'll take it in and heat it." He carried it off, thinking, "If Quonab won't let me give the bark extract, I'll make *him* give it." In the gloom of the kitchen he had no difficulty in adding to the tea, quite unseen, a quarter of the extract; when heated, he brought it again, and the Indian himself gave the dose.

As bedtime drew near, and she heard the red man say he would sleep there, the little one said feebly, "Mother, mother," then whispered in her mother's ear, "I want Rolf."

Rolf spread his blanket by the cot and slept lightly. Once or twice he rose to look at Annette. She was moving in her sleep, but did not awake. He saw to it that the mosquito bar was in place, and slept till morning.

There was no question that the child was better. The renewed interest in food was the first good symptom, and the partridge served the end of its creation. The snake-root and the quinine did noble work, and thenceforth her recovery was rapid. It was natural for her mother to wish the child back indoors. It was a matter of course that she should go. It was accepted as an unavoidable evil that they should always have those brown crawlers about the bed.

But Rolf felt differently. He knew what his mother would have thought and done. It meant another visit to Warren's, and the remedy he brought was a strong-smelling oil, called in those days "rock oil" — a crude petroleum. When all cracks in the bed and near wall were treated with this, it greatly mitigated, if it did not quite end, the nuisance of the "plague that walks in the dark."

Meanwhile, Quonab had made good his welcome by working on the farm. But when a week had flown, he showed signs of restlessness. "We have enough money, Nibowaka, why do we stay?"

Rolf was hauling a bucket of water from the well at the time. He stopped with his burden on the well-sweep, gazed into the well, and said slowly: "I don't know." If the truth were set forth, it would be that this was the only home circle he knew. It was the clan feeling that held him, and soon it was clearly the same reason that was driving Quonab to roam.

"I have heard," said the Indian, "that my people still dwell in Canada, beyond Rouse's Point. I would see them. I will come again in the Red Moon (August)."

So they hired a small canoe, and one bright morning, with Skookum in the bow, Quonab paddled away on his voyage of 120 miles on the placid waters of Lakes George and Champlain. His canoe became a dark spot on the water; slowly it faded till only the flashing paddle was seen, and that was lost around a headland.

The next day Rolf was sorry he let Quonab go alone, for it was evident that Van Trumper needed no help for a month yet; that is, he could not afford to hire, and while it was well enough for Rolf to stay a few days and work to equalize his board, the arrangement would not long continue satisfactory to both.

Yet there was one thing he must do before leaving, take Annette to pick out her dress. She was well again now, and they set off one morning in the canoe, she and Rolf. Neither father nor mother could leave the house. They had their misgivings, but what could they do? She was bright and happy, full of the childish joy that belongs to that age, and engaged on such an important errand for the first time in her life.

Rolf in the Woods

There was something more than childish joy showing in her face, an older person would have seen that, but it was largely lost on Rolf. There was a tendency to blush when she laughed, a disposition to tease her "big brother," to tyrannize over him in little things.

"Now, you tell me some more about *Robinson Crusoe*," she began, as soon as they were in the canoe, and Rolf resumed the ancient, inspiring tale to have it listened to eagerly, but criticized from the standpoint of a Lake George farm. "Where was his wife?" "How could he have a farm without hens?" "Dried grapes must be nice, but I'd rather have pork than goat," etc.

Rolf, of course, took the part of Robinson Crusoe, and it gave him a little shock to hear Quonab called his man Friday.

At the west side they were to invite Mrs. Callan to join their shopping trip, but in any case they were to borrow a horse and buckboard. Neither Mrs. Callan nor the buck-board was available, but they were welcome to the horse. So Annette was made comfortable on a bundle of blankets, and chattered incessantly while Rolf walked alongside with the grave interest and superiority of a much older brother. So they crossed the five-mile portage and came to Warren's store. Nervous and excited, with sparkling eyes, Annette laid down her marten skin, received five dollars, and set about the tremendous task of selecting her first dress of really, truly calico print; and Rolf realized that the joy he had found in his new rifle was a very small affair, compared with the epoch-making, soul-filling, life-absorbing, unspeakable, and cataclysmal bliss that a small girl can have in her first chance of unfettered action in choice of a cotton print.

"Beautiful?" How can mere words do justice to masses of yellow corn, mixed recklessly with green and scarlet poppies on a bright blue ground. No, you should have seen Annette's dress, or you cannot expect

MEAL
HOUSE

to get the adequate thrill. And when they found that there was enough cash left over to add a red cotton parasol to the glorious spoils, every one there beamed in a sort of friendly joy, and the trader, carried away by the emotions of the hour, contributed a set of buttons of *shining brass*.

Warren kept a "meal house," which phrase was a ruse that saved him from a burdensome hospitality. Determined to do it all in the best style, Rolf took Annette to the meal-house table. She was deeply awed by the grandeur of a table-cloth and white plates, but every one was kind.

Warren, talking to a stranger opposite, and evidently resuming a subject they had discussed, said:

"Yes, I'd like to send the hull lot down to Albany this week, if I could get another man for the canoe."

Rolf was interested at once and said: "What wages are you offering?"

"Twenty-five dollars and board."

"How will I do?"

"Well," said Warren, as though thinking it over: "I dunno but ye would. Could ye go to-morrow?"

"Yes, indeed, for one month."

"All right, it's a bargain."

And so Rolf took the plunge that influenced his whole life.

But Annette whispered gleefully and excitedly, "May I have some of that, and that?" pointing to every strange food she could see, and got them all.

After noon they set out on their return journey, Annette clutching her prizes, and prattling incessantly, while Rolf walked alongside, thinking deeply, replying to her chatter, but depressed by the thought of good-bye tomorrow. He was aroused at length by a scraping sound overhead and a sharp reprimand, "Rolf, you'll tear my new parasol, if you don't lead the horse better."

By two o'clock they were at Callan's. Another hour and they had crossed the lake, and Annette, shrill with joy, was displaying her treasures to the wonder and envy of her kin.

Making a dress was a simple matter in those days, and Marta promised: "Yah, soom day ven I one hour have, shall I it sew." Meanwhile, Annette was quaffing deep, soul-satisfying draughts in the mere contemplation of the yellow, red, green, and blue glories in which she was soon to appear in public. And when the bed hour came, she fell asleep holding the dress-goods stuff in her arms, and with the red parasol spread above her head, tired out, but inexpressibly happy.

LIII

Travelling to the Great City

"He's a bad failure that ain't king in some little corner."
—The Sayings of Si Sylvanne

THE children were not astir when Rolf was off in the morning. He caught a glimpse of Annette, still asleep under the red parasol, but the dress-goods and the brass buttons had fallen to the floor. He stepped into the canoe. The dead calm of early morning was on the water, and the little craft went skimming and wimpling across. In half an hour it was beached at Callan's. In a little more than an hour's jog and stride he was at Warren's, ready for work. As he marched in, strong and brisk, his colour up, his blue eyes kindled with the thought of seeing Albany, the trader could not help being struck by him, especially when he remembered each of their meetings — meetings in which he discerned a keen, young mind of good judgment, one that could decide quickly.

Gazing at the lithe, red-cheeked lad, he said: "Say, Rolf, air ye an Injun?"

"No sir."

"Air ye a half-breed?"

"No, I'm a Yank; my name is Kittering; born and bred in Redding, Connecticut."

"Well, I swan, ye look it. At fust I took ye fur an Injun; ye *did* look dark (and Rolf laughed inside, as he thought of that butternut dye), but I'm bound to say we're glad yer white."

"Here, Bill, this is Rolf, Rolf Kittering, he'll go with ye to Albany." Bill, a loose-jointed, middle-aged, flat-footed, large-handed, semi-loafer, with keen gray eyes, looked up from a bundle he was roping.

Then Warren took Rolf aside and explained: "I'm sending down all my fur this trip. There's ten bales of sixty pounds each, pretty near my hull fortune. I want it took straight to Vandam's, and, night or day,

219

don't leave it till ye git it there. He's close to the dock. I'm telling ye this for two reasons: The river's swarming with pirates and sneaks. They'd like nothing better than to get away with a five-hundred-dollar bundle of fur; and, next, while Bill is A1 on the river and true as steel, he's awful weak on the liquor; goes crazy, once it's in him. And I notice *you've* always refused it here. So don't stop at Troy, an' when ye get to Albany go straight past there to Vandam's. You'll have a letter that'll explain, and he'll supply the goods yer to bring back. He's a sort of a partner, and orders from him is same as from me.

"I suppose I ought to go myself, but this is the time all the fur is coming in here, an' I must be on hand to do the dickering, and there's too much moth to risk it any longer in the storehouse."

"Suppose," said Rolf, "Bill wants to stop at Troy?"

"He won't. He's all right, given he's sober. I've give him the letter."

"Couldn't you give me the letter, in case?"

"Law, Bill'd get mad and quit."

"He'll never know."

"That's so; I will." So when they paddled away, Bill had an important letter of instructions ostentanously tucked in his outer pocket. Rolf, unknown to any one else but Warren, had a duplicate, wrapped in waterproof, hidden in an inside pocket.

Bill *was* A1 on the river; a kind and gentle old woodman, much stronger than he looked. He knew the value of fur and the danger of wetting it, so he took no chances in doubtful rapids. This meant many portages and much hard labour.

I wonder if the world realizes the hard labour of the portage or carry? Let any man who seeks for light, take a fifty-pound sack of flour on his shoulders and walk a quarter of a mile on level ground in cool weather. Unless he is in training, he will find it a heavy burden long before he is half-way. Suppose, instead of a flour sack, the burden has sharp angles; the bearer is soon in torture. Suppose the weight carried be double; then the strain is far more than doubled. Suppose, finally, the road be not a quarter mile but a mile, and not on level but through swamps, over rocks, logs, and roots, and the weather not cool, but suffocating summer weather in the woods, with mosquitoes boring into every exposed part, while both hands are occupied, steadying the burden or holding on to branches for help up steep places — and then he

Start

Finish

will have some idea of the horror of the portage; and there were many of these, each one calling for six loaded and five light trips for each canoe-man. What wonder that men will often take chances in some fierce rapid, rather than to make a long carry through the fly-infested woods.

It was weighty evidence of Bill's fidelity that again and again they made a portage around rapids he had often run, because in the present case he was in sacred trust of that much prized commodity —*fur*.

Eighty miles they called it from Warren's to Albany, but there were many halts and carries which meant long delay, and a whole week was covered before Bill and Rolf had passed the settlements of Glens Falls, Fort Edward, and Schuylerville, and guided their heavily laden canoe on the tranquil river, past the little town of Troy. Loafers hailed them from the bank, but Bill turned a deaf ear to all temptation; and they pushed on happy in the thought that now their troubles were over; the last rapid was past; the broad, smooth waters extended to their port.

LIV

Albany

ONLY a man who in his youth has come at last in sight of some great city he had dreamed of all his life and longed to see, can enter into Rolf's feelings as they swept around the big bend, and Albany — *Albany*, hove in view. Albany, the first chartered city of the United States; Albany, the capital of all the Empire State; Albany, the thriving metropolis with nearly six thousand living human souls; Albany with its State House, beautiful and dignified, looking down the mighty Hudson highway that led to the open sea.

Rolf knew his Bible, and now he somewhat realized the feelings of St. Paul on that historic day when his life-long dream came true, when first he neared the Eternal City — when at last he glimpsed the towers of imperial, splendid Rome.

The long-strung docks were masted and webbed with ship rigging; the water was livened with boats and canoes; the wooden warehouses back of the docks were overtopped by wooden houses in tiers, until high above them all the Capitol itself was the fitting climax.

Rolf knew something of shipping, and amid all the masted boats his eyes fell on a strange, square-looking craft with a huge water-wheel on each side. Then, swinging into better view, he read her name, the *Clermont*, and knew that this was the famous Fulton steamer, the first of the steamboat age.

But Bill was swamped by no such emotion. Albany, Hudson, *Clermont*, and all, were familiar stories to him, and he stolidly headed the canoe for the dock he knew of old.

Loafers roosting on the snubbing posts hailed him, at first with raillery; but, coming nearer, he was recognized. "Hello, Bill; back again? Glad to see you," and there was superabundant help to land the canoe.

"Wall, wall, wall, so it's really you," said the touter of a fur house, in extremely friendly voice; "come in now, and we'll hev a drink."

"No, sir-ree," said Bill decisively, "I don't drink till business is done."

"Wall, now, Bill, here's Van Roost's not ten steps away, an' he hez tapped the finest bar'l in years."

"No, I tell ye, I'm not drinking — now."

"Wall, all right, ye know yer own business. I thought maybe ye'd be glad to see us."

"Well, ain't I?"

"Hello, Bill," and Bill's fat brother-in-law came up. "This does me good, an' yer sister is spilin' to see ye. We'll hev one on this."

"No, Sam, I ain't drinkin'; I've got biz to tend."

"Wall, hev just one to clear yer head. Then settle yer business and come back to us."

So Bill went to have *one* to clear his head. "I'll be back in two minutes, Rolf," but Rolf saw him no more for many days.

"You better come along, cub," called out a red-nosed member of the group. But Rolf shook his head.

"Here, I'll help you git them ashore," volunteered an effusive stranger, with one eye.

"I don't want help."

"How are ye goin' to handle 'em alone?"

"Well, there's one thing I'd be glad to have ye do; that is, go up there and bring Peter Vandam."

"I'll watch yer stuff while *you* go."

"No, I can't leave."

"Then go to blazes; d'y'e take me for yer errand boy?" And Rolf was left alone.

He was green at the business, but already he was realizing the power of that word *fur* and the importance of the peltry trade. Fur was the one valued product of the wilderness that only the hunter could bring. The merchants of the world were as greedy for fur as for gold, and far more so than for precious stones.

It was a commodity so light that, even in those days, a hundred weight of fur might range in value from one hundred to five thousand dollars, so that a man with a pack of fine furs was a capitalist. The profits of the business were good for trapper, very large for the trader, who doubled his first gain by paying in trade; but they were huge for the Albany middleman, and colossal for the New Yorker who shipped to London.

With such allurements, it was small wonder that more country was explored and opened for fur than fox settlement or even for gold; and there were more serious crime and high-handed robberies over the right to trade a few furs than over any other legitimate business. These things were new to Rolf within the year, but he was learning the lesson, and Warren's remarks about fur stuck in his memory with growing value. Every incident since the trip began had given them new points.

The morning passed without sign of Bill; so, when in the afternoon, some bare-legged boys came along, Rolf said to them: "Do any of ye know where Peter Vandam's house is?"

"Yeh, that's it right there," and they pointed to a large log house less than a hundred yards away.

"Do ye know him?"

"Yeh, he's my paw," said a sun-bleached freckle-face.

"If you bring him here right away, I'll give you a dime. Tell him I'm from Warren's with a cargo."

The dusty stampede that followed was like that of a mustang herd, for a dime was a dime in those days. And very soon, a tall, ruddy man appeared at the dock. He was a Dutchman in name only. At first sight he was much like the other loafers, but was bigger, and had a more business-like air when observed near at hand.

"Are you from Warren's?"

"Yes, sir."

"Alone?"

"No, sir. I came with Bill Bymus. But he went off early this morning; I haven't seen him since. I'm afraid he's in trouble."

"Where'd he go?"

"In there with some friends."

"Ha, just like him; he's in trouble all right. He'll be no good for a week. Last time he came near losing all our stuff. Now let's see what ye've got."

"Are you Mr. Peter Vandam?"

"Of course I am."

Still Rolf looked doubtful. There was a small group around, and Rolf heard several voices, "Yes, this is Peter; ye needn't a-worry." But

Rolf in the Woods

Rolf knew none of the speakers. His look of puzzlement at first annoyed then tickled the Dutchman, who exploded into a hearty guffaw.

"Wall, wall, you sure think ill of us. Here, now look at that," and he drew out a bundle of letters addressed to Master Peter Vandam. Then he displayed a gold watch inscribed on the back "Peter Vandam;" next he showed a fob seal with a scroll and an inscription, "Petrus Vandamus;" then he turned to a youngster and said, "Run, there is the Reverend Dr. Powellus, he may help us;" so the black-garbed, knee-breeched, shovel-hatted clergyman came and pompously said: "Yes, my young friend, without doubt you may rest assured that this is our very estimable parishioner, Master Peter Vandam; a man well accounted in the world of trade."

"And now," said Peter, "with the help of my birth-register and marriage-certificate, which will be placed at your service with all possible haste, I hope I may win your recognition." The situation, at first tense, had become more and more funny, and the bystanders laughed aloud. Rolf rose to it, and smiling said slowly, "I am inclined to think that you must be Master Peter Vandam, of Albany. If that's so, this letter is for you, also this cargo." And so the delivery was made.

Bill Bymus has not delivered the other letter to this day. Presumably he went to stay with his sister, but she saw little of him, for his stay at Albany was, as usual, one long spree. It was clear that, but for Rolf, there might have been serious loss of fur, and Vandam showed his appreciation by taking the lad to his own home, where the story of the difficult identification furnished ground for gusty laughter and primitive jest on many an after day.

The return cargo for Warren consisted of stores that the Vandam warehouse had in stock, and some stuff that took a day or more to collect in town.

As Rolf was sorting and packing next day, a tall, thin, well-dressed young man walked in with the air of one much at home.

"Good morrow, Peter."

"Good day to ye, sir," and they talked of crops and politics.

Presently Vandam said, "Rolf, come over here."

He came and was presented to the tall man, who was indeed very thin, and looked little better than an invalid. "This," said Peter, "is Master Henry van Cortlandt the son of his honour, the governor, and a very learned barrister. He wants to go on a long hunting trip for his health. I tell him that likely you are the man he needs."

This was so unexpected that Rolf turned red and gazed on the ground. Van Cortlandt at once began to clear things by interjecting: "You see, I'm not strong. I want to live outdoors for three months, where I can have some hunting and be beyond reach of business. Ill pay you a hundred dollars for the three months, to cover board and guidance. And providing I'm well pleased and have good hunting, I'll give you fifty dollars more when I get back to Albany."

"I'd like much to be your guide," said Rolf, "but I have a partner. I must find out if he's willing."

"Ye don't mean that drunken Bill Bymus?"

"No! My hunting partner; he's an Indian." Then, after a pause, he added, "You wouldn't go in fly-time, would you?"

"No, I want to be in peace. But any time after the first of August."

"I am bound to help Van Trumper with his harvest; that will take most of August."

As he talked, the young lawyer sized him up and said to himself, "This is my man."

And before they parted it was agreed that Rolf should come to Albany with Quonab as soon as he could return in August, to form the camping party for the governor's son.

LV

The Rescue of Bill

BALES were ready and the canoe newly gummed three days after their arrival, but still no sign of Bill. A messenger sent to the brother-in-law's home reported that he had not been seen for two days. In spite of the fact that Albany numbered nearly "six thousand living human souls," a brief search by the dock-sharps soon revealed the sinner's retreat. His worst enemy would have pitied him; a red-eyed wreck; a starved, sick and trembling weakling; conscience-stricken, for the letter intrusted to him was lost; the cargo stolen — so his comforters had said — and the raw country lad murdered and thrown out into the river. What wonder that he should shun the light of day! And when big Peter, with Rolf in the living flesh, instead of the sheriff, stood before him and told him to come out of that and get into the canoe, he wept bitter tears of repentance and vowed that *never, never, never,* as long as he lived, would he ever again let liquor touch his lips. A frame of mind which lasted in strength for nearly one day and a half, and did not entirely vanish for three.

They passed Troy without desiring to stop, and began their fight with the river. It was harder than when coming, for their course was against stream when paddling, up hill when portaging, the water was lower, the cargo was heavier, and Bill not so able. Ten days it took them to cover those eighty miles. But they came out safely, cargo and all, and landed at Warren's alive and well on the twenty-first day since leaving.

The two letters

Bill had recovered his usual form. Gravely and with pride he marched up to Warren and handed out a large letter which read outside, "Bill of Lading," and when opened, read: "The bearer of this, Bill Bymus, is no good. Don't trust him to Albany any more. (Signed) Peter Vandam."

Warren's eyes twinkled, but he said nothing. He took Rolf aside and said, "Let's have it." Rolf gave him the real letter that, unknown to Bill, he had carried, and Warren learned some things that he knew before.

Rolf's contract was for a month; it had ten days to run, and those ten days were put in weighing sugar, checking accounts, milking cows, and watching the buying of fur. Warren didn't want him to see too much of the fur business, but Rolf gathered quickly that these were the main principles: Fill the seller with liquor, if possible; "fire water for fur" was the idea; next, grade all fur as medium or second-class, when cash was demanded, but be easy as long as payment was to be in trade. That afforded many loopholes between weighing, grading, charging, and shrinkage, and finally he noticed that Albany prices were 30 to 50 per cent higher than Warren prices. Yet Warren was reckoned a first-class fellow, a good neighbour, and a member of the church. But it was understood everywhere that fur, like horseflesh, was a business with moral standards of its own.

A few days before their contract was up, Warren said: "How'd ye like to renew for a month?"

"Can't; I promised to help Van Trumper with his harvest."

"What does he pay ye?"

"Seventy-five cents a day and board."

"I'll make it a dollar."

"I've given my word," said Rolf, in surprise.

"Hev ye signed papers?"

"They're not needed. The only use of signed papers is to show ye *have* given your word," said Rolf, quoting his mother, with rising indignation.

The trader sniffed a little contemptuously and said nothing. But he realized the value of a lad who was a steady, intelligent worker, wouldn't drink, and was absolutely bound by a promise; so, after awhile, he said: "Wall, if Van don't want ye now, come back for a couple of weeks."

Early in the morning Rolf gathered the trifles he had secured for the little children and the book he had bought for Annette, a sweet story of a perfect girl who died and went to heaven, the front embellished with a thrilling wood-cut. Then he crossed the familiar five-mile portage at a pace that in an hour brought him to the lake.

The greeting at Van's was that of a brother come home.

The Rescue of Bill

"Vell, Rolf, it's goood to see ye back. It's choost vat I vanted. Hi, Marta, I told it you, yah. I say, now I hope ze good Gott send Rolf. Ach, how I am shpoil!"

Yes, indeed. The hay was ready; the barley was changing. So Rolf took up his life on the farm, doing work that a year before was beyond his strength, for the spirit of the hills was on him, with its impulse of growth, its joy in effort, its glory in strength. And all who saw the long-legged, long-armed, flat-backed youth plying fork or axe or hoe, in some sort ventured a guess: "He'll be a good 'un some day; the kind o' chap to keep friendly with."

LVI

The Sick Ox

THE Thunder Moon passed quickly by; the hay was in; the barley partly so. Day by day the white-faced oxen toiled at the creaking yoke, as the loads of hay and grain were jounced cumbrously over roots and stumps of the virgin fields. Everything was promising well, when, as usual, there came a thunderbolt out of the clear sky. Buck, the off ox, fell sick.

Those who know little about cattle have written much of the meek and patient ox. Those who know them well tell us that the ox is the "most cussedest of all cussed" animals; a sneak, a bully, a coward, a thief, a shirk, a schemer; and when he is not in mischief he is think-ing about it. The wickedest pack mule that ever bucked his burden is a pin-feathered turtle-dove compared with an average ox. There are some gentle oxen, but they are rare; most are treacherous, some are danger-ous, and these are best got rid of, as they mislead their yoke mates and mislay their drivers. Van's two oxen, Buck and Bright, manifested the usual variety and contrariety of disposition. They were all right when well handled, and this Rolf could do better than Van, for he was "raised on oxen," and Van's over voluble, sputtering, Dutch-English seemed ill comprehended of the massive yoke beasts. The simpler whip-waving and fewer orders of the Yankee were so obviously successful that Van had resigned the whip of authority and Rolf was driver.

Ordinarily, an ox driver walks on the haw (nigh or left) side, near the head of his team, shouting "gee" (right), "haw" (left), "get up," "steady," or "whoa" (stop), accompanying the order with a waving of the whip. Foolish drivers lash the oxen on the *haw* side when they wish them to *gee* — and *vice versa*; but it is notorious that all good drivers do little lashing. Spare the lash or spoil your team. So it was not long before Rolf could guide them from the top of the load, as they travelled from stook to stook in the field. This voice of command saved his life, or at least his limb, one morning, for he made a misstep that tumbled him down between the oxen and the wagon. At once the team started, but his ringing "Whoa!" brought them to a dead stop, and saved him; whereas, had it been Van's "Whoa!" it would have set them off at a run, for every shout from him meant a whiplick to follow.

Thus Rolf won the respect, if not the love, of the huge beasts; more and more they were his charge, and when, on that sad morning, in the last of the barley, Van came in, "Ach, vot shall I do! Vot shall I do! Dot Buck ox be nigh dead."

Alas! there he lay on the ground, his head sometimes raised, sometimes stretched out flat, while the huge creature uttered short moans at times.

Only four years before, Rolf had seen that same thing at Redding. The rolling eye, the working of the belly muscles, the straining and moaning. "It's colic; have you any ginger?"

"No, I haf only dot soft soap."

What soft soap had to do with ginger was not clear, and Rolf wondered if it had some rare occult medical power that had escaped his mother.

"Do you know where there's any slippery elm?"

"Yah."

"Then bring a big boiling of the bark, while I get some peppermint."

The elm bark was boiled till it made a kettleful of brown slime. The peppermint was dried above the stove till it could be powdered, and mixed with the slippery slush. Some sulphur and some soda were discovered and stirred in, on general principles, and they hastened to the huge, helpless creature in the field.

Poor Buck seemed worse than ever. He was flat on his side, with his spine humped up, moaning and straining at intervals. But now relief

was in sight — so thought the men. With a tin dipper they tried to pour some relief into the open mouth of the sufferer, who had so little appreciation that he simply taxed his remaining strength to blow it out in their faces. Several attempts ended the same way. Then the brute, in what looked like temper, swung his muzzle and dashed the whole dipper away. Next they tried the usual method, mixing it with a bran mash, considered a delicacy in the bovine world, but Buck again took notice, under pressure only, to dash it away and waste it all.

It occurred to them they might force it down his throat if they could raise his head. So they used a hand lever and a prop to elevate the muzzle, and were about to try another in-pour, when Buck leaped to his feet, and behaving like one who has been shamming, made at full gallop for the stable, nor stopped till safely in his stall, where at once he dropped in all the evident agony of a new spasm.

It is a common thing for oxen to sham sick, but this was the real thing, and it seemed they were going to lose the ox, which meant also lose a large part of the harvest.

In the stable, now, they had a better chance; they tied him, then raised his head with a lever till his snout was high above his shoulders. Now it seemed easy to pour the medicine down that long, sloping passage. But his mouth was tightly closed, any that entered his nostrils was blown afar, and the suffering beast strained at the rope till he seemed likely to strangle.

Both men and ox were worn out with the struggle; the brute was no better, but rather worse.

"Wall," said Rolf, "I've seen a good many ornery steers, but that's the orneriest I ever did handle, an' I reckon we'll lose him if he don't get that poison into him pretty soon."

Oxen never were studied as much as horses, for they were considered a temporary shift, and every farmer looked forward to replacing

them with the latter. Oxen were enormously strong, and they could flourish without grain when the grass was good; they never lost their head in a swamp hole, and ploughed steadily among all kinds of roots and stumps; but they were exasperatingly slow and eternally tricky. Bright, being the trickier of the two, was made the nigh ox, to be more under control. Ordinarily Rolf could manage Buck easily, but the present situation seemed hopeless. In his memory he harked back to Redding days, and he recalled old Eli Gooch, the ox expert, and wondered what he would have done. Then, as he sat, he caught sight of the sick ox reaching out its head and deftly licking up a few drops of bran mash that had fallen from his yoke fellow's portion. A smile spread over Rolf's face. "Just like you; you think nothing's good except it's stolen. All right; we'll see." He mixed a big dose of medicine, with bran, as before. Then he tied Bright's head so that he could not reach the ground, and set the bucket of mash half way between the two oxen. "Here ye are, Bright," he said, as a matter of form, and walked out of the stable; but, from a crack, he watched. Buck saw a chance to steal Bright's bran; he looked around; Oh, joy! his driver was away. He reached out cautiously; sniffed; his long tongue shot forth for a first taste, when Rolf gave a shout and ran in. "Hi, you old robber! Let that alone; that's for Bright."

The sick ox was very much in his own stall now, and stayed there for some time after Rolf went to resume his place at the peephole. But encouraged by a few minutes of silence, he again reached out, and hastily gulped down a mouthful of the mixture before Rolf shouted and rushed in armed with a switch to punish the thief. Poor Bright, by his efforts to reach the tempting mash, was unwittingly playing the game, for this was proof positive of its desirableness.

After giving Buck a few cuts with the switch, Rolf retired, as before. Again the sick ox waited for silence, and reaching out with greedy haste, he gulped down the rest and emptied the bucket; seeing which, Rolf ran in and gave the rogue a final trouncing for the sake of consistency.

Any one who knows what slippery elm, peppermint, soda, sulphur, colic, and ox do when thoroughly inter-incorporated will not be surprised to learn that in the morning the stable needed special treatment, and of all the mixture the ox was the only ingredient left on the active list. He was all right again, very thirsty, and not quite up to his usual standard, but, as Van said, after a careful look, "Ah, tell you vot, dot you vas a veil ox again, an' I t'ink I know not vot if you all tricky vas like Bright."

LVII

Rolf and Skookum at Albany

THE Red Moon (August) follows the Thunder Moon, and in the early part of its second week Rolf and Van, hauling in the barley and discussing the fitness of the oats, were startled by a most outrageous clatter among the hens. Horrid murder evidently was stalking abroad, and, hastening to the rescue, Rolf heard loud, angry barks; then a savage beast with a defunct "cackle party" appeared, but dropped the victim to bark and bound upon the "relief party" with ecstatic expressions of joy, in spite of Rolf's — "Skookum! You little brute!"

Yes! Quonab was back; that is, he was at the lake shore, and Skookum had made haste to plunge into the joys and gayeties of this social centre, without awaiting the formalities of greeting or even of dry-shod landing.

The next scene was — a big, high post, a long, strong chain and a small, sad dog.

"Ho, Quonab, you found your people? You had a good time?"

"Ugh," was the answer, the whole of it, and all the light Rolf got for many a day on the old man's trip to the North.

The prospect of going to Albany for Van Cortlandt was much more attractive to Quonab than that of the harvest field, so a compromise was agreed on. Callan's barley was in the stook; if all three helped Callan for three days, Callan would owe them for nine, and so it was arranged.

Again "good-bye," and Rolf, Quonab, and little dog Skookum went sailing down the Schroon toward the junction, where they left a *cache* of their supplies, and down the broadening Hudson toward Albany.

Rolf had been over the road twice; Quonab never before, yet his nose for water was so good and the sense of rapid and portage was so strong in the red man, that many times he was the pilot. "This is the way, because it must be;" "there it is deep because so narrow;" "that rapid is dangerous, because there is such a well-beaten portage trail;"

"that we can run, because I see it," or, "because there is no portage trail," etc. The eighty miles were covered in three sleeps, and in the mid-moon days of the Red Moon they landed at the dock in front of Peter Vandam's. If Quonab had any especial emotions for the occasion, he cloaked them perfectly under a calm and copper-coloured exterior of absolute immobility.

Their Albany experiences included a meeting with the governor and an encounter with a broad and burly river pirate, who, seeing a lone and peaceable-looking red man, went out of his way to insult him; and when Quonab's knife flashed out at last, it was only his recently established relations with the governor's son that saved him from some very sad results, for there were many loafers about. But burly Vandam appeared in the nick of time to halt the small mob with the warning: "Don't you know that's Mr. van Cortlandt's guide?" With the governor and Vandam to back him, Quonab soon had the mob on his side, and the dock loafer's own friends pelted him with mud as he escaped. But not a little credit is due to Skookum, for at the critical moment he had sprung on the ruffian's bare and abundant leg with such toothsome effect that the owner fell promptly backward and the knife thrust missed. It was quickly over and Quonab replaced his knife, contemptuous of the whole crowd before, during and after the incident. Not at the time, but days later, he said of his foe: "He was a talker; he was full of fear."

With the backwoods only thirty miles away, and the unbroken wilderness one hundred, it was hard to believe how little Henry van Cortlandt knew of the woods and its life. He belonged to the ultra-fashionable set, and it was rather their pose to affect ignorance of the savage world and its ways. But he had plenty of common-sense to fall back on, and the inspiring example of Washington, equally at home in the nation's Parliament, the army intrenchment, the glittering ball room, or the hunting lodge of the Indian, was a constant reminder that

the perfect man is a harmonious development of mind, morals, and physique.

His training had been somewhat warped by the ultra-classic fashion of the times, so he persisted in seeing in Quonab a sort of discoloured, barbaric clansman of Alaric or a camp follower of Xenophon's host, rather than an actual living, interesting, native American, exemplifying in the highest degree the sinewy, alert woodman, and the saturated mystic and pantheist of an age bygone and out of date, combined with a middle-measure intelligence. And Rolf, tall, blue-eyed with brown, curling hair, was made to pose as the youthful Achilles, rather than as a type of America's best young manhood, cleaner, saner, and of far higher ideals and traditions than ever were ascribed to Achilles by his most blinded worshippers. It recalled the case of Wordsworth and Southey living side by side in England; Southey, the famous, must needs seek in ancient India for material to write his twelve-volume romance that no one ever looks at; Wordsworth, the unknown, wrote of the things of his own time, about his own door, and produced immortal verse.

What should we think of Homer, had he sung his impressions of the ancient Egyptians? or of Thackeray, had he novelized the life of the Babylonians? It is an ancient blindness, with an ancient wall to bruise one's head. It is only those who seek ointment of the consecrated clay that gives back sight, who see the shining way at their feet, who beat their face against no wall, who safely climb the heights. Henry van Cortlandt was a man of rare parts, of every advantage, but still he had been taught steadfastly to live in the past. His eyes were yet to be opened. The living present was not his — but yet to be.

The young lawyer had been assembling his outfit at Vandam's warehouse, for, in spite of scoffing friends, he *knew* that Rolf was corning back to him.

When Rolf saw the pile of stuff that was gathered for that outfit, he stared at it aghast, then looked at Vandam, and together they roared. There was everything for light housekeeping and heavy doctoring, even chairs, a wash stand, a mirror, a mortar, and a pestle. Six canoes could scarcely have carried the lot.

"'Tain't so much the young man as his mother," explained Big Pete. "At first I tried to make 'em understand, but it was no use; so I says, 'All right, go ahead, as long as there's room in the warehouse.' I reckon I'll set on the fence and have some fun seein' Rolf entangle the affair."

"Phew, pheeeww — ph-e-e-e-e-w," was all Rolf could say in answer. But at last, "Wall, there's always a way. I sized *him* up as pretty level headed. We'll see."

There *was* a way and it was easy, for, in a secret session, Rolf, Pete, and Van Cortlandt together sorted out the things needed. A small tent, blankets, extra clothes, guns, ammunition, delicate food for three months, a few medicines and toilet articles — a pretty good load for one canoe, but a trifle compared with the mountain of stuff piled up on the floor.

"Now, Mr. van Cortlandt," said Rolf, "will you explain to your mother that we are going on with this so as to travel quickly, and will send back for the rest as we need it?"

A quiet chuckle was now heard from Big Pete. "Good! I wondered how he'd settle it."

The governor and his lady saw them off; therefore, there was a crowd. The mother never before had noted what a frail and dangerous thing a canoe is. She cautioned her son never to venture out alone, and to be sure that he rubbed his chest with the pectoral balm she had made from such and such a famous receipt, the one that saved the life but not the limb of old Governor Stuyvesant, and come right home if you catch a cold; and wait at the first camp till the other things come, and (in a whisper) keep away from that horrid red Indian with the knife, and never fail to let every one know who you are, and write regularly, and don't forget to take your calomel Monday, Wednesday, and Friday, alternating with Peruvian bark Tuesday, Thursday, and Saturday, and squills on Sunday, except every other week, when he should devote Tuesdays, Fridays, and Sundays to rhubarb and catnip tea, except in the full moon, when the catnip was to be replaced with graveyard bergamot and the squills with opodeldoc in which an iron nail had been left for a week.

So Henry was embraced, Rolf was hand-shaken, Quonab was nodded at, Skookum was wisely let alone, and the trim canoe swung from the dock. Amid hearty cheers, farewells, and "God speed ye's" it breasted the flood for the North.

Rolf and Skookum at Albany

And on the dock, with kerchief to her eyes, stood the mother, weeping to think that her boy was going far, far away from his home and friends in dear, cultured, refined Albany, away, away, to that remote and barbarous inaccessible region almost to the shore land of Lake Champlain.

LVIII

Back to Indian Lake

YOUNG Van Cortlandt, six feet two in his socks and thirty-four inches around the chest, was, as Rolf long afterward said, "awful good raw material, but awful raw." Two years out of college, half of which had been spent at the law, had done little but launch him as a physical weakling and a social star. But his mental make-up was more than good; it was of large promise. He lacked neither courage nor sense, and the course he now followed was surely the best for man-making.

Rolf never realized how much a farmer-woodman-canoe-man-hunter-camper had to know, until now he met a man who did not know anything, nor dreamed how many wrong ways there were of doing a job, till he saw his new companion try it.

There is no single simple thing that is a more complete measure of one's woodcraft than the lighting of a fire. There are a dozen good ways and a thousand wrong ones. A man who can light thirty fires on thirty successive days with thirty matches or thirty sparks from flint and steel is a graduated woodman, for the feat presupposes experience of many years and the skill that belongs to a winner.

When Quonab and Rolf came back from taking each a load over the first little portage, they found Van Cortlandt getting ready for a fire with a great, solid pile of small logs, most of them wet and green. He knew how to use flint and steel, because that was the established household way of the times. Since childhood had he lighted the candle at home by this primitive means. When his pile of soggy logs was ready, he struck his flint, caught a spark on the tinder that is always kept on hand, blew it to a flame, thrust in between two of the wet logs, waited for all to blaze up, and wondered why the tiny blaze went out at once, no matter how often he tried.

When the others came back, Van Cortlandt remarked: "It doesn't seem to burn." The Indian turned away in silent contempt. Rolf had hard work to keep the forms of respect, until the thought came: "I suppose I looked just as big a fool in his world at Albany."

"See," said he, "green wood and wet wood won't do, but yonder is some birch bark and there's a pine root." He took his axe and cut a few sticks from the root, then used his knife to make a sliver-fuzz of each; one piece, so resinous that it would not whittle, he smashed with the back of the axe into a lot of matchwood. With a handful of finely shredded birch bark he was now quite ready. A crack of the flint, a blowing of the spark caught on the tinder from the box, a little flame that at once was magnified by the birch bark, and in a minute the pine splinters made a sputtering fire. Quonab did not even pay Van Cortlandt the compliment of using one of his logs. He cut a growing poplar, built a fireplace of the green logs around the blaze that Rolf had made, and the meal was ready in a few minutes.

Van Cortlandt was not a fool; merely it was all new to him. But his attention was directed to fire-making now, and long before they reached their cabin he had learned this, the first of the woodman's arts — he could lay and light a fire. And when, weeks later, he not only made the flint fire, but learned in emergency to make the rubbing stick spark, his cup of joy was full. He felt he was learning.

Determined to be in everything, now he paddled all day; at first with vigour, then mechanically, at last feebly and painfully. Late in the afternoon they made the first long portage; it was a quarter mile. Rolf took a hundred pounds, Quonab half as much more, Van Cortlandt tottered slowly behind with his pill-kit and his paddle. That night, on his ample mattress, he slept the sleep of utter exhaustion. Next day he did little and said nothing. It came on to rain; he raised a huge umbrella and crouched under it till the storm was over. But the third day he began to show signs of new life, and before they reached the Schroon's mouth, on the fifth day, his young frame was already responding to the elixir of the hills.

Back to Indian Lake

It was very clear that they could not take half of the stuff that they had *cachéd* at the Schroon's mouth, so that a new adjustment was needed and still a *cache* to await another trip.

That night as they sat by their sixth camp fire, Van Cortlandt pondered over the recent days, and they seemed many since he had left home. He felt much older and stronger. He felt not only less strange, but positively intimate with the life, the river, the canoe, and his comrades; and, pleased with his winnings, he laid his hand on Skookum, slumbering near, only to arouse in response a savage growl, as that important animal arose and moved to the other side of the fire. Never did small dog give tall man a more deliberate snub. "You can't do that with Skookum; you must wait till he's ready," said Rolf.

The journey up the Hudson with its "mean" waters and its "carries" was much as before. Then they came to the eagle's nest and the easy waters of Jesup's River, and without important incident they landed at the cabin. The feeling of "home again" spread over the camp and every one was gay.

LIX

Van Cortlandt's Drugs

"AIN'T ye feeling' all right?" said Rolf, one bright, calomel morning, as he saw Van Cortlandt preparing his daily physic.

"Why, yes; I'm feeling fine; I'm better every day," was the jovial reply.

"Course I don't know, but my mother used to say: 'Med'cine's the stuff makes a sick man well, an' a well man sick.'"

"My mother and your mother would have fought at sight, as you may judge. B-u-t," he added with reflective slowness, and a merry twinkle in his eye, "if things were to be judged by their product, I am afraid your mother would win easily," and he laid his long, thin, scrawny hand beside the broad, strong hand of the growing youth.

"Old Sylvanne wasn't far astray when he said: 'There aren't any sick, 'cept them as *thinks* they are,'" said Rolf.

"I suppose I *ought* to begin to taper off," was the reply. But the tapering was very sudden. Before a week went by, it seemed desirable to go back for the stuff left in *cache* on the Schroon, where, of course, it was subject to several risks. There seemed no object in taking Van Cortlandt back, but they could not well leave him alone. He went. He had kept time with fair regularity — calomel, rhubarb; calomel, rhubarb; calomel, rhubarb, squills — but Rolf's remarks had sunk into his intelligence, as a red-hot shot will sink through shingles, letting in light and creating revolution.

This was a rhubarb morning. He drank his potion, then, carefully stoppering the bottle, he placed it with its companions in a box and stowed that near the middle of the canoe. "I'll be glad when it's finished," he said reflectively; "I don't believe I need it now. I wish sometimes I could run short of it all."

That was what Rolf had been hoping for. Without such a remark, he would not have dared do as he did. He threw the tent cover over the canoe amidships, causing the unstable craft to cant: "That won't do," he remarked, and took out several articles, including the medicine chest, put them ashore under the bushes, and, when he replaced them, contrived that the medicine should be forgotten.

Next morning Van Cortlandt, rising to prepare his calomel, got a shock to find it not.

"It strikes me," says Rolf, "the last time I saw that, it was on the bank when we trimmed the canoe."

Yes, there could be no doubt of it. Van must live his life in utter druglessness for a time. It gave him somewhat of a scare, much like that a young swimmer gets when he finds he has drifted away from his floats; and, like that same beginner, it braced him to help himself. So Van found that he *could swim without corks*.

They made a rapid journey down, and in a week they were back with the load.

There was the potion chest where they had left it. Van Cortlandt picked it up with a sheepish smile, and they sat down for evening meal. Presently Rolf said: "I mind once I seen three little hawks in a nest together. The mother was teaching them to fly. Two of them started off all right, and pretty soon were scooting among the tree-tops. The other was scared. He says: 'No, mother, I never did fly, and I'm scared I'd get killed if I tried.' At last the mother got mad and shoved him over. As soon as he felt he was gone, he spread out his wings to save himself. The wings were all right enough, and long before he struck the ground, he was flying."

LX

Van Cortlandt's Adventure

THE coming of Van had compelled the trappers to build a new and much larger cabin. When they were planning it, the lawyer said: "If I were you, I'd make it twenty by thirty, with a big stone fireplace."

"Why?"

"I might want to come back some day and bring a friend."

Rolf looked at him keenly. Here was an important possibility, but it was too difficult to handle such large logs without a team; so the new cabin was made fifteen by twenty, and the twenty-foot logs were very slim indeed. Van Cortlandt took much trouble to fix it up inside with two white birch bedsteads, balsam beds, and basswood mats on the floor.

After the first depression, he had recovered quickly since abandoning his apothecary diet, and now he was more and more in their life, one of themselves. But Quonab never liked him. The incident of the fire-making was one of many which reduced him far below zero in the red man's esteem. When he succeeded with the rubbing-stick fire, he rose a few points; since then he had fallen a little, nearly every day, and now an incident took place which reduced him even below his original low level.

In spite of his admirable perseverance, Van Cortlandt failed in his attempts to get a deer. This was depressing and unfortunate because of the Indian's evident contempt, shown, not in any act, but rather in his avoiding Van and never noticing him; while Van, on his part, discovered that, but for this, that, and the other negligence on Quonab's part, he himself might have done thus and so.

To relieve the situation, Rolf said privately to the Indian, "Can't we find some way of *giving* him a deer?"

"Humph," was the voluble reply.

"I've heard of that jack-light trick. Can ye work it?"

"Ugh!"

So it was arranged.

Quonab prepared a box which he filled with sand. On three sides of it he put a screen of bark, eighteen inches high, and in the middle he made a good torch of pine knots with a finely frizzled lighter of birch bark. Ordinarily this is placed on the bow of the canoe, and, at the right moment, is lighted by the sportsman. But Quonab distrusted Van as a lighter, so placed this ancient search-light on the after thwart in front of himself and pointing forward, but quartering.

The scheme is to go along the lake shore about dark, as the deer come to the water to drink or eat lily pads. As soon as a deer is located by the sound, the canoe is silently brought to the place, the torch is lighted, the deer stops to gaze at this strange sunrise; its body is not usually visible in the dim light, but the eyes reflect the glare like two lamps; and now the gunner, with a volley of buckshot, plays his part. It is the easiest and most unsportsmanlike of all methods. It has long been declared illegal; and was especially bad, because it victimized chiefly the does and fawns.

But now it seemed the proper way to "save Van Cortlandt's face."

So forth they went; Van armed with his double-barrelled shotgun and carrying in his belt a huge and ornamental hunting knife, the badge of woodcraft or of idiocy, according as you took Van's view or Quonab's. Rolf stayed in camp.

At dusk they set out, a slight easterly breeze compelling them to take the eastern shore, for the deer must not smell them. As they silently crossed the lake, the guide's quick eye caught sight of a long wimple on the surface, across the tiny ripples of the breeze — surely the wake of some large animal, most likely a deer. Good luck. Putting on all speed,

he sent the canoe flying after it, and in three or four minutes they sighted a large, dark creature moving fast to escape, but it was low on the water, and had no horns. They could not make out what it was. Van sat tensely gazing, with gun in hand, but the canoe overran the swimmer; it disappeared under the prow, and a moment later there scrambled over the gunwale a *huge black fisher*.

"Knife," cried Quonab, in mortal fear that Van would shoot and blow a hole throught the canoe.

The fisher went straight at the lawyer hissing and snarling with voice like a bear.

Van grasped his knife, and then and there began a most extraordinary fight; holding his assailant off as best he could, he stabbed again and again with that long blade. But the fisher seemed cased in iron. The knife glanced off or was solidly stopped again and again, while the fierce, active creature, squirming, struggling, clawing, and tearing had wounded the lawyer in a dozen places. Jab, jab went the knife in vain. The fisher seemed to gain in strength and fury. It fastened on Van's leg just below the knee, and growled and tore like a bulldog. Van seized its throat in both hands and choked with all his strength. The brute at length let go and sprang back to attack again, when Quonab saw his chance and felled it with a blow of the paddle across the nose. It tumbled forward; Van lunged to avoid what seemed a new attack, and in a moment the canoe upset, and all were swimming for their lives.

As luck would have it, they had drifted to the west side and the water was barely six feet deep. So Quonab swam ashore holding onto a paddle, and hauling the canoe, while Van waded ashore, hauling the dead fisher by the tail.

Quonab seized a drift pole and stuck it in the mud as near the place as possible, so they could come again in daylight to get the guns; then silently paddled back to camp.

Chestnut Oak

Rolf in the Woods

Next day, thanks to the pole, they found the plane and recovered first Van's gun, second, that mighty hunting knife; and learned to the amazement and disgust of all that it had not been out of its sheath: during all that stabbing and slashing, the keen edge was hidden and the knife was wearing its thick, round scabbard of leather and studs of brass.

LXI

Rolf Learns Something from Van

"A man can't handle hit own case, any more than a delirious doctor kin give himself the right physic."

— *The Sayings of Si Sylvanne*

HOWEVER superior Rolf might feel in the canoe or the woods, there was one place where Van Cortlandt took the lead, and that was in the long talks they had by the campfire or in Van's own shanty which Quonab rarely entered.

The most interesting subjects treated in these were ancient Greece and modern Albany. Van Cortlandt was a good Greek scholar, and, finding an intelligent listener, he told the stirring tales of royal Ilion, Athens, and Per-gamos, with the loving enthusiasm of one whom the teachers found it easy to instruct in classic lore. And when he recited or intoned the rolling Greek heroics of the siege of Troy, Rolf listened with an interest that was strange, considering that he knew not a word of it. But he said, "It sounded like real talk, and the tramp of men that were all astir with something big a-doing."

Albany and politics, too, were vital strains, and life at the Government House, with the struggling rings and cabals, social and political. These were extraordinarily funny and whimsical to Rolf. No doubt because Van Cortlandt presented them that way. And he more than once wondered how rational humans could waste their time in such tom-foolery and childish things as all conventionalities seemed to be. Van Cortlandt smiled at his remarks, but made no answer for long.

One day, the first after the completion of Van Cortlandt's cabin, as the two approached, the owner opened the door and stood aside for Rolf to enter.

"Go ahead," said Rolf.

"After you," was the polite reply.

"Oh, go on," rejoined the lad, in mixed amusement and impatience.

Van Cortlandt touched his hat and went in.

Inside, Rolf turned squarely and said: "The other day you said there was a reason for all kinds o' social tricks; now will you tell me what the dickens is the why of all these funny-do's? It 'pears to me a free-born American didn't ought to take off his hat to any one but God."

Van Cortlandt chuckled softly and said: "You may be very sure that everything that is done in the way of social usage is the result of common-sense, with the exception of one or two things that have continued after the reason for them has passed, like the buttons you have behind on your coat; they were put there originally to button the tails out of the way of your sword. Sword wearing and using have passed away, but still you see the buttons.

"As to taking off your hat to no man: it depends entirely on what you mean by it; and, being a social custom, you must accept its social meaning.

"In the days of knight errantry, every one meeting a stranger had to suppose him an enemy; ten to one he was. And the sign and proof of friendly intention was raising the right hand without a weapon in it. The hand was raised high, to be seen as far as they could shoot with a bow, and a further proof was added when they raised the vizor and exposed the face. The danger of the highway continued long after knights ceased to wear armour; so, with the same meaning, the same gesture was used, but with a lifting of the hat. If a man did not do it, he was either showing contempt, or hostility for the other, or proving himself an ignorant brute. So, in all civilized countries, lifting the hat is a sign of mutual confidence and respect."

"Well! that makes it all look different. But why should you touch your hat when you went ahead of me just now?"

Rolf Learns Something from Van

"Because this is my house; you are my guest. I am supposed to serve you in reasonable ways and give you precedence. Had I let you open my door for me, it would have been putting you in the place of my servant; to balance that, I give you the sign of equality and respect."

"H'm," said Rolf, "'it just shows,' as old Sylvanne sez, 'this yer steel-trap, hair-trigger, cocksure jedgment don't do. An' the more a man learns, the less sure he gits. An' things as hez lasted a long time ain't liable to be on a rotten foundation.'"

LXII

The Charm of Song

WITH a regular *túm ta túm ta*, came a weird sound from the sunrise rock one morning, as Van slipped out of his cabin.

"Ag-aj-wáy-o-sáy Pem-o-say Gezhik-om ena-bid ah-keen Ena-bid ah-keen"

"What's he doing, Rolf?"

"That's his sunrise prayer," was the answer.

"Do you know what it means?"

"Yes, it ain't much; jest 'Oh, thou that walkest in the sky in the morning, I greet thee.'"

"Why, I didn't know Indians had such performances; that's exactly like the priests of Osiris. Did any one teach him? I mean any white folk."

"No, it's always been the Indian way. They have a song or a prayer for most every big event, sunrise, sunset, moonrise, good hunting, and another for when they're sick, or when they're going on a journey, or when their heart is bad."

"You astonish me. I had no idea they were so human. It carries me back to the temple of Delphi. It is worthy of Cassandra of Ilion. I supposed an Indians were just savage Indians that hunted till their bellies were full and slept till they were empty again."

"H'm," rejoined Rolf, with a gentle laugh. "I see you also have been doing some 'hair-trigger, steel-trap, cocksure jedgin'.'"

"I wonder if he'd like to hear some of my songs?"

"It's worth trying; anyway, I would," said Rolf.

Rolf in the Woods

That night, by the fire, Van sang the "Gay Cavalier," "The Hunting of John Peel," and "Bonnie Dundee." He had a fine baritone voice. He was most acceptable in the musical circles of Albany. Rolf was delighted, Skookum moaned sympathetically, and Quonab sat nor moved till the music was over. He said nothing, but Rolf felt that it was a point gained, and, trying to follow it up, said:

"Here's your drum, Quonab; won't you sing 'The Song of the Wabanaki?'" But it was not well timed, and the Indian shook his head.

"Say, Van," said Rolf, (Van Cortlandt had suggested this abbreviation) "you'll never stand right with Quonab till you kill a deer."

"I've done some trying."

"Well, now, we'll go out to-morrow evening and try once more. What do you think of the weather, Quonab?"

"Storm begin noon and last three days," was the brief answer, as the red man walked away.

"That settles it," said Rolf, "we wait."

Van was surprised, and all the more so when in an hour the sky grew black and heavy rain set in, with squalls.

"How in the name of Belshazzar's weather bugler does he tell?"

"I guess you better *not* ask him, if you want to know. I'll find out and tell you later."

Rolf learned, not easily or at single talk:

"Yesterday the chipmunks worked hard; to-day there are none to be seen.

"Yesterday the loons were wailing; now they are still, and no small birds are about.

"Yesterday it was a yellow sunrise; to-day a rosy dawn.

"Last night the moon changed and had a thick little ring.

"It has not rained for ten days, and this is the third day of easterly winds.

"There was no dew last night. I saw Tongue Mountain at daybreak; my tom-tom will not sing.

"The smoke went three ways at dawn, and Skookum's nose was hot."

So they rested, not knowing, but forced to believe, and it was not till the third day that the sky broke; the west wind began to pay back its borrowings from the east, and the saying was proved that "three days' rain will empty any sky."

The Charm of Song

That evening, after their meal, Rolf and Van launched the canoe and paddled down the lake. A mile from camp they landed, for this was a favourite deer run. Very soon Rolf pointed to the ground. He had found a perfectly fresh track, but Van seemed not to comprehend. They went along it, Rolf softly and silently, Van with his long feet and legs making a dangerous amount of clatter. Rolf turned and whispered, "That won't do. You must not stand on dry sticks." Van endeavoured to move more cautiously and thought he was doing well, but Rolf found it very trying to his parience and began to understand how Quonab had felt about himself a year ago. "See," said Rolf, "lift your legs so; don't turn your feet out that way. Look at the place before you put it down again; feel with your toe to make sure there is no dead stick, then wriggle it down to the solid ground. Of course, you'd do better in moccasins. Never brush past any branches; lift them aside and don't let them scratch; ease them back to the place; never try to bend a dry branch; go around it," etc. Van had not thought of these things, but now he grasped them quickly, and they made a wonderful improvement in his way of going.

They came again to the water's edge; across a littie bay Rolf sighted at once the form of a buck, perfectly still, gazing their way, wondering, no doubt, what made those noises.

"Here's your chance," he whispered.

"Where?" was the eager query.

"There; see that gray and white thing?"

"I can't see him."

For five minutes Rolf tried in vain to make his friend see that statuesque form; for five minutes it never moved. Then, sensing danger, the buck gave a bound and was lost to view.

It was disheartening. Rolf sat down, nearly disgusted; then one of Sylvanne's remarks came to him: "It don't prove any one a fool, coz he can't play your game." Presently Rolf said, "Van, hev ye a book with ye?"

Rolf in the Woods

"Yes, I have my Virgil."

"Read me the first page."

Van read it, holding the book six inches from his nose.

"Let's see ye read this page there," and Rolf held it up four feet away.

"I can't; it's nothing but a dim white spot."

"Well, can ye see that loon out there?"

"You mean that long, dark thing in the bay?"

"No, that's a pine log close to," said Rolf, with a laugh, "away out half a mile."

"No, I can't see anything but shimmers."

"I thought so. It's no use your trying to shoot deer till ye get a pair of specs to fit yer eyes. You have brains enough, but you haven't got the eyesight of a hunter. You stay here till I go see if I have any luck."

Rolf melted into the woods. In twenty minutes Van heard a shot and very soon Rolf reappeared, carrying a two-year-old buck, and they returned to their camp by nightfall. Quonab glanced at their faces as they passed carrying the little buck. They tried to look inscrutable. But the Indian was not deceived. He gave out nothing but a sizzling "Humph!"

LXIII

The Redemption of Van

"WHEN things is looking black as black can be, it's a sure sign of luck corning your way." So said Si Sylvanne, and so it proved to Van Cortlandt. The Moon of the Falling Leaves was waning, October was nearly over, the day of his return to Albany was near, as he was to go out in time for the hunters to return in open water. He was wonderfully improved in strength and looks. His face was brown and ruddy. He had abandoned all drugs, and had gained fully twenty pounds in weight. He had learned to make a fire, paddle a canoe, and go through the woods in semi-silence. His scholarly talk had given him large place in Rolf's esteem, and his sweet singing had furnished a tiny little shelf for a modicum of Quonab's respect. But his attempts to get a deer were failures. "You come back next year with proper, farsight glasses and you'll be all right," said Rolf; and that seemed the one ray of hope.

The three days' storm had thrown so many trees that the hunters decided it would be worth while making a fast trip down to Eagle's Nest, to cut such timber as might have fallen across the stream, and so make an easy way for when they should have less time.

The surmise was quite right. Much new-fallen timber was now across the channel. They chopped over twenty-five trunks before they reached Eagle's Nest at noon, and, leaving the river in better shape than ever it was, they turned, for the swift, straight, silent run of ten miles home.

As they rounded the last point, a huge black form in the water loomed to view. Skookum's bristles rose. Quonab whispered, "Moose! Shoot quick!" Van was the only one with a gun. The great black beast stood for a moment, gazing at them with wide-open eyes, ears, and nostrils, then shook his broad horns, wheeled, and dashed for the shore. Van fired and the bull went down with a mighty splash among the lilies.

Rolf in the Woods

Rolf and Skookum let off a succession of most unhunterlike yells of triumph. But the giant sprang up again and reached the shore, only to fall to Van Cortlandt's second barrel. Yet the stop was momentary; he rose and dashed into the cover. Quonab turned the canoe at once and made for the land.

A great sob came from the bushes, then others at intervals. Quonab showed his teeth and pointed. Rolf seized his rifle, Skookum sprang from the boat, and a little later was heard letting off his war-cry in the bushes not far away.

The men rushed forward, guns in hand, but Quonab called, "Look out! Maybe he waiting."

"If he is, he'll likely get one of us," said Rolf, with a light laugh, for he had some hearsay knowledge of moose.

Covered each by a tree, they waited till Van had reloaded his double-barrelled, then cautiously approached. The great frothing sobs had resounded from time to time.

Skookum's voice also was heard in the thicket, and when they neared and glimpsed the place, it was to see the monster on the ground, lying at full length, flinging up his head at times when he uttered that horrid sound of pain.

The Indian sent a bullet through the moose's brain; then all was still, the tragedy was over.

But now their attention was turned to Van Cortlandt. He reeled, staggered, his knees trembled, his face turned white, and, to save himself from falling, he sank onto a log. Here he covered his face with his hands, his feet beat the ground, and his shoulders heaved up and down.

The others said nothing. They knew by the signs and the sounds that it was only through a mighty effort that young Van Cortlandt, grown man as he was, could keep himself from hysterical sobs and tears.

Not then, but the next day it was that Quonab said: "It comes to some *after* they kill, to some *before*, as it came to you, Rolf; to me

it came the day I killed my first chipmunk, that time when I stole my father's medicine."

They had ample work for several hours now, to skin the game and save the meat. It was fortunate they were so near home. A marvellous change there was in the atmosphere of the camp. Twice Quonab spoke to Van Cortlandt, as the latter laboured with them to save and store the meat of *his moose.* He was rubbed, doped, soiled, and anointed with its flesh, hair, and blood, and that night, as they sat by their camp fire, Skookum arose, stretched, yawned, walked around deliberately, put his nose in the lawyer's hand, gave it a lick, then lay down by his feet. Van Cortlandt glanced at Rolf, a merry twinkle was in the eyes of both. "It's all right. You can pat Skookum now, without risk of being crippled. He's sized you up. You are one of us at last;" and Quonab looked on with two long ivory rows a-gleaming in his smile.

LXIV

Dinner at the Governor's

WAS ever there a brighter blazing sunrise after such a night of gloom? Not only a deer, but the biggest of all deer, and Van himself the only one of the party that had ever killed a moose. The skin was removed and afterward made into a hunting coat for the victor. The head and horns were carefully preserved to be carried back to Albany, where they were mounted and still hang in the hall of a later generation of the name. The final days at the camp were days of happy feeling; they passed too soon, and the long-legged lawyer, bronzed and healthy looking, took his place in their canoe for the flying trip to Albany. With an empty canoe and three paddles (two and one half, Van said), they flew down the open stretch of Jesup's River in something over two hours, and camped that night fully thirty-five miles from their cabin. The next day they nearly reached the Schroon and in a week they rounded the great bend, and Albany hove in view.

How Van's heart did beat! How he did exult to come in triumph home, reestablished in health and strengthened in every way. They were sighted and recognized. Messengers were seen running; a heavy gun was fired, the flag run up on the Capitol, bells set a-ringing, many people came running, and more flags ran up on vessels.

A great crowd gathered by the dock.

"There's father, and mother too!" shouted Van, waving his hat.

"Hurrah," and the crowd took it up, while the bells went jingle, jangle, and Skookum in the bow sent back his best in answer.

The canoe was dragged ashore. Van seized his mother in his arms, as she cried: "My boy, my boy, my darling boy! How well you look. Oh, why didn't you write? But, thank God, you are back again, and looking so healthy and strong. I know you took your squills and opodeldoc. Thank God for that! Oh, I'm so happy! My boy, my boy! There's nothing like squills and God's blessing."

Rolf in the Woods

Rolf and Quonab were made to feel that they had a part in it all. The governor shook them warmly by the hand, and then a friendly voice was heard: "Wall, boy, here ye air agin; growed a little, settin' up and sassin' back, same as ever." Rolf turned to see the gigantic, angular form and kindly face of grizzly old Si Sylvanne and was still more surprised to hear him addressed "senator."

"Yes," said the senator, "one o' them freak elections that sometimes hits right; great luck for Albany, wa'nt it?"

"Ho," said Quonab, shaking the senator's hand, while Skookum looked puzzled and depressed.

"Now, remember," said the governor, addressing the Indian, the lad, and the senator, "we expect you to dine to-night at the mansion; seven o'clock."

Then the terror of the dragon conventionality, that guards the gate and hovers over the feast, loomed up in Rolf's imagination. He sought a private word with Van. "I'm afraid I have no fit clothes; I shan't know how to behave," he said.

"Then I'll show you. The first thing is to be perfectly clean and get a shave; put on the best clothes you have, and be sure they're clean; then you come at exactly seven o'clock, knowing that every one is going to be kind to you and you're bound to have a good time. As to any other 'funny-do' you watch me, and you'll have no trouble."

So when the seven o'clock assemblage came, and guests were ascending the steps of the governor's mansion, there also mounted a tall, slim youth, an easy-pacing Indian, and a prick-eared, yellow dog. Young Van Cortlandt was near the door, on watch to save them any embarrass-

ment. But what a swell he looked, cleanshaven, ruddy, tall, and handsome in the uniform of an American captain, surrounded by friends and immensely popular. How different it all was from that lonely cabin by the lake.

A butler who tried to remove Skookum was saved from mutilation by the intervention first of Quonab and next of Van; and when they sat down, this uncompromising four-legged child of the forest ensconced himself under Quonab's chair and growled whenever the silk stockings of the footman seemed to approach beyond the line of true respect.

Young Van Cortlandt was chief talker at the dinner, but a pompous military man was prominent in the company.

Dinner at the Governor's

Once or twice Rolf was addressed by the governor or Lady Van Cortlandt, and had to speak to the whole table; his cheeks were crimson, but he knew what he wanted to say and stopped when it was said, so suffered no real embarrassment.

After what seemed an interminable feast of countless dishes and hours' duration, an extraordinary change set in. Led by the hostess, all stood up, the chairs were lifted out of their way, and the ladies trooped into another room; the doors were closed, and the men sat down again at the end next the governor.

Van stayed by Rolf and explained: "This is another social custom that began with a different meaning. One hundred years ago, every man got drunk at every formal dinner, and carried on in a way that the ladies did not care to see, so to save their own feelings and give the men a free rein, the ladies withdrew. Nowadays, men are not supposed to indulge in any such orgy, but the custom continues, because it gives the men a chance to smoke, and the ladies a chance to discuss matters that do not interest the men. So again you see it is backed by common-sense."

This proved the best part of the dinner to Rolf. There was a peculiar sense of over-politeness, of insincerity, almost, while the ladies were present; the most of the talking had been done by young Van Cortlandt and certain young ladies, assisted by some very gay young men and the general. Their chatter was funny, but nothing more. Now a different air was on the group; different subjects were discussed, and by different men, in a totally different manner.

"We've stood just about all we can stand," said the governor, alluding to an incident newly told, of a British frigate boarding an American merchant vessel by force and carrying off half her crew, under pretence that they were British seamen in disguise. "That's been going on for three years now. It's either piracy or war, and, in either case, it's our duty to fight."

"Jersey's dead against war," said a legislator from down the river.

"Jersey always was dead against everything that was for the national good, sir," said a red-faced, puffy, military man, with a husky voice, a rolling eye, and a way of ending every sentence in "sir."

"So is Connecticut," said another. "They say, 'Look at all our defenceless coasts and harbour towns.'"

"They're not risking as much as New York," answered the governor, "with her harbours all the way up the Hudson and her back door open to invasion from Canada."

"Fortunately, sir, Pennyslvania, Maryland, and the West have not forgotten the glories of the past. All I ask — is a chance to show what we can do, sir. I long for the smell of powder once more, sir."

"I understand that President Madison has sent several protests, and, in spite of Connecticut and New Jersey, will send an ultimatum within three months. He believes that Britain has all she can manage, with Napoleon and his allies battering at her doors, and will not risk a war.

"It's my opinion," said Sylvanne, "that these Englishmen is too pig-headed an' ornery to care a whoop in hell whether we get mad or not. They've a notion Paul Jones is dead, but I reckon we've got plenty of the breed only waitin' a chance. Mor'n twenty-five of our merchantmen wrecked each year through being stripped of their crews by a 'friendly power.' 'Pears to me we couldn't be worse off going to war, an' might be a dum sight better."

"Your home an' holdings are three hundred safe miles from the seacoast," objected the man from Manhattan.

"Yes, and right next to Canada," was the reply.

"The continued insults to our flag, sir, and the personal indignities offered to our people are even worse than the actual loss in ships and goods. It makes my blood fairly boil," and the worthy general looked the part as his purple jowl quivered over his white cravat.

"Gosh all hemlock! The one pricks, but t'other festers. It's tarnal sure you steal a man's dinner and tell him he's one o' nature's noblemen, he's more apt to love you than if you give him five dollars to keep out o' your sight," said Sylvanne, with slow emphasis.

"There's something to be said on the other side," said the timid one. "You surely allow that the British government is trying to do right, and after all we must admit that that Jilson affair reflected very little credit on our own administration."

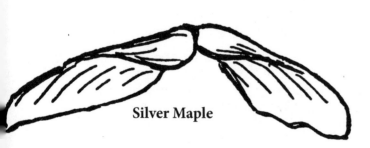

Silver Maple

Dinner at the Governor's

"A man ken make one awful big mistake an' still be all right, but he can't go on making a little mistake every day right along an' be fit company for a clean crowd," retorted the new senator.

At length the governor rose and led the way to the drawing-room, where they rejoined the ladies and the conversation took on a different colour and weight, by which it lost all value for those who knew not the art of twittering persiflage and found less joy in a handkerchief flirtation than in the nation's onward march. Rolf and Quonab enjoyed it now about as much as Skookum had done all the time.

Hickory

LXV

The Grebes and the Singing Mouse

QUONAB puzzled long over the amazing fact that young Van Cortlandt had evident high standing "in his own tribe." "He must be a wise counsellor, for I know he cannot fight and is a fool at hunting," was the ultimate decision.

They had a final interview with the governor and his son before they left. Rolf received for himself and his partner the promised one hundred and fifty dollars, and the hearty thanks of all in the governor's home. Next, each was presented with a handsome hunting knife, not unlike the one young Van had carried, but smaller. Quonab received his with "Ho!" — then, after a pause, "He pull out, maybe, when I need him." — "Ho! good!" he exclaimed, as the keen blade appeared.

"Now, Rolf," said the lawyer, "I want to come back next year and bring three companions, and we will pay you at the same rate per month for each. What do you say?"

"Glad to have you again," said Rolf. "We'll come for you on August fifteenth; but remember you should bring your guitar and your spectacles."

"One word," said the governor, "do you know the canoe route through Champlain to Canada?"

"Quonab does."

"Could you undertake to render scout service in that region?"

The Indian nodded.

Rolf in the Woods

"In case of war, we may need you both, so keep your ears open."

And once more the canoe made for the north, with Quonab in the stern and Skookum in the bow.

In less than a week they were home, and none too soon; for already the trees were bare, and they had to break the ice on the river before they ended their trip.

Rolf had gathered many ideas the last two months. He did not propose to continue all his life as a trapper. He wanted to see New York. He wanted to plan for the future. He needed money for his plans. He and Quonab had been running a hundred miles of traps, but some men run more than that single handed. They must get out two new lines at once, before the frost came. One of these they laid up the Hudson, above Eagle's Nest; the other northerly on Blue Mountain, toward Racquet River. Doing this was hard work, and when they came again to their cabin the robins had gone from the bleak and leafless woods; the grouse were making long night flights; the hollows had tracks of racing deer; there was a sense of omen, a length of gloom, for the Mad Moon was afloat in the shimmering sky; its wan light ghasted all the hills.

Next day the lake was covered with thin, glare ice; on the glassy surface near the shore were two ducks floundering. The men went as near as they could, and Quonab said, "No, not duck, but Shingebis, divers. They cannot rise except from water. In the night the new ice looks like water; they come down and cannot rise. I have often seen it." Two days after, a harder frost came on. The ice was safe for a dog; the divers or grebes were still on its surface. So they sent Skookum. He soon returned with two beautiful grebes, whose shining, white breast feathers are as much prized as some furs.

Quonab grunted as he held them up. "Ugh, it is often so in this Mad Moon. My father said it is because of Kaluskap's dancing."

"I don't remember that one."

"Yes, long ago. Kaluskap felt lazy. He wanted to eat, but did not wish to hunt, so he called the bluejay and said: 'Tell all the woods that to-morrow night Kaluskap gives a new dance and teaches a new song' and he told the hoot owl to do the same, so one kept it up all day — Kaluskap teaches a new dance to-morrow night and the other kept it up all night: 'Kaluskap teaches a new song at next council.'

The Grebes and the Singing Mouse

"Thus it came about that all the woods and waters sent their folk to the dance.

"Then Kaluskap took his song-drum and said: 'When I drum and sing you must dance in a circle the same way as the sun, close your eyes tightly, and each one shout his war whoop, as I cry "new songs"!'

"So all began, with Kaluskap drumming in the middle, singing:

"'New songs from the south, brothers,
Close your eyes tightly, brothers,
Dance and learn a new song.'

"As they danced around, he picked out the fattest, and, reaching out one hand, seized them and twisted their necks, shouting out, 'More war-cries, more noise! that's it; now you are learning!'

"At length Shingebis the diver began to have his doubts and he cautiously opened one eye, saw the trick, and shouted: 'Fly, brothers, fly! Kaluskap is killing us!'

"Then all was confusion. Every one tried to escape, and Kaluskap, in revenge, tried to kill the Shingebis. But the diver ran for the water and, just as he reached the edge, Kaluskap gave him a kick behind that sent him half a mile, but it knocked off all his tail feathers and twisted his shape so that ever since his legs have stuck out where his tail was, and he cannot rise from the land or the ice. I know it is so, for my father, Cos Cob, told me it was true, and we ourselves have seen it. It is ever so. To go against Kaluskap brings much evil to brood over."

A few nights later, as they sat by their fire in the cabin, a curious squeaking was heard behind the logs. They had often heard it before, but never so much as now. Skookum turned his head on one side, set his ears at forward cock. Presently, from a hole 'twixt logs and chimney, there appeared a small, white-breasted mouse.

Its nose and ears shivered a little; its black eyes danced in the firelight. It climbed up to a higher log, scratched its ribs, then rising on its hind legs, uttered one or two squeaks like those they had heard so often, but soon they became louder and continuous:

"Peo, peo, peo, peo, peo, peo, peo, peo, oo.
Tree, tree, tree, tree, trrrrrrr,
Turr, turr, turr, tur, tur,
Wee, wee, wee, we"—

The little creature was sitting up high on its hind legs, its belly muscles were working, its mouth was gaping as it poured out its music. For fully half a minute this went on, when Skookum made a dash; but the mouse was quick and it flashed into the safety of its cranny.

Rolf gazed at Quonab inquiringly.

"That is Mish-a-boh-quas, the singing mouse. He always comes to tell of war. In a little while there will be fighting."

Seeds of Ash Trees

LXVI

A Lesson in Stalking

"DID you ever see any fighting, Quonab?"

"Ugh! In Revolution, scouted for Gates."

"Judging by the talk, we're liable to be called on before a year. What will you do?"

"Fight."

"As soldier?"

"No! scout."

Scout or Scouting

"They may not want us."

"Always want scouts," replied the Indian.

"It seems to me *I* ought to start training now."

"You have been training."

"How is that?"

"A scout is everything that an army is, but it's all in one man. An' he don't have to keep step."

"I see, I see," replied Rolf, and he realized that a scout is merely a trained hunter who is compelled by war to hunt his country's foes instead of the beasts of the woods.

"See that?" said the Indian, and he pointed to a buck that was nosing for cranberries in the open expanse across the river where it left the lake. "Now, I show you scouting." He glanced at the smoke from the fire, found it right for his plan, and said: "See! I take my bow. No cover, yet I will come close and kill that deer."

Then began a performance that was new to Rolf, and showed that the Indian had indeed reached the highest pitch of woodcraft. He took his bow and three good arrows, tied a band around his head, and into this stuck a lot of twigs and vines, so that his head looked like a tussock of herbage. Then he left the shanty door, and, concealed by the last bushes on the edge, he reached the open plain. Two hundred yards off was the buck, nosing among the herbage,

Quonab glided swiftly forward

and, from time to time, raising its superb head and columnar neck to look around. There was no cover but creeping herbage. Rolf suspected that the Indian would decoy the buck by some whistle or challenge, for the thickness of its neck showed the deer to be in fighting humour.

Flat on his breast the Indian lay. His knees and elbow seemed to develop centipedic power; his head was a mere clump of growing stuff. He snaked his way quietly for twenty-five yards, then came to the open, sloping shore, with the river forty yards wide of level shining ice, all in plain view of the deer; how was this to be covered?

There is a well-known peculiarity of the white tail that the Indian was counting on; when its head is down grazing, even though not hidden, the deer does not see distant objects; before the head is raised, its tail is raised or shaken. Quonab knew that if he could keep the tail in view, he could avoid being viewed by the head. In a word, only an ill-timed movement or a whiff could betray him.

The open ice was, of course, a hard test, and the hunter might have failed, but that his long form looked like one of the logs that were lying about half stranded or frozen in the stream.

Watching ever the alert head and tail, he timed his approach, working hard and moving fast when the head was down; but when warned by a tail-jerk he turned to a log nor moved a muscle. Once the ice was crossed, the danger of being seen was less, but of being smelt was greater, for the deer was moving about, and Quonab watched the smoke from the cabin for knowledge of the wind. So he came within fifty yards, and the buck, still sniffing along and eagerly champing the few red cranberries it found above the frozen moss, was working toward a somewhat higher cover. The herbage was now fully eighteen inches high, and Quonab moved a little faster. The buck found a large patch of berries under a tussock and dropped on its knees to pick them out, while Quonab saw the chance and gained ten yards before the tail gave warning. After so long a feeding-spell, the buck took an extra long look-out, and then walked toward the timber, whereby the Indian lost all he had gained. But the browser's eye was drawn by a shining bunch of red, then another; and now the buck swung until there was danger of betrayal by the wind; then down went its head and Quonab retreated ten yards to keep the windward. Once the buck raised its muzzle and sniffed with flaring nostrils, as though its ancient friend had brought a warning. But soon he seemed reassured, for the landscape showed no foe, and nosed back and forth, while Quonab regained the yards he had lost. The buck worked now to the taller cover, and again a tempting bunch of berries under a low, dense bush caused it to kneel for farther under-reaching. Quonab glided swiftly forward, reached the twenty-five-yard limit, rose to one knee, bent the stark cedar bow. Rolf saw the buck bound in air, then make for the wood with great, high leaps; the dash of disappointment was on him, but Quonab stood erect, with right hand raised, and shouted:

"Ho —ho."

He knew that those bounds were unnecessarily high, and before the woods had swallowed up the buck, it fell — rose — and fell again, to rise not. The arrow had pierced its heart.

Then Rolf rushed up with kindled eye and exultant pride to slap his friend on the back, and exclaim:

"I never thought it possible; the greatest feat in hunting I ever saw; you are a wonder!"

To which the Indian softly replied, as he smiled:

"Ho! it was so I got eleven British sentries in the war. They gave me a medal with Washington's head."

"They did! how is it I never heard of it? Where is it?"

The Indian's face darkened. "I threw it after the ship that stole my Gamowini."

LXVII

Rolf Meets a Canuck

THE winter might have been considered eventful, had not so many of the events been repetitions of former experience. But there were several that by their newness deserve a place on these pages, as they did in Rolf's memory.

One of them happened soon after the first sharp frost. It had been an autumn of little rain, so that many ponds had dried up, with the result that hundreds of muskrats were forced out to seek more habitable quarters. The first time Rolf saw one of these stranded mariners on its overland journey, he gave heedless chase. At first it made awkward haste to escape; then a second muskrat was discovered just ahead, and a third. This added to Rolf's interest. In a few bounds he was among them, but it was to get a surprise. Finding themselves overtaken, the muskrats turned in desperation and attacked the common enemy with courage and fury. Rolf leaped over the first, but the second sprang, caught him by the slack of the trouser leg, and hung on. The third flung itself on his foot and drove its sharp teeth through the moccasin. Quickly the first rallied and sprang on his other leg with all the force of its puny paws, and powerful jaws.

Rolf in the Woods

Meanwhile Quonab was laughing aloud and holding back Skookum, who, breathing fire and slaughter, was mad to be in the fight.

"Ho! a good fight! good musquas! Ho, Skookum, you must not always take care of him, or he will not learn to go alone."

"Ugh, good!" as the third muskrat gripped Rolf by the calf.

There could be but one finish, and that not long delayed. A well-placed kick on one, the second swung by the tail, the third crushed under his heel, and the affair ended. Rolf had three muskrats and five cuts. Quonab had much joy and Skookum a sense of lost opportunity.

"This we should paint on the wigwam," said Quonab. "Three great warriors attacked one Sagamore. They were very brave, but he was Nibowaka and very strong; he struck them down as the Thunderbird, Hurakan, strikes the dead pines the fire has left on the hilltop against the sky. Now shall you eat their hearts, for they were brave. My father told me a fighting muskrat's heart is great medicine; for he seeks peace while it is possible, then he turns and fights without fear."

A few days later they sighted a fox. In order to have a joke on Skookum, they put him on its track, and away he went, letting off his joy-whoops at every jump. The men sat down to wait, knowing full well that after an hour Skookum would come back with a long tongue and an air of depression. But they were favoured with an unexpected view of the chase. It showed a fox bounding over the snow, and not twenty yards behind was their energetic four-legged colleague.

And, still more unexpected, the fox was overtaken in the next thicket, shaken to limpness, and dragged to be dropped at Quonab's feet. This glorious victory by Skookum was less surprising, when a closer examination showed that the fox had been in a bad way. Through some sad, sudden indiscretion, he had tackled a porcupine and paid the dire penalty. His mouth, jaws and face, neck and legs, were bristling with quills. He was sick and emaciated. He could not have lasted many days longer, and Skookum's summary lynching was a blessing in disguise.

The trappers' usual routine was varied by a more important happening. One day of deep snow in January, when they were running the northern line on Racquet River, they camped for the night at their shelter cabin, and were somewhat surprised at dusk to hear a loud challenge from Skookum replied to by a human voice, and a short man with black whiskers appeared. He raised one hand in token of friendliness and was invited to come in.

He was a French Canadian from La Colle Mills. He had trapped here for some years. The almost certainty of war between Canada and the States had kept his usual companions away. So he had trapped alone, always a dangerous business, and had gathered a lot of good fur, but had fallen on the ice and hurt himself inwardly, so that he had no strength. He could tramp out on snow-shoes, but could not carry his pack of furs. He had long known that he had neighbours on the south; the camp fire smoke proved that, and he had come now to offer all his furs for sale.

Quonab shook his head, but Rolf said, "We'll come over and see them."

A two-hours' tramp in the morning brought them to the Frenchman's cabin. He opened out his furs; several otter, many sable, some lynx, over thirty beaver — the whole lot for two hundred dollars. At Lyons Falls they were worth double that.

Rolf saw a chance for a bargain. He whispered, "We can double our money on it, Quonab. What do ye say?"

The reply was simply, "Ugh! you are Nibowaka."

"We'll take your offer, if we can fix it up about payment, for I have no money with me and barely two hundred dollars at the cabin."

"You haff tabac and grosairs?"

"Yes, plenty."

"You can go get 'em? Si?"

Rolf paused, looked down, then straight at the Frenchman.

"Will you trust me to take half the fur now; when I come back with the pay I can get the rest."

The Frenchman looked puzzled, then, "By Gar, you look de good look. I let um go. I tink you pretty good fellow, *parbleu*!"

So Rolf marched away with half the furs and four days later he was back and paid the pale-faced but happy Frenchman the one hundred and fifty dollars he had received from Van Cortlandt, with other bills making one hundred and ninety-five dollars and with groceries and tobacco enough to satisfy the trapper. The Frenchman proved a most amiable character. He and Rolf took to each other greatly, and when they shook hands at parting, it was in the hope of an early and happier meeting.

Rolf in the Woods

François la Colle turned bravely for the ninety-mile tramp over the snow to his home, while Rolf went south with the furs that were to prove a most profitable investment, shaping his life in several ways, and indirectly indeed of saving it on one occasion.

Tabac

Groceries

LXVIII

War

EIGHTEEN hundred and twelve had passed away. President Madison, driven by wrongs to his countrymen and indignities that no nation should meekly accept, had in the midsummer declared war on Great Britain. Unfitted to cope with the situation and surrounded by unfit counsellors, his little army of heroic men led by unfit commanders had suffered one reverse after another.

The loss of Fort Mackinaw, Chicago, Detroit, Browns-town, and the total destruction of the American army that attacked Queenstown were but poorly offset by the victory at Niagara and the successful defence of Ogdensburg.

Rolf and Quonab had repaired to Albany as arranged, but they left it as United States scouts, not as guides to the four young sportsmen who wished to hark back to the primitive.

Their first commission had been the bearing of despatches to Plattsburg.

With a selected light canoe and a minimum of baggage they reached Ticonderoga in two days, and there renewed their acquaintance with General Hampton, who was tossing about, and digging useless entrenchments as though he expected a mighty siege. Rolf was called before him to receive other despatches for Colonel Pike at Plattsburg. He got the papers and learned their destination, then immediately made a sad mistake. "Excuse me, sir," he began, "if I meet with—"

"Young man," said the general, severely, "I don't want any of your 'ifs' or 'buts'; your orders are 'go.' 'How' and 'if' are matters for you to find out; that's what you are paid for."

Rolf bowed; his cheeks were tingling. He was very angry at what he thought a most uncalled for rebuke, but he got over it, and he never forgot the lesson. It was Si Sylvanne that put it into rememberable form.

Rolf in the Woods

"A fool horse kin follow a turnpike, but it takes a man with wits to climb, swim, boat, skate, run, hide, go it blind, pick a lock, take the long way, round, when it's the short way across, run away at the right time, or fight when it's wise — all in one afternoon." Rolf set out for the north carrying a bombastic (meant to be reassuring) message from Hampton that he would annihilate any enemy who dared to desecrate the waters of the lake.

It was on this trip that Rolf learned from Quonab the details of the latter's visit to his people on the St. Regis. Apparently the joy of meeting a few of his own kin, with whom he could talk his own language, was offset by meeting with a large number of his ancient enemies the Mohawks. There had been much discussion of the possible war between the British and the Yankees. The Mohawks announced their intention to fight for the British, which was a sufficient reason for Quonab as a Sinawa remaining with the Americans; and when he left the St. Regis reserve the Indian was without any desire to reenter it.

At Plattsburg Rolf and Quonab met with another Albany acquaintance in General Wilkinson, and from him received despatches which they brought back to Albany, having covered the whole distance in eight days.

When 1812 was gone Rolf had done little but carry despatches up and down Lake Champlain. Next season found the Americans still under command of Generals Wilkinson and Hampton, whose utter incompetence was becoming daily more evident.

The year 1813 saw Rolf, eighteen years old and six feet one in his socks, a trained scout and despatch bearer.

By a flying trip on snowshoes in January he took letters, from General Hampton at Ticonderoga to Sackett's Harbour and back in eight days, nearly three hundred miles. It made him famous as a runner, but the tidings that he brought were sad. Through him they

**Scout
or
Scoutin**

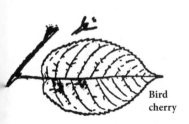

Bird
cherry

Norway
Maple

learned in detail of the total defeat and capture of the American army at Frenchtown. After a brief rest he was sent across country on snowshoes to bear a reassuring message to Ogdensburg. The weather was much colder now, and the single blanket bed was dangerously slight; so "Flying Kittering," as they named him, took a toboggan and secured Quonab as his running mate. Skookum was given into safe keeping. Blankets, pots, cups, food, guns, and despatches were strapped on the toboggan, and they sped away at dawn from Ticonderoga on the 18th of February 1813, headed northwestward, guided by little but the compass. Thirty miles that day they made in spite of piercing blasts and driving snow. But with the night there began a terrible storm with winds of zero chill. The air was filled with stinging, cutting snow. When they rose at daylight they were nearly buried in drifts, although their camp was in a dense, sheltered thicket. Guided wholly by the compass they travelled again, but blinded by the whirling white they stumbled and blundered into endless difficulties and made but poor headway. After dragging the toboggan for three hours, taking turns at breaking the way, they were changing places when Rolf noticed a large gray patch on Quonab's cheek and nose.

"Quonab, your face is frozen," he said.

"So is yours," was the reply.

Now they turned aside, followed a hollow until they reached a spruce grove, where they camped and took an observation, to learn that the compass and they held widely different views about the direction of travel. It was obviously useless to face the storm. They rubbed out their frozen features with dry snow and rested by the fire.

cout or scouting

No good scout seeks for hardship; he avoids the unnecessary trial of strength and saves himself for the unavoidable. With zero weather about them and twenty-four hours to wait in the storm, the scouts set about making themselves thoroughly comfortable.

With their snowshoes they dug away the snow in a circle a dozen feet across, piling it up on the outside so as to make that as high as possible. When they were down to the ground, the wall of snow around them was five feet high. Now they went forth with the hatchets, cut many small spruces, and piled them against the living spruces about the camp till there was a dense mass of evergreen foliage ten feet high around them, open only at the top, where was a space five feet across. With abundance of dry spruce wood, a thick bed of balsam boughs, and plenty of blankets they were in what most woodmen consider comfort complete.

They had nothing to do now but wait. Quonab sat placidly smoking, Rolf was sewing a rent in his coat, the storm hissed, and the wind-driven ice needles rattled through the trees to vary the crackle of the fire with a *siss* as they fell on the embers. The low monotony of sound was lulling in its evenness, when a faint crunch of a foot on the snow was heard. Rolf reached for his gun, the fir tree screen was shaken a little, and a minute later there bounded in upon them the snow covered form of little dog Skookum, expressing his good-will by excessive sign talk in which every limb and member had a part. They had left him behind, indeed, but not with his consent, so the bargain was incomplete.

There was no need to ask now, "What shall we do with him?" Skookum had settled that, and why or how he never attempted to explain.

He was wise who made it law that "as was his share who went forth to battle, so shall his be that abode with the stuff," for the hardest of all is the waiting. In the morning there was less doing in the elemental strife. There were even occasional periods of calm and at length it grew so light that surely the veil was breaking.

Quonab returned from a brief reconnoitre to say, "Ugh! — good going."

The clouds were broken and flying, the sun came out at times, but the wind was high, the cold intense, and the snow still drifting. Poor Skookum had it harder than the men, for they wore snowshoes; but he kept his troubles to himself and bravely trudged along behind. Had he been capable of such reflection he might have said, "What delightful weather, it keeps the fleas so quiet."

That day there was little to note but the intense cold, and again both men had their cheeks frost-bitten on the north side. A nook under an overhanging rock gave a good camp that night. Next day the bad weather resumed, but, anxious to push on they faced it, guided chiefly by the wind. It was northwest, and as long as they felt this fierce, burn-

ing cold mercilessly gnawing on their hapless tender right cheek bones, they knew they were keeping their proper main course.

They were glad indeed to rest at dusk and thaw their frozen faces. Next day at dawn they were off; at first it was calm, but the surging of the snow waves soon began again, and the air was filled with the spray of their lashing till it was hard to see fifty yards in any direction. They were making very bad time. The fourth day should have brought them to Ogdensburg, but they were still far off; how far they could only guess, for they had not come across a house or a settler.

LXIX

Ogdensburg

THE same blizzard was raging on the next day when Skookum gave unequivocal sign talk that he *smelled something.*

It is always well to find out what stirs your dog. Quonab looked hard at Skookum. That sagacious mongrel was sniffing vigorously, *up in the air*, not on the ground; his mane was *not bristling*, and the patch of dark hair that every gray or yellow dog has at the base of his tail, was *not lifted*.

"He smells smoke," was the Indian's quick diagnosis. Rolf pointed up the wind and made the sign-talk query. Quonab nodded.

It was their obvious duty to find out who was their smoky neighbour. They were now not so far from the St. Lawrence; there was a small chance of the smoke being from a party of the enemy; there was a large chance of it being from friends; and the largest chance was that it came from some settler's cabin where they could get necessary guidance.

They turned aside. The wind now, instead of on the right cheek, was square in their faces. Rolf went forward increasing his pace till he was as far ahead as was possible without being out of sight. After a mile their way led downward, the timber was thicker, the wind less, and the air no more befogged with flying snow. Rolf came to a long, deep trench that wound among the trees; the snow at the bottom of it was very hard. This was what he expected; the trail muffled under new, soft snow, but still a fresh trail and leading to the camp that Skookum had winded.

Rolf in the Woods

He turned and made the sign for them to halt and wait. Then strode cautiously along the winding guide line.

In twenty minutes the indications of a settlement increased, and the scout at length was peering from the woods across the open down to a broad stream on whose bank was a saw mill, with the usual wilderness of ramshackle shanties, sheds, and lumber piles about.

There was no work going on, which was a puzzle till Rolf remembered it was Sunday. He went boldly up and asked for the boss. His whole appearance was that of a hunter and as such the boss received him.

He was coming through from the other side and had missed his way in the storm, he explained.

"What are ye by trade?"

"A trapper."

"Where are ye bound now?"

"Well, I'll head for the nearest big settlement, whatever that is."

"It's just above an even thing between Alexandria Bay and Ogdensburg."

So Rolf inquired fully about the trail to Alexandria Bay that he did not want to go to. Why should he be so careful? The mill owner was clearly a good American, but the scout had no right to let any outsider know his business. This mill owner might be safe, but he might be unwise and blab to some one who was not all right.

Then in a casual way he learned that this was the Oswegatchie River and thirty miles down he would find the town of Ogdensburg.

No great recent events did he hear of, but evidently the British troops across the river were only awaiting the springtime before taking offensive measures.

For the looks of it, Rolf bought some tea and pork, but the hospitable mill man refused to take payment and, leaving in the direction of Alexandria Bay, Rolf presently circled back and rejoined his friends in the woods.

A long détour took them past the mill. It was too cold for outdoor idling. Every window was curtained with frost, and not a soul saw them as they tramped along past the place and down to continue on the ice of the Oswegatchie.

Pounded by the ceaseless wind, the snow on the ice was harder, travel was easier, and the same tireless blizzard wiped out the trail as soon as it was behind them.

Ogdensburg

Crooked is the river trail, but good the footing, and good time was made. When there was a north reach, the snow was extra hard or the ice clear and the scouts slipped off their snow shoes, and trotted at a good six-mile gait. Three times they halted for tea and rest, but the fact that they were the bearers of precious despatches, the bringers of inspiring good news, and their goal ever nearer, spurred them on and on. It was ten o'clock that morning when they left the mill, some thirty miles from Ogdensburg. It was now near sundown, but still they figured that by an effort they could reach the goal that night. It was their best day's travel, but they were nerved to it by the sense of triumph as they trotted; and the prospective joy of marching up to the commandant and handing over the eagerly looked for, reassuring documents, gave them new strength and ambition. Yes! they must push on at any price that night. Day was over now; Rolf was leading at a steady trot. In his hand he held the long trace of his toboggan, ten feet behind was Quonab with the short trace, while Skookum trotted before, beside, or behind, as was dictated by his general sense of responsibility.

It was quite dark now. There was no moon, the wooded shore was black. Their only guide was the broad, wide reach of the river, sometimes swept bare of snow by the wind, but good travelling at all times. They were trotting and walking in spells, going five miles an hour; Quonab was suffering, but Rolf was young and eager to finish. They rounded another reach, they were now on the last big bend, they were reeling off the miles; only ten more, and Rolf was so stirred that, instead of dropping to the usual walk on signal at the next one hundred yards spell, he added to his trot. Quonab, taken unawares, slipped and lost his hold of the trace. Rolf shot ahead and a moment later there was the crash of a breaking air-hole, and Rolf went through the ice, clutched at the broken edge and disappeared, while the toboggan was dragged to the hole.

Quonab sprung to his feet, and then to the lower side of the hole. The toboggan had swung to the same place and the long trace was tight;

without a moment's delay the Indian hauled at it steadily, heavily, and in a few seconds the head of his companion reappeared; still clutching that long trace he was safely dragged from the ice-cold flood, blowing and gasping, shivering and sopping, but otherwise unhurt.

Now here a new danger presented itself. The zero wind would soon turn his clothes to boards. They stiffened in a few minutes, and the Indian knew that frozen hands and feet were all too easy in frozen clothes.

He made at once for the shore, and, seeking the heart of a spruce thicket, lost no time in building two roaring fires between which Rolf stood while the Indian made the bed, in which, as soon as he could be stripped, the lad was glad to hide. Warm tea and warm blankets made him warm, but it would take an hour or two to dry his clothes. There is nothing more damaging than drying them too quickly. Quonab made racks of poles and spent the next two hours in regulating the fire, watching the clothes, and working the moccasins.

It was midnight when they were ready and any question of going on at once was settled by Quonab. "Ogdensburg is under arms," he said. "It is not wise to approach by night."

At six in the morning they were once more going, stiff with travel, sore-footed, face-frozen, and chafed by delay; but, swift and keen, trotting and walking, they went. They passed several settlements, but avoided them. At seven-thirty they had a distant glimpse of Ogdensburg and heard the inspiring roll of drums, and a few minutes later from the top of a hill they had a complete view of the heroic little town to see — yes! plainly enough — *that the British flag was flying from the flag pole.*

LXX

Saving the Despatches

OH, THE sickening shock of it! Rolf did not know till now how tired he was, how eager to deliver the heartening message, and to relax a little from the strain. He felt weak through and through. There could be no doubt that a disaster had befallen his country's arms.

His first care was to get out of sight with his sled and those precious despatches.

Now what should he do? Nothing till he had fuller information. He sent Quonab back with the sled, instructing him to go to a certain place two miles off, there camp out of sight and wait.

Then he went in alone. Again and again he was stung by the thought, "If I had come sooner they might have held out."

A number of teams gathered at the largest of a group of houses on the bank suggested a tavern. He went in and found many men sitting down to breakfast. He had no need to ask questions. It was the talk of the table. Ogdensburg had been captured the day before. The story is well known. Colonel MacDonnell with his Glengarry Highlanders at Prescott went to drill daily on the ice of the St. Lawrence opposite Ogdensburg. Sometimes they marched past just out of range, sometimes they charged and wheeled before coming too near. The few Americans that held the place watched these harmless exercises and often cheered some clever manœuvre. They felt quite safe behind their fortification. By an unwritten agreement both parties refrained from firing random shots at each other. There was little to suggest enemies entrenched; indeed, many men in each party had friends in the other, and the British had several times trotted past within easy range, without provoking a shot.

On February 22d, the day when Rolf and Quonab struck the Oswegatchie, the British colonel directed his men as usual, swinging them ever nearer the American fort, and then, at the nearest point, executed a very pretty charge. The Americans watched it as it neared, but instead of wheeling at the brink the little army scrambled up with merry shouts, and before the garrison could realize that this was war, they were over-powered and Ogdensburg was taken.

The American commander was captured. Captain Forsyth, the second in command, had been off on a snow-shoe trip, so had escaped. All the rest were prisoners, and what to do with the despatches or how to get official instructions was now a deep problem. "When you don't know a thing to do, don't do a thing," was one of Si Sylvanne's axioms; also, "In case of doubt lay low and say nothing." Rolf hung around the town all day waiting for light. About noon a tall, straight, alert man in a buffalo coat drove up with a cutter. He had a hasty meal in an inside room. Rolf sized him up for an American officer, but there was a possibility of his being a Canadian. Rolf tried in vain to get light on him but the inner door was kept closed; the landlord was evidently in the secret. When he came out he was again swaddled in the buffalo coat. Rolf brushed past him — there was something hard and long in the right pocket of the big coat.

The landlord, the guest, and the driver had a whispered conference. Rolf went as near as he dared, but got only a searching look. The driver spoke to another driver and Rolf heard the words "Black Lake." Yes, that was what he suspected. Black Lake was on the inland sleigh route to Alexandria Bay and Sackett's Harbour.

The driver, a fresh young fellow, was evidently interested in the landlord's daughter; the stranger was talking with the landlord. As soon as they had parted, Rolf went to the latter and remarked quietly: "The captain is in a hurry." The only reply was a cold look and: "Guess that's his business." So it *was* the *captain*. The driver's mitts were on the line back of the stove. Rolf shook them so that they fell in a dark corner. The driver missed his mitts, and glad of a chance went back in, leaving the

officer alone. "Captain Forsyth," whispered Rolf, "don't go till I have talked with you. I'll meet you a mile down the road."

"Who are you and what do you want?" was the curt and hostile reply, evidently admitting the identification correct however.

Rolf opened his coat and showed his scout badge.

"Why not talk now if you have any news — come inside." So the two went to the inner room. "Who is this?" asked Rolf cautiously as the landlord came in.

"He's all right. This is Titus Flack, the landlord."

"How am I to know that?"

"Haven't you heard him called by name all day?" said the captain.

Flack smiled, went out and returned with his license to sell liquor, and his commission as a magistrate of New York State. The latter bore his own signature. He took a pen and reproduced it. Now the captain threw back his overcoat and stood in the full uniform of an army officer. He opened his satchel and took out a paper, but Rolf caught sight of another packet addressed to General Hampton. The small one was merely a map. "I think that packet in there is meant for me," remarked Rolf.

"We haven't seen *your* credentials yet," said the officer. "I have them two miles back there," and Rolf pointed to the woods.

"Let's go," said the captain and they arose. Kittering had a way of inspiring confidence, but in the short, silent ride of two miles the captain began to have his doubts. The scout badge might have been stolen; Canadians often pass for Americans, etc. At length they stopped the sleigh, and Rolf led into the woods. Before a hundred yards the officer said, "Stop," and Rolf stopped to find a pistol pointed at his head. "Now, young fellow, you've played it pretty slick, and I don't know yet what to make of it. But I know this; at the very first sign of treachery I'll blow *your* brains out anyway."

Rolf in the Woods

It gave Rolf a jolt. This was the first time he had looked down a pistol barrel levelled at him. He used to think a pistol a little thing, an inch through and a foot long, but he found now it seemed as big as a flour barrel and long enough to reach eternity. He changed colour but quickly recovered, smiled, and said: "Don't worry; in five minutes you will know it's all right."

Very soon a sharp bark was heard in challenge, and the two stepped into camp to meet Quonab and little dog Skookum.

"Doesn't look much like a trap," thought the captain after he had cast his eyes about and made sure that no other person was in the camp; then aloud, "Now what have you to show me?"

"Excuse me, captain, but how am I to know you *are* Captain Forsyth? It is possible for a couple of spies to give all the proof you two gave me."

The captain opened his bag and showed first his instructions given before he left Ogdensburg four days ago; he bared his arm and showed a tattooed U. S. A., a relic of Academy days, then his linen marked J. F., and a signet ring with similar initials, and last the great packet of papers addressed to General Hampton. Then he said: "When you hand over your despatches to me I will give mine to you and we shall have good guarantee each of the other."

Rolf rose, produced his bundle of papers, and exchanged them for those held by Forsyth; each felt that the other was safe. They soon grew friendly, and Rolf heard of some stirring doings on the lake and preparations for a great campaign in the spring.

After half an hour the tall, handsome captain left them and strode away, a picture of manly vigour. Three hours later they were preparing their evening meal when Skookum gave notice of a stranger approaching. This was time of war; Rolf held his rifle ready, and a moment later in burst the young man who had been Captain Forsyth's driver.

His face was white; blood dripped from his left arm, and in his other hand was the despatch bag. He glanced keenly at Rolf. "Are you General Hampton's scout?" Rolf nodded and showed the badge on his breast. "Captain Forsyth sent this back," he gasped. "His last words were,' Burn the despatches rather than let the British get them.' They got him — a foraging party — there was a spy at the hotel. I got away, but my tracks are easy to follow unless it drifts. Don't wait."

**Scout
or
Scoutin**

Saving the Despatches

Poor boy, his arm was broken, but he carried out the dead officer's command, then left them to seek for relief in the settlement.

Night was near, but Rolf broke camp at once and started eastward with the double packet. He did not know it then, but learned afterward that these despatches made clear the weakness of Oswego, Rochester, and Sackett's Harbour, their urgent need of help, and gave the whole plan for an American counter attack on Montreal. But he knew they were valuable, and they must at once be taken to General Hampton.

It was rough, hard going in the thick woods and swamps away from the river, for he did not dare take the ice route now, but they pushed on for three hours, then, in the gloom, made a miserable camp in a cedar swamp.

At dawn they were off again. To their disgust the weather now was dead calm; there was no drift to hide their tracks; the trail was as plain as a highway wherever they went. They came to a beaten road, followed that for half a mile, then struck off on the true line. But they had no idea that they were followed until, after an hour of travel, the sun came up and on a far distant slope, full two miles away, they saw a thin black line of many spots, at least a dozen British soldiers in pursuit.

The enemy was on snowshoes, and without baggage evidently, for they travelled fast. Rolf and Quonab burdened with the sled were making a losing race. But they pushed on as fast as possible — toiling and sweating at that precious load. Rolf was pondering whether the time had not yet come to stop and burn the packet, when, glancing back from a high ridge that gave an outlook, he glimpsed a row of heads that dropped behind some rocks half a mile away, and a scheme came into his mind. He marched boldly across the twenty feet opening that was in the enemy's view, dropped behind the spruce thickets, called Quonab to follow, ran around the thicket, and again crossed the open view. So he and Quonab continued for five minutes, as fast as they could go, knowing perfectly well that they were watched. Round and round that bush they went, sometimes close together, carrying the guns, sometimes dragging the sled, sometimes with blankets on their shoulders, sometimes with a short bag or even a large cake of snow on their backs. They did everything they could to vary the scene, and before five minutes the British officer in charge had counted fifty-six armed Americans marching in single fire up the bank with ample stores, accompanied by five yellow dogs. Had Skookum been allowed to carry out his ideas, there would have been fifty or sixty yellow dogs, so thoroughly did he enter into the spirit of the game.

The track gave no hint of such a troop, but of course not, how could it? Since the toboggan left all smooth after they had passed, or maybe this was a reinforcement arriving. What could *he* do with his ten men against fifty of the enemy? He thanked his stars that he had so cleverly evaded the trap, and without further attempt to gauge the enemy's strength, he turned and made all possible haste back to the shelter of Ogdensburg.

LXXI

Sackett's Harbour

IT WAS hours before Rolf was sure that he had stopped the pursuit, and the thing that finally set his mind at rest was the rising wind that soon was a raging and drifting snow storm. "Oh, blessed storm!" he said in his heart, as he marked all trail disappear within a few seconds of its being made. And he thought: "How I cursed the wind that held me back — really from being made prisoner. How vexed I was at that ducking in the river, that really saved my despatches from the enemy. How thankful I am now for the storm that a little while back seemed so bitterly cruel."

That forenoon they struck the big bend of the river and now did not hesitate to use the easy travel on the ice as far as Rensselaer Falls, where, having got their bearings from a settler, they struck across the country through the storm, and at night were encamped some forty miles from Ogdensburg.

Box Elder

Marvellously few signs of game had they seen in this hard trip; everything that could hide away was avoiding the weather. But in a cedar bottom land near Cranberry Lake they found a "yard" that seemed to be the winter home of hundreds of deer. It extended two or three miles one way and a half a mile the other. In spite of the deep snow this was nearly all in beaten paths. The scouts saw at least fifty deer in going through, so, of course, had no difficulty in selecting a young buck for table use.

The going from there on was of little interest. It was the same old daily battle with the frost, but less rigorous than before, for now the cold winds were behind, and on the 27th of February, nine days after leaving, they trotted into Ticonderoga and reported at the commandant's headquarters.

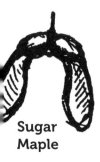

Sugar Maple

The general was still digging entrenchments and threatening to annihilate all Canada. But the contents of the despatches gave him new topics for thought and speech. The part he must play in the proposed descent on Montreal was flattering, but it made the Ticonderoga entrenchments ridiculous.

For three days Rolf was kept cutting wood, then he went with despatches to Albany.

Many minor labours, from hog-killing to stable-cleaning and trenching, varied the month of March. Then came the uncertain time of April when it was neither canoeing nor snow-shoeing and all communication from the north was cut off.

But May, great, glorious May came on, with its inspiring airs and livening influence. Canoes were afloat, the woods were brown beneath and gold above.

Rolf felt like a young stag in his strength. He was spoiling for a run and volunteered eagerly to carry despatches to Sackett's Harbour. He would go alone, for now one blanket was sufficient bed, and a couple of pounds of dry meat was enough food for each day. A small hatchet would be useful, but his rifle seemed too heavy to carry; as he halted in doubt, a junior officer offered him a pistol instead, and he gladly stuck it in his belt.

Taller than ever, considerably over six feet now, somewhat lanky, but supple of joint and square of shoulder, he strode with the easy stride of a strong traveller. His colour was up, his blue-gray eyes ablaze as he took the long trail in a crow line across country for Sackett's Harbour. The sentry saluted, and the officer of the day, struck by his figure and his glowing face as much as by the nature of his errand, stopped to shake hands and say, "Well, good luck, Kittering, and may you bring us better news than the last two times."

Rolf knew how to travel now; he began softly. At a long, easy stride he went for half an hour, then at a swinging trot for a mile or two. Five miles an hour he could make, but there was one great obstacle to speed at this season — every stream was at flood, all were difficult to cross. The brooks he could wade or sometimes could fell a tree across them, but the rivers were too wide to bridge, too cold and dangerous to swim. In nearly every case he had to make a raft. A good scout takes no chances. A slight raft means a risky passage; a good one, a safe crossing but loss of time in preparations. Fifteen good rafts did Rolf make in that cross-country journey of three days: dry spruce logs he found each time and bound them together with leather-wood and withes of willow. It meant a delay of at least an hour each time; that is five hours each day. But the time was wisely spent. The days were lengthening; he could travel much at dusk. Soon he was among settlements. Rumours he got at a settler's cabin of Sir George Prevost's attack on Sackett's Harbour and the gallant repulse and at morning of the fourth day he came on the hill above Sackett's Harbour — the same hill where he had stood three months before. It was with something like a clutching of his breath that he gazed; his past experiences suggested dreadful thoughts but no — thank God, "Old Glory" floated from the pole. He identified himself to the sentinels and the guard, entered the fort at a trot, and reported at headquarters.

There was joy on every side. At last the tide had turned. Commodore Chauncey, after sweeping Lake Ontario, had made a sudden descent on York (Toronto now) the capital of Upper Canada, had seized and destroyed it. Sir George Prevost, taking advantage of Chauncey's being away, had attacked Sackett's Harbour, but, in spite of the absence of the fleet, the resistance had been so vigorous that in a few days the siege was abandoned.

There were shot holes in walls and roofs, there were a few wounded in the hospital, the green embankments were torn, and the flag-pole splintered; but the enemy was gone, the starry flag was floating on the wind, and the sturdy little garrison filled with a spirit that grows only in heroes fighting for their homes.

How joyfully different from Ogdensburg.

LXXII

Scouting Across Country

THAT very night, Rolf turned again with the latest news and the commandant's reports.

He was learning the country well now, and, with the wonderful place-memory of a woodman, he was able to follow his exact back trail. It might not have been the best way, but it gave him this advantage — in nearly every case he was able to use again the raft he had made in coming, and thereby saved many hours of precious time.

On the way out he had seen a good many deer and one bear, and had heard the howling of wolves every night; but always at a distance. On the second night, in the very heart of the wilderness, the wolves were noisy and seemed very near. Rolf was camping in the darkness. He made a small fire with such stuff as he could find by groping, then, when the fire blazed, he discovered by its light a dead spruce some twenty yards away. Taking his hatchet he went toward this, and, as he did so, a wolf rose up, with its forefeet on a log, only five yards beyond the tree and gazed curiously at him. Others were heard calling; presently this wolf raised its muzzle and uttered a long, smooth howl.

Rolf had left his pistol back at the fire; he dared not throw his hatchet, as that would have left him unarmed. He stooped, picked up a stick, and threw that; the wolf ducked so that it passed over, then, stepping back from the log, stood gazing without obvious fear or menace. The others were howling; Rolf felt afraid. He backed cautiously to the fire, got his pistol and came again to the place, but nothing more did he see of the wolf, though he heard them all night and kept up two great fires for a protection.

In the morning he started as usual, and before half an hour he was aware of a wolf, and later of two, trotting along his trail, a few hundred yards behind. They did not try to overtake him; indeed, when he stopped, they did the same; and when he trotted, they, true to their

The others were howling; Rolf felt afraid

dog-like nature, ran more rapidly in pursuit. How Rolf did wish for his long rifle; but they gave no opportunity for a shot with the pistol. They acted, indeed, as though they knew their safe distance and the exact range of the junior gun. The scout made a trap for them by stealing back after he had crossed a ridge, and hiding near his own trail. But the wind conveyed a warning, and the wolves merely sat down and waited till he came out and went on. All day long these two strange ban dogs followed him and gave no sign of hunger or malice; then, after he crossed a river, at three in the afternoon, he saw no more of them. Years after, when Rolf knew them better, he believed they followed him out of mild curiosity, or possibly in the hope that he would kill a deer in which they might share. And when they left him, it was because they were near the edge of their own home region; they had seen him off their hunting grounds.

That night he camped sixty miles from Ticonderoga, but he was resolved to cover the distance in one day. Had he not promised to be back in a week? The older hands had shaken their heads incredulously, and he, in the pride of his legs, was determined to be as good as his promise. He scarcely dared sleep lest he should oversleep. At ten he lay down. At eleven the moon was due to rise; as soon as that was three hours high there would be light enough, and he proposed to go on. At least half a dozen times he woke with a start, fearing he had overslept, but reassured by a glance at the low-hung moon, he had slumbered again.

At last the moon was four hours high, and the woods were plain in the soft light. A horned owl "hoo-hoo-ed," and a far-off wolf uttered a drawn-out, soft, melancholy cry, as Rolf finished his dried meat, tightened his belt, and set out on a long, hard run that, in the days of Greece, would have furnished the theme of many a noble epic poem.

No need to consult his compass. The blazing lamp of the dark sky was his guide, straight east his course, varied a little by hills and lakes, but nearly the crow-flight line. At first his pace was a steady, swinging stride; then after a mile he came to an open lake shore down which he went at a six-mile trot; and then an alder thicket through which his progress was very slow; but that soon passed, and for half a mile he splashed through swamps with water a foot deep: nor was he surprised at length to see it open into a little lake with a dozen beaver huts in view. *Splash plong* their builders went at his approach, but he made for the hillside;

the woods were open, the moonlight brilliant now, and here he trotted at full swing as long as the way was level or down, but always walked on the uphill. A sudden noise ahead was followed by a tremendous crashing and crackling of the brush. For a moment it continued, and what it meant, Rolf never knew or guessed.

Trot, trot, he went, reeling off six miles in the open, two or perhaps three in the thickets, but on and on, ever eastward. Hill after hill, swamp after swamp, he crossed, lake after lake he skirted round, and, when he reached some little stream, he sought a log bridge or prodded with a pole till he found a ford and crossed, then ran a mile or two to make up loss of time.

Tramp, tramp, tramp, and his steady breath and his steady heart kept unremitting rhythm.

LXXIII

Rolf Makes a Record

TWELVE miles were gone when the foreglow — the first cold dawn-light — showed, and shining across his path ahead was a mighty rolling stream. Guided by the now familiar form of Goodenow Peak he made for this, the Hudson's lordly flood. There was his raft securely held, with paddle and pole near by, and he pushed off with all the force of his young vigour. Jumping and careening with the stream in its freshet flood, the raft and its hardy pilot were served with many a whirl and some round spins, but the long pole found bottom nearly everywhere, and not ten minutes passed before the traveller sprang ashore, tied up his craft, then swung and tramped and swung.

Over the hills of Vanderwhacker, under the woods of Boreas. *Tramp, tramp, splash, tramp,* wringing and sopping, but strong and hot, *tramp, tramp, tramp, tramp.* The partridge whirred from his path, the gray deer snorted, and the panther sneaked aside. *Tramp, tramp, trot, trot,* and the Washburn Ridge was blue against the sunrise. *Trot, trot,* over the low, level, mile-long slope he went, and when the Day-god burnt the upper hill-rim he was by brown Tahawus flood and had covered eighteen miles.

By the stream he stopped to drink. A partridge cock, in the pride of spring, strutted arrogantly on a log. Rolf drew his pistol, fired, then hung the headless body while he made a camper's blaze: an oatcake, the partridge, and river water were his meal. His impulse was to go on at once. His reason, said "go slow." So he waited for fifteen minutes. Then again, beginning with a slow walk, he ere long added to his pace. In half an hour he was striding and in an hour the steady *trot, trot,* that slackened only for the hills or swamps. In an hour more he was on the Washburn Ridge, and far away in the east saw Schroon Lake that empties in the river Schroon; and as he strode along, exulting in his strength,

White
Oak

he sang in his heart for joy. Again a gray wolf cantered on his trail, and the runner laughed, without a thought of fear. He seemed to know the creature better now; knew it as a brother, for it gave no hostile sound, but only seemed to *trot, trot,* for the small joy of running with a runner, as a swallow or an antelope will skim along by a speeding train. For an hour or more it matched his pace, then left as though its pleasant stroll was done, and Rolf kept on and on and on.

The spring sun soared on high, the day grew warm at noon. Schroon River just above the lake was in his path, and here he stopped to rest. Here, with the last of his oatcake and a little tea, he made his final meal; thirty-eight miles had he covered since he rose; his clothes were torn, his moccasins worn, but his legs were strong, his purpose sure; only twenty-two miles now, and his duty would be done; his honours won. What should he do, push on at once? No, he meant to rest an hour. He made a good fire by a little pool, and using a great mass of caribou moss as a sponge, he had a thorough rub-down. He got out his ever-ready needle and put his moccasins in good shape; he dried his clothes and lay on his back till the hour was nearly gone. Then he girded himself for this the final run. He was weary, indeed, but he was far from spent, and the iron will that had yearly grown in force was there with its unconquerable support.

Slowly at start, soon striding, and at last in the famous jog trot of the scout he went. The sky was blackened with clouds at length, and the jealous, howling east wind rolled up in rain; the spindrift blurred the way; the heavy showers of spring came down and drenched him; but his pack was safe and he trotted on and on. Then long, deep swamps of alder barred his path, and, guided only by the compass, Rolf pushed in and through and ever east. Barely a mile an hour in the thickest part he made, but lagged not; drenched and footsore, warm and torn, but doggedly, steadily on. At three he had made a scant seven miles; then the level, open wood of Thunderbolt was reached and his stride became a run; *trot, trot, trot,* at six-mile gait, for but fifteen miles remained. Sustained, inspired, the bringer of good news, he halted not and faltered not, but on and on.

Tramp tramp, tramp tramp — endless, tireless, hour by hour. At five he was on Thunder Creek, scarce eight miles more to the

Red oak

goal; his limbs were sore, his feet were sore; bone tired was he, but his heart was filled with joy.

"News of battle, news of victory" he was bringing, and the thought lent strength; the five miles passed, the way was plain with good roads now, but the runner was so weary. He was striding, his running was done, the sun was low in the west, his feet were bleeding, the courier was brain worn and leg worn, but he strode and strode. He passed by homes but heeded them not.

"Come in and rest," called one who saw nothing but a weary traveller. Rolf shook his head, but gave no word and strode along. A mile — a short mile now; he *must* hold out; if he sat down he feared he could not rise. He came at last in sight of the fort; then, gathering all his force, he broke into a trot, weak, so weak that had he fallen, he could scarcely have got up, and slow, but faster than a walk: and so, as the red sun sank, he passed the gate. He had no right to give ridings to any but the general, yet they read it in his eyes. The guard broke into a cheer, and trotting still, though reeling, Rolf had kept his word, had made his run, had brought the news, and had safely reached his goal.

LXXIV

Van Trumper's Again

WHY should the scout bringing good news be differently received from the one that brings the ill? He did not make the news, he simply did his duty; the same in both cases. He is merely the telegraph instrument. Yet it is so ever. King Pharaoh slew the bearer of ill-tidings; that was human nature. And General Hampton brought in the tall stripling to his table, to honour him, to get the fullest details, to glory in every item as though it all were due to himself. Rolf's wonderful journey was dilated on, and in the reports to Albany he was honourably mentioned for exceptionally meritorious service as a bearer of despatches.

Scout or Scouting

For three days Flying Kittering was hero of the post; then other runners came with other news and life went on.

Hitherto the scouts had worn no uniform, but the execution of one of their number, who was captured by the British and treated as a spy, resulted in orders that all be formally enlisted and put in uniform.

Not a few withdrew from the service; some, like Quonab, reluctantly consented, but Rolf was developing the fighting spirit, and was proud to wear the colours.

The drill was tedious enough, but it was of short duration for him. Despatches were to go to Albany. The general, partly to honour Rolf, selected him.

"Are you ready for another run, Kittering?"

"Yes, sir."

"Then prepare to start as soon as possible for Fort George and Albany. Do you want a mate?"

"I should like a paddler as far as Fort George."

"Well, pick your man."

"Quonab."

Rolf in the Woods

And when they set out, *for the first time Rolf was in the stern*, the post of guidance and command. So once more the two were travelling again with Skookum in the bow. It was afternoon when they started and the four-mile passage of the creek was slow, but down the long, glorious vista of the noble George they went at full canoe-flight, five miles an hour, and twenty-five miles of the great fair-way were reeled and past when they lighted their nightly fire.

At dawn-cry of the hawk they sped away, and in spite of a rising wind they made six miles in two hours.

As they approached the familiar landing of Van Trumpers farm, Skookum began to show a most zestful interest that recalled the blackened pages of his past. "Quonab, better use that," and Rolf handed a line with which Skookum was secured and thus led to make a new record, for this was the first time in his life that he landed at Van Trumper's without sacrificing a chicken in honour of the joyful occasion.

They entered the house as the family were sitting down to breakfast.

"Mein Hemel! Mein Hemel! It is Roif and Quonab; and vere is dot tarn dog? Marta, vere is de chickens? Vy, Rolf, you bin now a giant, yah. Mein Gott, it is I am glad! I did tink der cannibals you had eat; is it dem Canadian or cannibal? I tink it all one the same, yah!"

Marta was actually crying, the little ones were climbing over Rolf's knee, and Annette, tall and sixteen now, stood shyly by, awaiting a chance to shake hands.

Home is the abiding place of those we love; it may be a castle or a cave, a shanty or a chateau, a moving van, a tepee, or a canal boat, a fortress or the shady side of a bush, but it is home, if there indeed we meet the faces that are ever in the heart, and find the hands whose touch conveys the friendly glow. Was there any other spot on Earth where he could sit by the fire and feel that "hereabout are mine own, the people I love?" Rolf knew it now — Van Trumpers was his home.

Talks of the war, of disasters by land, and of glorious victories on the sea, where England, long the unquestioned mistress of the waves, had been humbled again and again by the dauntless seamen of her Western blood; talks of big doings by the nation, and, yet more interesting, small doings by the travellers, and the breakfast passed all too soon. The young scout rose, for he was on duty, but

the long rollers on the lake forbade the going forth. Van's was a pleasant place to wait, but he chafed at the delay; his pride would have him make a record on every journey. But wait he must. Skookum tied safely to his purgatorial post whined indignantly — and with head cocked on one side, picked out the very hen he would like to utilize — as soon as released from his temporary embarrassment. Quonab went out on a rock to burn some tobacco and pray for calm, and Rolf, ever active, followed Van to look over the stock and buildings, and hear of minor troubles. The chimney was unaccountably given to smoking this year. Rolf took an axe and with two blows cut down a vigorous growth of shrubbery that stood above the chimney on the west, and the smoking ceased. Buck ox had a lame foot and would allow no one even to examine it. But a skilful ox-handler easily hobbles an ox, throws him near some small tree, and then, by binding the lame foot to the tree, can have a free hand. It proved a simple matter, a deep-sunk, rusty nail. And when the nail was drawn and the place washed clean with hot brine, kind nature was left in confidence to do the rest. They drifted back to the house now. Tomas met them shouting out a mixture of Dutch and English and holding by the cover Annette's book of the *Good Girl*. But its rightful owner rescued the precious volume and put it on the shelf.

"Have you read it through, Annette?"

"Yes," was the reply, for she had learned to read before they left Schuylervule.

"How do you like it?"

"Didn't like it a bit; I like *Robinson Crusoe*," was the candid reply.

The noon hour came, still the white rollers were pounding the shore.

"If it does not calm by one o'clock I'll go on afoot." So off he went with the packet, leaving Quonab to follow and await his return at Fort George. In Schuyler settlement he spent the night and at noon next day was in Albany.

How it stirred his soul to see the busy interest, the marching of men, the sailing of vessels, and above all to hear of more victories on the high seas. What mattered a few frontier defeats in the north, when the arrogant foe that had spurned and insulted them before the world had now been humbled again and again.

Young Van Cortlandt was away, but the governor's reception of him reflected the electric atmosphere — the country's pride in her sons.

Rolf in the Woods

Rolf had a matter of his own to settle. At the bookseller's he asked for and actually secured a copy of the great book — *Robinson Crusoe*. It was with a thrilling feeling of triumph that he wrote Annette's name in it and stowed it in his bag.

He left Albany next day in the gray dawn. Thanks to his uniform, he got a twenty-five mile lift with a traveller who drove a fast team, and the blue water was glinting back the stars when he joined Quonab at Fort George, some sixty miles away.

In the calm betwixt star-peep and sun-up they were afloat. It was a great temptation to stop at Hendrik's for a spell, but breakfast was over, the water was calm, and duty called him. He hallooed, then they drew near enough to hand the book ashore. Skookum growled, probably at the hens, and the family waved their aprons as he sped on. Thirty miles of lake and four miles of Ticonderoga Creek they passed and the packet was delivered in four days and three hours since leaving.

The general smiled and his short but amply sufficient praise was merely, "You're a good 'un."

Swamp white oak

LXXV

Scouting in Canada

"THAR is two things," said Si Sylvanne to the senate, "that every national crisis is bound to show up: first, a lot o' dum fools in command; second a lot o great commanders in the ranks. An' fortunately before the crisis is over the hull thing is sure set right, and the men is where they oughter be."

How true this was the nation was just beginning to learn. The fools in command were already demonstrated, and the summer of 1813 was replete with additional evidence. May, June, and July passed with many journeyings for Rolf and many times with sad news. The disasters at Stony Creek, Beaver Dam, and Niagara were severe blows to the army on the western frontier. In June on Lake Champlain the brave but reckless Lieutenant Sidney Smith had run his two sloops into a trap. Thus the *Growler* and the *Eagle* were lost to the Americans, and strengthened by that much the British navy on the lake.

Encouraged by these successes, the British north of Lake Champlain made raid after raid into American territory, destroying what they could not carry off.

Rolf and Quonab were sent to scout in that country and if possible give timely notice of raiders in force.

The Americans were averse to employing Indians in warfare; the British entertained no such scruples and had many red-skinned allies. Quonab's case, however, was unusual, since he was guaranteed by his white partner, and now he did good service, for he knew a little French and could prowl among the settlers without anyone suspecting him of being an American scout.

Thus he went alone and travelled far. He knew the country nearly to Montreal and late in July was lurking about Odletown, when he overheard scattered words of a conversation that made him eager for more. "Colonel Murray — twelve hundred men — four hundred men—"

Rolf in the Woods

Meanwhile Rolf was hiding in the woods about La Colle Mill. Company after company of soldiers he saw enter, until at least five hundred were there. When night came down, he decided to risk a nearer approach. He left the woods and walked cautiously across the open lands about.

The hay had been cut and most of it drawn in, but there was in the middle of the field a hay-cock. Rolf was near this when he heard sounds of soldiers from the mill. Soon large numbers came out, carrying their blankets. Evidently there was not room for them in the mill, and they were to camp on the field.

The scout began to retreat when sounds behind showed that another body of soldiers was approaching from that direction and he was caught between the two. There was only one place to hide and that was beneath the haycock. He lifted its edge and crawled under, but it was full of thistles and brambles; indeed, that was why it was left, and he had the benefit of all the spines about him.

His heart beat fast as he heard the dank of arms and the trampling; they came nearer, then the voices became more distinct. He heard unmistakable evidence too that both bodies were camping for the night, and that he was nearly surrounded. Not knowing what move was best he kept quiet. The men were talking aloud, then they began preparing their beds and he heard some one say, "There's a hay-cock; bring some of that."

A soldier approached to get an armful of the hay, but sputtered out a chapter of malediction as his bare hands touched the masses of thistle and briers. His companions laughed at his mishap. He went to the fire and vowed he'd stick a brand in it and back he came with a burning stick.

Rolf was all ready to make a dash for his life as soon as the cover should take fire, and he peered up into the soldier's face as the latter blew on the brand; but the flame had died, the thistles were not dry, and the fire was a failure; so, growling again, the soldier threw down the smoking stick and went away. As soon as he was safely afar, Rolf gathered a handful of soil and covered the red embers.

Scouting in Canada

It was a critical moment and his waiting alone had saved him.

Two soldiers came with their blankets and spread them near. For a time they smoked and talked. One of them was short of tobacco; the other said, "Never mind, we'll get plenty in Plattsburg," and they guffawed.

Then he heard, "As soon as the colonel" and other broken phrases.

It was a most difficult place for Rolf; he was tormented with thistles in his face and down his neck; he dared not change his position; and how long he must stay was a problem. He would try to escape when all was still.

The nearer soldiers settled to rest now. All was very quiet when Rolf cautiously peeped forth to see two dreadful things: first, a couple of sentries pacing up and down the edges of the camp; second, a broad, brilliant, rising moon. How horrible that lovely orb could be Rolf never before knew.

Now, what next? He was trapped in the middle of a military camp and undoubtedly La Colle Mill was the rendezvous for some important expedition.

He had ample time to think it all over. Unless he could get away before day he would surely be discovered. His uniform might save his life, but soldiers have an awkward, hasty way of dealing summarily with a spy — then discovering too late that he was in uniform.

From time to time he peered forth, but the scene was unchanged — the sleeping regiment, the pacing sentries, the ever-brightening moon. Then the guard was changed, and the sentries relieved selected of all places for their beds, the bank beside the hay-cock. Again one of them went to help himself to some hay for a couch; and again the comic anger as he discovered it to be a bed of thorns. How thankful Rolf was for those annoying things that pricked his face and neck.

He was now hemmed in on every side and, not knowing what to do, did nothing. For a couple of hours he lay still, then actually fell asleep. He was awakened by a faint rustling near his head and peered forth to see a couple of field mice playing about.

The moon was very bright now, and the movements of the mice were plain; they were feeding on the seeds of plants in the hay-cock, and from time to time dashed under the hay. Then they gambolled farther off and were making merry over a pod of wild peas when a light form came skimming noiselessly over the held. There was a flash, a hurried rush, a clutch, a faint squeak, and one of the mice was borne away in the claws of its feathered foe. The survivor scrambled under the hay over Rolf's face and somewhere into hiding.

The night passed in many short naps. The bugle sounded at daybreak and the soldiers arose to make breakfast. Again one approached to use a handful of hay for fire-kindler, and again the friendly thistles did their part. More and more now his ear caught suggestive words and sounds—"Plattsburg"— "the colonel"— etc.

The breakfast smelt wonderfully captivating — poor Rolf was famished. The alluring aroma of coffee permeated the hay-cock. He had his dried meat, but his need was water; he was tormented with thirst, and stiff and tortured; he was making the hardest fight of his life. It seemed long, though doubtless it was less than half an hour before the meal was finished, and to Rolf's relief there were sounds of marching and the noises were drowned in the distance.

By keeping his head covered with hay and slowly raising it, he was safe to take a look around. It was a bright, sunny morning. The hay-cock, or thistle-cock, was one of several that had been rejected. It was a quarter-mile from cover; the soldiers were at work cutting timber and building a stockade around the mill; and, most dreadful to relate, a small dog was prowling about, looking for scraps on the scene of the soldiers' breakfast. If that dog came near his hiding-place, he knew the game was up. At such close quarters, you can fool a man but not a dog.

Fortunately the breakfast tailings proved abundant, and the dog went off to assist a friend of his in making sundry interesting smell analyses along the gate posts of the stockade.

Red acorn

LXXVI

The Duel

THIS was temporary relief, but left no suggestion of complete escape. He lay there till nearly noon suffering more and more from the cramped position and thirst, and utterly puzzled as to the next move.

"When ye don't like whar ye air, git up without any fuss, and go whar ye want to be," was what Sylvanne once said to him, and it came to Rolf with something like a comic shock. The soldiers were busy in the woods and around the forges. In half an hour it would be noon and they might come back to eat.

Rolf rose without attempting any further concealment, then stopped, made a bundle of the stuff that had sheltered him, and, carrying this on his shoulder, strode boldly across the field toward the woods.

His scout uniform was inconspicuous; the scouts on duty at the mill saw only one of themselves taking a bundle of hay round to the stables.

He reached the woods absolutely unchallenged. After a few yards in its friendly shade, he dropped the thorny bundle and strode swiftly toward his own camp. He had not gone a hundred yards before a voice of French type cried "'Alt," and he was face to face with a sentry whose musket was levelled at him.

A quick glance interchanged, and each gasped out the other's name. "François la Colle!"

"Rolf Kittering! Mon Dieu! I ought to shoot you, Rolf; I cannot, I cannot! But run, run! I'll shoot over your head," and his kindly eyes filled with tears.

Rolf needed no second hint; he ran like a deer, and the musket ball rattled the branches above his shoulders.

"Run! I'll shoot over your head"

The Duel

In a few minutes other soldiers came running and from La Colle they heard of the hostile spy in camp.

"I shoot; I t'ink maybe I not hit eem; maybe some blood dere? No, dat notting."

There were both runners and trackers in camp. They were like bloodhounds and they took up the trail of the fugitive. But Rolf was playing his own game now; he was Flying Kittering. A crooked trail is hard to follow, and, going at the long stride that had made his success, he left many a crook and turn. Before two miles they gave it up and the fugitive coming to the river drank a deep and cooling draught, the first he had had that day. Five miles through is the dense forest that lies between La Colle and the border. He struck a creek affluent of the Richelieu River and followed to its forks, which was the place of rendezvous with Quonab.

It was evening as he drew near and after long, attentive listening he gave the cry of the barred owl:

> *Wa, wáh, wa, wáh,*
> *Wa, wáh, wa, hoóóoooo-aw.*

The answer came: a repetition of the last line, and a minute later the two scouts were together.

As they stood, they were startled by a new, sudden answer, an enact repetition of the first call. Rolf had recovered his rifle from its hiding place and instantly both made ready for some hostile prowler; then after a long silence he gave the final wail like "hoooo-aw" and that in the woods means, "Who are you?"

Promptly the reply came:

> *Wa wáh wa wáh*
> *Wa wáh wa hoóoo-aw.*

But this was the wrong reply. It should have been only the last half. The imitation was perfect, except, perhaps, on the last note, which was a trifle too human. But the signal was well done; it was an expert calling, either an Indian or some thoroughly seasoned scout; yet Quonab was not deceived into thinking it an owl. He touched his cheek and his coat, which, in the scout sign language, means "red coat," *i.e.,* Britisher.

Rolf and his partner got silently out of sight, each with his rifle cocked and ready to make a hole in any red uniform or badge that might show itself. Then commenced a very peculiar duel, for evidently the enemy was as clever as themselves and equally anxious to draw them out of cover.

Wa-wáh-wa hooó-aw called the stranger, giving the right answer in the wrong place. He was barely a hundred yards off, and, as the two strained their senses to locate him, they heard a faint click that told of his approach.

Rolf turned his head and behind a tree uttered again the *Wa-wáh -wa - hóo* which muffled by his position would convince the foe that he was retreating. The answer came promptly and much nearer:

Wa - wáh -wa- hoooo-aw.

Good! the medicine was working. So Rolf softened his voice still more, while Quonab got ready to shoot.

The *Wa - wa - hooo-aw* that came in answer this time was startlingly clear and loud and nearly perfect in intonation, but again betrayed by the human timbre of the *aw*. A minute or two more and they would reach a climax.

After another wait, Rolf muffled his voice and gave the single *hooo-aw*, and a great broad-winged owl came swooping through the forest, alighted on a tree overhead, peered about, then thrilled them with his weird:

Wa - hóo - wa - hoo
Wa - hóo- -wa - hooóoooooo-aw,

the last note with the singular human quality that had incompletely set them astray.

LXXVII

Why Plattsburg Was Raided

"The owl's hull reputation for wisdom is built up on lookin' wise and keepin' mum."

— *The Sayings of Si Sylvanne*

THE owl incident was one of the comedies of their life, now they had business on hand. The scraps of news brought by Quonab pieced out with those secured by Rolf, spelt clearly this: that Colonel Murray with about a thousand men was planning a raid on Plattsburg.

Their duty was to notify General Hampton without delay.

Burlington, forty miles away, was headquarters. Plattsburg, twenty miles away, was marked for spoil.

One more item they must add: Was the raid to be by land or water? If the latter, then they must know what preparations were being made at the British naval station, Isle au Noix. They travelled all night through the dark woods to get there, though it was but seven miles away, and in the first full light they saw the gallant array of two warships, three gunboats, and about fifty long boats, all ready, undoubtedly waiting only for a change in the wind, which at this season blew on Champlain almost steadily from the south.

A three-hour, ten-mile tramp through ways now familiar brought Rolf and his partner to the north of the Big Chazy where the canoe was hidden, and without loss of time they pushed off for Burlington, thirty miles away. The wind was head on, and when four hours later they stopped for noon, they had made not more than a dozen miles.

All that afternoon they had to fight a heavy sea; this meant they must keep near shore in case of an upset, and so lengthened the course; but it also meant that the enemy would not move so long as this wind kept up.

Rolf in the Woods

It was six at night before the scouts ran into Burlington Harbour and made for Hampton's headquarters.

His aide received them and, after learning that they had news, went in to the general. From the inner room now they heard in unnecessarily loud tones the great man's orders to, "Bring them in, sah."

The bottles on the table, his purple visage, and thick-tongued speech told how well-founded were the current whispers.

"Raid on Plattsburg? Ha! I hope so. I only hope so. Gentlemen," and he turned to his staff, "all I ask is a chance to get at them — Ha, Ha! Here, help yourself, Macomb," and the general pushed the decanter to a grave young officer who was standing by.

"No, thank you, sir," was the only reply.

The general waved his hand, the scouts went out, puzzled and ashamed. Was this the brains of the army? No wonder our men are slaughtered.

Now Macomb ventured to suggest: "Have you any orders, sir? These scouts are considered quite reliable. I understand from them that the British await only a change of wind. They have between one thousand and two thousand men."

"Plenty of time in the morning, sah. Plattsburg will be the bait of my trap, not one of them shall return alive," and the general dismissed his staff that he might fortify himself against a threatened cold.

Another young man, Lieut. Thomas MacDonough, the naval commandant, now endeavoured to stir him by a sense of danger. First he announced that his long boats and gunboats were ready and in six hours he could transfer three thousand troops from Burlington to Plattsburg. Then he ventured to urge the necessity for action.

Champlain is a lake of two winds. It had blown from the south for two weeks; now a north wind was likely to begin any day. MacDonough urged this point, but all in vain, and, shocked and humiliated, the young man obeyed the order "to wait till his advice was asked."

The next day Hampton ordered a *review*, not an embarkation, and was not well enough to appear in person.

The whole army knew now of the situation of affairs, and the militia in particular were not backward in expressing their minds.

Why Plattsburg Was Raided

Next day, July 30th, the wind changed. Hampton did nothing. On the morning of July 31st they heard the booming of guns in the north, and at night their scouts came with the news that the raid was on. Plattsburg was taken and pillaged by a force less than one third of those held at Burlington.

There were bitter, burning words on the lips of the rank and file, and perfunctory rebukes on the lips of the young officers when they chanced to overhear. The law was surely working out as set forth by Si Sylvanne: "The fools in command, the leaders in the ranks."

And now came news of fresh disasters — the battles of Beaverdam, Stony Creek, and Niagara River. It was the same story in nearly every case — brave fighting men, ill-drilled, but dead shots, led into traps by incompetent commanders.

In September Lieutenant Macomb was appointed to command at Plattsburg. This proved as happy an omen as it was a wise move. Immediately after, in all this gloom, came the news of Perry's famous victory on Lake Erie, marking a new era for the American cause, followed by the destruction of Moraviantown and the British army which held it.

Stirred at last to action General Wilkinson sent despatches to Hampton to arrange an attack on Montreal. There was no possibility of failure, he said, for the sole defence of Montreal was 600 marines. His army consisted of 8000 men. Hampton's consisted of 4000. By a union of these at the mouth of Chateaugay River, they would form an invincible array.

So it seemed. Rolf had not yet seen any actual fighting and began to long for the front. But his powers as a courier kept him ever busy bearing despatches. The road to Sackett's Harbour and thence to Ogdensburg and Covington, and back to Plattsburg he knew thoroughly, and in his canoe he had visited every port on Lakes Champlain and George.

He was absent at Albany in the latter half of October and first of November, but the ill news travelled fast. Hampton requested MacDonough to "swoop down on Isle au Noix" — an insane request, compliance with which would have meant certain destruction to the American

fleet. MacDonough's general instructions were: "Cooperate with the army, but at any price retain supremacy of the lake," and he *declined to receive Hampton's order.*

Threatening court-martials and vengeance on his return, Hampton now set out by land; but at Chateaugay he was met by a much smaller force of Canadians who resisted him so successfully that he ordered a retreat and his army retired to Plattsburg.

Meanwhile General Wilkinson had done even worse. His army numbered 8000. Of these the rear guard were 2500. A body of 800 Canadians harassed their line of march. Turning to brush away this annoyance, the Americans were wholly defeated at Chrystler's farm and, giving up the attack on Montreal, Wilkinson crossed the St. Lawrence and settled for the winter at Chateaugay.

In December, America scored an important advance by relieving Hampton of his command.

As the spring drew near, it was clearly Wilkinson's first play to capture La Colle Mill, which had been turned into a fortress of considerable strength and a base for attack on the American border, some five miles away.

Of all the scouts Rolf best knew that region, yet he was the one left out of consideration and despatched with papers to Plattsburg. The attack was bungled from first to last, and when Wilkinson was finally repulsed, it was due to Macomb that the retreat was not a rout.

But good came out of this evil, for Wilkinson was recalled and the law was nearly fulfilled — the incompetents were gone. General Macomb was in command of the land force and MacDonough of the Lake.

Oak

LXXVIII

Rumours and Papers

MACDONOUGH'S orders were to hold control of the lake. How he did it will be seen. The British fleet at Isle au Noix was slightly stronger than his own, therefore he established a navy yard at Vergennes, in Vermont, seven miles up the Otter River, and at the mouth erected earthworks and batteries. He sent for Brown,* a famous New York shipbuilder. Brown agreed to launch a ship of twenty-four guns in sixty days. The trees were standing in the forest on March 2d, the keel was laid March 7th, and on April 11th the *Saratoga* was launched — forty days after the timbers were green standing trees on the hills.

Other vessels were begun and pushed as expeditiously. And now MacDonough's wisdom in choice of the navy yard was seen, for a British squadron was sent to destroy his infant fleet, or at least sink stone-boats across the exit so as to bottle it up.

But their attempts were baffled by the batteries which the far-seeing American had placed at the river's mouth.

The American victory at Chippewa was followed by the defeat at Lundy's Lane, and on August 25 th the city of Washington was captured by the British and its public buildings destroyed. These calamities, instead of dampening the spirits of the army, roused the whole nation at last to a realization of the fact that they were at war. Fresh troops and plentiful supplies were voted, the dead wood commanders were retired, and the real men revealed by the two campaigns were given place and power.

---

* Of the firm of Adam and Noah Brown

Choke cherry

Rolf in the Woods

At the same time, Great Britain, having crushed Napoleon, was in a position to greatly reinforce her American army, and troops seasoned in Continental campaigns were poured into Canada.

All summer Rolf was busied bearing despatches. During the winter he and Quonab had built a birch canoe on special lines for speed; it would carry two men but no baggage.

With this he could make fully six miles an hour for a short time, and average five on smooth water. In this he had crossed and recrossed Champlain, and paddled its length, till he knew every bay and headland. The overland way to Sackett's Harbour he had traversed several times; the trail from Plattsburg to Covington he knew in all weathers, and had repeatedly covered its sixty miles in less than twenty-four hours on foot. The route he picked and followed was in later years the line selected for the military highway between these two camps.

But the chief scene of his activities was the Canadian wilderness at the north end of Lake Champlain. Chazy, Champlain, Odelltown, La Colle Mill, Isle au Noix, and Richelieu River he knew intimately and had also acquired a good deal of French in learning their country.

It was characteristic of General Wilkinson to ignore the scout who knew, and equally characteristic of his successors, Izard and Macomb, to seek and rely on the best man.

The news that he brought in many different forms was that the British were again concentrating an army to strike at Plattsburg and Albany.

Izard on the land at Plattsburg and Champlain, and Macomb at Burlington strained all their resources to meet the invader at fair terms. Izard had 4000 men assembled, when an extraordinary and devastating order from Washington compelled him to abandon the battle front at Champlain and lead his troops to Sackett's Harbour where all was peace. He protested like a statesman, then obeyed like a soldier, leaving Macomb in command of the land forces of Lake Champlain, with, all told, some 3400 men.

On the day that Izard left Champlain, the British troops, under Brisbane, advanced and occupied his camp.

Rumours and Papers

As soon as Rolf had seen them arrive, and had gauged their number, he sent Quonab back to report, and later retired by night ten miles up the road to Chazy. He was well known to many of the settlers and was welcome whereever known, not only because he was a patriot fighting his country's battles, but for his own sake, for he was developing into a handsome, alert, rather silent youth. It is notorious that in the drawing-room, given equal opportunity, the hunter has the advantage over the farmer. He has less self-consciousness, more calm poise. He is not troubled about what to do with his feet and hands, and is more convinced of his native dignity and claims to respect. In the drawing-room Rolf was a hunter; the leading inhabitants of the region around received him gladly and honoured him. He was guest at Judge Hubbell's in Chazy, in September of 1814. Every day he scouted in the neighbourhood and at night returned to the hospitable home of the judge.

On the 12th of September, from the top of a tall tree on a distant wooded hill, he estimated the force at Champlain to be 10,000 to 15,000 men. Already their bodyguard was advancing on Chazy.

Judge Hubbell and anxious neighbours hastily assembled now, discussed with Rolf the situation and above all, "What shall we do with our families?" One man broke into a storm of hate and vituperation against the British. "Remember the burning of Washington and the way they treated the women at Bladensburg."

"All of which about the women was utterly disproved, except in one case, and in that the criminal was shot by order of his own commander," retorted Hubbell.

At Plattsburg others maintained that the British had harmed no one. Colonel Murray had given strict orders that all private property be absolutely respected. Nothing but government property was destroyed and only that which could be construed into war stores and buildings. What further damage was done was the result of accident or error. Officers were indeed quartered on the inhabitants, but they paid for what they got, and even a carpet destroyed by accident was replaced months afterward by a British officer who had not the means at the time.

So it was agreed that Hubbell with Rolf and the village fathers and brothers should join their country's army, leaving wives and children behind.

There were wet bearded cheeks among the strong, rugged men as they kissed their wives and little ones and prepared to go, then stopped, as horrible misgivings rose within. "This was war, and yet again, 'We have had proofs that the British harmed no woman or child.'" So they dashed away the tears, suppressed the choking in their throats, shouldered their guns, and marched away to the front, commending their dear ones to the mercy of God and the British invaders.

None had any cause to regret this trust. Under pain of death, Sir George Prevost enforced his order that the persons of women and children and all private property be held inviolate. As on the previous raid, no damage was done to non-combatants, and the only hardships endured were by the few who, knowing nothing, feared much, and sought the precarious safety of life among the hills.

Sir George Prevost and his staff of ten officers were quartered in Judge Hubbell's house. Mrs. Hubbell was hard put to furnish them with meals, but they treated her with perfect respect, and every night, not knowing how long they might stay, they left on the table the price of their board and lodging.

For three days they waited, then all was ready for the advance.

"Now for Plattsburg this week and Albany next, so good-bye, madam," they said politely, and turned to ride away, a gay and splendid group.

"Good-bye, sirs, for a very little while, but I know you'll soon be back and hanging your heads as you come," was the retort.

Sir George replied: "If a man had said that, I would call him out; but since it is a fair lady that has been our charming hostess, I reply that when your prophecy comes true, every officer here shall throw his purse on your door step as he passes."

So they rode away, 13,000 trained men with nothing between them and Albany but 2000 troops, double as many raw militia, and — MacDonough of the Lake.

Ten times did Rolf cover that highway north of Plattsburg in the week that followed, and each day his tidings were the same — the British steadily advance.

Witch hazel

LXXIX

McGlassin's Exploit

THERE was a wonderful spirit on everything in Plattsburg, and the earthly tabernacle in which it dwelt, was the tall, grave young man who had protested against Hampton's behaviour at Burlington — Captain, now General Macomb. Nothing was neglected, every emergency was planned for, every available man was under arms. Personally tireless, he was ever alert and seemed to know every man in his command; and every man of it had implicit confidence in the leader. We have heard of soldiers escaping from a besieged fortress by night; but such was the inspiring power of this commander that there was a steady *leaking in* of men from the hills, undrilled and raw, but of superb physique and dead shots with the rifle.

A typical case was that of a sturdy old farmer who was marching through the woods that morning to take his place with those who manned the breastworks and was overheard to address his visibly trembling legs: "Shake, damn you, shake; and if ye knew where I was leading you, you'd be ten times worse."

His mind was more valiant than his body, and his mind kept control — this is true courage.

No one had a better comprehension of all this than Macomb. He knew that all these men needed was a little training to make of them the best soldiers on earth. To supply that training he mixed them with veterans, and arranged a series of unimportant skirmishes as coolly and easily as though he were laying out a programme for an evening's entertainment.

The first of these was at Culver's Hill. Here a barricade was thrown up along the highway, a gun was mounted, and several hundred riflemen were posted under leaders skilled in the arts of harrying a foe and giving him no chance to strike back.

Rolf in the Woods

Among the men appointed for the barricade's defence was Rolf and near him Quonab. The latter had been seasoned in the Revolution, but it was the former's first experience at the battle front, and he felt as most men do when the enemy in brave array comes marching up. As soon as they were within long range, his leader gave the order "Fire!" The rifles rattled and the return fire came at once. Balls pattered on the barricade or whistled above. The man next to him was struck and dropped with a groan; another fell back dead. The horror and roar were overmuch. Rolf was nervous enough when he entered the fight. Now he was unstrung, almost stunned, his hands and knees were shaking, he was nearly panic-stricken and could not resist the temptation to duck, as the balls hissed *murder* over his head. He was blazing away, without aiming, when an old soldier, noting his white face and shaking form, laid a hand on his shoulder and, in kindly tones, said: "Steady, boy, steady; yer losing yer head; see, this is how," and he calmly took aim, then, without firing, moved the gun again and put a little stick to raise the muzzle and make a better rest, then fired as though at target practice. "Now rest for a minute. Look at Quonab there; you can see he's been through it before. He is making a hit with every shot."

Rolf did as he was told, and in a few minutes his colour came back, his hand was steady, and thenceforth he began to forget the danger and thought only of doing his work.

When at length it was seen that the British were preparing to charge, the Americans withdrew quickly and safely to Halsey's Corner, where was another barricade and a fresh lot of recruits awaiting to receive their baptism of fire. And the scene was repeated. Little damage was done to the foe but enormous benefit was gained by the Americans, because it took only one or two of these skirmishes to turn a lot of shaky-kneed volunteers into a band of steady soldiers — for they had it all inside. Thus their powder terror died.

McGlassin's Exploit

That night the British occupied the part of the town that was north of the Saranac, and began a desultory bombardment of the fortification opposite. Not a very serious one, for they considered they could take the town at any time, but preferred to await the arrival of their fleet under Downie.

The fight for the northern half of the town was not serious, merely part of Macomb's prearranged training course; but when the Americans retired across the Saranac, the planks of the bridges were torn up, loop-holed barricades were built along the southern bank, and no effort spared to prepare for a desperate resistance.

Every man that could hold up a gun was posted on the lines of Plattsburg. The school-boys, even, to the number of five hundred formed a brigade, and were assigned to places where their squirrel-hunting experiences could be made of service to their country.

Meanwhile the British had established a battery opposite Fort Brown. It was in a position to do some material and enormous moral damage. On the ninth it was nearly ready for bloody work, and would probably begin next morning. That night, however, an extraordinary event took place, and showed how far from terror-palsy were the motley troops in Plattsburg. A sturdy Vermonter, named Captain McGlassin, got permission of Macomb to attempt a very Spartan sortie.

He called for fifty volunteers to go on a most hazardous enterprise. He got one thousand at once. Then he ordered all over twenty-five and under eighteen to retire. This reduced the number to three hundred. Then, all married men were retired, and thus again they were halved Next he ordered away all who smoked — Ah, deep philosopher that he was! — and from the remnant he selected his fifty. Among them was Rolf. Then he divulged his plan. It was nothing less than a dash on the new-made fort to spike those awful guns — fifty men to dash into a camp of thirteen thousand.

Again he announced, "Any who wish to withdraw now may do so." Not a man stirred.

Twenty of those known to be expert with tools were provided with hammers and spikes for the guns, and Rolf was proud to be one of them.

In a night of storm and blackness they crossed the Saranac; dividing in two bodies they crawled unseen, one on each side of the battery. Three hundred British soldiers were sleeping near, only the sentries peered into the storm-sleet.

Rolf in the Woods

All was ready when McGlassin's tremendous voice was heard, "Charge front and rear!" Yelling, pounding, making all the noise they could, the American boys rushed forth. The British were completely surprised, the sentries were struck down, and the rest assured that Macomb's army was on them recoiled for a few minutes. The sharp *click, click, click* of the hammers was heard. An iron spike was driven into every touch hole; the guns were made harmless as logs and quickly wheeling, to avoid the return attack, these bold Yankee boys leaped from the muzzled redoubt and reached their own camp without losing one of their number.

LXXX

The Bloody Saranac

SIR GEORGE PREVOST had had no intention of taking Plattsburg, till Plattsburg's navy was captured. But the moral effect of McGlassin's exploit must be offset at once. He decided to carry the city by storm — a matter probably of three hours' work.

He apportioned a regiment to each bridge, another to each ford near the town, another to cross the river at Pike's Cantonment, and yet another to cross twenty miles above, where they were to harry the fragments of the American army as it fled.

That morning Plattsburg was wakened by a renewal of the bombardment. The heavy firing killed a few men, knocked down a few walls and chimneys, but did little damage to the earthworks.

It was surprising to all how soon the defenders lost their gun-shyness. The very school-boys and their sisters went calmly about their business, with cannon and musket balls whistling overhead, striking the walls and windows, or, on rare occasions, dropping some rifleman who was over-rash as he worked or walked on the ramparts.

There were big things doing in the British camp — regiments marching and taking their places — storms of rifle and cannon balls raging fiercely. By ten o'clock there was a lull. The Americans, from the grandfathers to the school-boys, were posted, each with his rifle and his pouch full of balls; there were pale faces among the youngsters, and nervous fingers, but there was no giving way. Many a man there was, no doubt, who, under the impulse of patriotism, rushed with his gun to join the ranks, and when the bloody front was reached, he wished in his heart he was safe at home. But they did not go. Something kept them staunch.

Although the lines were complete all along the ramparts, there were four places where the men were massed. These were on the embankments opposite the bridges and the fords. Here the best shots were placed and among them was Rolf, with others of McGlassin's band.

The plank of the bridges had been torn up and used with earth to form breastworks; but the stringers of the bridges were there, and a body of red-coats approaching, each of them showed plainly what their plan was.

The farthest effective range of rifle fire in those days was reckoned at a hundred yards. The Americans were ordered to hold their fire till the enemy reached the oaks, a grove one hundred yards from the main bridge — on the other bank.

The British came on in perfect review-day style. Now a hush fell on all. The British officer in command was heard clearly giving his orders. How strange it must have been to the veterans of wars in Spain, France, and the Rhine, to advance against a force with whom they needed no interpreter.

McGlassin's deep voice now rang along the defences, "Don't fire till I give the order."

The red-coats came on at a trot, they reached the hundred-yard-mark.

"Now, aim low and fire!" from McGlassin, and the rattle of the Yankee guns was followed by reeling ranks of red in the oaks.

"Charge!" shouted the British officer and the red-coats charged to the bridge, but the fire from the embankment was incessant; the trail of the charging men was cluttered with those who fell.

"Forward!" and the gallant British captain leaped on the central stringer of the bridge and, waving his sword, led on. Instantly three lines of men were formed, one on each stringer.

They were only fifty yards from the barricade, with five hundred rifles, all concentrated on these stringers. The first to fall was the captain, shot through the heart, and the river bore him away. But on and on came the three ranks into the whistling, withering fire of lead. It was like slaughtering sheep. Yet on and on they marched steadily for half an hour. Not a man held back or turned, though all knew they were marching to their certain death. Not one of them ever reached the centre of the span, and those who dropped, not dead, were swallowed by the swollen stream. How many hundred brave men were sacrificed that day, no one ever knew. He who gave the word to charge was dead with his second and third in command and before another could come to change the order, the river ran red — the Bloody Saranac they call it ever since.

The regiment was wrecked, and the assault for the time was over.

Rolf had plied his rifle with the rest, but it sickened him to see the horrible waste of human valour. It was such ghastly work that he was glad indeed when a messenger came to say he was needed at headquarters. And in an hour he was crossing the lake with news and instructions for the officer in command at Burlington.

LXXXI

The Battle of Plattsburg

IN BROAD daylight he skimmed away in his one-man canoe.

For five hours he paddled, and at star-peep he reached the dock at Burlington. The howl of a lost dog caught his ear; and when he traced the sound, there, on the outmost plank, with his nose to the skies, was the familiar form of Skookum, wailing and sadly alone.

What a change he showed when Rolf landed; he barked, leaped, growled, tail-wagged, head-wagged, feet-wagged, body-wagged, wig-wagged and zigzagged for joy; he raced in circles, looking for a sacrificial hen, and finally uttered a long and conversational whine that doubtless was full of information for those who could get it out.

Rolf delivered his budget at once. It was good news, but not conclusive. Everything depended now on MacDonough. In the morning all available troops should hurry to the defence of Plattsburg; not less than fifteen hundred men were ready to embark at daylight.

That night Rolf slept with Skookum in the barracks. At daybreak, much to the latter's disgust, he was locked up in a cellar, and the troops embarked for the front.

It was a brisk north wind they had to face in crossing and passing down the lake. There were many sturdy oarsmen at the sweeps, but they could not hope to reach their goal in less than five hours.

When they were half way over, they heard the cannon roar; the booming became incessant; without question, a great naval battle was on, for this north wind was what the British had been awaiting.

The rowers bent to their task and added to the speed. Their brothers were hard pressed; they knew it, they must make haste. The long boats flew. In an hour they could see the masts, the sails, the smoke of the battle, but nothing gather of the portentous result. Albany and New York, as well as Plattsburg, were in the balance, and the oarsmen rowed and rowed and rowed.

Rolf in the Woods

The cannon roared louder and louder, though less continuously, as another hour passed. Now they could see the vessels only four miles away. The jets of smoke were intermittent from the guns; masts went down. They could see it plainly. The rowers only set their lips and rowed and rowed and rowed.

Sir George had reckoned on but one obstacle in his march to Albany, an obstruction named MacDonough; but he now found there was another called Macomb.

It was obviously a waste of men to take Plattsburg by front assault, when he could easily force a passage of the river higher up and take it on the rear; and it was equally clear that when his fleet arrived and crushed the American fleet, it would be a simple matter for the war vessels to blow the town to pieces, without risking a man.

Already a favouring wind had made it possible for Downie to leave Isle au Noix and sail down the lake with his gallant crew, under gallant canvas clouds.

Tried men and true in control of every ship, out-numbering Mac-Donough, outweighing him, outpointing him in everything but seamanship, they came on, sure of success.

Three chief moves were in MacDonough's strategy. He anchored to the northward of the bay, so that any fleet coming down the lake would have to beat up against the wind to reach him; so close to land that any fleet trying to flank him would come within range of the forts; and left only one apparent gap that a foe might try to use, a gap in front of which was a dangerous sunken reef. This was indeed a baited trap. Finally he put out cables, kedges, anchors, and springs, so that with the capstan he could turn his vessels and bring either side to bear on the foe.

All was ready, that morning of September the 11th, as the British fleet, ably handled, swung around the Cumberland Head.

The young commander of the Yankee fleet now kneeled bareheaded with his crew and prayed to the God of Battles as only those going into

battle pray. The gallant foe came on, and who that knows him doubts that he, too, raised his heart in reverent prayer? The first broadside from the British broke open a chicken coop on the *Saratoga* from which a game-cock flew, and, perching on a gun, flapped his wings and crowed; so all the seamen cheered at such a happy omen.

Then followed the fighting, with its bravery and its horrors — its brutish wickedness broke loose.

Early in the action, the British sloop, *Finch*, fell into Mac-Donough's trap and grounded on the reef.

The British commander was killed, with many of his officers. Still, the heavy fire of the guns would have given them the victory, but for MacDonough's foresight in providing for swinging his ships. When one broadside was entirely out of action, he used his cables, kedges, and springs, and brought the other batteries to bear.

It was one of the most desperate naval fights the world has ever seen. Of the three hundred men on the British flag-ship not more than five, we are told, escaped uninjured; and at the close there was not left on any one of the eight vessels a mast that could carry sail, or a sail that could render service. In less than two hours and a half the fight was won, and the British fleet destroyed.

To the God of Battles each had committed his cause: and the God of Battles had spoken.

Far away to the southward in the boats were the Vermont troops with their general and Rolf in the foremost. Every sign of the fight they had watched as men whose country's fate is being tried.

It was a quarter after eleven when the thunder died away; and the Vermonters were headed on shore, for a hasty landing, if need be, when down from the peak of the British flag-ship went the Union Jack, and the Stars and Stripes was hauled to take its place.

"Thank God!" a soft, murmuring sigh ran through all the boats and many a bronzed and bearded cheek was wet with tears. Each man clasped hands with his neighbour; all were deeply moved, and even as an audience melted renders no applause, so none felt any wish to vent his deep emotion in a cheer.

LXXXII

Scouting for Macomb

GENERAL MACOMB knew that Sir George Prevost was a cautious and experienced commander. The loss of his fleet would certainly make a radical change in his plans, but what change? Would he make a flank move and dash on to Albany, or retreat to Canada, or entrench himself to await reinforcements at Plattsburg, or try to retrieve his laurels by an overwhelming assault on the town?

Whatever his plan, he would set about it quickly, and Macomb studied the enemy's camp with a keen, discerning eye, but nothing suggesting a change was visible when the sun sank in the rainy west.

It was vital that he know it at once when an important move was begun, and as soon as the night came down, a score of the swiftest scouts were called for. All were young men; most of them had been in McGlassin's band. Rolf was conspicuous among them for his tall figure, but there was a Vermont boy named Seymour, who had the reputation of being the swiftest runner of them all.

They had two duties laid before them: first, to find whether Prevost's army was really retreating; second, what of the regiment he sent up the Saranac to perform the flank movement.

Each was given the country he knew best. Some went westerly, some followed up the river. Rolf, Seymour, and Fiske, another Vermonter, skimmed out of Plattsburg harbour in the dusk, rounded Cumberland Bend, and at nine o'clock landed at Point au Roche, at the north side of Treadwell's Bay.

Here they hid the canoe and agreeing to meet again at midnight, set off in three different westerly directions to strike the highway at different points. Seymour, as the fast racer, was given the northmost route; Rolf took the middle. Their signals were arranged — in the woods the barred-owl cry, by the water the loon; and they parted.

Rolf in the Woods

The woods seemed very solemn to Rolf that historic September night, as he strode along at speed, stopping now and again when he thought he heard some signal, and opened wide his mouth to relieve his ear-drums of the heart-beat or to still the rushing of his breath.

In half an hour he reached the high-road. It was deserted. Then he heard a cry of the barred owl:

Wa — wah — wa — wah
Wa — wah — wa — hooooo-aw.

He replied with the last line, and the answer came a repeat of the whole chant, showing that it might be owl, it might be man; but it was not the right man, for the final response should have been the *hooooo-aw*. Rolf never knew whence it came, but gave no further heed.

For a long time he sat in a dark corner, where he could watch the road. There were sounds of stir in the direction of Plattsburg. Then later, and much nearer, a couple of shots were fired. He learned afterward that those shots were meant for one of his friends. At length there was a faint *tump ta tump ta*. He drew his knife, stuck it deep in the ground, then held the handle in his teeth. This acted like a magnifier, for now he heard it plainly enough — the sound of a horse at full gallop — but so far away that it was five minutes before he could clearly hear it while standing. As the sound neared, he heard the clank of arms, and when it passed, Rolf knew that this was a mounted British officer. But why, and whither?

In order to learn the rider's route, Rolf followed at a trot for a mile. This brought him to a hilltop, whither in the silent night, that fateful north wind carried still the sound—

te — rump te — rump te — rump

As it was nearly lost, Rolf used his knife again; that brought the rider back within a mile it seemed, and again the hoof beat faded, *te — rump te— rump te — rump.*

"Bound for Canada all right," Rolf chuckled to himself. But there was nothing to show whether this was a mere despatch rider, or an advance scout, or a call for reinforcements.

So again he had a long wait. About half-past ten a new and larger sound came from the south. The knife in the ground increased but did not explain it. The night was moonless, dark now, and it was safe to sit very near the road. In twenty minutes the sound was near at hand, in five, a dark mass was passing along the road. There is no mistaking the language of drivers. There is never any question about such and such a voice being that of an English officer. There can be no doubt about the clank of heavy wheels — a rich, tangy voice from someone in advance said: "Oui. Parbleu, tous ce que je sais, c'est par là." A body of about one hundred Britishers, two or three wagons, guns, and a Frenchman for guide. Rolf thought he knew that voice; yes, he was almost sure it was the voice of François la Colle.

This was important but far from conclusive. It was now eleven. He was due at the canoe by midnight. He made for the place as fast as he could go, which, on such a night, was slow, but guided by occasional glimpses of the stars he reached the lake, and pausing a furlong from the landing, he gave the rolling, quivering loon call:

Ho-o-o-o-000-0
Ho-o-o-o-000-0.
Hooo-ooo.

After ten seconds the answer came:

Ho-o-o-o-o-o-o-o
Hoo-ooo.

And again after ten seconds Rolf's reply:

Hoo-ooo.

Both his friends were there; Fiske with a bullet-hole through his arm. It seemed their duty to go back at once to headquarters with the meagre information and their wounded comrade. But Fiske made light of his trouble — it was a mere scratch — and reminded them that their orders were to make sure of the enemy's movements. Therefore, it was arranged that Seymour take back Fiske and what news they had, while Rolf went on to complete his scouting.

By one o'clock he was again on the hill where he had marked the horseman's outward flight and the escorted guns. Now, as he waited, there were sounds in the north that faded, and in the south were similar sounds that grew. Within an hour he was viewing a still larger body of troops with drivers and wheels that clanked. There were only two explanations possible: Either the British were concentrating on Chazy

Landing, where, protected from MacDonough by the north wind, they could bring enough stores and forces from the north to march overland independent of the ships, or else they were in full retreat for Canada. There was but one point where this could be made sure, namely, at the forks of the road in Chazy village. So he set out at a jog trot for Chazy, six miles away.

The troops ahead were going three miles an hour. Rolf could go five. In twenty minutes he overtook them and now was embarrassed by their slowness. What should he do? It was nearly impossible to make speed through the woods in the darkness, so as to pass them. He was forced to content himself by marching a few yards in their rear.

Once or twice when a group fell back, he was uncomfortably close and heard scraps of their talk.

These left little doubt that the army was in retreat. Still this was the mere chatter of the ranks. He curbed his impatience and trudged with the troop. Once a man dropped back to light his pipe. He almost touched Rolf, and seeing a marching figure, asked in unmistakable accents "Oi soi, matey, 'ave ye a loight?"

Rolf assumed the low south country English dialect, already familiar through talking with prisoners, and replied: "Naow, oi oin't a-smowking," then gradually dropped out of sight.

They were nearly two hours in reaching Chazy where they passed the Forks, going straight on north. Without doubt, now, the army was bound for Canada! Rolf sat on a fence near by as their footsteps went *tramp, tramp, tramp* — with the wagons, *clank, clank, clank,* and were lost in the northern distance.

He had seen perhaps three hundred men; there were thirteen thousand to account for, and he sat and waited. He did not have long to wait; within half an hour a much larger body of troops evidently was approaching from the south; several lanterns gleamed ahead of them, so Rolf got over the fence, but it was low and its pickets offered poor shelter. Farther back was Judge Hubbell's familiar abode with dense

348

shrubbery. He hastened to it and in a minute was hidden where he could see something of the approaching troops. They were much like those that had gone before, but much more numerous, at least a regiment, and as they filled the village way, an officer cried "Halt!" and gave new orders. Evidently they were about to bivouac for the night. A soldier approached the picket fence to use it for firewood, but an officer rebuked him. Other fuel, chiefly fence rails, was found, and a score or more of fires were lighted on the highway and in the adjoining pasture. Rolf found himself in something like a trap, for in less than two hours now would be the dawn.

The simplest way out was to go in; he crawled quietly round the house to the window of Mrs. Hubbell's room. These were times of nervous tension, and three or four taps on the pane were enough to arouse the good lady. Her husband had come that way more than once.

"Who is it?" she demanded, through a small opening of the sash.

"Rolf Kittering," he whispered, "the place is surrounded by soldiers; can't you hide me?"

Could she? Imagine an American woman saying "No" at such a time.

He slipped in quietly.

"What news?" she said. "They say that MacDonough has won on the Lake, but Plattsburg is taken."

"No, indeed; Pittsburgh is safe; MacDonough has captured the fleet. I am nearly sure that the whole British army is retiring to Canada."

"Thank God, thank God," she said fervently, "I knew it must be so; the women have met here and prayed together every day, morning and night. But hush!" she laid a warning finger on her lips and pointed up toward one of the rooms —"British officer."

She brought two blankets from a press and led up to the garret. At the lowest part of the roof was a tiny door to a lumber closet. In this Rolf spread his blankets, stretched his weary limbs, and soon was sound asleep.

Rolf in the Woods

At dawn the bugles blew, the camp was astir. The officer in the house arose and took his post on the porch. He was there on guard to protect the house. His brother officers joined him. Mrs. Hubbell prepared breakfast. It was eaten silently, so far as Rolf could learn. They paid for it and, heading their regiment, went away northward, leaving the officer still on the porch.

Presently Rolf heard a stealthy step in his garret, the closed door was pushed open, and Mrs. Hubbell's calm, handsome face appeared, as, with a reassuring nod, she set down a mug of coffee, some bread, and a bowl of mush and milk. And only those who have travelled and fasted for twelve hours when they were nineteen know how good it tasted.

From a tiny window ventilator Rolf had a view of the road in front. A growing din of men prepared him for more troops, but still he was surprised to see ten regiments march past with all their stores — a brave army, but no one could mistake their looks; they wore the despondent air of an army in full retreat.

LXXXIII

The Last of Sir George Prevost

THE battle was over at Plattsburg town, though it had not been fought; for the spirit of MacDonough was on land and water, and it was felt by the British general, as well as the Yankee riflemen, as soon as the Union Jack had been hauled from the mast of the *Confiance.*

Now Sir George Prevost had to face a momentous decision: He could force the passage of the Saranac and march on to Albany, but his communications would be cut, and he must rely on a hostile country for supplies. Every day drew fresh bands of riflemen from the hills. Before he could get to Albany their number might exceed his, and then what? Unless Great Britain could send a new army or a fleet to support him, he must meet the fate of Burgoyne. Prevost proposed to take no such chances and the night of the 11th, eight hours after MacDonough's victory, he gave the order "Retire to Canada."

To hide the move as long as possible, no change was made till after sundown; no hint was given to the beleaguered town; they must have no opportunity to reap the enormous advantages, moral and material, of harrying a retreating foe. They must arise in the morning to find the enemy safely over the border. The plan was perfect, and would have been literally carried out, had not he had to deal with a foe as clever as himself.

How eagerly Rolf took in the scene on Chazy Road; how much it meant! How he longed to fly at his fastest famous speed with the stirring news. In two hours and a half he could surely let his leader know. And he gazed with a sort of superior pride at the martial pomp and bravery of the invaders driven forth.

Near the last was a gallant array of gentlemen in gorgeous uniforms of scarlet and gold; how warlike they looked, how splendid beside the ill-clad riflemen of Vermont and the rude hunters of the Adirondacks.

How much more beautiful is an iron sword with jewels, than a sword of plain gray steel.

Dame Hubbell stood in her door as they went by. Each and all saluted politely; her guard was ordered to join his regiment. The lady waved her sun-bonnet in response to their courteous good-bye, and could not refrain from calling out:

"How about my prophecy, Sir George, and those purses?"

Rolf could not see his hostess, but he heard her voice, and he saw the astonishing effect:

The British general reined in his horse. "A gentleman's word is his bond, madam," he said. "Let every officer now throw his purse at the lady's feet," and he set the example. A dozen rattling thuds were heard and a dozen officers saluting, purseless, rode away.

Around thousand dollars in gold the lady gathered on her porch that morning, and to this day her grand-kin tell the tale.

LXXXIV

Rolf Unmasks the Ambush

ROLF'S information was complete now, and all that remained was to report at Plattsburg. Ten regiments he had counted from his peep hole. The rear guard passed at ten o'clock. At eleven Mrs. Hubbell did a little scouting and reported that all was quiet as far as she could see both ways, and no enemy in sight anywhere.

With a grateful hand shake he left the house to cover the fourteen miles that lay between Chazy and Plattsburg.

Refreshed and fed, young and strong, the representative of a just and victorious cause, how he exulted in that run, rejoicing in his youth, his country, his strength, his legs, his fame as a runner. Starting at a stride he soon was trotting; then, when the noon hour came, he had covered a good six miles. Now he heard faint, far shots, and going more slowly was soon conscious that a running fight was on between his own people and the body of British sent westward to hold the upper Saranac.

True to the instinct of the scout, his first business was to find out exactly what and where they were. From a thick tree top he saw the red-coats spotting an opening of the distant country. Then they were lost sight of in the woods. The desultory firing became volley firing, once or twice. Then there was an interval of silence. At length a mass of red-coats appeared on the highway within half a mile. They were travelling very fast, in full retreat, and were coming his way. On the crest of the hill over which the road ran, Rolf saw them suddenly drop to the ground and take up position to form a most dangerous ambuscade, and half a mile away, straggling through the woods, running or striding, were the men in the colours he loved. They had swept the enemy before them, so far, but trained troops speedily recover from a panic, if they have a leader of nerve, and seeing a noble chance in the angle of this deep-sunk road, the British fugitives turned like boars at bay. Not a sign of them was visible to the Americans. The latter were suffering from too much success. Their usual caution seemed to have deserted them, and trotting in a body they came along the narrow road, hemmed in by a forest and soon to be hedged with cliffs of clay. They were heading for a death-trap. At any price he must warn them. He slid down the tree, and keeping cover ran as fast as possible toward the ambush. It was the only hill near — Beekman's Rise, they call it. As far as possible from the red-coats, but still on the hill that gave a view, he leaped on to a high stump and yelled as he never did before: "Go back, go back! A trap! A trap!" And lifting high his outspread hands he flung their palms toward his friends, the old-time signal for "go back."

Not twice did they need warning. Like hunted wolves they flashed from view in the nearest cover. A harmless volley from the baffled ambush rattled amongst them, and leaping from his stump Rolf ran for life.

Furious at their failure, a score of red-coats, reloading as they ran, came hot-footed after him. Down into cover of an alder swamp he plunged, and confident of his speed, ran on, dashing through thickets and mudholes. He knew that the red-coats would not follow far in such a place, and his comrades were near. But the alder thicket ended at a field. He heard the bushes crashing close at hand, and dashed down a little ravine at whose lower edge the friendly forest recommenced. That was his fatal mistake. The moment he took to the open there was a rattle of rifles from the hill above, and Rolf fell on his face as dead.

It was after noontide when he fell; he must have lain unconscious for an hour; when he came to himself he was lying still in that hollow, absolutely alone. The red-coats doubtless had continued their flight with the Yankee boys behind them. His face was covered with blood. His coat was torn and bloody; his trousers showed a ragged rent that was reddened and sopping. His head was aching, and in his leg was the pain of a cripplement. He knew it as soon as he tried to move; his right leg was shattered below the knee. The other shots had grazed his arm and head; the latter had stunned him for a time, but did no deeper damage.

Rolf Unmasks the Ambush

He lay still for a long time, in hopes that some of his friends might come. He tried to raise his voice, but had no strength. Then he remembered the smoke signal that had saved him when he was lost in the woods. In spite of his wounded arm, he got out his flint and steel, and prepared to make a fire. But all the small wood he could reach was wet with recent rains. An old pine stump was on the bank not far away; he might cut kindling-wood from that to start his fire, and he reached for his knife. Alas! its case was empty. Had Rolf been four years younger, he might have broken down and wept at this. It did seem such an unnecessary accumulation of disasters. Without gun or knife, how was he to call his friends?

He straightened his mangled limb in the position of least pain and lay for a while. The September sun fell on his back and warmed him. He was parched with thirst, but only thirty yards away was a little rill. With a long and fearful crawling on his breast, he dragged himself to the stream and drank till he could drink no more, then rested, washed his head and hands, and tried to crawl again to the warm place. But the sun had dropped behind the river bank, the little ravine was in shadow, and the chill of the grave was on the young man's pain-racked frame.

Shadows crossed his brain, among them Si Sylvanne with his quaint sayings, and one above all was clear:

"Trouble is only sent to make ye do yer best. When ye hev done yer best, keep calm and wait. Things is comin' all right." Yes, that was what he said, and the mockery of it hurt him now.

The sunset slowly ended; the night wind blew; the dragging hours brought gloom that entered in. This seemed indeed the direst strait of his lot. Crippled, dying of cold, helpless, nothing to do but wait and die, and from his groaning lips there came the half-forgotten prayer his mother taught him long ago, "O God, have mercy on me!" and then he forgot.

When he awoke, the stars were shining; he was numb with cold, but his mind was clear.

"This is war," he thought, "and God knows we never sought it." And again the thought: "When I offered to serve my country, I offered

355

In the chill, dark hour . . . he heard the sweet music of Skookum's bark

my life. I am willing to die, but this is not a way of my choosing," and a blessed, forgetfulness came upon him again.

But his was a stubborn-fibred race; his spark of life was not so quickly quenched; its blazing torch might waver, wane, and wax again. In the chill, dark hour when the life-lamp nickers most, he wakened to hear the sweet, sweet music of a dog's loud bark; in a minute he heard it nearer, and yet again at hand, and Skookum, erratic, unruly, faithful Skookum, was bounding around and barking madly at the calm, unblinking stars.

A human "halloo" rang not far away; then others, and Skookum barked and barked.

Now the bushes rustled near, a man came out, kneeled down, laid hand on the dying soldier's brow, and his heart. He opened his eyes, the man bent over him and softly said, "Nibowaka! It's Quonab."

That night when the victorious rangers had returned to Plattsburg it was a town of glad, thankful hearts, and human love ran strong. The thrilling stories of the day were told, the crucial moment, the providential way in which at every hopeless pass, some easy, natural miracle took place to fight their battle and back their country's

In the chill, dark hour . . . he heard the sweet music of Skookum's bark cause. The harrying of the flying rear-guard, the ambuscade over the hill, the appearance of an American scout at the nick of time to warn them — the shooting, and his disappearance — all were discussed.

Then rollicking Seymour and silent Fiske told of their scouting on the trail of the beaten foe; and all asked, "Where is Kittering?" So talk was rife, and there was one who showed a knife he had picked up near the ambuscade with R. K. on the shaft.

Now a dark-faced scout rose up, stared at the knife, and quickly left the room. In three minutes he stood before General Macomb, his words were few, but from his heart:

"It is my boy, Nibowaka; it is Rolf; my heart tells me. Let me go. I feel him praying for me to come. Let me go, general. I must go."

It takes a great man to gauge the heart of a man who seldom speaks. "You may go, but how can you find him to-night?"

"Ugh, I find him," and the Indian pointed to a little, prick-eared, yellow cur that sneaked at his heels.

Rolf in the Woods

"Success to you; he was one of the best we had," said the general, as the Indian left, then added: "Take a couple of men along, and, here, take this," and he held out a flask.

Thus it was that the dawning saw Rolf on a stretcher carried by his three scouting partners, while Skookum trotted ahead, looking this way and that — they should surely not be ambushed this time.

And thus the crowning misfortune, the culminating apex of disaster — the loss of his knife — the thing of all others that roused in Rolf the spirit of rebellion, was the way of life, his dungeon's key, the golden chain that haled him from the pit.

LXXXV

The Hospital, the Prisoners, and Home

THERE were wagons and buckboards to be had, but the road was rough, so the three changed off as litter-bearers and brought him to the lake where the swift and smooth canoe was ready, and two hours later they carried him into the hospital at Plattsburg.

The leg was set at once, his wounds were dressed, he was warmed, cleaned, and fed; and when the morning sun shone in the room, it was a room of calm and peace.

The general came and sat beside him for a time, and the words he spoke were ample, joyful compensation for his wounds. MacDonough, too, passed through the ward, and the warm vibrations of his presence drove death from many a bed whose inmate's force ebbed low, whose soul was walking on the brink, was near surrender.

Rolf did not fully realize it then, but long afterward it was clear that this was the meaning of the well-worn words, "He filled them with a new spirit."

There was not a man in the town but believed the war was over; there was not a man in the town who doubted that his country's cause was won.

Three weeks is a long time to a youth near manhood, but there was much of joy to while away the hours. The mothers of the town came and read and talked. There was news from the front. There were victories on the high seas. His comrades came to sit beside him; Seymour, the sprinter, as merry a soul as ever hankered for the stage and the red cups of life; Fiske, the silent, and Mc-Glassin, too, with his dry, humorous talk; these were the bright and funny hours. There were others. There came a bright-cheeked Vermont mother whose three sons had died in service at MacDonough's guns; and she told of it in a calm voice, as one who speaks of her proudest honour. Yes, she rejoiced that God had given her three such sons, and had taken again His gifts in such a day of

Rolf in the Woods

glory. Had England's rulers only known, that this was the spirit of the land that spoke, how well they might have asked: "What boots it if we win a few battles, and burn a few towns; it is a little gain and passing; for there is one thing that no armies, ships, or laws, or power on earth, or hell itself can down or crush — that alone is the thing that counts or endures — the thing that permeates these men, that finds its focal centre in such souls as that of the Vermont mother, steadfast, proud, and rejoicing in her bereavement."

But these were forms that came and went; there were two that seldom were away — the tall and supple one of the dark face and the easy tread, and his yellow shadow — the ever unpopular, snappish, prick-eared cur, that held by force of arms all territories at floor level contiguous to, under, comprised, and bounded by, the four square legs and corners of the bed.

Quonab's nightly couch was a blanket not far away, and his daily, self-given task to watch the wounded and try by devious ways and plots to trick him into eating ever larger meals.

Garrison duty was light now, so Quonab sought the woods where the flocks of partridge swarmed, with Skookum as his aid. It was the latter's joyful duty to find and tree the birds, and "yap" below, till Quonab came up quietly with bow and blunt arrows, to fill his game-bag; and thus the best of fare was ever by the invalid's bed.

Rolf's was easily a winning fight from the first, and in a week he was eating well, sleeping well, and growing visibly daily stronger.

Then on a fleckless dawn that heralded a sun triumphant, the Indian borrowed a drum from the bandsman, and, standing on the highest breastwork, he gazed across the dark waters to the whitening hills. There on a tiny fire he laid tobacco and kinnikinnik, as Gisiss the Shinning One burnt the rugged world rim at Vermont, and, tapping softly with one stick, he gazed upward, after the sacrificial thread of smoke, and sang in his own tongue:

> "Father, I burn tobacco, I smoke to Thee.
> I sing for my heart is singing."

Pleasant chatter of the East was current by Rolf's bedside. Stories of homes in the hills he heard, tales of hearths by far away lakes and streams, memories of golden-haired children waiting for father's or brother's return from the wars. Wives came to claim their husbands, mothers to bring away their boys, to gain again their strength at home. And his own heart went back, and ever back, to the rugged farm on the shores of the noble George.

In two weeks he was able to sit up. In three he could hobble, and he moved about the town when the days were warm.

And now he made the acquaintance of the prisoners. They were closely guarded and numbered over a hundred. It gave him a peculiar sensation to see them there. It seemed un-American to hold a human captive; but he realized that it was necessary to keep them for use as hostages and exchanges.

Some of them he found to be sullen brutes, but many were kind and friendly, and proved to be jolly good fellows.

On the occasion of his second visit, a familiar voice saluted him with, "Well, Rolf! *Comment ça va?*" and he had the painful joy of greeting François la Colle.

"You'll help me get away, Rolf, won't you?" and the little Frenchman whispered and winked. "I have seven little ones now on La Rivière, dat have no flour, and tinks dere pa is dead."

"I'll do all I can, François," and the picture of the desolate home, brought a husk in his voice and a choke in his throat. He remembered too the musket ball that by intent had whistled harmless overhead. "But," he added in a shaky voice, "I cannot help my country's enemy to escape."

Then Rolf took counsel with McGlassin, told him all about the affair at the mill, and McGlassin with a heart worthy of his mighty shoulders, entered into the spirit of the situation, went to General Macomb presenting such a tale and petition that six hours later François bearing a passport through the lines was trudging away to Canada, paroled for the rest of the war.

Rolf in the Woods

There was another face that Rolf recognized — hollow-cheeked, flabby-jowled and purplish-gray. The man was one of the oldest of the prisoners. He wore a white beard and moustache. He did not recognize Rolf, but Rolf knew him, for this was Micky Kittering. How he escaped from jail and joined the enemy was an episode of the war's first year. Rolf was shocked to see what a miserable wreck his uncle was. He could not do him any good. To identify him would have resulted in his being treated as a renegade, so on the plea that he was an old man, Rolf saw that the prisoner had extra accommodation and out of his own pocket kept him abundantly supplied with tobacco. Then in his heart he forgave him, and kept away. They never met again.

The bulk of the militia had been disbanded after the great battle. A few of the scouts and enough men to garrison the fort and guard the prisoners were retained. Each day there were joyful partings — the men with homes, going home. And the thought that ever waxed in Rolf came on in strength. He hobbled to headquarters. "General, can I get leave — to go" — he hesitated — "home?"

"Why, Kittering, I didn't know you had a home. But, certainly, I'll give you a month's leave and pay to date."

Champlain is the lake of the two winds; the north wind blows for six months with a few variations, and the south wind for the other six months with trifling changes.

Next morning a bark canoe was seen skimming southward before as much north wind as it could stand, with Rolf reclining in the middle, Quonab at the stern, and Skookum in the bow.

In two days they were at Ticonderoga. Here help was easily got at the portage and on the evening of the third day, Quonab put a rope on Skookum's neck and they landed at Hendrik's farm.

The hickory logs were blazing bright, and the evening pot was reeking as they opened the door and found the family gathered for the meal.

"I didn't know you had a home," the general had said. He should have been present now to see the wanderer's welcome. If war breeds such a spirit in the land, it is as much a blessing as a curse. The air was full of it, and the Van Trumpers, when they saw their hero hobble in, were melted. Love, pity, pride, and tenderness were surging in storms through every heart that knew. "Their brother, their son come back, wounded, but proven and glorious." Yes, Rolf *had* a home, and in that intoxicating realization he kissed them all, even Annette of the glowing cheeks and eyes; though in truth he paid for it, for it conjured up in her a shy aloofness that lasted many days.

Old Hendrik sputtered around. "Och, I am smile; dis is goood, yah. Vere is that tam dog? Yah! tie him not, he shall dis time von chicken have for joy."

"Marta," said Rolf, "you told me to come here if I got hurt. Well, I've come, and I've brought a boat-load of stuff in case I cannot do my share in the fields."

"Pless you, my poy, you didn't oughter brung dot stuff; you know we loff you here, and effery time it is you coom I get gladsomer, and dot Annette she just cried ven you vent to de war."

"Oh, mother, I did not; it was you and little Hendrick!" and Annette turned her scarlet cheeks away.

October, with its trees of flame and gold, was on the hills; purple and orange, the oaks and the birches; blue blocked with white was the sky above, and the blue, bright lake was limpid.

"Oh, God of my fathers," Quonab used to pray, "when I reach the Happy Hunting, let it be ever the Leaf-falling Moon, for that is the only perfect time." And in that unmarred month of sunny sky and woodlands purged of every plague, there is but one menace in the vales. For who can bring the glowing coal to the dry-leafed woods without these two begetting the dread red fury that devastates the hills?

Who can bring the fire in touch with tow and wonder at the blaze? Who, indeed? And would any but a dreamer expect young manhood in its growing strength, and girlhood just across the blush-line, to meet in daily meals and talk and still keep up the brother and sister play? It needs only a Virginia on the sea-girt island to turn the comrade into Paul.

"Marta, I tink dot Rolf an Annette don't quarrel bad, ain't it?"

"Hendrik, you vas von blind old bat-mole," said Marta, "I tink dat farm next ours purty good, but Rolf he say 'No! Lake George no good.' Better he like all his folks move over on dat Hudson."

LXXXVI

The New Era of Prosperity

A
S NOVEMBER neared and his leave of absence ended, Rolf
was himself again; had been, indeed, for two weeks, and, swinging fork or axe, he had helped with many an urgent job on the
farm.

A fine log stable they had rolled up together, with corners dove-
tailed like cabinet work, and roof of birch bark breadths above the hay.

But there was another building, too, that Rolf had worked at night
and day. It was no frontier shack, but a tall and towering castle, splendid and roomy, filled with loved ones and love. Not by the lake near by,
not by the river of his choice, but higher up than the tops of the high
mountains it loomed, and he built and built until the month was nearly
gone. Then only did he venture to ask for aid, and Annette it was who
promised to help him finish the building.

Yes, the Lake George shore was a land of hungry farms. It was
off the line of travel, too. It was neither Champlain nor Hudson; and
Hendrik, after ten years' toil with barely a living to show, was easily convinced. Next summer they must make a new choice of home. But now
it was back to Plattsburg.

On November 1st, Rolf and Quonab reported to General Macomb.
There was little doing but preparations for the winter. There were no
prospects of further trouble from their neighbours in the north. Most of
the militia were already disbanded, and the two returned to Plattsburg,
only to receive their honourable discharge, to be presented each with
the medal of war, with an extra clasp on Rolf's for that dauntless dash
that spiked the British guns.

Wicked war with its wickedness was done at last. "The greatest
evil that can befall a country," some call it, and yet out of this end
came three great goods: The interstate distrust had died away, for now
they were soldiers who had camped together, who had "drunk from the

same canteen"; little Canada, until then a thing of shreds and scraps, had been fused in the furnace, welded into a young nation, already capable of defending her own. England, arrogant with long success at sea, was taught a lesson of courtesy and justice, for now the foe whom she had despised and insulted had shown himself her equal, a king of the sea-king stock. The unnecessary battle of New Orleans, fought two weeks after the war was officially closed, showed that the raw riflemen of Tennessee were more than a match for the seasoned veterans who had overcome the great Napoleon, and thus on land redeemed the Stars and Stripes.

The war brought unmeasured material loss on all concerned, but some weighty lasting gains to two at least. On December 24, 1814, the Treaty of Ghent was signed and the long rifles were hung up on the cabin walls. Nothing was said in the treaty about the cause of war — the right of search. Why should they speak of it? If a big boy bullies a smaller one and gets an unexpected knock-down blow, it is not necessary to have it all set forth in terms before they shake hands that "I, John, of the first part, to wit, the bully, do hereby agree, promise, and contract to refrain in future forevermore from bullying you, Jonathan, of the second part, to wit, the bullied." That point had, already been settled by the logic of events. The right of search was dead before the peace was born, and the very place of its bones is forgotten to-day.

Rolf with Quonab returned to the trapping that winter; and as soon as the springtime came and seeding was over, he and Van Trumper made their choice of farms. Every dollar they could raise was invested in the beautiful sloping lands of the upper Hudson. Rolf urged the largest possible purchase now. Hendrick looked somewhat aghast at such a bridge-burning move. But a purchaser for his farm was found with unexpected promptness, one who was not on farming bent and the way kept opening up.

The wedding did not take place till another year, when Annette was nineteen and Rolf twenty-one. And the home they moved to was not exactly a castle, but much more complete and human.

This was the beginning of a new settlement. Given good land in plenty, and all the rest is easy; neighbours came in increasing numbers; every claim was taken up; Rolf and Hendrik saw themselves growing rich, and at length the latter was thankful for the policy that he once thought so rash, of securing all the land he could. Now it was his making, for in later years his grown-up sons were thus provided for, and kept at home.

The falls of the river offered, as Rolf had foreseen, a noble chance for power. Very early he had started a store and traded for fur. Now, with the careful savings, he was able to build his sawmill; and about it grew a village with a post-office that had Rolf's name on the signboard.

Quonab had come, of course, with Rolf, but he shunned the house, and the more so as it grew in size. In a remote and sheltered place he built a wigwam of his own.

Skookum was divided in his allegiance, but he solved the puzzle by dividing his time between them. He did not change much, but he did rise in a measure to the fundamental zoological fact that hens are not partridges; and so acquired a haughty toleration of the cackle-party throng that assembled in the morning at Annette's call. Yes, he made even another step of progress, for on one occasion he valiantly routed the unenlightened dog of a neighbour, a "cur of low degree," whose ideas of ornithology were as crude as his own had been in the beginning.

All of which was greatly to his credit, for he found it hard to learn now; he was no longer young, and before he had seen eight springs dissolve the snow, he was called to the Land of Happy Hunting, where the porcupine is not, but where hens abound on every side, and there is no man near to meddle with his joy.

Yet, when he died, he lived. His memory was kept ever green, for Skookum Number 2 was there to fill his room, and he gave place to Skookum 3, and so they keep their line on to this very day.

LXXXVII

Quonab Goes Home

"The public has a kind of crawlin' common-sense, that is always right and fair in the end, only it's slow."

—The Sayings of Si Sylanne

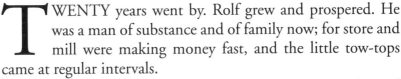

TWENTY years went by. Rolf grew and prospered. He was a man of substance and of family now; for store and mill were making money fast, and the little tow-tops came at regular intervals.

And when the years had added ripeness to his thought, and the kind gods of gold had filled his scrip, it was that his ampler life began to bloom. His was a mind of the best begetting, born and bred of ancient, clean-blooded stock; inflexibly principled, trained by a God-fearing mother, nurtured in a cradle of adversity, schooled in a school of hardship, developed in the big outdoors, wise in the ways of the woods, burnt in the fire of affliction, forced into self-reliance, inspired with the lofty inspiration of sacrificial patriotism — the good stuff of his make-up shone, as shines the gold in the fervent heat; the hard blows that prove or crush, had proved; the metal had rung true; and in the great valley, Rolf Kittering was a man of mark.

The country's need of such is ever present and ever seeking. Those in power who know and measure men, soon sought him out, and their messenger was the grisly old Si Sylvanne.

Because he was a busy man, Rolf feared to add to his activities. Because he was a very busy man, the party knew they needed him. So at length it was settled, and in a little while, Rolf stood in the Halls of Albany and grasped the hand of the ancient mill-man as a colleague, filling an honoured place in the councils of the state.

Each change brought him new activities. Each year he was more of a public man, and his life grew larger. From Albany he went to New

Rolf in the Woods

York, in the world of business and men's affairs; and at last in Washington, his tall, manly figure was well known, and his good common-sense and clean business ways were respected. Yet each year during hunting time he managed to spend a few weeks with Quonab in the woods. Tramping on their ancient trapping grounds, living over the days of their early hunts; and double zest was added when Rolf the second joined them and lived and loved it all.

But this was no longer Kittering's life, rather the rare precarious interval, and more and more old Quonab realized that they were meeting only in the past. When the big house went up on the river-bank, he indeed had felt that they were at the parting of the ways. His respect for Nibowaka had grown to be almost a worship, and yet he knew that their trails had yearly less in common. Rolf had outgrown him; he was alone again, as on the day of their meeting. His years had brought a certain insight; and this he grasped — that the times were changed, and his was the way of a bygone day.

"Mine is the wisdom of the woods," he said, "but the woods are going fast; in a few years there will be no more trees, and my wisdom will be foolishness. There is in this land now a big, strong thing called 'trade,' that will eat up all things and the people themselves. You are wise enough, Nibowaka, to paddle with the stream, you have turned so the big giant is on your side, and his power is making you great. But this is not for me; so only I have enough to eat, and comfort to sleep, I am content to watch for the light."

Across the valley from the big store he dwelt, in a lodge from which he could easily see the sunrise. Twenty-five years added to the fifty he spent in the land of Mayn Mayano had dimmed his eye, had robbed his foot of its spring, and sprinkled his brow with the winter time; but they had not changed his spirit, nor taught him less to love the pine woods and the sunrise. Yes, even more than in former days did he take his song-drum to the rock of worship, to his *idaho* — as the western red man would have called it. And there, because it was high and the wind blew cold, he made a little eastward-facing lodge.

He was old and hunting was too hard for him, but there was a strong arm about him now; he dimly thought of it at times — the arm of the fifteen-year-old boy that one time he had shielded. There was no lack of food or blankets in the wigwam, or of freedom in the woods under the sun-up rock. But there was a hunger that not far-seeing Nibowaka could appease, not even talk about. And Quonab built another medicine lodge to watch the sun go down over the hill. Sitting by a little fire to tune his song-drum, he often crooned to the blazing skies. "I am of the sunset now, I and my people," he sang, "the night is closing over us."

One day a stranger came to the hills; his clothes were those of a white man, but his head, his feet, and his eyes — his blood, his walk, and his soul were those of a red Indian of the West. He came from the unknown with a message to those who knew him not: "The Messiah was coming; the deliverer that Hiawatha bade them look for. He was coming in power to deliver the red race, and his people must sing the song of the ghost-dance till the spirit came, and in a vision taught them wisdom and his will!"

Not to the white man, but to the lonely Indian in the hill cleft he came, and the song that he brought and taught him was of a sorrowing people seeking their father.

> "Father have pity on us!
> Our souls are hungry for Thee.
> There is nothing here to satisfy us
> Father we bow to Thy will."

By the fire that night they sang, and prayed as the Indian prays—"Father have pity and guide us." So Quonab sang the new song, and knew its message was for him.

The stranger went on, for he was a messenger, but Quonab sang again and again, and then the vision came, as it must, and the knowledge that he sought.

None saw him go, but ten miles southward on the river he met a hunter and said: "Tell the wise one that I have heard the new song. Tell him I have seen the vision. We are of the sunset, but the new day comes. I must see the land of Mayn Mayano, the dawn-land, where the sun rises out of the sea."

They saw no more of him. But a day later, Rolf heard of it, and set out in haste next morning for Albany. Skookum the fourth leaped into the canoe as he pushed off. Rolf was minded to send him back, but the dog begged hard with his eyes and tail. It seemed he ought to go, when it was the old man they sought. At Albany they got news. "Yes, the Indian went on the steamboat a few days ago." At New York, Rolf

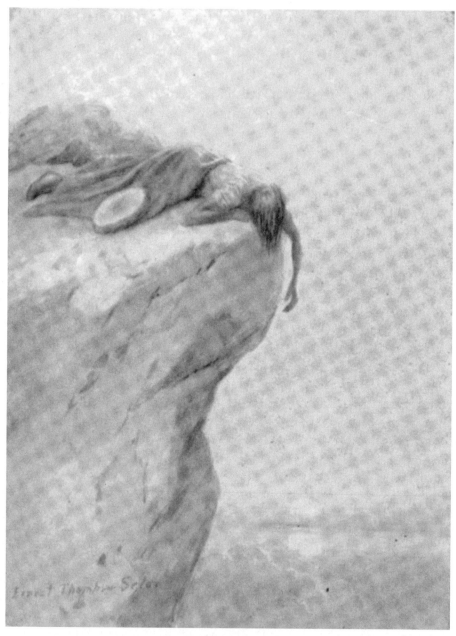

Quonab goes home

made no attempt to track his friend, but took the Stanford boat and hurried to the old familiar woods, where he had lived and suffered and wakened as a boy.

There was a house now near the rock that is yet called "Quonab's." From the tenants he learned that in the stillest hours of the night before, they had heard the beating of an Indian drum, and the cadence of a chant that came not from throat of white man's blood.

In the morning when it was light Rolf hastened to the place, expecting to find at least an Indian camp, where once had stood the lodge. There was no camp; and as he climbed for a higher view, the Skookum of to-day gave bristling proof of fear at some strange object there — a man that moved not. His long straight hair was nearly white, and by his side, forever still, lay the song-drum of his people.

And those who heard the mournful strains the night before, knew now from Rolf that it was Quonab come back to his rest, and the song that he sang was the song of the ghost dance.

> "Pity me, Wahkonda.
> My soul is ever hungry.
> There is nothing here to satisfy me,
> I walk in darkness;
> Pity me, Wahkonda !"